The Return

by

Noel Primrose

© **Noel Primrose**
2025

ISBN: 978-1-917778-22-0

This book is a work of fiction. Names, characters, places and incidents are products of the author's imagination or are used fictitiously. Any resemblance to real persons, living or dead, is purely coincidental.

All rights reserved, including the rights to reproduce this book, or portions thereof, in any form whatsoever.

Other books by the author

A Fall to the Top
Treachery
Betrayal
Deception

WHAT IF?

there was to be a Second Coming? How the world react to a man who sets out to rescue it from the myriad of disastrous military, environmental and human situations it has created, before it enters an irreversible downward spiral to extinction?

WHAT IF?

one of the World's leading political figures set out to change the course of mankind? The man is John Lincoln, Vice-President of the United States, he's talented, he's black and he's destined to be the next President.

WHAT IF?

he found a very powerful supporter along the way; perhaps the most powerful supporter of all?

I dedicate this book to my wife and to my family, all three generations of whom, along with their partners, have tolerated me, supported me, and been so very kind to me over the years, far beyond the call of familial duty.

Thank you and bless you all.

STATEMENT BY THE AUTHOR

Before writing this book, I want to begin with an apology to anyone who is upset by any of its contents. I recognise that religious beliefs can be a sensitive issue and hope that the reader will see this story for what it is a work of fantasy intended to entertain.

Over time there have been over 2,500 Gods or Deities dating from the most ancient to the most contemporary. The five largest religions are Buddhism, Hinduism, Islam, Christianity and Judaism. It is thought there are over 10,000 sects and sub-sects within these religions.

Some groups such as Atheists, Agnostics, Humanists, the Secular, the Bright and the Freethinkers are examples of groups which do not have a belief in a god.

Of the foregoing religions, only Islam and Christianity believe in a Second Coming. Jews believe that the Messiah has yet to arrive on Earth. Islamists do not worship Jesus, Christians do. I mention these few facts to give a sense of how diverse religious beliefs are.

I am of Scots-Irish heritage, both my mother and father were raised in Christian households. My Irish forebears were for the most part staunch Christians, my Scottish forebears less so. My Irish grandmother's parents were French Huguenots driven from their home by religious persecution.

As for me, I believe that Jesus, son of Joseph and Mary, was the greatest man to have set foot on Earth. I believe that he set the ground rules for the laws and ethical standards that govern life in the western world. In the Bible, Matthew Chapter 22, Jesus asks us to "love thy neighbour as thyself." Who would argue with those wise words? I have no quarrel with religions and beliefs but sadly they all to often fall into the wrong hands; think of some past Popes, Archbishops, Bishops, Vicars, Priests and Nuns.

CHAPTER 1

A place called Heaven: Early in the 21ˢᵗ Century.

"Father, I'm sorry to interrupt, but I must talk with you." The younger man's voice held urgency and concern; his face taut with the anxiety that welled within him.

His Father was a very old man although time had been kind to him; his face unlined by the passing of the years. His eyes and countenance projected wisdom and tolerance.

He smiled and nodded, seeking to calm his son. "I'm sorry, I'm totally engrossed with my own problems at the moment; can we talk later?"

The younger man shook his head violently, the very thought of delay added to his agitation. "No." He responded sharply, then thought better of it and softened his tone. "Please Father, please, we must talk now." He knew all too well from experience that when his Father said 'later' it could mean much, much later. "Please, Father" he entreated "it really is important."

*The older man sighed resignedly, everything seemed to be important to the younger generation, whenever **they** decided it was. "I'm sure it's important my son, but what I am contemplating is also important, also urgent. What matter is troubling you so much? And why can you not deal with it yourself? Have I not given you the authority to act in my name as you will?"*

The younger man drew a deep breath before replying, attempting to phrase his words carefully; he knew that his father would not be pleased. "I cannot deal with this problem; you and only you have the authority to authorise what needs to be done. It is the same matter we discussed previously, mankind on Earth. We must find a way of helping them. We cannot let matters continue as they are."

*"We can and we will." The old man was firm, unyielding, his expression stern. "I will not discuss this matter further. They must be free to choose what path to follow; they must be free to develop and mould their own destiny. Their freedom to choose is paramount; we cannot control and direct them in pursuit of **our** ideals. Choice is paramount. What would be the point of forcing them along a path they do not wish to follow? We ask them to have faith, we must also have faith. No, we must not interfere. Now leave me, please."*

"But Father," the son began to protest.

The old man held up his hand, silencing his son He had no wish to listen to argument. His son was persuasive, perhaps too persuasive, and there was much that he said with which he agreed. He was increasingly finding that his resistance to his son's entreaties was weakening, and had reached the point where he relied on his authority rather than on winning the argument. "Now, make that an end to it. Leave me please, I have work to do."

The young man shook his head sadly and turned to leave. "I will do as you ask Father, but you are wrong in this matter." The old man made no reply; he too had his doubts.

The Oval Office, Washington: 12th August 2001

"Mr President, turn on your television; there's been terrorist attacks in Los Angeles and Chicago." Secretary of State Al Weinberger almost shouted his words as he burst into the Oval Office.

The President was taken aback; nobody entered the Oval Office unannounced, well not until now. "For Christ's sake Al, calm down, you'll give yourself a heart attack. If something big was going down, those phones would be bouncing off my desk."

But Al Weinberger's wasn't given to panic, something major must be in the air so Jack Caswell, President of the United States, rose rapidly from behind his desk and crossed the room to switch on his television.

Terrorist attacks in Chicago and Los Angeles. The words echoed in his head, his jaw dropped, his pulse was already racing, his gut knotting as he tried to guess at what he was about to witness. *Thousands believed to have died.* Even as the picture filled the screen, he could hear the shock and panic in the voice of the broadcasters and discern the cries of horror amongst the cacophony of background noises emerging from the television. The screen showed a skyscraper collapsing, people running away in terror.

He drew breath as he vaguely recalled that there had been recent mention on the internet of possible terrorist attacks but nothing specific. He hadn't been concerned; some group, somewhere, was always threatening the United States. The warning had been filed away with countless similar warnings in the past, the vast majority unfulfilled.

Jack Caswell, the most powerful man in the world stood transfixed as the media presenters sought scenes of devastation; his eyes were seeing what his brain couldn't believe. It wasn't possible, not in his backyard; it couldn't be happening, but it was. His heart sank as he witnessed an event unfolding that should only happen in a disaster movie. He couldn't believe what he was witnessing. Half the screen showed a large passenger jet on the point of colliding with a skyscraper in Los Angeles – the other half of the screen showed smoke and flames billowing from a crumbling skyscraper in central Chicago. He wanted to look away, pray it wasn't happening, wanted to wake up from a ghastly nightmare but the images wouldn't go away.

He glanced at his watch; it showed 9.03. "Christ Al, what's happening to us? This can't be happening here in America. Why wasn't I informed immediately? I'll have somebody's balls for this." Even as he spoke the line of telephones on his desk began to ring, almost simultaneously; their strident shrills filling the Oval Office. "Get those Al." He didn't want to watch the destruction and mayhem, but he couldn't tear his eyes away from the screen.

The Secretary of State moved over to the President's desk and picked up the nearest telephone, his hand shaking as he lifted the handset.

"Al Weinberger speaking. The President has been informed; he's dealing with the emergency even as I speak. He'll get back to you when he can." He made a note on the telephone pad, then picked up the next phone repeating the message, leaving it off the cradle. He lifted the third phone and was part way through his statement when the caller interrupted him.

"What? Repeat that please. Are you certain? Oh My God. Thank you, we'll get back to you as soon as we can."

He turned to Jack Caswell, his mouth dry, "Mr President, two more planes have been hijacked and they might be headed for Washington. We must get you to safety."

"Fuck it, what do you mean, **might** be headed for Washington? Fuck me, has nobody got a handle on this outrage? I'm staying put till we've got some better intelligence on this."

For the second time that morning the door to the Oval Office burst open and two burly members of his protection squad moved purposefully towards their President.

"Sorry, Mr President, we've got to take you to a place of safety."

Caswell's mouth dropped open. One of the agents was taking his arm, making ready to lead him away. Irritated, he shrugged the hand away.

"No fucking terrorists are going to drive me out of the White House, my place is here."

The agent stood back wondering what to do next. "We have our orders Mr President. Two planes are on their way to Washington, perhaps to attack the White House, we must get you out."

"And now you have new orders, **executive** orders. I'm staying right here in the Oval Office, but you can take the First Lady to a place of safety, and that is an order." The two agents looked at each other non-plussed, the President was the top man. An executive order, was an executive order. The senior agent looked to Al Weinberger inviting him to intervene, but the Secretary of State made no comment. Consummate politician that he was, he knew what was at stake and was keeping out of this particular dilemma; if the nation ended up with a dead President, or one who might be accused of running away, he wouldn't be involved.

The senior agent gave way. "We'll do what you ask, Mr President, but under protest."

Caswell smiled grimly, trying to ease their concerns. "I know you're doing your job, now go and rescue the First Lady."

The agents made their exit, they had new orders. But first they would report back; someone else could deal with the President.

Jack Caswell was ashen faced, his brain numbed with overload as he tried to deal with the human tragedy he was witnessing; his eyes darted back and forth between the television and his Secretary of State. He felt that a part of him was dying as he watched the screen; people were leaping from the building to escape the horror of being burned alive, death their only future. *Dear God, how can you let this happen?*

The sheer enormity of the disaster was sending him into paralysis. The images on the screen were translating themselves into the loss of human life. Thousands would die, thousands more would be orphaned, or widowed, or have their loved ones taken from them. Unimaginable misery had been created in a few savage moments of time.

'Damn it.' He had less than eighteen months to run in the first term of a successful Presidency. 'Why does have to happen under my watch?'

His policies had strengthened America; at least that's how it looked from his viewpoint. Uncle Sam was the one remaining Super-Power; the world's Super-Hero and all thanks to him. Ever since he won occupancy of the White House his unwritten dictum had been, *'What America wants, America gets.'* And yet the unthinkable had happened. Some, Third-World extremists had attacked the very heart of Uncle Sam's commerce and administration. How could Los Angeles, Chicago and Washington, all bastions of American supremacy, have been so vulnerable to attack?

He shook his thoughts free from the horrors of the screen; he was the President. He had to take command of the situation, not stand watching television, a mere observer of a burgeoning crisis. Stepping forward, he made to switch off the television but stopped himself; however horrific, however disturbing it was the best source of communication currently available to him. But the sounds of the disaster were intrusive and impeding his thinking, so he pressed the mute button.

"Al, find out what's happening to our communications. Why wasn't I informed about this disaster as soon as it happened? And why didn't we have planes in the air ready to shoot the aircrafts down when we learned they had been hijacked and diverted from their authorised flight paths? Christ, you strategists and military people cost the nation trillions and still this happens. The American people will never forgive us; we've failed to protect our Homeland." His mind was flooding with practical questions, but post-mortems were for another day; the present was what mattered. He had to take control.

Caswell straightened his back, raised his head and made his way to the reception area outside the Oval Office where three of his secretarial staff had gathered to watch television. All eyes were upon him from the instant he stepped through the door; their spirits rallied when they saw the President.

"Sorry, but this is not the time for watching television, we must all get back to work; there are people out there who need our help."

He turned to his personal assistant, the ever-reliable Mary O'Halloran who had been with him since his Senate days.

"Mary, hold all calls till I tell you otherwise, and that includes the Hotline. Say the right things; tell whoever calls that I'll get back to them whenever I can. Same goes for the First Lady, Foreign Heads of State etc. Make notes of everything that comes in and let me have a typed bulletin every ten minutes. If you think something can't wait then stick your head round the door and check, but don't put anybody through without my say so."

Mary O'Halloran was a fifty-one-year-old single woman who had devoted almost her entire career to Jack Caswell. She was out of the top drawer and was one of the few people the President trusted implicitly, perhaps the only one. She stood poised, notebook ready in hand, knowing there was more to come.

"Set up a meeting of the National Emergency Committee for two hours' time; make sure everyone gets here, no excuses personal or otherwise." He knew that many of his colleagues had family and friends in Chicago, Los Angeles and Washington; they would be worried but personal concerns would have to wait.

"The media will be hammering on the door, get Diane Phelps in here as soon as you can track her down. Tell her she's to handle all media contacts and that I want to make a brief nation-wide broadcast one hour from now. I'll follow that up with a detailed statement, probably three hours hence, after I've met with the National Emergency Committee. Tell her I'll want some inspirational phrases for my address. And finally, before you do anything else put me through to Mayor Orsini in Los Angeles and Mayor Casey in Chicago. Oh, nearly forgot, best tell the First Lady I'll be in touch as soon as I can; give her my love."

Mary O'Halloran shared her employer's pain; he looked drained. "I'll put all that in hand Mr President. I'm so sorry for all those poor people; I know you'll do everything possible for them."

Caswell returned to the Oval Office, closing the door behind him. Al Weinberger watched as he took his seat behind the desk that had been used by so many great men. The President looked ruefully at the small silver plaque left behind by one of his predecessors 'THE BUCK STOPS HERE'; he pointed at it. "Never a truer word Al, this is the biggest fucking buck of my life and it feels like it has landed square on top of me."

His friend and colleague shared his dismay. "Sure is, Jack. I can't believe this is happening to us right here in America, the greatest country in the world. We'll make sure that some bastard pays big time, just as soon as we find out who is responsible."

"I don't know how it could happen, Al; it's a question that's going to be asked time and time again, and at this moment I don't have any answers. The public are going to crucify us if we can't explain this debacle and avenge it."

"Christ, what the fuck is happening now?" A new picture had filled the television screen; it was 10.07 and the Pentagon had been hit by American Airlines Flight 83. Carswell buried his head in his hands. "Fuck it, do we have an air force? Don't we have fucking radar? How can this be happening?"

CHAPTER 2

The White House 11.00
Meeting of the National Emergency Committee

Eight men and four women were seated round the table; Jack Caswell at its head. They had gathered outside the Meeting Room and entered en masse; he had acknowledged each of them in turn but conversation didn't travel beyond a polite greeting. All were traumatised to a greater or lesser extent.

Two stenographers followed and sat apart from the table. They had been briefed by the President to record everything that was said, and each was to produce a typed copy of the notes, for his eyes only in the first instance. He didn't know what might be said and he would have sole control over the minutes that were subsequently circulated.

They would use the stand-alone computer in his private office to type the notes and would be under Mary O'Halloran's watchful eye during the entire process; there would be no leaks of sensitive material this time round. Caswell was probably being over-cautious but he was determined to control all the formal White House records associated with the aftermath of the disaster until he knew all there was to know about it. His political future, his reputation, his very epitaph would be governed by how he dealt with this crisis.

Nothing on this scale had happened since Pearl Harbour, and even then, heinous as it had been, at least it had been a military attack on a military target. Sixty years had passed, and historians and upstarts were still picking over the bones of that incident. Who knows what might be said in the heat of the moment, or what accusations might emerge in the course of the meeting. His instincts were telling him that something embarrassing might crawl out of the CIA and FBI woodwork. He was determined that when the shit the fan, it wasn't going to blow in his direction.

The President rose to his feet, on this occasion it seemed important to stand; there was no need to ask for silence, the usual round-the-table banter was absent.

"Just in case you're wondering, I've refused to go to a place of safety; my personal protection squad isn't happy about that, but I'm not going to driven out of the White House by a gang of terrorists." He paused to let the words sink in, wanting them to be remembered for posterity.

"You all know by now why we're here; there's been a co-ordinated terrorist attacks on Los Angeles and Chicago, and most recently on the Pentagon right here in Washington. All the attacks involved hijacked civilian aircraft. As near as we can estimate, up to eight thousand people have perished so far, most of them American citizens but many foreign nationals have also lost their lives. Three aircraft have hit skyscrapers and the damage sustained has resulted in their collapse; another aircraft hit the Pentagon and it has incurred significant damage. A fourth aircraft crashed in open country with no survivors; as far as we know some passengers fought back and overcame some of the hijackers but weren't able to regain control of the plane.

"Damnable as it was, the whole attack was well planned and well executed, though it galls me to give even the slightest praise to the perpetrators. I say it, to make it clear, that we're not dealing with a bunch of fanatical amateurs; whoever did this has access to huge resources and intelligence.

"Now, before we go into detailed reporting and discussion, I'm going to lay down my ground rules. We have two prime objectives. Number one, render every assistance to those killed, injured, traumatised or bereaved as a result of this tragedy, and, number two find and take revenge on the terrorists who committed this atrocity.

"At this point, just to make it absolutely clear, I don't want anybody coming to me about financial implications; do what needs to be done, and do it quickly; we'll add up the costs another day. Anybody who abuses the situation will be subject to very serious retribution. Finally, with regards to the bastards who did this I don't care what we do, or who we upset, seek them out and bring them to justice. Bring them back in body bags if you have to, but bring them back.

"In the short term I want maximum publicity for this outrage; I'm going on nation-wide television following this meeting. I want every American and the entire world to know the full horrific scale of what's happened today. I want them to know what we are doing to alleviate the situation, virtually as we do it. I want the world to know that there will be no let up until we find and deal with the terrorists involved. I want to see plenty of arrests, bring in every dubious character on your records for questioning. I want the people to see that we mean business. There must be no doubt in anybody's mind that Uncle Sam is going to kick ass here on in."

Caswell paused and looked at those seated round the table, seeking the support of everyone present; some spoke affirmatively, some just nodded. "OK the meeting is open to report, reaction and discussion; let's have your ideas."

Oliver Dacre, Chief of CIA, raised his hand. "Mr President, I think we may know who did this." He spoke nervously, knowing he was moving into dangerous territory. If the CIA had some kind of prior knowledge, everyone would be asking why it hadn't taken action?

Every head in the room turned to look at the speaker; he could almost feel their collective gaze bear down on him. The President voiced their thoughts. "But how can you know so soon, Olly, smoke is still pouring out of those buildings, the dust has hardly settled?" He wagged a finger at the CIA Director, "Don't tell me that you had some sort of prior knowledge of this? Please don't tell me that."

"No, Mr President, no specific warning." Oliver Dacre fought to keep his voice steady, the slightest tremor or hesitancy would send out a signal of guilt.

Caswell was onto him in a flash. "Cut out the fucking weasel words, Olly. What do you mean, **no specific warning**? Did you or did you not know of the likelihood of these attacks?"

"No Mr President, unequivocally, I did not. Nor to the best of my knowledge did anyone at the Agency."

Caswell wasn't convinced; there was more to come, he was sure of it. "I'll come back to you."

He turned his attention to Lionel Jackson, Head of the FBI. He wasn't going to let the Bureau Chief take a back seat and let the CIA take all the flak. "And what about you, Lionel? Did you, or anyone at the Bureau, have any prior warning?"

"No Mr President, we did not." He responded emphatically.

Caswell eyed him searchingly. "Do you know what outfit is responsible?"

"Mr President, I don't know for sure but I could hazard a guess; I suspect Oliver and I are on the same wavelength. Best if he reports though, his information comes from better sources than mine."

Caswell glared at them both. "This is no time for arse-covering, cut to the fucking chase; Olly just who do you think is responsible?"

Oliver Dacre inwardly cursed Jackson, they met regularly to update each other on terrorist activity; the FBI knew as much as CIA did, but his colleague had neatly side- stepped a reply leaving him in the hot seat.

"Mr President, Lionel and I have discussed the terrorist scenario on many occasions, the last time only a few days ago. So, we're both in the picture as far as it goes. I want it to be understood that at this stage, any accusation I make is no more than informed conjecture. As I speak, I have no evidence as to who carried out this outrage."

"Yeah, yeah Oliver, spare me the health warning, get on with it." Caswell was becoming impatient and always resorted to full first names when he moved into uptight mode.

"Very well Mr President; my belief is that the organisation responsible is known as Al Qaeda and is led and funded by Osama Bin Laden. We believe he's hiding out in Afghanistan. I'll need time to gather proof but we know he's been threatening action against mainland United States and its citizens for some years now. It's highly likely that he was responsible for the attack on our Embassy in Kenya. He certainly has the resources and the network to carry out an attack of this scale. I'm sure Lionel will confirm what I've just said."

Caswell pointed a finger at the FBI Head. "Lionel, do you go along with that?"

"Yes, I do Mr President, Al Qaeda is capable of an operation of this scale; it's possibly the only terrorist organisation in the world with the capability."

Caswell maintained a calm voice, seeking to control the anger swelling within him; the two men knew more than they were saying, or at least it seemed that way to him. "Right, you two get together, provide me with proof of this guy's guilt, and get it quickly. Bear in mind this isn't a Court of Law I'll accept best probability. If it is this Bin Laden guy, we're going into Afghanistan to get him."

Caswell fixed his stare on his military representatives. "You military guys start taking stock; I'll want to know what we need to do to go after this guy and how quickly we can do it. I don't want to know the difficulties, just give me the solutions. You all clear on that?"

The three military men responded in unison. "Yes, Mr President." They sounded confident enough, but they knew that an almost impossible task lay ahead; Afghanistan was hostile territory well suited to guerrilla warfare. The Soviet-Afghan war had lasted throughout the eighties, well over a million lives had been lost and the local Mujahideen forces had come out on top. The Soviet Union had abandoned the war.

The meeting continued, the focus turning to what needed to be done to help the victims. It was well into its second hour when the President decided he had to leave to prepare for his Address to the Nation. "Right, I'm closing the meeting down. I have to get my speech together; it'll be the most difficult of my life, I wish like Hell I didn't have to make it. Keep Mary informed of your whereabouts on a 24/7 basis until further notice. We'll meet again same time tomorrow."

The President watched as they gathered their papers to leave, he believed he had a good team, but he would find out one way or another just how good they were over the course of the next month or so. They all stood back respectfully as he moved into the corridor on his way back to the Oval Office.

"Diane, you come with me, I need your advice."

Diane Phelps was a stunning twenty-six years old Harvard graduate in Politics and Economics. She was the youngest Head of Communications the White House had ever had. She was black and she was ambitious; she believed she could be the first woman President of the United States.

The pair made their way to the Oval Office where the President slumped into his chair; his adrenaline was draining away leaving him weary and fragile. He nestled his head in his hands shaking it slowly from side-to-side striving to come to terms with the gravity of the situation in which he found himself.

"Why has this happened Diane? Why do they hate us so much? We try so hard but still they turn on us."

Phelps admired the President, not only for his political achievements, but also as a man. Jack Caswell was forty-eight and good-looking, his fair hair somewhat unruly. He had a ruggedly handsome face with a square chin, but it was his sky-blue eyes that attracted immediate attention. He topped six feet and his regular workouts ensured that he remained fit and trim.

She was ambitious and would need his support if she wanted to further her political ambitions. And she was attracted to him but had never made it obvious, content to wait for the right moment. Maybe the time had come; she sensed that he was vulnerable and might welcome her attentions. She moved across behind him and put a consoling arm round his shoulders. "Lots of people are envious of our success Mr President. It's a tough one but you'll come through it, whatever it takes, and I'll be right here for you whenever you need me."

Caswell turned his head to look at her, aware of her closeness and her sensuality. Her perfume filled the air, his eyes were level with her breasts, just inches away from his face. He looked up and his eyes met hers; her mouth opened slightly but she didn't say anything. He wanted to pull her head down and kiss her, take her there and then. *Christ what a time to think of sex.* He sighed and shook his head but he wanted her.

"What is it Mr President?" A smile played round her lips as she spoke; she had recognised what had been in his thoughts.

"Nothing Diane, it's nothing. Please call me Jack when we're alone."

She smiled. "I'd like that, Jack. We could talk some more later if you want to? She didn't wait for him to reply; she had sown the seed; it was up to him now. "In the meantime, I've drafted your speech to the Nation; there are three areas to concentrate on, sympathy for the victims, praise for the heroes and of course retribution for the terrorists. It's only a draft of course; I know you'll want to put your own inimitable touches to it."

She handed Caswell a six-page speech; the President took it gratefully and began to read, nodding as he absorbed its contents. The American people would like what he was going to tell them. "Thank you, Diane; its absolutely first class Just a few minor changes needed here and there."

She leaned forward across the desk to stroke his cheek, her eyes holding his. "I'll leave you with it then Jack; go show the people what a great President you are."

"You'll come back after the broadcast?" Half question, half request.

"That would be nice Jack; we can review how your speech went down together."

He watched as she stood to leave; she was a beautiful woman. She was slim but rounded where it mattered, and her five feet seven inches carried her curves to perfection. He hadn't noticed how short her skirt was until now. His gaze didn't leave her as she walked away, her hips swaying gently; those long slender legs were playing havoc with his baser thoughts. She turned at the door, catching him staring at her, pleased that he didn't look away.

"Good luck with the speech, Mr President." Then she was gone.

Christ what's wrong with you Jack? Sex on your mind when people are dead and dying out there.

CHAPTER 3

Heaven, 13th August 2001

"Father I'm sorry I must speak with you again. You will know what has happened on Earth, in the United States."

The Old Man nodded wearily, sadness lined his face, his voice coated with sorrow. "I know; Man's inhumanity to Man, there seems to be no end to it. I've been expecting you, my son. I knew you would come."

"So, you've finally acknowledged that we can't let things continue as they are?" There was a note of triumph in his son's voice. "You must intervene Father, you must; these inhuman acts cannot be allowed to continue."

"And what would you have me do? Turn them all into obedient followers, doing only what I thought was right? What would be the point? It's not like those far off days; time has moved on, it's more complex now. There's too much history to unravel; people are not so easily impressed no. They are better informed, but at the same time misled daily by their media and politicians. There are so many divisions; greed abounds, there is temptation and evil at every turn. Yet they survive, they go on, and it has to be said that not everything is bad, there are many good deeds."

"But where is it all leading, Father? As each year passes, killing, starvation, plague, and destruction increase, Evil seems to take a greater hold. You intervened all those years ago, you must do so again."

"Send you back my son? I cannot."

"Yes, you can, Father, and you must. I am willing."

"I won't, and even if I did, they wouldn't accept you for what you are. They would judge you to be mad, hold you up to ridicule. Sadly, it just wouldn't work. I accept I may have let them go unchecked for too long, and now I think it's too late.

They must accept the destiny they are making for themselves, whatever it might be."

"Please Father, I beg you. I believe I can help them. Over two thousand years ago you promised I would return; you must keep that promise. How can you expect them to have faith if you do not do what you have promised. You say that mankind must have freedom of purpose, a free will to make their own choices; I am asking for that same right, that same freedom. I can show them the way. I want to go; I still love them dearly. I sincerely believe that with my help they could become all that you wish."

The Old Man shook his head. "What's done is done; history must take its course. I am working on a new venture; the same mistakes will not be repeated."

"Please Father, I beg you, don't give up on them now. They are having to cope with so much more than we ever envisaged. Think about the advances in technology, the environmental crisis, the conflicts between nations throughout the world, the computerisation of society and the perils of social media."

The Old Man looked sorrowfully at his son, for a second not sure what to say; the younger man saw the moment of indecision and seized his opportunity.

"I have a plan, Father. I believe it can work. I believe that I can show them the way."

The Old Man sighed resignedly; in his heart he didn't want to see mankind fail, but was it right to intervene again? Still, it would do no harm to listen to what his son had to say.

"Very well, tell me your plan my son."

The younger man spoke for two hours, answering questions and criticisms as he went along. When he had no more to say he fell silent and waited for the older man's response. After a few minutes it came. "It might work; I have to admit it has a chance of success."

The younger man breathed a sigh of relief and smiled for the first time. "So, when can I go Father?"

"You'll have to be patient, there are others I have to consult and persuade; others who went before you. I want to take their counsel before I make a final decision. Earth has waited over two thousand years for your return, it can wait a little longer."

The young man was disappointed but he knew his father was right. Nevertheless, he protested. "But it's your decision Father, is it not?"

The Old Man smiled benignly but ignored his son's entreaty, "I will speak with you again when I am ready. Leave me now; go and develop your plan, there is much to be done."

When his son had gone the Old Man lapsed into deep thought; ultimately the decision was his alone to make, but others would have their opinions and he knew that difficult negotiations lay ahead.

Oval Office, some weeks later

The intercom in the Oval Office buzzed and the President answered, irritation in his voice "What is it, Mary? I asked not to be disturbed; I'm in discussion with Diane Phelps."

Mary O'Halloran ignored her boss's unspoken reprimand. "The Vice-President is here; he's asking to see you."

Caswell breathed deeply, calming himself. He had other things on his mind, like seducing his Head of Communications. Things hadn't advanced between them since terrorist attacks; even when he had got her on her own, there had always been a distraction of one kind or another. It had proved surprisingly difficult to get uninterrupted time alone together. Added to that the tide of meetings he had to attend showed no sign of abatement. And he **was** nervous about getting into a relationship so close to home, very nervous. The Press would have a field day if it ever came to light, but lust had won, and sooner or later he would make it happen.

He didn't really want to see John Lincoln, but he was a good friend and trusted colleague. They had fought a great campaign together and there were many who considered Lincoln to be the better man. If the polls were to be believed he was destined to become America's first black President. Caswell believed Lincoln to be loyal, although of late he had noticed awkward changes in his friend's outlook; he had become a touch too altruistic, too ready to compromise, too willing to accept the other side's viewpoint. And there had been occasions when

Lincoln had seemed to be on the point of rebellion making it clear that he wasn't wholeheartedly on board in some key policy areas. To his credit he had never gone public with his differences, and as long as he continued to tow the party line, Lincoln could think what he liked.

Caswell put on his warm, welcoming tone. "Thank you, Mary, you were right to interrupt; I'll always make time for the Vice-President. Just give me a minute to finish up here; show John in when Diane leaves."

He turned and sighed. "Diane, you heard that, it's the Vice-President, I have to see him. Sorry, I'd much rather spend more time with you."

Their eyes locked for a second; she let her disappointment show. "Another time Jack but don't leave it too long."

Caswell smiled at what he saw as an invitation; he was sure that she wanted him as much as he wanted her. "I promise I'll check my diary later to see if we can fit in some **quality** time in the near future."

She nodded, moistening her lips provocatively. "I'd like that."

"By the way I saw your picture in the Post last night with Will O'Neill. He's the Post's political editor, isn't he? I hope he wasn't offering you a job." Caswell had been disappointed, jealous in fact, when he'd seen the photo.

Phelps laughed, pleased at the insecurity she detected in his voice. "Just business Jack, believe me. In fact, I was telling him what an outstanding President you were, promoting your image to the great American people."

"I hope it stays that way; I wouldn't want a rival for your services, professional or otherwise."

"You don't have any competition, Jack, I assure you. I hope I don't either?"

He smiled and shook his head. "You know you don't."

Phelps reached across the desk and squeezed the President's hand. "I'd better go; we mustn't keep the Vice-President waiting."

As Phelps left, she held the door open for the Vice-President letting him pass. "After you Mr Vice-President, age before beauty."

"More like substance before sham, Diane."

They didn't like each other much and made little attempt to disguise their feelings.

For her part Phelps saw Lincoln as a barrier to her political ambitions. America was ready for a black President. Not that she was ready for the Presidency, but she had a good chance of getting the President's support for her to be his running mate, if as expected, he chose to run for a second term.

She was fairly certain, Caswell would win a second term, and when he did, she wanted to be right there alongside him. *Vice-President Phelps, that's who I want to be.* However, if Caswell didn't run and Lincoln was chosen as the next candidate for the Presidency, it was unlikely that he'd want a black running mate, especially not her. For that reason, she wanted to see him go out of favour and she had resolved to do what she could to damage his position whenever the opportunity arose.

For his part, Lincoln saw Phelps as scheming, manipulative and ambitious. An old and trusted media friend had fed back to him some of the off-the-record derogatory statements she had made about himself and other colleagues. He had long since recognised her political ambitions, but she had Caswell's support and he hadn't pressed the issue.

Caswell interrupted the exchange; he didn't want warring factions in the White House and he needed both of them for now. "Come in John, it's good to see you. Have a seat; I'll get you a drink. What brings you to the Oval Office? Checking it out for size, perhaps; this term hasn't got long to run?" Lincoln shook his head. "I'm happy with things exactly as they are Jack." He laughed, and added. "In fact, I'm relieved that you're dealing with the current crisis and not me. I'm sure you'll have cleared up this mess long before I would be ready to move in."

The President respected his partner and they were friends though not close; they socialised when they had to, but rarely sought each other's company for other than official business.

"Nothing to drink thanks, Jack. How is Beth these days?"

"She's doing just fine, John, it's kind of you to ask; I'll pass on your regards. While we're on the subject of spouses, how is Carol?"

"She's happy as always, Jack, and of course asked to be remembered to both of you when she knew I was coming." Lincoln lied easily when he had to.

"That's kind of her, pass on our best wishes; we must all get together sometime, it's been a while."

Lincoln smiled, "Yes we must." But he knew it wouldn't happen if it was at all avoidable; the two women didn't like each other much.

Beth Caswell was sophisticated, a socialite and only wanted to mix with people of public standing. If it didn't have a designer label she wouldn't wear it; she was an out and out snob and generally flaunted her position as First Lady. She took very little interest in politics.

Carol Lincoln was her opposite in most respects; she was one of life's good people and devoted her life to doing what she could for the underprivileged, black or white it didn't matter.

"But you didn't come here to talk about our beautiful ladies, much as they deserve our attention, so what's on your mind John?"

The Vice President took a deep breath, he knew the man opposite wasn't going to like what he was about to hear. "You're right, I do have got something on my mind, Jack. He sighed. "It's been there for a while and it's time I gave it an airing. I guess the terrorist attacks have pushed it to the top of the agenda."

Caswell felt his mouth dry; anything related to the attacks was certain to prove difficult, especially if the Vice-President was about to launch one of his persuasive intellectual arguments.

"Sounds ominous John; I'm not sure I'm going to enjoy this."

Lincoln paused, choosing his words carefully. "Well Jack, it's kind of hard to get started, but I guess, that like me, many American citizens wake up each morning wondering why those attacks took place. They just can't understand why so many folks hate us. We of course both know that the American public don't know half the things we get up to in their name."

"Hell John, get real; it's inevitable don't you think? We're involved in so many trouble spots around the world, trying to put things right in more places than I can remember. And in every case, there are two sides to the story, so we're bound to upset one of them.

There are requests for aid all around the world and we can't respond to them all; we've got limited resources like everybody else, but people don't seem to recognise that. Stands to reason we're going to upset some Governments, and get up the noses of dozens of factions, rebels, extremists, freedom fighters or whatever they call themselves. Time and time again the UN, NATO or that European lot ask us to intervene, then criticise us when we do. You know the old saying as well as I do - *You can't make an omelette without breaking eggs*."

Lincoln nodded; there were no easy solutions. "There's a lot of truth in what you say Jack but the point is, it's not always our eggs and maybe we shouldn't be making the omelette.

I've supported you in everything you've tried to do, before, during and since September 11; I'm one hundred percent behind you in the fight against terrorism, be clear about that. But I don't think we've got an eye on the longer term; we need a strategy for World peace, we can't go on forever just fighting forest fires. If we carry on conducting our business as we do now, the current sorry mess will just perpetuate itself. We dampen down one hot spot, and another immediately flares up in its place. We've got to have an overall plan that most folks will sign up to."

The President shook his head, puzzled and wary; Lincoln had something big on his mind. "You've lost me John; we've got to live in the real world, deal with real issues. What are you getting at? I don't have some magic wand that I can wave and somehow everything's OK. This isn't some Disney movie with a guaranteed fairytale ending. All I can do, is what's best for America, note that, America. That's why I'm here, that's why I was elected."

Caswell jerked back when Lincoln reacted by slamming his fist down on the desk. "That's exactly it, Jack, you've hit the nail on the head. I think you said, **we** were *'trying to put things right in more places than you can remember'*, and of course." he added sarcastically, "it's all done in a good cause, provided that it's in Uncle Sam's best interests."

It was Caswell's turn to slam the desk. "You're damn right that's what I said. We've become the World's policeman, the World's peacemaker; we're bigger and more powerful than anybody else so it's easier for us, or at least that's what all the onlooking hands-in-pockets brigade like to believe."

The Vice-President shook his head. "Think about it Jack, all our power and resources didn't save us from the tragedies we suffered a few weeks ago. We mean well, of course we do, but people still hate us."

Caswell sat back in his chair, wondering for a moment where the conversation was headed, wondering what the man opposite was going to come up with. "Sure, some folks hate us, I'll grant you that, but it doesn't mean they're right. And we've got some good friends, lots of them in fact; others will come along sooner or later if they know what's good for them."

Lincoln snorted. "There you go again Jack, that's sums up your approach succinctly, if the carrot doesn't work hit them with a big stick."

The President nodded and shrugged. "I guess at the end of the day that's exactly how it is, John. I can see that you obviously have a problem with that approach though many have done very well out of it so far."

Lincoln shook his head; the crunch point had arrived. "Well, I don't think we've got it right Jack, we need a new strategy, a new beginning. We've got to give leadership, try to show the right direction, but we must make sure we have the support of the world in general not just friends and allies. We've got to stop going it alone, stop being the bully boy and stop making ourselves rich with the resources of the poor. There are times when we should help countries and people do what's best for them, even if it's not in America's best interests. There's a whole world out there and we're just a part of it, we need others just as much as they need us. We've got to take the longer view, Jack; democracy will win out in the long run given half a chance. It did here, it did in Great Britain when it gave up its Empire, it did all over Europe right back into Roman times. It's beginning to happen in Russia and China; we've got to give people time to do what's best for themselves."

"We've got to draw back, set good examples and encourage our friends and allies to do likewise. As a matter of fact, I think Europe is ahead of us in this regard. Whether you like it or not, whether the American people like it or not, there are times when we must put World interests before those of America. This is a small planet; we must find ways of pulling in the same direction. If we don't, then I fear we are all doomed."

The President stared at his colleague, incredulity showing in his expression. "And while we're carrying out this grand design of yours, who's going to bankroll this fucking dream? You sound like some screwball evangelist; you know its pie in the sky, it's idealism in the first degree. The American people would never stand for it."

Lincoln stood his ground. "They certainly won't Jack if we don't give them a chance, don't show them the way. The World is getting smaller and we're all dependent on each other to a greater or lesser extent. I **am** looking for a grand design Jack, one drawn up and brokered by the United States; one that will turn the tide of history before mankind marches into oblivion.

"Those terrorist outrages were horrific, but if weapons of mass destruction are ever used by terrorists, the result will be a disaster of cataclysmic proportions. It could end mankind; we'd follow the dinosaurs into extinction. You have a chance to be the greatest President ever, but you have to change course."

Caswell clenched his fist, shaking it for emphasis, "But that's exactly what I'm trying to achieve, you know that. And we do have support; the British Prime Minister is a staunch ally."

Lincoln shook his head, smiling wryly, he could see he wasn't getting anywhere. "Can't you see that people like Saddam Hussein and Osama Bin Laden are just today's terrorists, Jack? If we don't change how we go about our business others will come along to take their place. Of course, the Brits **are** our closest Allies, some would say our puppets, and it's true the special relationship **has** always come through when it mattered. But times are changing and even you must accept that their approach is less hawkish than ours? Increasingly they've got to take account of the European dimension; someday they might be forced to line up against us. Then what?"

Caswell smiled derisively. "Not much chance of that, they benefit too much from the so-called special relationship. The fact is, we are the major partner in any alliance, that's why we call the shots."

Lincoln sighed. "It always come down to that, doesn't it Jack? Might is right. Do it our way or not at all; play the game to our rules or we'll take our ball away. That's about it, isn't it, Jack?"

Caswell was getting impatient; he wasn't going to back down. "You're damn right it is John, damn right."

"Well, I'm sorry but I won't let this one go. I'm going to raise it at the next meeting of the Cabinet with or without your support. I just thought it was fair to give you prior warning of what I had in mind. I suspect I'm not the only American who feels this way."

Caswell shrugged dismissively. "You can raise whatever you want; you'll get laughed right out of the room. I'll bet nobody throws their hat into the ring alongside yours."

Lincoln nodded; he couldn't think of anyone on the team who would challenge the President. "You're probably right about that, but I feel very strongly about this; I've thought about it a long time and if I have to, I'll find other ways of taking my ideas forward."

The President gathered his thoughts rapidly, the politician in him woke up; Lincoln would make a troublesome enemy, and an increasing number of Americans were expressing similar views. "I don't agree with you John but I'll tell you what, put some flesh on that Utopian skeleton of yours and I'll see that you get a fair hearing at the next meeting. Can we break off now? I've got some urgent business to attend to. Thanks for sharing your views with me in private; I'm sure we can work something out."

When his Vice-President had gone Caswell sat thinking about the exchange for a long time. Lincoln was at best misguided, but his hypothesis was just about plausible; he was a billionaire and had the resources to promote them extensively in every corner of the country. He had accumulated his vast fortune from his publishing and communications interests and he owned several television channels, which could be used to further his approach. He would have no trouble generating a large following.

Lincoln was America's first black Vice-President, with claims that his ancestry could be traced back to the slave days on Abe Lincoln's plantation. He had charisma by the bucketful, and strong support across the country; everybody seemed to admire him no matter their colour or creed. Somehow, he had avoided bad headlines in his private life and had always been the voice of reason and fair play. Caswell nodded reflectively; yes, Lincoln could be troublesome.

He reached forward and buzzed his Personal Assistant, "Mary, would you get Diane in here as soon as possible please, and let the First Lady know I'll be an hour or so later than planned. And no calls please, no interruptions; I have some important issues to deal with courtesy of the Vice-President's visit"

The Head of Communications reported to the Oval Office just ten minutes later. Phelps liked to be summoned at short notice; it made her feel important and maybe this was the opportunity she had been waiting for.

"How can I help Mr President?"

Caswell's eyes strayed over her cleavage, the short skirt, those legs; he wanted her right there and then, but first there was some business to attend to. "I need your advice Diane and I stress it's a sensitive matter for your ears only."

Caswell explained what had transpired during his meeting with Lincoln and the threat he believed could emerge if he didn't co-operate.

This was the moment Phelps had prayed for, a split between the President and John Lincoln.

"Well now, that's a toughie, but I'm sure we can handle it."

"Tell me how Diane; the Vice-President is a popular guy; he has a strong media base and he excels at persuading people to his viewpoint."

"Sure, he's popular, for the moment anyway, but that can change and change can be arranged, if you get my meaning. I'll need to think things through, but I reckon we should give him enough rope to hang himself. Let's find a lion's den and send him into it. Leave it with me and I'll come up with some firm ideas in the next day or so. I won't let you down I promise."

Puzzlement crept over Caswell's face and he started to speak but she put a finger to his lips. "Later Jack, it's time we got to know each other better." She took his hand and led him round to the front of the desk, her eyes never leaving his. The moment had come; he reached for her, his lips finding hers, their tongues colliding, their hands searching. She pushed herself against him and stepped back into the desk pulling him down on top of her. She let him take the lead then, there was only one way it was going to end. Their coupling didn't last long, just long enough to relieve the emotion that had built up in recent weeks. Afterwards they stood facing each other composing themselves, re-arranging their clothes, both thinking of what had just taken place.

"My God, I needed that Diane, needed you so badly, sorry it was so short a time."

"Not as much as I needed you, I want more of you."

He looked at her unsure of what she meant, praying to God she didn't have anything permanent in mind; he really did love his wife. She sensed his hesitancy saw the doubt in his eyes. "I want you in bed Jack, I want you naked."

A smile wreathed his face; he nearly sighed with relief. "I'd like that Diane, maybe you could arrange to stay over in one of the White House guest rooms; we can't risk the Oval Office again."

"Leave it to me Jack. I'd better be going; I need time to think about our other problem."

Phelps was smiling as she stepped into the outer office and closed the door behind her. She could hardly believe her luck; she had compromised the President and an opportunity had been created to damage the Vice-President.

'You're looking pleased with yourself Diane." Mary O'Halloran's voice cut into her thoughts.

"Yes, I think I've been able to help the President with a personnel problem that's been gnawing at him for some time." She smiled wickedly as she thought of herself stretched out on his desk. "Two problems in fact."

Mary O'Halloran nodded sympathetically. "Poor man needs all the help he; it's good to have people he can rely on around him."

The Head of Communications nodded. "You can rest assured I'll be there for him whenever he needs me, and you can tell him I said that."

CHAPTER 4

Heaven : August 2001

"You sent for me Father, have you come to a decision?"

"Yes, I have my son and the others are in agreement. I've persuaded them to accept your plan, but it took a great deal of argument and exhortation. They are greatly troubled and concerned about the precedent I'm creating. They have demanded a high price if you decide to go ahead."

"I'll pay whatever price is demanded Father, as long as you support me."

"I know you will, but I don't know if I want to pay the price."

The young man recognised the gravity in his father's voice, and for the first time saw pain in his eyes. "What is it, Father? You will help me, won't you?"

"I'll always be there for you my son but...."

The young man interrupted, "Then that's all that matters Father, I'll go."

"You don't know the price they have demanded. I can help but I cannot lead you. I can support you but not act directly and..."

The young man interrupted again keen to put his plans into action., "That's alright Father, I understand."

"No, you do not." The old man hesitated, reluctant to speak the words that were troubling him, "You can go back, but they will be against you being allowed to return."

"Not allowed to return? What do you mean, Father?" Concern replaced the young man's eagerness.

"What you do, what you achieve, the results of your intercession, will be judged by the Council and you may not be allowed to return."

"And you agreed to this?"

"There was no other way to get their agreement and I knew how much this meant to you. I will help, even they will help, but

whether or not you are allowed to return is in their hands. It's not too late to change your mind; you don't need to go."

The Old Man watched as the younger man grappled with the difficult decision now facing him, praying inwardly that he would change his mind, but knowing that he would not.

The young man looked deeply into his father's eyes; he had made up his mind.

"I will go Father, whatever the cost."

"So be it my son, I expected no less from you. You will take the powers with you that you have gained over time but, as I've told you, I will be restricted in what assistance I can give. Now, go through your plan again, I want to be sure that it has a chance of success."

When they had done the young man bowed his head, "Thank you Father, you have shown me the way yet again."

CHAPTER 5

The Lincoln Residence

"How did it go with the President, Honey?" She kept her tone light, Carol Lincoln was worried about her husband; he had become increasingly introspect and irritable over the last six months, but had shown no inclination to discuss whatever was troubling him.

The Lincolns had been married for twenty-seven years and had known each other since their childhood days in Washington. He had wanted to be a politician since college days. For her part, she was neither ambitious nor political; her vocation in life was working for religious charities of all denominations. She used her status as the Vice-President's wife to bring about many donations from the wealthy. They had gone down different educational routes, but had got back together as soon as they completed their studies, marrying when they were both twenty-three.

She had probed, gently at first as wives do, trying to get to the root of the problem she knew was weighing heavily on her husband. In the end, recognising that his mood swings were becoming deeper and more extreme, she had pressed hard and uncompromisingly for an explanation. He had sought to evade a reply, seeking refuge behind a political screen of confidentiality and security. In the end she had used a ploy she had never resorted to in their twenty-seven years of marriage.

"Is it me John? Have you fallen out of love with me? Is there someone else in your life?

Lincoln had been shocked, filled with dismay that she should have to ask such a question, but she had explained that it was the only possible reason for his behaviour that she could identify. He was overwhelmed with guilt. He recognised the depth of his wife's anguish, and realised for the first time just how much he had withdrawn from their marriage. He had never stopped caring for her for an instant, but at that moment he realised that he had stopped sharing.

He had told her the nature of his concerns, told her of his growing disillusionment with the Executive's current policies and actions in relation to World affairs.

She had held him close. "Two things John, we have each other, no matter what. I don't care if you walk out on this job; believe me you're not the only one who feels as you do about how our country conducts itself. Many Americans are uneasy about our role in the World, and how we go about our business. If we were honest with ourselves, we would admit that we've got too big for our boots."

"Thanks, Honey, you're right, but I'm the Vice-President, a big cog in the machinery of State; if anything happened to Jack, I would have to take over. I find myself going along with policy whether I agree with it or not. I feel that I'm duty bound to support the President; we campaigned together, got elected together. We're supposed to be a team, but increasingly I'm becoming more alienated from his approach to policy. But I can't resign, just run away from it; as Vice-President, at least I have a chance to influence policy."

Carol Lincoln loved her husband dearly, always had done and always would; when she had taken her marriage vows, she had meant them. She was an attractive woman, though not a classic beauty; she was petite and nicely proportioned with a winning smile. She, like her husband, was a product of a mixed-race marriage. Her knowledge of, and interest in politics was limited; her husband and her children, two daughters and a son, along with her religion, were the mainstays of her life.

"You and Jack are supposed to be a team, but if he's not working with you to formulate policy, he can hardly expect your unqualified support. There comes a time when good men have to stand up and be counted, it's been like that all through our history. You owe it to yourself, and to America, to stand up for what you believe, maybe more so because you **are** Vice-President. If you can't say what you believe in, then maybe it is time you got out of politics. What hope is there for the rest of us if the Vice-President is gagged and can't make a difference?

There are lots of doubts out there, many Americans have reservations about our foreign policy; they just need a powerful voice to articulate those doubts, just like Our Lord did long ago, and Winston Churchill did in more recent times. You could be that voice, John; maybe it's your destiny."

Lincoln's discussion with his wife turned out to be a wake-up call; subsequently he had searched his conscience over and over, weighing his wife's simple words carefully, accepting finally that there were only two options open to him. He had to step down as Vice-President or try to persuade Caswell to his way of thinking. He made his decision and determined that it was irrevocable; he would raise his concerns with the President at the earliest opportunity. Carol, bless her, had nagged him almost every day and the terrorist attacks had finally driven him to confront Caswell with his views. He had promised to report back and he was now telling her the outcome of his discussion in the Oval Office.

"Well let's just say he wasn't all together enthusiastic Honey. As matter of fact, he was downright dismissive; he probably thinks I'm crazy. I suspect he would get rid of me if he thought I'd go quietly."

"I can't see that happening John," she said emphatically "you're America's favourite son last poll I saw. He needed you to get elected and he still needs you to win over Congress and the Senate when a controversial issue comes along."

"That may be so, Carol, but I didn't get too far with him; though he eventually agreed I could raise the subject at the next Cabinet meeting. He said that he would support me as far as he's able, which I suspect doesn't add up to a handful of beans. It's sad, but I just don't feel I can trust him anymore. I guess I'll have to wait and see what the day brings."

"Don't worry, Honey, you'll bring them all round to your way of thinking in the long run, you mark my words. Have faith in the Lord, he'll be at your side."

"Bless you, I can always rely on you to boost my morale; I just hope I'm half the man you think I am. I often wonder what would happen if your Lord was on Earth today, and faced with the magnitude of today's complex problems."

"He'd find a way to solve them John, somehow he'd find a way."

The White House: Two weeks later.

Caswell had gathered his team to discuss progress in the crusade against terrorism; he had come to regard himself as the world's torchbearer against all things evil, albeit he never lost sight of Uncle Sam's commercial interests. Domestic politics and other issues would get an airing, but Afghanistan, Al-Queda and Iraq would dominate discussion.

Lincoln sat patiently, waiting for the President to make the introduction he'd promised, all the time wondering if he'd keep his promise. But the moment arrived when Caswell caught his eye nodding a forewarning.

"And now, there's one final matter, and it's an important one; one in fact that I've been in discussion with Vice-President on and off for some time. He's going to lead on this one, so I'll leave it to him to explain."

Lincoln couldn't restrain a raised eyebrow; this wasn't quite what he had expected. *Was the President lending his support? His introduction had been less than positive; it had been non-specific and non-committal. Still, he had allowed it onto the agenda.* He took a deep breath and looked round the table, trying to read expressions, making eye contact here and there as he prepared to speak, all the time trying to identify where sympathy to his viewpoint might emerge.

"What I've got to say isn't easy; it represents a whole new approach, so bear with me. I'm grateful to the President for giving me an opportunity to put forward what you'll find is a clear departure from our current approach to world affairs."

Most of those present sharpened their attention, a few leaned forward in their seats, an air of expectancy filled in the air.

"I think most of us would agree that America's standing in the world isn't what it should be; it certainly isn't what it deserves to be, given the effort and resources involved. In fact, nowadays we regularly receive more criticism, than we receive praise." Lincoln spoke slowly, placing emphasis on key words.

There were murmurs of agreement, and he paused, looking round the table again, searching out further reaction but nobody spoke.

"It shouldn't be like that, and that's what I want to talk about; you might not like what I have to say. But here goes - I think we are too introverted as a nation, we're too self-interested. When we get involved in a foreign country, far too often it's to safeguard what's best for us, rather than do what's good for the other guy."

His colleagues reacted instantly to his words; surprise, puzzlement and anger filled expressions round the table; this wasn't what they wanted to hear.

Undeterred Lincoln pressed on. "We've got to look at things differently and come up with a new approach; we have to replace force and extortion with partnership and persuasion. Sure, we've got to continue to set an example, give leadership where it's needed, but that doesn't mean we get to shoehorn the other guy into doing what's best for Uncle Sam, whether or not it's of benefit to the local situation. And we've got to start giving more weight to what's best for Planet Earth, not just the good old US of A. We've got to make some sacrifices in respect of what we always refer to as, **our interests**, if we're going to earn global respect."

Around the table, jaws dropped ever lower, not one head nodded in support, but he did have their undivided attention and nobody was interrupting. His audience was transfixed, all of them wondering where the Vice-President was heading. Why wasn't the President saying anything; did he agree with Lincoln's views? They tried to recall his introduction; had he supported what Lincoln putting forward? He hadn't really said he was in support, but he hadn't interrupted or criticised the presentation either, and he was in charge. They all knew that it was what President thought that mattered, and for the moment at least, they kept their collective heads below the parapets. It was best to say nothing at this point, best to wait and see how things developed, best to wait and hear how the President reacted.

The Vice-President took a sip of water from the glass in front of him; he knew they were playing a waiting game, waiting for the President to speak, but Caswell was saying nothing. *What are you up to Jack?*

"As I said, we want to further the interests of the United States, but not at the expense, nor the integrity, nor the welfare of other countries. We have to look to the future; we have to change the world's perception that what America wants, America gets, no matter who gets hurt in the process. We don't need to keep using force to prove that we're the most powerful nation on Earth, the entire planet knows we are. Though keep in mind places like Korea, Vietnam and Cambodia, where we didn't achieve unqualified success. I want to show that alongside our power, lies compassion in equal measure. I want us to formulate a vision for the future that ensures the independence, as well as the interdependence, of countries throughout the World."

Rebecca Wright, the Defence Secretary spoke up. "I like the sound of what John is saying Mr President; we do have the firepower to produce any result we want, but peace built on alliances and partnerships is more likely to last than one derived from conflict and force."

Lincoln stifled his surprise at support from this quarter; Rebecca Wright was an out and out hawk of the highest order. Her usual response to any looming crisis was to send out the biggest aircraft carrier available.

Secretary of State Al Weinberger joined in. "Might be worthwhile considering Mr President but, no offence intended John, we need some substance to wrap round those ideals. How are we supposed to go about this grand design that you've sprung on us?"

Caswell interrupted before his Vice-President could respond. "Don't rush it Al, its early days; John and I haven't got a fully worked up plan. This is embryonic policy we're talking about here; I'm ready to put my little toe in the water, and that's about all at this stage. We need to take soundings and examine options before moving ahead. As I said in my opening, the Vice-President is going to lead on this; I'd like him to go on a fact-finding mission, speak with those who are friendly towards us **and,** to those who are less than friendly. He'll have freedom to go where he wants, talk to whosoever he wants, then come back here with some firm ideas."

Caswell turned to Lincoln, smiling invitingly. "John, how does that sound to you? Have you got anything to add at this time?"

Lincoln smiled wryly. *Agreement had come all too easily; what's your game plan Jack?* He was beginning to sense a set-up but he wasn't going to turn tail now. He returned the President's smile and tried to sound confident. "Not really Jack, this is the beginning of what's going to be a very long, very torturous process. What I'd like to do next, is discuss with you just how flexible you're prepared to be with some of the existing policies? When I know that, I can put some ideas together and bring them back here for discussion. I'm sure that round the table there are anxieties about what I'm proposing and we need to talk those through."

Al Weinberger nodded, "That's for sure John; I for one wouldn't want to see any sudden changes in direction that might have our enemies thinking we'd gone soft, but I'm willing to give it a go."

Lincoln was puzzled the exchanges had been lightweight; there had been no real resistance to his ideas. The outcome was way beyond his most optimistic dreams. How come Caswell, Wright and Weinberger, all hawks by nature, had so readily gone along with his concept? But no matter, for the moment he was in the driving seat.

Caswell was speaking again, "Any comments, thoughts, ideas? If not I'm keen to move on." He glanced quickly round the table, then continued almost immediately. "Good, that's settled; I'm releasing the Vice-President from all domestic duties with immediate effect. If we're going down this path we might as well start straightaway. I'm sure that we all wish him well; he's taking on a huge task and I know that I'm throwing him in at the deep end. I do have one specific I'd like you to tackle John, and I know we haven't discussed this, but it occurred to me that our Middle East policy is constantly under fire. Everybody is convinced we favour the Israelis and our prime concern is oil. I reckon if you could broker a resolution of the Arab-Israeli conflict, you would be making a major contribution to World Peace.

Towards this end I've gone ahead and set up for you to meet Prime Minister Dayan and Chairman Musrah, in Jerusalem, in two weeks time. Sorry I'm springing this on you, but quite by chance I had a call from Dayan last night asking me to visit Israel, as a show of support, and I took the opportunity for you to go in my place. I followed that up with a call to Musrah, and he would be happy to meet you. It does seem to be in line with the policy you're advocating. So, the ball is in your court, John, they're both expecting a call from you."

Lincoln glimpsed the trace of a smile form on Rebecca Wright's lips and knew that he had been outmanoeuvred; he was being dispatched to the Middle East to resolve the most insoluble of all problems. He had walked into the simplest of traps with his eyes wide open; he'd hoped for something easy to begin the process, something that money could resolve. On the other hand, it was a problem that would have to be addressed sooner or later; he wasn't going to back off now. He fixed a stare on Jack Caswell and drew up an ingenuous smile. *OK you bastard, you've been clever, but try this on.*

"Thank you, Mr President, I'm grateful that you've allowed my proposal to move forward so quickly. I'm sure that it took all your political skills to persuade those two leaders to meet with me. I just hope that I'm up to the challenge, but you've given me a completely free hand to negotiate any deal I can, so I can't ask for more."

Weinberger and Wright looked anxiously at the President; the Defence Secretary voiced her thoughts. "I hope that the Vice-President will remember our interests in the Middle East, military bases, oil etc."

"How could I possibly forget them Rebecca, but as the President and I have agreed, we'll be looking at what's best for **all Parties,** not just the United States. That's what this is all about, isn't that the case Jack?"

Caswell's mouth dried up; he was caught in his own trap "That is what we discussed John, but as Rebecca says, I'm sure you'll give due regard to our interests."

Weinberger pushed forward, both hands on the table, "Well John, looks like you have a completely free hand within the remit of existing policy."

"No Al, you've misunderstood the President, I've got a **completely free hand**. The current policy hasn't brought a resolution; it's a starting point but no more than that. We have to move on, work out new solutions if we're going to resolve the problem of peace in the Middle East. But I'll say this, I'm as patriotic as any American; count my medals when we attend the next Remembrance Day Parade."

Weinberger's eyes narrowed; one way or other he had managed to avoid military service and he knew that Lincoln was getting him. Caswell was inwardly squirming but he wanted to close down discussion before it got out of hand; free hand or no free hand his Vice-President wasn't going to solve the Arab-Israeli deadlock, nobody could.

"What John the Vice-President says is fact, Al, but I'm sure he'll represent our interests properly; he'll report back here as and when issues develop. In any case, the Middle East is only one of the World's trouble spots; we'll want to know more about his plans for other strife-torn countries on this planet of ours. I'm going to end the meeting at this juncture. Let the Vice-President have any ideas that occur to you outside the meeting."

Nobody spoke to Lincoln as he stood and moved across to the door; he knew he was on his own, no matter what had been said in support during the meeting. There were now two camps in the White House; he was in one, the President and everybody else was in the other. Still, he was further on than he had been a month ago.

The President made his way back to the Oval Office quickly, the meeting hadn't gone entirely to plan; Lincoln had outflanked him. In the outer office he stopped and instructed Mary O'Halloran to get Phelps on the line.

"Hello, you wanted me Mr President?"

"Diane, I have a job for you, get here right away."

The Oval Office

Ten minutes later the Head of Communications seated herself opposite the President and enquired about the outcome of the meeting. She had come up with the Middle East idea knowing that it was bound to fail, and failure would take away some of the Vice-President's shine. On her own initiative she was planning an occasional White House leak about Lincoln's increasingly un-American ideas.

"Well, it went more or less as planned, Diane, but right at the end Lincoln outsmarted us and he's going off to Israel with freedom to change policy. Nothing we won't be able to handle though, and I think your plan will still work. But we will need to keep an eye on him; he's a very determined and resourceful guy.

"Rebecca and Al know what's going on and I'm sure the four of us are more than capable of containing his aspirations but I am worried. Let's leave that for now, I didn't request your presence just to discuss business. Have a drink and let's move over to the sofa where it's more comfortable; I've told Mary we aren't to be disturbed."

"I don't think I need a drink for what you have in mind, Jack. I've been hoping all day that you would have some time to spare this evening."

CHAPTER 6

Lincoln Residence

Lincoln drove home faster than usual, leaving his car on the drive outside the front door of his colonial style mansion house, shouting loudly for his wife as soon as he stepped through the door.

"Carol, Carol, where are you? Where are you, Carol?"

"Calm down Honey, I'm here in the library, I heard you the first time. My, my, we are excited today."

He threw his arms round his wife and hugged her tightly. "We've done it, Carol, I've got the go-ahead. I'm making a start week after next. It means I'll be going away for a few days, but guess what, I'm meeting Prime Minister Dayan and Chairman Musrat in Jerusalem."

Carol beamed with happiness for her husband. "Well done, Darling, that's as tough an assignment as Caswell could have landed you with, but somehow, with the good Lord's help, I think you'll handle it. Now get yourself freshened up and you can tell me all about your meeting over dinner."

As they ate their meal, Lincoln related what had transpired, but made no mention of his belief that Caswell was deliberately setting him up to fail. There was no sense in worrying her by complicating the issue, and in any case, he was going to succeed.

Ben Gurion Airport, Israel

It was three o'clock in the afternoon as Lincoln made his way down the short flight of steps from Air Force Two. The airport was bathed in bright sunshine and, although early February, it was warm, with the temperature approaching twenty-two degrees; the mild weather was a welcome change from the chilly dampness he'd left behind in Washington. He thought it ironic that his personal mission to change the World was beginning here in Israel, one of the cradles of civilisation. Would he succeed? Was he on the threshold of a historic visit which would take its place in history by bringing to an end the Arab-Israeli conflict or would it end in failure like all previous initiatives?

Prime Minister Dayan moved forward to greet him. "Welcome to Israel, Mr Vice President. I believe this is your first visit to my country?"

"It is indeed Prime Minister; the President keeps all the best visits for himself."

Ezer Dayan smiled broadly at his guest's politeness.

In the past, Lincoln had read about the origins of Israel and the Middle East in general and he had refreshed his knowledge of Israel during the flight, thanks to the wonders of the internet. He had learned that it was a country of six million people, occupying around eight thousand square miles, mostly mountains and sand by all accounts. He had concluded that Israel was arguably the cornerstone of the Bible's Holy Land. It had become a theatre of war for Jews, Arabs, Christians and others since the beginnings of recorded history. Some of the early names associated with those times would appear in the most elite edition of Who's Who, such as Abraham, Moses, Saul, David, Solomon, Jesus.

The region had been a scene of strife since time immemorial. Conflicts had been simple in those very early days and throughout the Crusades for that matter, but around the beginning of the twentieth century the area had become a hotbed of politics, nationalism and terrorism. The British, United Nations and Uncle Sam had all tried to establish lasting peace without success, and all sides seemed further apart than ever.

He had persevered with his homework, but the more research he had undertaken, the more confusing the situation had seemed to him. Layer upon layer of history seemed designed to bedevil any attempt at compromise. But he was certain of one fact, the future of Jerusalem lay at the heart of any solution. Jerusalem had been capital of Israel since 1980, although not recognised as such by the United Nations. The Israelis had appropriated the eastern half of Jerusalem from Jordan following the Six Days War in 1967. The United Nations continued to recognise Tel Aviv as the capital. Lincoln believed that a basic knowledge of Middle East geography and history was essential if he was to have any success in the negotiations that lay ahead.

The Vice-President gazed around Ben Gurion Airport, taking in his surroundings; the waiting officials, a strong security presence, a military guard of honour and an aircraft ready for take-off. It was an impressive turn out. In those few brief seconds Lincoln considered the enormity of the task that lay ahead. There had to be a Palestine, the Bible's Promised Land, located in what had been a Jewish Kingdom since the 11th Century. And there had to be a State of Israel; this was now accepted by even the most extremist of Arab leaders. Somehow the Palestinian Arabs had to get a fair deal, and of course there was the hitherto intractable problem of Jerusalem itself.

"This way Mr Vice-President." Prime Minister Dayan brought him back to the business of the moment and led him along the line of military and civic dignitaries. Only a few smiles were on offer as he walked along; he was under scrutiny. Lincoln could understand why they were suspicious of the motives behind his visit; they would reason that he had an agenda and would sense change; change that might not benefit Israel.

The Vice-President smiled and nodded as he walked along the Israeli guard of honour. The line-up was a mix of young men and women; a reflection of the fact that Israel was one of the few countries in the Western world that still had conscription. "A fine body of men and women, Prime Minister, their fighting ability is recognised and respected throughout the World." He raised his voice so that it could be heard by the soldiers, stopping now and then to talk to one of them. He had resolved to take every opportunity to create a good impression on his hosts, and he genuinely held the Israeli military in high regard.

The welcoming ceremony completed, the two men walked to the waiting limousine and settled in the rear seat. The driver and a security guard sat in front. The guard, hand on gun, his eyes darting back and forth was on full alert. Meanwhile, the entourage of American and Israeli officials, made its way to their allocated vehicles and the small cavalcade made ready to depart.

Ezer Dayan was first to speak. "Your stay is short Mr Vice-President, just three days and already half a day has passed Not long to get to know us."

"I agree Prime Minister, but this is just the beginning; I've been well briefed and I hope to have good cause to come back in the very near future. I wonder if we could dispense with the formalities, titles are such a mouthful, don't you think? Call me John; it's quicker, and easier on the vocal chords."

"As you wish John; I answer to Ezer."

"Thank you Ezer. I presume that the President has briefed you on the purpose of my visit? It isn't just about Israel, or the Middle East as a whole for that matter. It's about a new order of World politics. I'm assuming that whatever President Caswell said has been classified as confidential to you and will remain so until the time is right? If we are successful in what I hope to achieve it will set an example for the rest of the World. I'm hoping that you and your colleagues will give me a fair hearing."

Dayan grimaced. "I fully understand what lies behind your visit John, but I confess that I am sceptical about the whole venture; my belief in miracles has long since deserted me."

"Understood Ezer, but there is everything to gain and nothing to lose, just listen to my ideas. During my visit I will gain a first-hand insight into the Israeli-Palestinian problems from all interested parties, then it's back to the States to talk things over with the President. After that I'll return with some firm proposals."

"Firm proposals," Dayan echoed his guest "there have been many firm proposals John, but no instances of lasting acceptance. You can't trust the Palestinians to abide by any agreement brokered by you or anyone else on this planet."

"That's an attitude I hope to change; the Palestinians say the same thing about the Israelis, as you well know. I suspect there are faults on both sides of the divide and I've come with an open mind, believing that everybody wants peace in the long run. We have to move forward, consign past differences to history; we owe it to our children and our children's children." Lincoln had decided that alluding to children's future would regularly feature in his presentations.

Dayan shook his head. "You're an idealist John; your President said as much. Of course, we all want peace, that goes without saying. But not at any price and the price the Palestinians demand is too high."

"Let's not create any immovable objects, Ezer. There has to be give and take on all sides; I want to hear first hand what your bottom line is, then I want to listen to Chairman Musrat's demands. Once I establish the boundaries, I'll talk to other leaders in the region and try to broker a deal. There has to be a package that everyone can live with and it's our job to find it. The President has given me carte blanche, and I warn you now, I intend to be even-handed; I won't favour either side regardless of the votes back home."

The Israeli Prime Minister was taken aback, these were strong words and not what Caswell had led him to expect. But time would show, as it always did, whether or not there was any substance to the Vice-President's rhetoric.

"I'm not hopeful John, we can but try. It's a long drive to Jerusalem and I thought we could begin to explore the issues on the way and continue our discussion after tonight's formal reception. Tomorrow morning you will meet with the Israeli Cabinet and you'll get a feel for the range of opinions on our side; do bear in mind that I will not agree with everything my colleagues might say. I regretfully have to acknowledge that there are extremists on my Cabinet. After the meeting, you and I will have lunch, and then you'll be taken to a secret meeting with Chairman Abdul Musrat the self-styled leader of the Palestinian Authority. Personally, I question just how much authority he actually has nowadays. This meeting will not be afforded any media access."

Lincoln frowned. "Why is there no publicity Ezer? If this initiative is to have any chance of success Chairman Musrat has to be afforded proper respect. The President made no mention of a media ban."

Dayan smiled. "I suspect that the President has been less than frank with either of us, John. I would ask you to be reasonable. In the current circumstances I cannot be seen to be facilitating formal discussions with the Palestinians. Our policy is quite clear on this. I thought I had the President's assurances on this."

Lincoln spoke sharply; he had his own ideas. "Your policies haven't brought peace Ezer. I will honour the President's undertaking for the moment, but on one condition."

Dayan raised his eyebrows; it wasn't for the American, not even if he was the Vice-President, to tell him what he could and couldn't do. "Condition, what condition?" His voice betrayed his annoyance.

Lincoln locked eyes with his host. "I want to go to into the heart of Jerusalem, to the Church of the Holy Sepulchre, to visit Christ's birthplace, and I want you and Chairman Musrat to accompany me. And I'm insistent on media coverage; this is a unique opportunity. Think of it, an Arab, a Jew and Christian standing together at Christ's birthplace. It's highly symbolic, the three of us standing together; it has the right feel to it given the nature of my initiative. I understand the church is also known as the Church of Resurrection."

Dayan nodded, but couldn't conceal his surprise at the nature of the request; it appeared to be nothing more than a publicity stunt.

"I understand your surprise, Ezer; you'll find that I work as much on the basis of instinct as I do on intellect. I like to do the simple things and leave aside political mumbo-jumbo whenever I can. I've set my heart on this and I won't take no for an answer."

"You haven't given me a chance to respond." Dayan chided. "But you are correct in your assumption; I am unwilling to attend such a meeting."

Lincoln knew that he had to make a stand. "All right Ezer, if that's how you feel you can turn this car round and take me back to Air Force Two this very minute."

Dayan looked at the Vice- President in astonishment "You aren't serious? Such an occurrence would be interpreted as a gross insult to me personally and to Israel."

Lincoln made no attempt to conceal the threat in his tone of voice. "You are damned right it would, Ezer. I'll make no attempt to deny my feelings on the matter. The choice is yours."

Dayan sighed, and thought deeply about the political consequences. "Very well, I'll make the necessary arrangements. Purely in the interest of preserving good relations with the United States I'm conceding to your request. But there will be no media presence." His tone was formal, any trace of familiarity was absent.

Lincoln shook his head and dug in; he wasn't going to back down. "Sorry, Ezer but there has to be media presence; I don't mind what spin you put on the occasion, within reason of course. And if there is any problem with Chairman Musrat, I'll speak to him directly."

Dayan gritted his teeth; he was angry but nodded. "Very well, if you insist; I'll make the approach to Musrat but I'll be emphasising that this is not a political meeting." Dayan was shocked. This wasn't the sort of diplomacy he had expected, and he wondered if his guest would have gone through with his threat.

Lincoln eyed his host and sensed his doubts, "I know what you're thinking, and I can assure you I wasn't bluffing; this visit is too important to play games, believe me." He could tell from the Israeli's expression that he'd struck home.

"So be it, John. By the way, I don't know if you have been advised, but you'll be staying with me in the Prime Minister's Official Residence throughout your visit. You'll find it to be comfortable and security arrangements are well established and, I would add, have the approval of your security people. The Official Reception will be held there, and you'll have an evening of opportunities to meet those who are influential in Israeli politics. You and I will talk afterwards, and again tomorrow morning at breakfast, after which you'll have the session with the Israeli Cabinet."

"And no doubt this is a part of my trip that **will** receive maximum publicity." Lincoln smiled at Dayan's unease. "It's not a problem Ezer; you can wring as much political capital out of my visit as you wish."

The remainder of the drive to Jerusalem was uneventful and the two men talked at length about the realities and nuances of Middle East politics.

Prime Minister's Official Residence, Jerusalem

The Official Reception and Dinner were exactly as Lincoln had anticipated, opulent surroundings, excellent cuisine and invigorating conversation, punctuated with a liberal exchange of ideas. Predictably, all the local individuals to whom he was introduced, were hard line Israelis, all keen to advance their views to the Vice-President of the United States, and invariably blaming the Arabs for all the problems of the Middle East.

Without fail Lincoln made minimal comment, other than to make it clear that he was there to listen and not make judgements. The sprinkling of Ambassadors, Consuls and Envoys attending from other countries sat on their respective fences of neutrality.

When the Reception was over and the guests had dispersed, Dayan and Lincoln undid their ties and cast aside their jackets to reflect on the day. They talked long into the early hours, covering random subjects - history from the Holocaust to the Yom Kippur War - ancestors to grandchildren. Dayan spoke with pride of his six grandchildren, three girls and three boys.

Lincoln decided to end their conversation on the latter topic. "I wonder what the future holds for them Ezer, and for their children? Will they live in times of peace or war? Will they respect their Arab neighbours, or hate them? Will they inherit a legacy of love, or of bitterness? One thing for sure, whatever happens, it's in our hands. Forgive me but I'm feeling tired, it's time to hit the hay as we Americans say. Thank you for a great start to my visit, I'll see you at breakfast."

Lincoln slept well and felt fully refreshed when he went and went down to breakfast at eight-thirty; he felt ready to tackle whatever the Israeli Cabinet had to throw at him. Dayan briefed him fully on the make-up of his Cabinet.

"I wish you good fortune John. Tere are so many shades of Zionism in the Cabinet, achieving consensus is a daily nightmare for me, though to give them credit, once a decision is taken, we present a united front. By the way, you'll be pleased to learn that Musrat has agreed to meet us, at the Church of the Holy Sepulchre as you requested. And, as you requested, an invitation has been extended to the media to be in attendance; I have restricted numbers though, around thirty or so."

"Good news indeed Ezer, thanks for that. As for your Cabinet, I doubt if it's much different from any other power-sharing group, the Senate and Congress is no different. I promise not to stir them up any more than might be necessary."

The Cabinet Meeting

In the event, the meeting went as well as Lincoln could have wished for. He had entreated them to think of the future they would leave behind for their children and grandchildren. He had stressed that the current situation could not, and would not, be allowed to continue; the United States was seeking change and its ongoing support would be dependent on the outcome of his visit. He had asked them what they would like to see happen, but to bear in mind that their opponents also had their view of the future.

When they'd had their say he invited them to consider if their Arab neighbours would find their aspirations acceptable. Would these sustainable if the United States no longer felt able to provide Israel with its current level of support; he made it sound like a barely concealed threat. The exchanges in the second half of the meeting were initially bitter, but with tact and persuasion on his part the tenor of debate began to soften. When it had gone far enough, he thanked them and promised that their views would remain confidential until he discussed them with the President.

"I'm now going to meet with Chairman Musrat; I'm sure his views will be equally enlightening. Following that, I'll then report back to President Caswell and then go on a round trip to Jordan, Egypt, Iran, Saudi Arabia, Syria and Iraq, to learn what they have to say."

"Iraq?" Dayan expressed his surprise. "In current circumstances I can't imagine that President Caswell would agree to you visiting Iraq."

Lincoln shrugged. "The President is my problem, but is on record as having given me a free hand on this trip. Iraq is a player in the game whether we like it or not; there would be limited value in getting everyone else on board if there's still a loose cannon in the region."

Dayan shook his head, unconvinced, "May your God, and everyone else's God, be with you. I applaud your objectives but moving them from idealism to reality will require divine intervention."

During lunch Dayan explained that a diversion had been arranged to ensure that he would not be followed to the meeting with Musrat. The Prime Minister's official car complete with a passenger somewhat resembling the Vice-President, would leave via the main gate to distract media attention; they would leave by a side exit in an armoured but unpretentious vehicle. A limited escort would meet up with them en route.

"I would just like to offer you my personal assurances, John, that the Church interior is completely free of any surveillance devices." He smiled wryly. "Not that you'll take my word for it; your team will no doubt check it out in any case."

Lincoln just smiled. His host was wrong he was completely relaxed about the meeting, more than that, for some reason he didn't comprehend, felt that his moment of destiny had come.

CHAPTER 7

Secret location in Jerusalem

Abdul Musrat was a tall, slim man dressed in plain army khaki-brown trousers and a dark green jacket; a pistol hung at his side. Lincoln wondered if it had ever been fired in anger. He was accompanied by three others, all wearing traditional Arab dress. His smile gleamed as he welcomed the Vice-President, his handshake was firm.

"Thank you for meeting with me Mr Lincoln; it is an honour to meet the Vice-President of the United States. These are my advisors, though they will leave discussions entirely to me."

Lincoln nodded, "Sure, no problem." He appraised the three men. *Were they advisors? Were they security? Or were they the real power behind the Abdul Musrat?*

Musrat frowned and spoke. "I'm disappointed that no publicity has been given to our meeting; I note that the Israelis took maximum advantage of your visit, the media has provided full coverage of you and Dayan. Subterfuge of this kind serves to perpetuate the view that the United States is not an honest broker and gives the impression that you will support the Israelis at the expense of everyone else in the region."

Lincoln nodded. "I accept that criticism, Chairman Musrat; it is entirely unsatisfactory but my hands were tied on this occasion. Let us hope that the time will come when all parties sit at the same table. We are due to meet at the Church of the Holy Sepulchre tomorrow and you have my assurance that the media will be present."

"The Israelis will not meet with me Mr Vice-President; if they were reasonable people there could be peace between us tomorrow."

Lincoln nodded, "You will not be surprised to learn that that is precisely what they say about you."

"No doubt they would Mr Vice-President. Now to business, why have you asked to meet with me?"

Lincoln reiterated the statement he had made to the Israeli Cabinet and explained how he intended to conduct his negotiations.

Musrat was sceptical, slightly disappointed. "It all sounds good Mr Vice-President. I've heard similar utterances from other high-placed Politicians in the past, but in the final analysis the United States sides with Israel. Successive Presidents have needed the Jewish vote to secure their election; it's as simple as that."

Lincoln grimaced; history supported what the Arab said. "That's an over-simplification if I might say so, though I confess it's got a fair measure of truth in it. But can you honestly say that have you have always delivered on your undertakings? There's no need to answer that; it doesn't matter. I'm trying to dispense with the baggage of history. I'm not here to dwell on the past or carry out a post mortem on failures; I'm looking to the future, and only the future. The recent terrorist attacks have changed American thinking. My visit is proof of that. What I want to know at this moment in time is - what do we have to do to move from where we are now – how do we get to where you would like to be? When I've heard what you have to say, I'll have both sides of the picture."

Musrat shrugged his shoulders, 'We shall see.'

Lincoln smiled and continued. 'If I recall correctly, the Palestine Liberation Organisation was founded in 1964, you became its President in 1969 and here we are, more than thirty years later, and still no permanent solution. Many have been killed on both sides, and if we fail to deliver, many more will die in the future, including women and children. I believe we can avoid further pain and hardship; this is an opportunity to move forward, but all parties must compromise and I include the United States. I want everyone involved to bear in mind the future their children and grandchildren will inherit if we don't all agree to compromise and tolerance."

Musrat nodded. "I assure you that we want peace, Mr Vice-President, of that you can be sure. But we have stopped believing everything we are told even, with respect, by Presidents and Vice-Presidents of the United States."

"I appreciate that I have to earn your trust and I'd like to start doing that right now. Let me put some questions to you and see where it takes us."

Their discussion lasted three hours during which Lincoln discreetly observed the faces of the three advisors as they reacted to the issues raised. He was clear at the end of the meeting that they would be influential within Musrat's circle of advisors; disappointingly, as far as he could tell, they showed no willingness to compromise, particularly with regard to the future of Jerusalem.

The meeting over, Lincoln rose to his feet and shook hands with the Palestinian leader. "Thank you, Chairman Musrat, most of our discussion has been useful, all of it has been informative. We meet tomorrow in Bethlehem, thank you for agreeing to come."

Musrat smiled. "I shall be there though I confess that I was, and remain, puzzled by your request. Dayan invited me although he offered no real explanation as to why I should accept, other than it was your specific request. Not everyone would support my attendance at a Christian edifice in the presence of a Jew."

"Rest assured it is indeed entirely my idea and there's no hidden agenda, no planned speeches. I just believe that there is something highly symbolic about an Arab, a Jew and a Christian meeting at the Church of the Holy Sepulchre. It's in your territory and there will be a big media presence outside the Church. We'll be seen going in together, but there's no need for the usual handshakes if that's what's worrying you?"

"I'm not worried, but I am cautious; when you've been around as long as I have, you'll realise what a deceitful business politics is."

Lincoln nodded. "I learned that lesson long ago but it needn't be that way; I'd look upon it as a personal favour if you do turn up."

Musrat looked at his advisors, one nodded almost imperceptibly in support. "I promise I'll attend, though I can't see that the meeting will have any lasting value. If your Bible is to be believed, your Deity on Earth, Jesus Christ, was a man of great wisdom and humanity with many followers through the ages, but where are those followers now?"

Lincoln smiled, "His wisdom remains even if many of his followers have closed their ears. I look forward to seeing you tomorrow and perhaps we could be less formal and move onto first name terms."

Musrat nodded, smiling broadly; he liked this American. "As you wish, John." The two men exchanged a final warm handshake and departed.

Lincoln lapsed deep into thought as he was driven back to the Prime Minister's Residence; no immediate solutions had emerged from the discussions but the two sides weren't as far apart as they believed themselves to be and, more importantly, neither meeting had been as contentious as he imagined. Hopefully tomorrow's meeting would bring the new beginning he was seeking. He smiled as his thoughts went to Carol. If his wife were with him, she would be engaged in silent prayer; she probably was and he needed all the help he could get.

Official Residence of the Israeli Prime Minister

Back at the Official Residence, Lincoln asked if could see Dayan and was taken to the Prime Minister's office.

"Welcome back John, do take a seat. How did you get on with our friend Musrat?"

"I got on very well Ezer. He has a different perspective to you of course, but that was to be expected.'

The Israeli pressed further. "So, what did he have to say for himself?"

"Sorry Ezer, I didn't tell Abdul Musrat what your side said, and I'm not telling you, his position. When I get back Stateside, I'll put both halves of the equation together and see what comes out. There are gaps, but you would expect that, and that's where the involvement of other Middle East leaders will be so important. I hope you have some friends in this part of the world."

Dayan frowned. "You almost make it sound as if any proposals are dependent on the result of a vote; if that were to be the case I doubt if the result would be one that Israel could accept."

"Please, Ezer, try to accept me as an honest broker. My job is to come up with a solution which is acceptable to **everyone**."

"I wish you success; I hope you will not be too disappointed when things don't go your way. Now to more pleasant matters, dinner will be served in one hour."

After dinner, both men, each to the other's relief, steered clear of the politics of the Middle East, dwelling instead on broader issues and the increasingly important environmental situation, where Lincoln had to acknowledge America's disgraceful withdrawal from the Kyoto Agreement undertakings.

Dayan voiced a note of despondency. "The world is in a mess; personally, I think we've all sunk too far into the quagmire of politics to rescue it now."

Lincoln countered, expressing his optimism. "I just don't accept that; we've never really tried to break the dreadful mould we've created. We're all so consumed with our own need and greed that we've lost sight of the big picture. We in the West live off the backs of the under-developed nations; we've got to stop taking advantage of their poverty and cheap labour. The world gets ever smaller and if we don't give more regard to the far future, it won't be around for any of us."

The Israeli sighed. "Ever since the first images of Earth were sent back to us from space, we've recognised that we have a beautiful planet and that its resources are finite but it's made little difference. Its resources are not shared equitably; the West is the major beneficiary by far, and is determined to remain so. The poverty, deprivation, sickness, terrorism and wars continue and as some poet said more than two centuries ago, *'Man's inhumanity to Man makes countless thousands mourn.'* Sadly, I fear it will be ever thus."

Lincoln put an encouraging hand on the Israeli's shoulder. "That's where we differ, Ezer. I believe we can succeed if we are prepared to set self-interest aside, and that applies more to my own country than most. Remember too that the poet you referred to, Robert Burns, ended on an optimistic note when he wrote, '*But it's coming yet for all that, that Man to Man the world over will brothers be.*' I believe that can be the case if we all want it to be."

Dayan pursed his lips. "I hope you're right; I wonder if he would continue to believe his words when he saw that little had changed with regard to exploitation in over two hundred years. As an American you know better than most, that the iron fist still rules and sadly, **might** still seems to be **right**." The Israeli sighed and rose to his feet. "But we cannot solve all of the world's problems tonight my friend, so I suggest at this point we retire and see what tomorrow brings."

As his head settled into his pillow Lincoln's last thoughts went to his wife. *Carol, if you're listening, I could do with the help of a mighty big prayer.*

CHAPTER 8

Breakfast next morning.

"What time do we have to get to the church, Ezer?" The Israeli Prime Minister continued to be unhappy about the three-way meeting and the tone of his voice conveyed as much. "I told Musrat that we would arrive at 11.00am prompt."

The Vice-President pursed his lips. "I've been giving our little gathering some thought Ezer; if you don't mind, I think we should travel in separate vehicles."

Dayan was taken aback with the request. "I hope you're not concerned about security? I can assure you it's all perfectly safe; we've doubled the security that would normally be provided for me."

Lincoln shook his head and sought to re-assure his host. "Hell no, I'm a fatalist; whatever will be, will be, that's my outlook on life generally. It's just that, if we arrive together, it could be construed as an Israeli-American event with Musrat just making up the numbers. Maybe I'm being a touch sensitive on this, but I'd prefer to travel alone and aim to arrive first, at say ten forty-five. That way I can welcome you both in equal measure and deal with the media."

Dayan nodded his agreement enthusiastically. "Very shrewd John, I've got no objections to that; in fact, it means that there will be clear diplomatic space between Musrat and me. If I had my way I wouldn't be there. I'm doing a close ally a great favour and just to make it absolutely clear, I will not be shaking his hand so you can drop any thoughts of a smiley-smiley diplomatic photo shot of the three of us."

Lincoln shrugged. "Fair enough, I won't push you on this one. I guess it doesn't matter which of you arrives first though there is some merit in Musrat getting there before you."

"We're on the same wavelength, John; my spies will be watching the routes to the Church and you can be certain I'll be the last to arrive."

On the way to the church, Israel's towering concrete and barbed wire barrier filled Lincoln with dismay; he knew why it had been constructed, but it was another shameful example of mankind's failure to deal with its problems. *Had nothing been learned since the Berlin Wall?*

The Church of the Holy Sepulchre is located in Manger Square in the Church Quarter of Old Jerusalem and the journey had taken twenty minutes. It was ten forty-five precisely when Lincoln's car drew up outside the church. He was mildly surprised at the media numbers in attendance, Dayan, true to his word had managed to ensure that there were only thirty or so reporters and photographers present. In the normal course of events, he would have expected three times that number; there was no doubt that the Israeli authorities had restricted media attendance. Still, access to the internet would ensure that the meeting would get publicity in goodly measure.

He got out of the car and was immediately surrounded by Israeli security guards forming a protective shield, then quickly funnelled through the media and spectators to the entrance to the Church. He took his place in the doorway and waved an acknowledgement at the assembled throng.

The journalists formed an arc around the Church entrance and Lincoln braced himself to deal with the inevitable questions. Amidst the sea of flashing cameras, he listened carefully for questions that were uncontroversial.

"Why are you here Mr Vice-President?"

Lincoln smiled broadly. "Why not, seems to me this is a pretty important place if you're a Christian, besides Mrs Lincoln insisted."

"Surely there's must be more to your visit than that?"

"Seriously, I really do want to see the Birthplace of Jesus Christ."

"Will anyone else be coming, Mr Vice-President?"

"What's the matter with you guys, don't you like surprises? You'll have to wait and see."

"Will Prime Minister Dayan be coming?"

"You'll have to wait and see."

"There's a rumour that Chairman Musrat is coming, is that true?"

"There are always rumours and you guys start most of them."

"You're not giving much away Mr Vice-President."

"No, I'm not, am I? As I told you, I like surprises."

"So, there is going to be a surprise? If, they both attend, will it lead to any formal discussions?"

"The reason for my presence here is personal; I really do feel the need to take this opportunity to pay homage at one of the great religious shrines in the world."

One of the smarter journalists, or one who was better informed, tried to pin him down. "You're clearly waiting for someone Mr Vice-President or you would have gone inside by now; have you invited them both to attend?"

"I haven't gone inside because I'm talking to you guys. Maybe you've had enough of me?" Lincoln smiled. It was time to stop teasing them. "Now, as it happens, Prime Minister Dayan and Chairman Musrat both know that I'm here today, and it would certainly enhance my visit if they shared the occasion with me. That's as much as I'm going to say on that subject."

"Just why did you come to Israel, Mr Vice-President?"

"Firstly, I've never been to Israel and I wanted to see it; this whole area has been important since Biblical times. Secondly, there is a lot of unrest in this part of the world and I wanted to hear what the problems are at first hand. And I stress I want to hear both sides of the argument."

"And then what Mr Vice-President?"

"I go back to America a more informed politician."

The journalists and news reporters could see that they were being stonewalled and were moving on to more personal questions when Abdul Musrat's car arrived. The frenzy of camera activity was renewed as he left his vehicle and was shepherded towards the Vice-President.

Lincoln smiled broadly as he shook hands with the Chairman of the Palestinian Authority. "Thank you for coming Chairman Musrat, I'm pleased to see you."

"And I you Mr Vice-President.' He lowered his voice to a whisper, 'I see that Prime Minister Dayan has not arrived."

"I'm sure he won't be much longer; he wanted to be the last to arrive."

Musrat pursed his lips and smiled. "Now why am I not surprised?"

"Why are you here Chairman Musrat?" The waiting throng took up its questioning again; it had a new victim.

"I'm here to meet Vice-President Lincoln."

"What have you come to discuss?"

"I haven't come to discuss anything. I just wanted to be photographed with the Vice-President, thank you for bringing your cameras. No more questions, please."

The arrival of Prime Minister Dayan's limousine diverted their attention, and once more cameras clicked and whirred into life to record the moment.

"Why are you here Prime Minister?"

"I'm simply being a good host and joining my guest on a sightseeing visit."

"Were you expecting to meet Chairman Musrat?"

"The Chairman and I do not share a diary; he is here for his own purposes." The Israeli replied coolly and remained slightly apart from the others.

Lincoln moved forward smiling, clasping the Israeli's hand, "Thank you for coming, Prime Minister."

Abdul Musrat stood nearby watching the two men, but made no attempt to acknowledge the Israeli. The Vice-President beckoned him to join him and put an arm the shoulders of both; he felt the Israeli stiffen but Dayan make no attempt to pull away. Lincoln gave the photographers ample opportunity to do their work then, his goal achieved, he ushered the two men towards the Church.

"That's all folks. No more questions, we're moving inside now, thank you for coming. After you Prime Minister."

Arab and Jew, political adversaries eyed each other warily, neither making a move; Lincoln gently pushed Dayan forward.

Dayan took the opportunity to whisper angrily. 'That was sneaky of you, John, I told you I didn't want any formal photos of the three of us."

Lincoln pointedly ignored him. "And now you Chairman Musrat."

The Church of the Holy Sepulchre

As the three men entered the basilica, one of the oldest churches in continuous use in the world, Security took up position outside the entrance and Israeli soldiers stationed themselves around the perimeter of the church. Lincoln had insisted that each of them be allowed to nominate one media representative each and that these three favoured journalists would be allowed to enter the church. The building and its immediate environs had been thoroughly searched earlier had been under guard since. Dayan had taken every precaution to ensure his guests' safety.

The local Priest, who had watched the arrivals from the church vestibule, introduced himself as Father Paul, and shook hand warmly with each politician.

"It's an honour to have you visit our Church gentlemen, even if we don't all share the same Faith. I pray my God, and your God, will help you all in the pursuit of peace and understanding. Now, if you will follow me, I will take you down to see the very place where we believe the Lord entered this world."

Lincoln bowed his head respectfully, noting that his companions had the good grace to nod in agreement. "Thank you, Father Paul, I'm most grateful that you have allowed us to visit your Church. I hope that a modicum of enlightenment and spiritual goodness rubs off on us all."

The Priest nodded sombrely then led the trio through the small Door of Humility and on down the narrow stone staircase to the Grotto. Dayan was small of stature and made his way without stooping, but Lincoln and Musrat had to stoop to avoid bumping their heads on the rocky roof. At the bottom of the stairs a short passageway opened out into what could only be described as a small cave or grotto.

The Priest crossed himself and spoke in a reverent voice to the three men. "Here we are gentlemen, the birthplace of Jesus of Nazareth, the Son of God and Saviour of Mankind."

The three nominated media representatives were taking photographs and videos nonstop but were under strict instructions not to use flash lighting of any kind.

As Lincoln's eyes adjusted to the low-level lighting, he looked round for Christian artefacts and was pleased to find that there were none; after all there wouldn't have been any in the stable referred to in the Bible. The earthen floor and the plain undecorated rock wall seemed more in keeping with the surroundings that welcomed Christ into the world two thousand years ago.

Set into the floor in the middle of the grotto was a white mosaic circle about one metre in diameter; in the centre of this was the fourteen-point star that marked the place where the faithful believe Mary gave birth to Jesus Christ. In the centre of the Star a small flame burned continuously, symbolising eternal life. Lincoln gazed into the flame. *Was this really where the Son of God was born all those years ago?*

Lincoln felt genuinely humbled as he took in his surroundings, in awe that a man who had changed the face of history, had been born in such lowly circumstances. He couldn't help but wonder what Christ would make of today's world. How would he deal with the evils that pervaded mankind? The Priest was looking at him, waiting for some comment, a reaction.

"How certain are you that this is the actual birthplace, Father?"

"As certain as we can be Mr Vice-President. I have little knowledge of archaeology but ancient maps and writings suggest that there was an inn on this site, and excavations of various artefacts and materials seem to confirm that there was almost certainly a stable on this very spot. As for my personal belief, each time I visit, I experience a great sense of serenity. I never fail to achieve great inspiration and comfort when I come here to pray. And of course, no other place has laid claim to be the Lord's birthplace."

Lincoln nodded. "I can understand your feelings, Father. I wonder if you would say a short prayer for us? I am a very poor Christian, and of course my companions are of other faiths but I'm sure they wouldn't object."

Dayan shook his head. "I have no objection."

Musrat shrugged. "If we go back to the ancient Semitic People, we find that the origins of Islam, Judaism and Christianity stem from a single deity, and back in those times all Faiths shared David's temple."

Lincoln expressed his surprise. "Really? I have to confess that I didn't know that, Chairman Musrat."

The Priest bowed his head and folded his hands in prayer. "Father, we beseech you, help those present in their search for lasting Peace. Enter their souls at this very moment and guide them along a path of righteousness in the interests of all those they seek to serve and lead."

The Priest and Lincoln intoned. "Amen"

Dayan and Musrat looked on impassively but said nothing. His prayer said, Father Paul explained that he had arrangements made for others to visit the grotto and asked the politicians to leave as soon as possible. "You have my sincere apologies, gentlemen, but I received very little notice of your visit, and there are many others who would pay homage to the Son of God."

Something was happening. Even as the Priest spoke an ethereal aura appeared in the corner of the Grotto, growing and slowly taking form, until finally, a ghostly figure of a man, surrounded by a luminous radiation stood just two metres away from the astonished group. The four men and the three media representatives watched in amazement as the manifestation gained living form and colour.

The man was dressed in a simple white gown; bare feet showed beneath its hem. Dark brown hair fell to his shoulders and a small beard adorned his chin; pale blue eyes contrasted with his Middle Eastern skin colour. On his head the man wore a diadem of thorns; the apparition could be none other than Christ.

The Priest fell to his knees and prostrated himself, sobbing.

The others watched open-mouthed as the luminescence faded away and the Christ-like figure looked from one to the other saying nothing.

Musrat was the first to speak, anger in his voice as he addressed Dayan. "What trickery is this?"

The man looked at the Arab, smiling, shaking his head, "This is no trick Abdul Musrat, I have come again into this world."

Lincoln's voice quavered as he spoke, "I can feel it; we're witnessing a miracle. We are being visited by the Son of God."

Musrat shook his head. "It's not possible, I don't believe it; the Israelis are behind this." The Arab gazed wide-eyed, a wave of fear swept through his body, disbelieving what he was seeing, but afraid nevertheless.

Lincoln felt strangely calm. "This is no man-made deception, Abdul. I tell you it's a miracle. There is no other explanation; the Lord's son is standing right there in front of us. We are witnessing the Second Coming, Christ has returned."

Dayan stood silently, deep in thought, his heart pounding. It was a miracle, there could be no doubt about it. As a Jew and politician, he was already thinking through the consequences of what he was witnessing. In his religion, the Messiah had yet to be born. *Could this be him? No, it was impossible, or was it?*

Father Paul had risen to his knees and was fingering his rosary and murmuring prayers.

The figure spoke once more. "Mankind is forever full of doubt; behold even now I will give you proof." He pointed to his right inviting the men's attention.

The four men gazed in awe as successive scenes from the life of Christ materialised as miniature holograms; the Nativity, the Moneylenders in the Temple, the Garden of Gethsemane, the Last Supper and finally the Crucifixion.

Dayan and Musrat watched dumbstruck; Father Paul fell to the ground and prostrated himself. Lincoln watched calmly as the hologram of the Crucifixion faded from view and the manifestation of Christ turned to face the group and spoke again. "John Lincoln, come hither to me."

The vision extended his arms, beckoning Lincoln with his hands, smiling and nodding his head encouragingly.

Heaven

The Old Man watched the scene from afar and spoke to his son. "Are you certain, my son? When the bonding takes place, you will have to follow the path wherever it takes you."

"Yes Father, it is the only way. I must go now."

"Are you sure? Even now I can bring you back. If you need more time to consider, it's not too late."

"No Father, I must go."

"So be it, my son; you may take your leave."

The Old Man looked on sadly as his son dematerialised before him and was gone.

The Grotto

Lincoln shuffled hesitantly towards the earthly form that he believed was the Son of God. He was calm and unafraid, but still numbed by the wonder of the miracle he was witnessing. He reached the man and stood before him, head bowed in reverence, waiting for whatever was about to happen. As the others watched the man reached forward and lifted Lincoln's chin, raising his head till their eyes locked together. Lincoln knew his head had been raised but had no sense of the man's touch. He tried to find words, but speech had left him and, in any case, he wasn't sure what he should say.

The man took a step forward and put his arms around Lincoln's shoulders, pulling him close; then it began to happen. The others watched in amazement, as the form of the man they all accepted was Jesus Christ, was absorbed into the Vice-President of the United States.

Lincoln could feel the transfer taking place, but would never find words to adequately describe the change he had undergone in mind and in body. His body changed in ways too subtle to define, he was himself, yet someone else at the same time; his mind was filling with knowledge and understanding. His instincts and senses were being moulded to perfection; he was climbing a staircase of wisdom, but he had no idea where it was leading or where it would end.

His head was spinning under the sheer intensity and magnitude of the transference; he felt that his brain was on the verge of overload and about to explode. He began to feel faint; his legs were giving way and he sank slowly to the ground. Before he lost consciousness, he heard an inner voice speaking to him. "You are ready now John Lincoln; go forth and do my work."

As Dayan, Musrat and Father Paul looked on, the luminous aura disappeared as suddenly as it came.

Father Paul felt traumatised, but crawled forward to help the unconscious Vice-President. Musrat was moving to assist when he was pulled back by Dayan. The Israeli whispered in his ear. "We must say nothing about what we have witnessed until we've had a chance to talk; the implications for Judaism and Islam are immense. Quickly, before he recovers, are we agreed?"

Musrat's thoughts raced; his sworn enemy was right, but alignment with an Israeli against the Vice-President? For the moment at least he had to countenance the unthinkable.

"Agreed, but I need time to think; what is done is done. And don't forget, there is the Priest to consider, and the Press."

Dayan nodded. "The Priest is a minnow, leave him to me. Now, keep an eye on Lincoln whilst I summon assistance, there is an ambulance on standby for emergencies."

The media representatives were dumbstruck; they had witnessed one of the greatest events in history and had recorded it. Flashbulbs had been forbidden but their cameras were the best available; the whole occurrence was on record. Unfortunately, there was no internet signal in the grotto so knowledge of the miracle at this stage remained with those present.

The Israeli leader turned and hurried up the narrow staircase; his thoughts in a turmoil as he grappled with the event he had just witnessed. Options were already forming in his head; the situation had to be contained, there was no time to be lost.

Whilst he helped the priest attend to the Vice-President, Musrat wrestled with his thoughts, trying to make sense of the spectacle he had witnessed. He could think of no logical explanation. If it was a trick, what was its purpose? If it was a miracle the implications were unthinkable, but how else could the apparition be described? He put his dilemma to one side as Lincoln groaned and attempted to sit up. Father Paul supported the Vice-President, his voice trembling as he spoke.

"How are you Mr Lincoln? Do you remember what happened to you? Do you remember where you are?"

Lincoln's head was clearing rapidly and he pushed himself to his feet. "I'm fine Father Paul, really, I am. I can recall everything."

The priest stood back, eyeing the Vice-President warily. "Are you sure? We saw Christ enter your body; we have all witnessed the return of the Son of God."

At that moment Dayan returned. "Mr Vice-President, how are you feeling? An ambulance has been called and assistance will be with us shortly. I have not alerted your security staff to the fact that it is you that is unwell; I thought you might not want to publicise that you fainted."

Lincoln nodded his thanks. "I'm fine and you're right, I don't want any fuss." Looking beyond the Israeli Prime Minister, he saw the ambulance men approach carrying a stretcher and shook his head emphatically. "No way am I going out on that thing. The media would have a field day if the I had to be carried out of here. He turned to the three media observers, 'If any report of my fainting becomes public, I will ensure that you or your employers are not allowed to enter the United States at any time in the future."

Dayan nodded his agreement; wily politician that he was, he had anticipated that Lincoln would react in this manner. All politicians, especially world leaders, were averse to displaying any vulnerability. "You heard the Vice-President, the same will apply to Israel."

Dayan turned to Father Paul; he had devised a plan and needed the Priest's cooperation. "Father, I wonder if you could spare the Vice-President some embarrassment and take his place on the stretcher? The media will expect it to be used, they know something is amiss."

The Priest hesitated, reluctant to be part of a deception.

Lincoln looked imploringly at the Priest. "Please Father, I would be most grateful if you could. We all need time to reflect on the momentous event that has just occurred."

Father Paul fought his natural instincts. "Deception however small is wrong, Mr Vice-President but in these very exceptional circumstances, I will allow myself to be carried out in your place as long as I don't have to answer any questions, or tell any untruths."

"Thank you, Father Paul, I'm in your debt."

Dayan addressed the priest. "Father Paul, I too have a request; we have all shared a very special experience." He chose his words carefully not wishing to alert the nearby ambulance staff to what had taken place. "By your leave, could I ask that it isn't discussed with anyone until we all meet together again?"

"I will do what God wills me to do Prime Minister, no more, no less."

Dayan nodded, smiling. "Of course, Father, but for the moment it would help the Vice-President if you could avoid any immediate publicity." He turned to the medics and issued his instructions. "Look after the good Father, take him straight to the ambulance and don't let those journalists bother him. I think its best that he is taken to my official residence so that he isn't hounded by reporters."

The two men complied and made their way up the narrow stairs, through the Church of the Holy Sepulchre to the porch where they were surrounded by the waiting throng of onlookers and media personnel. Dayan followed closely behind; he would deal with the inevitable questions.

"Let them through." He ordered. "We are taking the priest to hospital."

Father Paul had his eyes closed feigning unconsciousness. As Dayan had hoped, the reporters and cameramen bustled around him, ignoring the Priest. He watched with relief as the priest was lifted into the ambulance; he had cleared another hurdle.

"What's happened, Prime Minister?"

"Is he ill?"

"Did he fall?"

"Where is he being taken?"

"Where are the Vice-President and Chairman Musrat?"

Question after question emanated from the crowd. Dayan raised his hands for silence. "I'll make a brief statement. Father Paul has indeed been taken ill. At this stage we don't know how serious it is; hopefully he will make a speedy recovery. He is being taken to hospital for examination, and treatment should it prove necessary. The Vice-President and Chairman Musrat will be here shortly. Now no more questions please."

As the ambulance pulled away, Lincoln and Musrat joined Dayan, steadfastly ignoring the questions being shouted at them from the crowd. Security staff quickly took control and formed a cordon round the three men as they made their way to the Prime Minister's car.

."Where is he being taken, Ezer?"

"He's being taken to hospital John; we'll talk to him later." It was a blatant lie; the Priest would be taken to Dayan's Official Residence. He had instructed one of his aides to ensure that the Priest was held in the Residence's clinical treatment room immediately on arrival. He didn't want the Priest to be left unattended where he could inform the Church hierarchy of the events at the church, or worse still make contact with the media. Dayan had also instructed his Security staff to take the three Press representatives to a local army command station for debriefing.

"Chairman Musrat, will you please accompany the Vice-President and me to my Official Residence? There is much to discuss before we issue formal statements."

Musrat eyed the crowd nervously, "What will they make of it?"

"We will say nothing. It doesn't matter what they think; this is too important."

Lincoln intervened. "I think Ezer is right Abdul, we do have to agree our story. They can put it down to our concerns for the Priest, or conclude that my personal charm has somehow persuaded you two to talk to each other. I'd be very grateful if you would." Lincoln sensed an opportunity and wasn't going to let it pass. He looked appealingly at the Arab, breathing a sigh of relief when Musrat nodded his acquiescence.

"Ezer, you're in control around here; I'm sure that you can arrange for your men to guarantee Abdul and I a head start out of here to make sure we aren't followed."

"No problem, John, give me a few minutes to issue the necessary instructions and get the routes covered. I suggest you two get in my car; I'll join you when I've spoken to the military command."

Dayan speedily made arrangements for roadblocks to be set up on the roads to the Official Residence, making it clear to his staff that he wanted the ambulance to get to there before he did. He also telephoned a Physician and requested that he made his way covertly to the Official Residence as a matter of urgency.

Having issued his instructions, Dayan made his way back to his limousine; a solid line of soldiers protected him from a curious Press. They would remain in place when the officials departed and prevent other vehicles following. Sooner or later the journalists would find a circuitous route out of the Old Quarter, but they would encounter further delays when they reached the roadblocks on the approaches to the Prime Minister's residence.

CHAPTER 9

Prime Minister's Official Residence

The ambulance transporting Father Paul arrived at the Prime Minister's residence and the priest was stretchered into a small clinical room reserved for emergencies. The two stretcher bearers left immediately, leaving the priest alone with an Israeli guard.

"Why have I been brought here and placed under guard? This is quite unnecessary; there is nothing wrong with me. I have to get to a telephone; I must contact my Bishop."

The Israeli guard shook his head. "I'm sorry, I have my orders; you are to remain in this room, Father. A doctor will be along shortly to examine you; I'm sure he won't be long. I'm surprised he's not already here."

"But I tell you, there's nothing wrong with me. It was the Vice-President who was unwell."

"Sorry, but I have my instructions. Wait here for the doctor please; the Prime Minister will be along shortly to speak to you personally."

The priest was about to protest further when the door opened and a small, middle-aged, portly man entered and introduced himself. "Father Paul, I'm the Prime Minister's personal physician, he's asked me to examine you." He turned to the guard "Can you wait outside please."

The priest's annoyance was increasing. "Now look here, as the Prime Minister well knows there is nothing whatsoever wrong with me and I want to leave."

The doctor shrugged his shoulders, "As you will Father Paul but I'm confused, the Prime Minister was most explicit that you had gone through a traumatic experience and should be examined. I obviously can't insist, but on the other hand what harm can it do to let me examine you? What was the nature of the experience the Prime Minister is referring to?"

The priest pondered for a moment; he didn't want to betray his undertaking to say nothing about the event if he could avoid doing so. "I'd rather not talk about it, if you don't mind. But if it will satisfy your concerns, you can examine me."

The doctor nodded. "Thank you, Father. Just open up your shirt for me please."

The doctor removed his stethoscope from his valise and listened to the Priest's heartbeat, then took his pulse. "Well, there's nothing to worry about, though your pulse rate is higher than I would expect. May I take your blood pressure?"

Father Paul sighed resignedly, "If you feel it's necessary."

"Hmm, that's much, much higher than it should be for a man of your age; I'd guess you're about forty."

"Forty-one actually doctor, a good guess."

The doctor rummaged in his valise and produced a small bottle of tablets, which he handed to the Priest. "I suggest that you take one of these now, and then one every eight hours or so for a few days. They'll help you to relax and get over this secret trauma you've experienced."

He waited expectantly for the Priest's response. Father Paul sighed wearily. "Very well doctor, though I feel a bit of a fraud."

"Good man, have one now. I'll get you a glass of water."

Father Paul popped a tablet into his mouth and swallowed as the doctor looked on.

"There you are, satisfied?" Even as he spoke, he felt waves of giddiness flow through his body, gasping as a pain took a vice-like grip on his heart. He gazed helplessly at the doctor forcing one last word from his lips. "Why?"

The physician smiled benignly. "I don't really know Father, politics I suppose."

The doctor gathered up the bottle of tablets that had fallen from the Priest's hand, then crossed to the door to instruct the guard. "The Priest has collapsed; it looks like a heart attack. Call an ambulance and have him taken to the nearest hospital immediately, I'll travel with him."

Lincoln steadfastly refused to discuss the manifestation during the journey back to Dayan's Official Residence. "I need time to consider what's happened to me. We can discuss the implications of what we witnessed over dinner."

And so, the three had travelled in silence, each man deep in thought.

Prime Minister's Official Residence

Back in the Prime Minister's residence they gathered together at dinner, eating in virtual silence. The Vice-President ignored all prompting until afterwards when they gathered in the Prime Minister's study.

Dayan's patience finally deserted him. "Right John, we've humoured you long enough. You can't postpone discussion any longer; we're all involved in this business. You obviously recognise the impact this occurrence could have; the apparent appearance of Jesus Christ, the bonding of his Spirit with yours. I'm not sure what the world would make of it. The Pope will probably want to move his headquarters here, or make you an Honorary Saint or something similar. How do you feel physically by the way?"

Lincoln shrugged. "I feel fine physically, but I'm totally confused, psychologically and emotionally. I've just had a thought; where is Father Paul? He should be here."

Dayan had anticipated the question and replied with false concern in his voice. "They've taken him to hospital; he became quite unwell. I'm sure the occasion has devastated him. I'll enquire about his health later."

Lincoln nodded. "Understandable I suppose, not every day you get to witness a miracle."

Musrat stroked his chin. "Truly it was some kind of divine intervention but to what purpose is difficult to imagine."

"I have concerns, John." Dayan chose his words carefully. "Happening where it did, and the form it took, could have unimaginable implications for Judaism, and of course Islam." He looked at the Arab pointedly. "The Christian Church, especially the Vatican, could if it chose make use of this happening to the detriment of all other religions."

"I too have deep concerns." Musrat looked strained. "The alignment of the risen Christ with the Vice-President of the United States can only add to the dominance your country already exercises in world affairs. And yet it has happened, that we cannot deny."

Lincoln understood and sympathised with their concerns. He wasn't a deeply religious man, but he believed the manifestation could only have one purpose - to somehow render him support in pursuit of his mission. The circumstances were such that it must be a Divine Intervention, but what was the best way to use what had taken place? He had to act wisely; he had to exercise statesmanship and allay their concerns. He gathered his thoughts and chose his words carefully. "I understand how you must both feel, but let me say this - I've got no wish to benefit in any personal way, or see my country derive any benefit. I've got no personal wish for ecclesiastical recognition, or to be subjected to interrogation by theocrats for the rest of my life. Nor do I want the media delving into every crevice of my existence trying to discover why I was chosen."

He paused, watching as Dayan and Musrat visibly relaxed, before going on. "Nevertheless, it has happened, and I believe it happened for a reason. And we mustn't forget the priest, he won't want to keep quiet about this; he's duty bound to report this miracle to the church authorities. There can be no doubt now that the Church of the Holy Sepulchre is indeed the birthplace of Christ. And," he paused for effect, "given what we witnessed, it will strengthen belief in the contents of the New Testament. His appearance itself would be regarded as a miracle by every Christian church. His creation of the holograms depicting events in his life add credence to the event and his powers. My priority is to work out why I, John Lincoln, have been chosen to be the subject of this miracle. And, when I've done that, more importantly, what is expected of me hereon. What purpose is it intended to serve? What direction am I expected to follow? It cannot be a co-incidence that I came to

Israel to investigate what scope there is to negotiate a lasting peace."

Dayan was quick to put forward a way out of the situation. "We could deny it ever happened. The priest was seen being taken to hospital; we could claim he was delusional. Nobody would take his word over ours."

Lincoln shook his head. "I won't go down that path Ezer; we could try to persuade him, but I doubt if he would agree. In any case I want to give more thought to why it happened. We weren't gathered together in that place by accident; I arranged it and I'm the key to this conundrum."

Before he could continue there was a knock on the study door.

"Come." Dayan shouted angrily, annoyed at the interruption. A member of the staff entered carrying a telephone.

"A call for you, from your Physician; he says that it's urgent."

"Dayan speaking. - Oh dear, when was this? And the cause? Thank you for letting me know."

The aide took the telephone and left the study. Dayan gazed at the others his expression mournful. "Bad news I'm afraid. That was the hospital, Father Paul has died from a heart attack. The whole thing has been too much for him."

Musrat seized the opportunity that had arisen. "Another sign from your God, Mr Vice-President? The matter is now entirely in your hands. A sad happening, but it does simplify matters, does it not?"

Lincoln felt uneasy; it was an extraordinary coincidence, the priest dying so conveniently. *I wonder, providence or design?*

"I think we should agree to say nothing about this incident, John? It would seem to be in all our best interests; this is one thing upon which Chairman Musrat and I are in agreement."

"Not so fast Ezer, what right have I to deny the Christian world knowledge of this miracle?"

Dayan adopted a conciliarity tone, "I understand what you are saying John, but a lone voice may not be convincing." He smiled to ease the impact of his threat and went on. "It was, shall we say, a very atmospheric environment, an emotional occasion for you; travel weariness, the imagination working overtime, political pressures. Who knows what people would believe; your reputation could get damaged in the process."

Lincoln fixed the Israeli with a steely stare. "That almost sounds like a threat Ezer; I assume implying that you and Abdul would deny that the manifestation occurred. Well, let me tell you, I don't take kindly to threats and, with my political and media clout, I'm a sizeable player on the world stage. You would do well to remember what America's support means to Israel. And I'm wondering what brought about Father Paul's heart attack? He seemed to me to be a perfectly healthy young man, as perhaps an autopsy would confirm. Could you arrange for me to talk to the Physician who examined him, please."

Dayan backed off a little; he didn't want the Vice-President of the United States as an enemy. "You are misunderstanding me, John; I'm saying that it would be difficult for us to lend support to something that clearly isn't in our best interests. And who knows, perhaps as non-Christians, Musrat and I weren't privileged to see what your God allowed you to see." Dayan smiled wickedly before going on, "Or at least what you imagined, you saw."

Lincoln snorted angrily. "Don't fuck with me, know exactly what I saw. And I'd remind you again that the Vice-President of the United States packs a heavy punch, and I've got no previous history of hearing or seeing things. Millions of Christians all over the world would want to believe me and I reckon I would be a very convincing witness. The world press would certainly be on my side and I wouldn't hesitate to claim that you were trying to refute my testimony purely in the interests of Judaism. And I think you're forgetting that there were three other witnesses to what I believe was a miracle - the media representatives. I know that Dan Schultz, my nominee will back me up."

Dayan shrugged, "My nominee had already been persuaded that nothing untoward took place and I believe Abdul's representative has adopted a similar position.'

Lincoln nodded. 'Good to see an Arab and a Jew agreeing about something. You're forgetting Dan Schultz.'

The Israeli smiled, "I would attribute his statement to bribery - you have aspirations to be the next President of the United States and a happening of this nature, fanciful as it is, would enhance your status throughout the Western world. Abdul and I would continue to debunk your claim, you would be seen as deranged." He looked across to Musrat for support but the Arab did nothing other than emit a soft sigh.

Lincoln held Dayan's gaze. "And photographic evidence? How will you deal with that?"

"All cameras were confiscated by Israeli security and spools etc removed. I have them in my office, so you have no physical evidence."

Lincoln laughed. "You're sure about that, Ezer?" His thoughts were racing, he was formulating a bluff. "I'm going to be blunt - you made your reluctance to media presence clear - you were against their presence in the Grotto. So, I arranged for Dan Schultz, a fellow collegiate to have a concealed camera, a microchip spy camera, concealed in his belt buckle; the very latest technology. Sorry, I had to be so underhand, but sometimes you have to fight fire with fire."

Dayan was furious. "Damn you. You'll excuse me for a moment I have to make a telephone call." He smiled, "I'll have to arrange for security to deal with Mr Schultz."

It was Lincoln's turn to smile. "Go ahead, but you're wasting your time. Dan has a lot of experience of Middle East politics and so-called security; the micro-chip camera has been passed on, and is on its way to a safe destination. I doubt if it's still in Israel."

'Fuck you, John, I don't believe you. I'm phoning security.'

"You're getting boring Ezer, stop making threats and get on with it." Lincoln played his final card. *Will your bluff work?*

He was relieved when Musrat intervened seeking to restore calm. "I understand where you're coming from, John, but there must be an area of compromise we could all live with. Could it be that the manifestation took place as we were leaving? We were on our way out; you stayed behind to say a private prayer and the spirit appeared to you."

Dayan shook his head. "I'm all for compromise but that won't work; the fact would remain that a figure resembling Jesus Christ had manifested itself in the Church of the Holy Sepulchre. If this becomes known, it would cause a great upheaval within both Jewish and Islamic faiths. I really can't see your solution helping us in the long run but, if it's the best we can come up with I won't dissent."

Lincoln had a glimmer of an idea. He could now press for what he really wanted, a way to further his aims for a solution to the Middle East problem.

"Thank you for your suggestion though, Abdul, we might have the genesis of a solution; let's build on it. It occurs to me that here we are, an Arab, a Jew and a Christian, working together for compromise. In fact, it's a minor miracle to have you both ganging up on me. We're talking together on first name terms and, most importantly, we're all three of us concerned about the effect our decisions will have on the lives of people all round the world. Before I make my mind up about what I'm going to do about the manifestation, I suggest we take this opportunity to find a solution to the problem that brought us all together in the first place. I'm referring to the sovereignty of the State of Israel. If we can make good progress in that direction, I'm sure I can be persuaded to a deal on the miracle we all witnessed."

Musrat responded instantly. "With respect, the sovereignty of the State of Israel is **not** the issue; it is the expansionist policy of its current Government and the independence of the Palestinian Authority that is the real issue." He was beginning to worry about the Vice-President's intentions. Before Lincoln could respond Dayan interjected, bristling with anger.

"It is the Palestine Liberation Organisation's terrorist actions which are at the root of conflict in the Middle East."

Lincoln held up his hands for silence. "Stop it you two. Hold it right there, or I'm going off this very instant to report on my personal experience at the birthplace of Christ. You're both getting hung up on words and history as usual. I want to deal with the future not the past. We can't do anything about the dead, or the wrongs of the past, except perhaps to say sorry and that would be no bad thing. I'm going to start the ball rolling and by outlining my solution and I want you both to tell me why they can't work."

Dayan and Musrat both glowered at each other but fell silent. They had to listen to the Vice-President; United States policy would be central to Middle East politics for the foreseeable future.

Lincoln smiled. "That's better, now this is how I see it. First off, we go back to the terms of the 1993 Peace Accord; they were the right solutions then and still hold good today.

"Second, any properly constituted Palestinian Authority will be absolutely autonomous with unhindered right of passage for its citizens.

"Third, you **both** crack down on terrorists." He looked pointedly at Dayan, "and that includes those wearing Israeli uniforms." He turned to Musrat, "And similarly, Hamas and other terrorist groups acting on your behalf."

"Fourth, the 1998 Wye Peace Agreement is enacted in full.

"Fifth, Israel withdraws from all occupied territories.

"And finally, the big one, Jerusalem."

Both men looked at the Vice-President intently; Jerusalem was the permanent thorn in the flesh of any settlement; all the other elements had been muted before.

"I'm proposing that Jerusalem be given similar status to that afforded to the Vatican in Rome. It should be given independent status for ten years and, at the end of this period, its legitimate residents would vote on whether to align with Israel, or the Palestinian Authority, or to retain its independence and become a sovereign State.

"Any breaches of the foregoing agreements and conditions would be dealt with by the International Court of Justice.

"As part of the deal, during the first two or three years the Israeli settlements in East Jerusalem and other sensitive areas should be subject to review, and ideally, withdraw on a voluntary basis. The United States will bankroll the whole operation or at least contribute to it substantially.

"The existing Governing body in Jerusalem will represent the main players in the immediate future but will be replaced by locally elected politicians at the end of the second year. This body will report to a committee constituted by the United Nations Security Council, but will not be subservient to it. The United Nations Security Council will guarantee the integrity of the foregoing.

"Now, I think there is something for everybody in that lot and it could be made to work if you guys support it. I confess I don't know the detail of some of the previous agreements so we'll have to go through those."

Dayan was first to respond. "That all sounds promising but I'll need to reflect on the whole package; you've thrown a lot at us. I think that I personally could live with it, but I doubt very much if I could get it through the Knesset; the hardliners will reject the offer out of hand. Jerusalem will be a major stumbling block."

Lincoln nodded. "I appreciate it's not an easy task but you **are** Israel's Prime Minister and maybe it's time you held a referendum and put your case to the people of Israel? Hear what they have to say, trust them. I think a genuine Peace Accord would command support."

Lincoln turned to Musrat. "And what about you Abdul, what do you think?"

"I must be honest; it seems to me that Palestinians have most to gain from your proposals, but I too would have great difficulties persuading the militants and extremists amongst my followers to accept what you propose."

"But would you try? This might be the best deal you'll ever be offered."

Musrat lowered his eyes and shook his head slowly, "I don't know, I just don't know; I'll have to think about it."

Dayan was genuinely interested in the package; the Israeli people were tiring of war and strife, but he didn't want to run the risk of selling out his country. "Will you draft a proposal reflecting what you've just described John, one which would be clearly seen as your idea?"

Lincoln nodded, recognising the Israeli's political dilemma. "I understand; you want to distance yourself from the package. I can go along with that, provided you promise to support the package. Will you do that?”

Dayan drew a deep breath and nodded, “I will try but I’m not sure I would go as far as sacrificing my political future.”

Lincoln was disappointed at this statement of self-interest but didn’t comment. “And you Abdul, what is your position?’

Musrat buried his face in his hands, rubbing his brow; then looked up and nodded. “I will try to persuade my people to accept your proposals. I promise.”

Dayan was worried about the enormity of his personal commitment and wanted to gain more concessions from the Vice-President. “Two further conditions, John. I would require that you personally mediate with the other Arab States including Iraq?” He hoped that the Vice-President might baulk at Iraq but he was wrong.

Lincoln nodded enthusiastically. “I was going to suggest that; I want to meet all Middle Eastern rulers. Everybody has got to be on board if this Accord is going to work.”

“Let me be absolutely clear John.” Dayan wanted an unequivocal commitment. “You will meet the leadership of Iraq?”

“I acknowledge the gravity of your question and the answer is still yes, I will visit Iraq. Persuading President Caswell will be my problem. And the second matter?”

“The occurrence at the Church of the Holy Sepulchre. Can it be put to one side?”

Both men looked at the Vice-President expectantly.

Lincoln nodded. “Let me put it this way; as long as you guys are making progress in the right direction, I will refrain from announcing what took place.”

The Israeli breathed a sigh of relief; the longer the announcement was delayed the less credible the incident was likely to appear, especially if it were to be denied subsequently by himself and Musrat.

“Are we agreed then?” Lincoln held his breath. Was his grand design about to be given birth?

The two Middle East leaders looked at each other, each wondering if he could or should trust the other. They were fearful of how their colleagues would react. The Palestinian had most to gain and was the first to speak, "Yes, you have my word."

Dayan controlled a smirk; he didn't think the word of an Arab was worth much.

"It's down to you Ezer." Lincoln held the gaze of the Israeli Prime Minister; he believed he was on the verge of a decision history would record as a watershed in Middle East politics.

The Israeli shook his head apprehensively then shrugged. "It will probably bring about my downfall and end my political career, but you have my word."

Lincoln laughed. "Who knows, it might be the end for all of us, but at least we will have tried. Now I want to see you two shake hands on the deal; I wish I had a camera to record the moment."

Arab and Jew faced each other and extended their hands, shaking slowly at first; then taken with the gravity of what they had achieved, pumping them up and down with exhilaration, their faces wreathed in smiles.

Lincoln smiled broadly and took Musrat's hand; he had been the first to speak. As he did so he felt a flow of energy; images and voices filled his mind at breathless speed and he found himself witness to scenes and conversations from the man's life. He shook his head involuntarily, trying to stabilise his thoughts, seeking to control and make sense of what was happening. *What was happening to him? Somehow, he was able to delve into the thoughts and memories of the Arab.* He now knew a great deal about Musrat's political intrigues and concerns.

"Are you all right, John?" Musrat was genuinely concerned.

"Yes, yes, I'm just overwhelmed with what we have achieved. I'm fine." As he spoke the flow of energy ceased, leaving his mind in turmoil.

Dayan reached forward to shake hands; Lincoln braced himself for what was about to take place and was ready when the thought transmission process began. His mind's eye worked tirelessly to absorb the conveyor belt of images and information flowing from the Israeli. His inner ear operated at computer speed to comprehend what it was hearing. He now knew what had happened to Father Paul and had an unprecedented insight into Israeli politics.

As the transfer continued, he began to understand the full implications of what had taken place at the Church of the Holy Sepulchre. The gift he now possessed had unlimited possibilities; he had to be alone to think. He needed time to consider the knowledge he now had and how best to use it to further his aims.

"Gentlemen, I wonder if this is a real turning point for politics in the Middle East? I hope that in time history will record it as such. As for now, I fear I must take my leave; I suddenly feel quite weary."

Dayan and Musrat looked at each other, their brows wrinkled, eyebrows raised; the Arab shrugged his shoulders and smiled. "These younger New World politicians can't keep up with we old ones, Ezer. Still, the hour is late and perhaps he has a point; I expect we all need to be alone with our thoughts."

Dayan knew that he should be inviting his one-time enemy to stay overnight but the political consequences were unacceptable; he hesitated, not wishing to give offence, searching for the right words, relief arriving when the Musray sensed the awkwardness of the situation. "It's all right Ezer, I cannot be seen to stay here no more than you can be seen to ask me; we both have our respective images to protect, for the time being at least."

When Musrat had gone, Dayan eyed his guest respectfully. "A good day's work, John; you've travelled far in a single day; a proposal for Middle East peace and a miracle."

"Yes, one miracle for certain and another to be negotiated. I'm just sorry that it resulted in a death."

"A death?"

"You surely haven't forgotten Father Paul?"

The Israeli looked sorrowful. "Of course, a sad outcome."

"But one that was avoidable."

Dayan shook his head. "I think not, a heart attack comes when it comes, it's not really avoidable."

"Don't fucking lie to me." Lincoln spat out the words. "You arranged for him to be murdered; murdered right here in this residence by the doctor you so kindly made available. Your brother Abraham was the doctor involved; he gave Father Paul a lethal tablet."

"Preposterous! Have you taken leave of your senses?" Dayan blustered desperately, astounded that the American knew so much. "The post mortem will confirm that it was a heart attack."

"Of course it will Ezer, the pathologist will say anything you want. Please don't lie to me; I could take you to the very room where the deed was done, I could even tell you the time of death. But God forgive me, I'm going to do nothing about it provided you do what you've promised."

Dayan regained his composure and put on a show of bravado. "The world will think you've gone mad. Asserting that there has been a miracle and then claiming that the Prime Minister of Israel is involved in the murder of a priest. What fantasy will you come up with next?"

"I don't know what will happen next; I'm going to bed to consider just that. We'll talk further in the morning. Meantime you might like to consider how I came to know about the priest's murder. You might like to consider what new powers I inherited when Christ's apparition melded into my body. I warn you, be very careful."

CHAPTER 10

Official Residence of the Israeli Prime Minister

Lincoln lay in bed trying to find sleep but the events of the day kept him awake and led him to experiment with his new power of insight. He focussed on Abdul Musrat and as he did his mind filled with images of the Arab's life; the pictures were random and unstructured, time consuming. He needed to quicken the process and be more selective. Through trial and error, he learned how to focus on a chosen issue and access the information his mind had acquired. With practice it became as easy as accessing a computer hard disc.

He discovered that the Arab was going to support the Peace proposals but didn't expect them to gain the approval of his key advisors. There were four extremists who would reject any compromise with Israel; the fate of the proposals and perhaps the Musrat's own lay in their hands. Lincoln was able to visualise them; he knew their names and he could see their faces. He could sense Musrat's fear; the Arab lived under constant threat of death from some of his own supporters. *I wonder what you are doing now, Abdul? Good luck to you; it would be better for you if those four extremists weren't around.*

An Arab Camp

A hundred miles away, in the early hours of the morning, Musrat was reporting to his Council on the nature of his meeting with the Lincoln. He wasn't going into too much detail; he exercised great caution as he outlined the American's proposals. He didn't encourage discussion; there would be time for discussion when Lincoln formally circulated a detailed document. His Council's reaction was predictable; some welcomed the ideas put forward, but the extremists were steadfast in their objection to any compromise with Israel. Unless this hard-core faction changed its stance the likelihood of the proposals being accepted and implemented were negligible.

When the meeting ended, the various groups set off for their respective camps. The extremist group of four headed towards El Ariba. They were already plotting how to forestall any agreement with Israel, even if this necessitated the elimination of Abdul Musrat. His death could easily be arranged and blamed on the Israelis; one of the four felt Musrat was getting soft and had already decided to bring about his assassination.

As they travelled, their fervour rose, their threats became more extreme; they would never compromise their dreams of a true Palestinian homeland. The driver was caught up in the passion of the moment and neither he nor his passengers seemed aware of the vehicle's ever-increasing speed. They were all taken by surprise, when suddenly, the sky turned black and visibility dropped to zero; the driver pressed his headlight switch, swearing when the headlights didn't respond. He knew he had to reduce speed and took his foot off the accelerator – too late – the car hit a sand mound and swerved sharply, tumbling down a steep embankment before hitting the bottom where it overturned and burst into flames. Subsequent investigation would not determine that the sky's blackout and headlamp failure was the cause of the accident; the driver would be blamed for the accident. Not that he would care. He along, with the four militants died in the flames; the opponents of Abdul Musrat had perished. An impediment to peace had been eliminated.

Official Residence of the Israeli Prime Minister

Lincoln woke from his slumbers with a start; in his dream he had witnessed the accident. The incident had been vivid, his heart was pounding with its reality, but what alarmed him most, was the fact that his unvoiced wish had been enacted in his dreams in such a violent and unexpected manner. He remembered that his last thoughts as he fell asleep were the removal of Musrat's extremist advisors from the equation.

Anxiety flowed over him; surely, he couldn't possibly have inherited the power to intercede in such a manner. The taking of life was contrary to Christian doctrine. He dismissed his thoughts as a flight of fancy, but nevertheless it worried him and many minutes passed before he found the solace of sleep.

Next Morning

Lincoln and Dayan explored the details of the Peace proposals over a late breakfast; the death of Father Paul wasn't mentioned.

"I wouldn't get your hopes up, John; Musrat will not be able to persuade his thugs to accept these proposals. They don't want peace with Israel, they don't even accept there should be an Israel. You'll find that those on his Council who would compromise, are terrified of those who will not. Your proposals will be rejected, you'll see."

"There are extremists in all political Parties, Ezer, including yours; they have to be controlled one way or another and I believe a way will be found to do that."

Dayan shook his head and chuckled. "Never. I'm coming to believe that President Caswell is right about you when he says you are a dreamer."

Their conversation was interrupted when the Dayan's Private Secretary entered the room and approached the table. "Some bulletins you should be aware of Prime Minister; one of them is probably significant."

Dayan eyed them superficially, leafing through till one held his attention. He glanced up at his guest. "How extraordinary." He shook his head in amazement. "This is truly unbelievable; four of Abdul Musrat's top advisors, all known terrorists, have been killed in a car accident on the road to El Ariba. It's good news for Abdul and a blessing for Israel."

Lincoln felt his heart pound, he could scarcely believe what he was hearing; his dream, or was it his wish, had been fulfilled. It just couldn't be a coincidence. Unease gnawed at his gut. Was he, the Vice-President of the United States, directly responsible for the death of five men? His thoughts took over;

names surfaced involuntarily. "Would the advisors involved, perchance be the two Al Hassad brothers, El Hassim and Habanti?"

Dayan nodded without thinking, "Only the Hassad brothers have been identified in this bulletin but two of the other badly burned bodies could well be those you name; it's a notorious group."

He paused, realising the significance of Lincoln's question, his expression puzzled, troubled almost. "How can you possibly know their names? Have you had a call from your intelligent sources? If so, they are better informed than I realised."

Lincoln fought to control his inner emotions, instinctively afraid of what appeared to be a devastating power, more fearful still of his ability to control it. "No comment Ezer." He answered enigmatically; it suited him to leave Dayan uncertain. "Now it's eleven-o'clock and I fly out at 13.00 hours; tell me who you think is likely to prove to be your strongest opposition?"

Dayan grimaced. "That's easy, they are all around me; but the main players will be there in the airport farewell line-up, watchful to the very end. They will all want to be interviewed by the media after your departure to make it clear to the public that they are immune to your political overtures."

Lincoln smiled grimly; his new powers could well prove to be useful. "I look forward to meeting them. Hopefully I'll be able to exert some last-minute influence on their thinking."

The Israeli Prime Minister smiled. "And as they say in your country, John, 'pigs might fly."

Israeli Military Airport

At 12.40, Lincoln moved slowly along the line of Israeli dignitaries who had gathered to witness his farewell. Air Force Two stood ready nearby, gleaming in the midday sun. Far above four Israeli fighter-jets were circling the sky to ensure that his flight out would be protected whilst it was in Israeli air space.

There were twelve members of the Knesset in the lineup and Lincoln stopped to talk to each of them, shaking hands as he did so, ostensibly thanking them for the hospitality he had enjoyed during his visit. In six instances he leaned forward and whispered into the politician's ear then stood back to witness their reaction. He had spoken only a sentence or two in each case but it was enough; expressions changed in an instant and he could see fear and dismay register in their eyes.

Those six men would never sleep easily again, now that such a powerful politician was aware of their individual failings, sexual perversion, drug abuse, tax evasion, rape, murder, even incest, whichever applied. If Lincoln told Dayan, he would inform the Speaker, and they would be summarily dismissed from the Knesset; their careers would be ended and criminal charges would follow.

Finally, Lincoln reached the end of the line and stood opposite the Israeli Prime Minister. He made no attempt to lower his voice; he wanted everyone to hear what he had to say. "Goodbye Ezer, thank you for your co-operation and hospitality. I will make a record of all that I have learned during this very informative visit. I hope that you and your colleagues will be able to support the Peace Accord. Let me know if I can help in any way." He looked pointedly along the line of watching politicians. "I've sown a few seeds here and there and it's just possible you'll encounter less opposition than you anticipate."

Dayan nodded. "I hope that you have a good trip back to America, John, and will pray that your mission meets with the success that it deserves. President Caswell contacted me this morning seeking a perspective on your visit; I was able to tell him, that it had been thought- provoking and that you had left us with much to consider. He appears to support the Peace Accord to some extent, but expressed surprise that you had even considered the possibility of a visit to Iraq."

Lincoln winced. "I'm sorry that you felt it necessary to be specific about Iraq; you must have realised how sensitive it would be. But no matter, just make sure you keep to your undertakings and I'll keep to mine."

Dayan smile was smug, he had sown a few seeds of his own with President Caswell.

I'll wipe that smile off your face, Dayan. Lincoln bent forward to whisper as he shook hands. "Oh, by the way, Ezer. It's come to my attention that, as well as the matter of Father Paul's death, you've been transferring large sums of money into a Swiss Bank account." He stood back, smiling at the Israeli's obvious discomfort. "Don't look so anxious, I know how to keep a confidence - if it suits me, that is."

Lincoln felt very satisfied as he climbed the steps to Air Force Two, turning at the top to smile and wave; the success of his visit had been beyond his wildest dreams. *Thank you, Lord, we will make a formidable team in the years that lie ahead.*

Air Force Two

Air Force Two was half way across the Atlantic when an aide alerted Lincoln to a telephone call from the President.

"Hi John, how are you?"

"I'm fine, looking forward to getting home. We'll have a lot to discuss."

"How have things gone? I've kept my nose out and left you to do things your own way."

"Thanks, Jack, I appreciate that greatly. I guess you would say that the situation is finely balanced, but moving in the right way. Dayan and Musrat are talking to each other; I'd say that was significant progress in itself. Ezer did mention that you had been in touch; I wondered if he'd briefed you?"

"It was just a courtesy call; we didn't talk for long. I hope you didn't make any promises you can't deliver on? There's a limit to how far we can go and how much loot we can put in the pot."

"You gave me a free hand Jack, so you'll have to live with it. Any solution is going to have a cost, but a lasting Arab-Israeli Peace Accord would be a good investment. It must be better for all concerned if we invest in their infra-structure instead of weapons of destruction."

"Spare me the idealism; it's the price tag that's worrying me, and even if you do get lucky with that pair, there are the other Middle East leaders to deal with. They will all want their say, believe me. A word of warning, no dealings with that bastard Saddam Hussein." Briefed by Dayan, Caswell was laying down a warning.

"We'll talk when I get back Jack. It's already been a long day for me and I don't feel much like entering into a debate right now."

"OK, I'll leave you in peace for the moment, but I want to see you as soon as you get back."

Lincoln leaned back in his seat. *Oh dear, Jack, I hope you're not going to be too troublesome; I've got a major player in my corner now.*

Heaven

The Old Man had observed all that had taken place and was deeply concerned. "I pray you know what you are doing my son. I won't be able to protect you if you go too far; we all have to abide by our rules."

The White House, Washington

Caswell was troubled; something had to be done to curb his Vice-President's ambitions. He thought for a moment and, as was frequently the case in recent months, he sent for his lover and confidant Diane Phelps.

'Diane, our Middle East venture might have back-fired on us. Lincoln has made more progress than I would have thought possible. I'm really worried about the direction he's taking us; he's rapidly becoming a loose cannon. We need to tie him down before he does some real damage. I want you to gather together some ideas as to how we might put a few dents in that shiny reputation of his. Find out anything you can about him, or his wife. I'm sure Lionel Cruz over at the FBI will let you have access to anything he has, and Olly Dacre might have something on his CIA files. Be careful how you approach Olly; I'm not sure of his loyalty. Needless to say, this requires your utmost discretion."

"Sure thing, Darling, just leave it to me; I'll get right onto it. I can always say we're looking forward to the next election campaign and need to be sure there are no skeletons hidden away in the cupboard. Do you want me to hang around? It's been nearly a week since we had some quality time together?"

"There's nothing I'd want more, but Weinberger is due any minute now. Call me later this afternoon; I'm sure we can arrange one of those do-not-disturb meetings of ours."

She leaned over the desk and kissed him, running her tongue along his lips. "Can't wait, don't leave it too long."

CHAPTER 11

The Lincoln Residence: Washington

Carol Lincoln was working upstairs, in what she referred to as her leisure room, when she heard her husband's car crunching on the drive gravel. She had been expecting him for the last hour or so, praying that there had been no last-minute changes to his plans. She wanted him back home; life wasn't quite the same when he wasn't around. She ran downstairs and across the oak-floored hall to the front door, pulling it open before he had time to unload his luggage from the car. He turned when he heard the door, his spirits lifting when he saw her standing there in the porch, her smile lighting up her face as it always did.

"Hi Honey; I've missed you." He climbed the three stone steps on to the pillared portico, dropping his luggage when he reached her, his arms extending to embrace her. Even as he did so, he remembered his new powers and for a brief instant felt confused. He trusted her implicitly, he had no reason to fear her innermost thoughts, and yet he wished he had a switch to disengage the gift he had inherited. *'What secrets might she have; what shortcomings might she see in him that she had never revealed? Damn it, I don't want to know.'*

His fears left almost as quickly as they arrived and they threw their arms around each other, hugging, kissing, cuddling, making up for the time they had been apart. He felt the energy between them and steeled himself for what he was about to learn, but this time there were no images, no revelations or life history Just an overwhelming feeling of love and trust. Tears gathered in his eyes, tiny droplets rolling down his cheeks as relief and emotion combined.

"Why John you're crying. What's wrong, Honey?"

"Nothing's wrong, Darling, nothing at all; I'm just so happy to be back with you. I have so much to tell you, some of it very important. I'm going to need your advice and support more than I've ever done before."

"Goodness me, what on Earth has happened to you? No!" She put a finger to his lips before he could reply, "Don't tell me, not just yet. I think you should freshen up, have a bath and relax; whatever it is can wait. Whilst you're doing that, I'll get us something to eat."

She was in the kitchen when the telephone rang and even before she picked it up, she guessed it would be Jack Caswell.

"Carol its Jack; how are you?"

"Just fine, and what about you and Beth?"

"We're both well, thanks. I know that John landed safely and I presume he's home by now, unless he's gone cruising the sidewalks."

"You speak for yourself Jack Caswell; my man has no need to do such a thing."

"Only joking. I had hoped he'd call in at the White House on his way past. I need some feed back on his trip."

"Well, that'll have to wait until tomorrow.' She spoke firmly, 'I'm the most important person in my husband's life right now. He's tired and gone straight to bed, jet-lag I guess. Nothing a good night's sleep won't put right."

Caswell knew she was protecting her husband and pressed further. "Sorry to intrude, but I wonder if I could have a quick word?"

Carol Lincoln was resolute. "I'm afraid not, Jack. Unless, you're invoking some Presidential powers I don't know about, I'd rather not disturb him. The exception being that it's some kind of emergency. I'm sure if he had had anything urgent or vital to tell you, he would have made contact. I'll tell him you rang and ask him to see you first thing tomorrow. Bye for now, and do give my regards to Beth." She smiled to herself; she didn't care much for Jack Caswell.

She restored the telephone to its cradle and turned to find her husband, in his dressing gown, watching her with amusement.

"Tut, tut, Carol Lincoln, telling lies to the President; I'm sure that's an indictable offence."

"I didn't tell him any lies; I just didn't go in for the whole truth, that's all."

"I see; what you would call a white lie I suppose?"

She laughed. "I'm not sure if black folks can tell white lies; let's say it was a black truth. Now let's have our meal, and I don't want to hear about any problems while we're eating; you can tell me about the places you've been to in Israel though, especially Jerusalem and the Church of the Holy Sepulchre where our Lord was born. Just leave out the politics until we're done."

Lincoln caught his breath and reflected briefly on the account of events he would have to tell his wife, wondering how it would be received by someone as devout as she.

Afterwards they sat together in their lounge in front of the huge open log fire, sipping the Jack Daniels they both enjoyed. He took his usual place at one end of the sofa, she at the other her feet on his lap. She waited patiently when he lapsed into silence, knew he was searching his thoughts, thinking out what he was going to say. She didn't hurry him, knowing he would begin when he was comfortable with what he had to tell her. The moment came and he looked deep into her eyes, giving emphasis to what he was about to reveal.

"Carol, I have to ask you to promise never to repeat what I'm about to tell you, not even after I die."

She thought she detected a tremor in her husband's voice. "Heavens John, whatever has happened? What can you possibly have to tell me that's affecting you in this way? Of course I'll give my promise, that's easy; it's not breaking it someday that might be the difficulty. But are you sure you want to tell me this secret of yours?"

"I need to tell you. You're the only one I can tell, the only one I want to tell. I trust you implicitly and I know you'll keep your promise if you possibly can. And, before I start, I swear that what I'm about to tell you is the absolute truth."

"I have no doubt about that." She looked at him searchingly. "I'm dying to know what can be so important."

Lincoln took a deep breath and began to tell his story, watching for her reaction, hoping she didn't think he was mad. "I've witnessed a miracle, Carol; I believe I've seen Jesus Christ, right there at his birthplace. And it wasn't just me; Prime Minister Dayan and Chairman Musrat were there with me in the Church of the Holy Sepulchre when it happened."

Carol Lincoln didn't speak; she didn't know what to think or say, but she had faith in her man's belief. She could sense the profound feelings that lay within her husband.

"And it wasn't just that I saw him, Carol; it was much more than that. He put his arms around me in full view of the others." He watched as his wife absorbed his revelation; she was calmer than he had anticipated, but she was after all a devout Christian and had no difficulty accepting the occurrence of miracles. Over the centuries, Church history recorded that they happened from time to time and usually involved very ordinary people.

She squeezed his hand. "Tell me all about it. Whatever you saw, what makes you think it was the Lord? Tell me what you think it means, and what you are going to do about it. One thing is for sure; if it was the Lord, it's a sign that he believes in you and in what took you to the Middle East."

"It was the Lord, I'm sure of it. I haven't told you everything."

Their conversation lasted for nearly an hour during which he described the manifestation and told her of his hopes and fears, explaining why he didn't want to publicise the event. He kept one thing from her; he didn't tell her about the powers he had acquired. He was afraid it might affect their close relationship in some unforeseen way.

"And that's about it. I feel so undeserving; we both know I'm not a practising Christian. Why me? What if I do something wrong?"

She shook her head. "You're forgetting something John; he chose you – you didn't choose him. You are not his partner - you are his servant. He picked you for a reason, and from that moment, you've been doing what he expected you to do. If you stray from his chosen path, he'll let you know soon enough."

Lincoln smiled; he envied his wife's simple belief that good would prevail no matter what. "I wish I had your faith, Darling, you're always so sure of things. But bless you; you've said just what I hoped you would say. I wish you could have been there with me."

"So do I, John, so do I."

"Carol, I'm emotionally drained, do you mind if we have an early night?"

"Sounds good to me."

Before they went to sleep, they made love; he'd had his concerns momentarily, wondering if it would be different than before, but nothing had changed. Somehow, she had sensed his disquiet. "There you are Honey; you're still my husband even though the good Lord has blessed you. And you've been fibbing, John, you didn't seem at all tired to me."

Lincoln fell asleep re-assured, his belief in the future strengthened.

The White House

Next morning he made the short drive to the White House, for once unconcerned by the snail-paced traffic generated by the morning rush hour, using the slow journey to rehearse his meeting with the President.

"Good morning, Mary, nice outfit you're wearing."

"Thank you, John, and welcome back. Ms Phelps is in with him at the moment, but you can go straight in; I buzzed him when I saw you start along the corridor."

"If it's all the same, I'll wait till Phelps leaves, there's no hurry."

She raised an eyebrow but made no comment; not many people liked the Head of Communications.

Lincoln didn't have to wait long, barely a few minutes had elapsed before the door opened and Phelps stepped out, wearing her usual public relations smile.

"Good morning, Mr Vice-President, nice to have you back on board; the place isn't the same without you."

He had never invited her to use his first name and didn't
intend to. The Head of Communications was at her most
gushing and manufactured a generous smile accompanied by a
little bow.

*You ingenuous little toad; you belong in the pond with the
rest of the low life.* But he returned her smile and didn't betray
his inner disapproval.

"Why thank you, it's always nice to come home, no matter
what part of the world I visit. Could be, when I've conversed
with the President, you and I might have to work together on
some ideas I have for the Middle East peace process. We
haven't always seen eye to eye, but I guess we could shake
hands on the past and look forward to the future." He extended
his hand. She was surprised and showed it, but her public
relations reflexes took over and she shook hands warmly.

"Sure thing, Mr Vice-President. As soon as the President
gives the word, I'll be happy to work alongside you."

The energy flow started, as he knew it would, astounding
him with the images it released. Her liaisons with Caswell were
revealed, the approaches to the FBI and CIA for his life history
and the plotting to bring about his downfall.

She tried to pull her hand away. "You can let go now I'm
getting cramp in my hand."

Lincoln looked deep into her eyes, so deep that she looked
away. "Sure, sorry, I guess it's just so good to be back amongst
friends, I got carried away."

She nodded, but she sensed that something lay behind the
handshake. *That look he had given her, meant something. But
what?*

The Oval Office

"Come on in John." Caswell called out. "I'm keen to get
some feedback on this trip of yours."

Lincoln felt numb, almost in a daze, as he walked slowly
forward, his gaze fixed on the man he thought was his friend.
*There must be a mistake; the wires have got crossed somehow.
Diane Phelps and the President, it was impossible.* His thoughts

raced; there was one way to find out. He fought to regain his composure, but Caswell had seen the look of dismay on his face.

"What's wrong? Carol said you were very tired but I have to confess I thought you were just avoiding me."

"No, no, I'm fine Jack; I guess jet-lag still has me in its clutches. I wouldn't miss this session for the world, believe me."

He reached out and took the President's hand, putting his other hand on the President's shoulder, seeking out what lay in his innermost thoughts, steeling himself for what he was about to learn. The process began immediately and he struggled to summon up a smile to hide his reactions to the images flooding into his mind. He barely suppressed a groan as everything he learned from the Phelps' transfer was confirmed; the truth he hadn't wanted to believe couldn't be denied. She and Caswell were engaged in an adulterous affair right here in the Oval Office.

Instances of political chicanery were laid bare. Corruption and intrigue emerged, mostly in the years before Caswell became President were revealed. Lincoln was totally dismayed; his friend's image had been shattered in a moment's exposure.

Caswell was staring at him open-mouthed. "John, what in the hell is the matter with you? You look like you've seen a ghost. Come and sit down. If these trips are going to have this kind of effect, we'll have to keep you back home in the USA."

"Sorry Jack, my thoughts are full of this Middle East business; let's get started. You've had a copy of my proposals for the Peace Accord, and of course you've already spoken to Dayan."

"Yes, and you've done a first-class job. As far as I can see, it can be made to work but just talk me through it."

The two men explored the details and implications of the Draft Peace Accord for the next hour during which Lincoln tried to allay the President's fears. In fact, to his surprise, Caswell was generally more accommodating than he had expected, but eventually the President's reservations surfaced.

"The way I see it John, there are three problems we need to address though I expect, given time, we can iron them out."

Lincoln shook his head; no way was he going to let the President put a brake on the process. "There isn't a lot of time, I want the momentum maintained. I've got Dayan and Musrat running with these proposals; I need your wholehearted support, and I need it now."

Caswell raised his hands in protest. "Just hold on, hear me out. Number one, this resettlement angle and all the rebuilding could be costly; Congress and the Senate may not go for it."

"They'll support it if you ask them to, correction, if **we** ask them to. We're pouring money into Israel even as we speak, like we have done for years. If we got pulled into a war in the region it would cost us billions, so I don't accept the financial argument. Folks are divided on the issue even now, and when body-bags started to come home, opinion would shift against you overnight."

Caswell nodded. "I'll concede you that point for the moment. Number two, when you go round talking to the Heads of State, I want our oil interests safeguarded."

"There you go again Jack; this is about what's best for the region, not what's best for America. We have our own oil sources and if needs be we can buy oil on the open market like everybody else, and probably can afford it more readily than most other nations. Ukraine, Russia and Venezuela have got vast oil resources; if we have to, we can start buying more from them and build better relationships in the process. In any case, the Middle East relies on its oil sales to survive; we'll always be able to buy from them. They need us as much as we need them."

"Maybe you have a point,", Caswell was wavering, "though you haven't entirely convinced me; we can research that assertion. It isn't just the security of supply that counts, it's the price we have to pay for it."

Lincoln snorted. "With our purchasing power, alongside that of our friends and allies, I can't see it will be a problem. What's the third point?"

Caswell's expression hardened. "Put at its simplest, there's no way you're going to Iraq to be seen talking to that bastard Saddam Hussein. He's completely off limits with his germ warfare resources; until you drop that madman from the equation, your proposals are going nowhere."

Lincoln knew he reached a crunch point, but he wasn't going to give way. "Whether we like it or not, he governs a major Middle East country. We don't need to like him to do business with him. He knows he can't win in a fight with the US; I reckon he'll negotiate if he thinks there's something in it for him."

"Let me put it this way. You don't speak to him until he gives up his so-called 'weapons of mass destruction."

"That's all he's got. Think about it for a moment. Assuming he does have them, he's not going to concede them until he feels his position is secure."

"There's no compromise on this; you go off and sleep on it."

Lincoln regarded the President sombrely. Now wasn't the time to argue; they had reached an impasse and he needed some leverage to get his way.

"I'll give the matter some serious thought, Jack but, in the meantime, I want your unequivocal support for the Peace Accord itself. I want to tell the Israelis and the Palestinians that you're on board and that they can formally take steps to find out what support they have for the Accord amongst their colleagues and people. I'd like you to make this initiative your top priority"

Caswell nodded reluctantly, "OK, you have my support, go ahead."

Lincoln was pensive as he left the Oval Office; he had lethal information about the President but no proof to back it up. And what if he did? He wouldn't do anything to damage America in the eyes of the world, but neither was he going to let the Iraq issue fall at the first hurdle. He walked along the corridor to his office and sank into his favourite chair deep in thought. As he relaxed, a plan took shape in his mind; he knew now what he had to do. But first he had to update Dayan and Musrat. He put out calls requesting that they got in touch as soon as possible.

The Arab was the first to return his call. "How can I help, John?"

"Abdul, thanks for getting back to me. The President supports the Peace Accord we discussed and wants you to sound out your people. Can you do that and let me know how things stand? The President has asked that we don't publicise the proposals just yet."

"I've already taken soundings John, it looks promising. Providence removed some of my militant colleagues; I'll need another seventy-two hours before I can be certain."

Dayan called soon afterwards. "Ezer, thanks for calling back. We're going ahead with the Peace Accord. The President is in full agreement and would like you to discuss the matter formally with your Cabinet and the Knesset. No publicity at this stage and we'd like an answer in seventy-two hours."

"I'll need longer than that John and what about your consultations with the other Middle East Heads of State."

"Seventy-two hours is all you've got Ezer; you guys are always meeting in emergency session; this is just another day at the office. As for the consultations, President Caswell and I are working on them."

"I don't like being bulldozed."

"I don't either Ezer, but that's how it is this time round."

"Have it your way; I'll do my best, but can't promise."

Lincoln's secretary had learned from a friend that the FBI and CIA were about to carry out searches of his personal files and she had told him.

'I'm sure it's just a precaution, Sue-Ellen but thanks for letting me know.' He had some concerns; they would go back to his college and university days and rake over the ashes of his political and personal life. And they were checking out Carol. He smiled at the thought; they were wasting their time on her.

Politically he had little to fear; he had been very left wing in his early years, most students were but he hadn't gone as far as supporting Communist ideals. There were no political scandals to be rooted out, and no underhand business dealings to embarrass him. He pushed his thoughts back in time; there had been some indiscreet criticisms of American policy in the presence of a handful of foreign leaders with whom he had found an affinity, but nothing that couldn't be explained or denied.

It was his personal life that concerned him. He had gone down the soft drug trail at university, mild usage by the standards of the present day, but he was currently an outspoken critic of the whole drug scene. Exposure might just damage his influence, especially if the drug-taking was exaggerated. And there had been a sprinkling of outrageous sex parties during one semester, but that too was expected of students and he'd told Carol all about them before they married.

It was his early years of marriage that really concerned him. In the years before the children came along, he had spent many nights away from home building his political and business careers; he had been a rising star and many women had admired him. He had no excuses for the indiscretions he had committed when uncontrolled testosterone and vanity had taken over. The arrival of his first daughter had changed his outlook on life completely, and he had been faithful to his wife ever since. But given the chance the media would crawl all over those early days, exaggerate what had occurred, and put it in the public domain. Carol would be humiliated; he couldn't let that happen.

Ever since the Hoover days, the FBI had contrived to find the dirt on all public figures and release it to the media when the stakes got high enough. He wasn't too concerned about his image; most politicians managed to rise above the muck and leave it behind. It was his family that concerned him most; he just couldn't bear to be the instrument of shame for Carol and his daughters. *What can I do about those sins? I only have myself to blame but I can't let some cheap blackmail on Caswell's part scupper this whole process.*

The President and Phelps didn't know anything yet, the Agencies hadn't reported but it wouldn't be long before they did. Well, he'd fight fire with fire; he'd play them at their own game. He knew now exactly what he was going to do. Hmm, I'm not sure what you would think about my tactics, Lord but I can't come up with anything else.'

He dialled Mary O'Halloran, "Mary, I might need to see the President later on. Am I right in thinking he's seeing Phelps this evening?"

"He is indeed, the meeting is set for five o'clock in her office; he reckoned it would take about an hour. Shall I book you in after that?"

"Not sure yet, I'll let you know when I've worked through my other commitments. I've been away such a lot recently and Carol might want me home early tonight."

The offices of the Vice-President and the Head of Communications were separated by a small bedroom suite, which could be used by either official when the situation required an overnight stay. Lincoln had never had cause to make use of it; as Vice-President, and a friend of Caswell's, he had always been invited to stay in the President's private residential quarters when the need had arisen. Over time the room had become increasingly associated with Phelps but nevertheless it could still be accessed from both offices.

"Jane, does Diane have any free time today? I'm working on something that might require her expertise."

Phelps' secretary ran through the appointments. "She's not around at the moment Mr Vice-President and she's booked out for most of the day. The best time to catch her is probably between four and five, after that she's with the President. I guess she might come in around lunchtime, I'm not sure. Shall I give you a call when she's around?"

"Thanks Jane, leave it with me and I'll see what progress I make. It might not be necessary."

Lincoln crossed the room to his wall safe and removed two Minrecs, miniature wafer-thin recording devices, as used by the CIA. They were intended primarily for covert purposes but he occasionally used them to record discussions at meetings, always with the knowledge of those attending. He set the time delay on the Minrecs to activate at 16.45 and to run for their full capacity of three hours. What he planned was totally out of character, but there was too much at stake to be squeamish. He used his White House passkey to access the overnight room via the connecting door from his office. Concealment of one of the Minrecs in the bedroom was straightforward. He slid it under the bed against the headboard wall; in the shadow it was unlikely to be seen even if someone chanced to look.

Next, he listened at the door to Phelps' office; silence. The door was unlocked and he eased it open far enough to see into the room. To his dismay the connecting door to the secretary's office was partly open and he could hear her going about her duties. Fortunately, she didn't have a significant line of vision into her boss's office and he had time to scan the room for a suitable hiding place for the second Minrec. There was one obvious place, behind the books on a bookcase that stood to the right of the door. He crossed the floor swiftly, making no sound on the thick carpet, praying that Jane Dolan wouldn't choose to enter the office. Luck, if it was luck, and not a divine helping hand, continued to be on his side; he deposited the Minrec behind a line of large reference books and within seconds had left the room. *Phew, glad that's over with, job done,* His pulse was racing. *I'm obviously not CIA material. Let's hope the technology works.*

Back in his office he contacted Mary O'Halloran again. "What's the earliest I can see the President tomorrow morning?"

"He's usually here by eight and his first meeting tomorrow isn't until ten."

"What about booking me in for nine; that'll give him time to go through his post. I'll join him for a cup of your very best coffee."

"No problem, John; I'll book you in."

Next, he made his way to Jane Dolan's office. "Jane, I'm going out now so I won't catch up with Diane today. What are her movements tomorrow? I'm with the President from 9.00am to 10.00am."

"Nothing near that I'm afraid; she's not coming in first thing and is out most of the morning."

"No matter, I'll leave it for now; I'm sure we'll catch up with each other sooner or later."

Next morning

Lincoln made an early start and was in the White House shortly after seven. Staff came and went around the clock and his early appearance was entirely unremarkable; a nod of the head, a brief good morning, a wave of acknowledgement was the sum of his encounters as he made his way to his office. He anticipated no difficulties in retrieving the Minrecs; Phelps wouldn't be in until later on and as he walked past the open door of Jane Dolan's office, he was relieved to see it was empty. Security cameras would record his presence; those in the main corridor would subsequently show that he went straight to his office and stayed there until his meeting with the President.

The bed in the overnight room looked like it hadn't been disturbed. *Shit, I hope you two didn't change your mind.* The Minrecs were exactly where he had left them and he was back in the safety of his office within a few minutes. It had all been too easy.

Lincoln locked the doors to his office and the overnight room; he didn't want an unscheduled interruption whilst he played back the recordings. They confirmed what he already knew; the content was explicit and he doubted if the President's career would survive if they ever reached the public arena. He made a number of notes, and it was eight forty-five by the time he completed his task; he was now ready to confront Caswell.

The security of the Minrecs could prove problematic following his meeting and he pondered putting them in his wall safe, but felt sure that it could be opened by White House security staff at the President's direction. In fact, under the watchful lenses of the security cameras, he doubted if there was a safe hiding place in the White House. Instead, he put each of them in an envelope and slid them into his inside jacket pocket; even Caswell would be unlikely to require the Vice-President to undergo a personal search.

CHAPTER 12

The Oval Office

The short time remaining until his meeting with the President passed slowly, but eventually the moment came and he made his way along the corridor to the Oval Office.

"Good morning, Mary. Is he ready for me?"

"Sure is, go right on in; the coffee jug is at the already."

"John," Caswell looked up smiling and waved a hand at one of the armchairs, "come on in and take a pew. I hadn't expected you to come back to me this quickly. Looks like that problem you went away with hasn't proved as tough as I thought."

"I've come up with a solution Jack, though I suspect it's not one you'll be happy with."

"Sounds ominous; I didn't cut you much slack. Tell you what, you take a few minutes to reflect on what you've come up with and I'll take a leak; sounds like this one isn't a quickie."

Left alone in the Oval Office, Lincoln had a brainwave and he moved across to the large glass-fronted oak bookcase and dropped the envelopes containing the Minrecs behind some ancient leather-bound tomes. They were unlikely to have been moved in the last fifty years. The entire White House might be searched but he doubted if the President's office would come under scrutiny.

Caswell returned to find his Vice-President patiently lounging in one of the armchairs and seated himself opposite. "Coffee?"

"Sure, I need the caffeine; black as usual."

"OK you have the floor, fire away."

"I hope there's no chance of us being overheard Jack?"

Caswell wrinkled his brow. 'Overheard? Mary wouldn't think of listening in, you surely know that. What's bugging you?"

"I was thinking of something more subtle."

The President smiled. "Ah, I see what you're getting at; I assure you there are no secret recording devices in here. All that shit went out with Nixon; I promise you. You're getting more intriguing by the minute; what's troubling you?"

"Nothing's troubling me; I'm more concerned about you, believe me."

Caswell pursed his lips. 'Now you're really starting to worry me fire away.'

Lincoln took a deep breath, the moment had arrived, their relationship would never be the same again. 'Firstly, I contacted Dayan and Musrat and told them to go ahead and consult formally on the Peace Accord proposals. I also told them the package had your blessing. I've given them seventy-two hours to deliver their reply. OK so far?"

Caswell nodded his head warily and shrugged. "That's the easy bit done."

"Next, I asked President Marak of Egypt to use his good offices to arrange for me to meet the various Middle East leaders. I've made clear it's a top-of-the office affair; told him I didn't want a tribe of advisors massing round the table. I've indicated that I'll meet them either individually or in groups; whatever suits their commitments. I had to give Marak an insight into what was happening and he was very supportive; I told him I'd be available all next week. You might like to see a list of those involved, I hadn't quite realised just how many States could have an interest."

Caswell seized the list proffered to him and scrutinised it closely, nodding as he did so; Bahrain, Egypt, Iran, Jordan, Kuwait, Lebanon, Oman, Qatar, Saudi Arabia, Syria, United Arab Emirates and Yemen. "Christ, you haven't let the dust settle on this one, have you? They aren't all major players you know; we don't need to consult everybody."

Lincoln wagged his finger at the President. "Yes, we do Jack; if I listened to you, you would have me believe America was the only major player. We've got to start including **all** the players if our foreign policy is to gain wider acceptance. Every country in the Middle East will be affected by the Peace Accord; I want them all on board. And you're right, I am deliberately moving things along fast; I want to maintain the momentum that's been generated this far."

Caswell stroked his chin pensively. "You must be very confident of Dayan and Musrat going along with the proposals. I would have briefed one of my aides to arrange the meetings if you had asked, but no harm done. One thing for sure though, I'm pleased to see that you've come to your senses about talking to that bastard Saddam Hussein."

Lincoln smirked openly; he had deliberately made no reference to Iraq on the list knowing that Caswell would seize on the omission, seeing it as a victory of some sort. "Oh, did I forget to include Iraq? I'm sorry about that; let me add it to the list. He's included in the party, although in deference to your wishes, I insisted on meeting him in secret. There will be no publicity whatsoever; I promise you."

"Don't play fucking games." Caswell snarled. "I told you he was off limits. You seem to be overlooking the fact that I'm the boss around here. You even try talking to him on the phone and I'll see that your career is in ruins before the week is out. You had better believe me on this one, I mean business."

Lincoln shook his head. "I thought you might take it badly, but nevertheless, I will be meeting him; in fact, Marak already has it in hand."

"You fucking won't, I'll get on to Marak right this minute and cancel the whole show until you come to your senses."

He reached forward and lifted his phone, then paged through his private telephone directory.

Lincoln reached forward and pressed down the phone rest. "Before you do that, tell me how your meeting, with the Head of Communications, went yesterday evening?

Caswell was nonplussed; he couldn't figure out what lay behind the question. "What? Have you lost the plot altogether? What's my meeting with Diane got to do with anything? Keep to the fucking point."

"You'll see what the point is soon enough. Let me tell you how it went. You arrived at her office," Lincoln glanced at his notes before going on, "at eleven minutes after five and left at fourteen minutes after six. During that hour you were very busy."

Caswell exploded, not seeing where it was headed. "So, fucking what? Have you been checking the CCTV footage? If you carry on like this, you'll find yourself writing your resignation before the day is out."

"Back off, Jack, I hope that **neither** of us has to resign. You had a whisky; Diane had a dry martini. Am I right so far? Are you starting to get the picture? Am I keeping to the fucking point?"

Caswell's eyes narrowed, his hands started to shake, sweat broke out on his brow. "What of it; we had a drink, no harm in that. Have you taken to marking the bottles?" He knew his bravado wasn't having any effect; his stomach knotted as he tried to figure out how Lincoln knew so much.

"You didn't confine your business to her office, did you? How was the overnight room? The bed was comfortable, I hope? Good mattress, plenty of spring in it?"

Caswell rose to his feet, livid with anger, pointing a shaking finger at his accuser. "What are you insinuating? There's nothing between Diane and me. It would be your word against ours."

"Calm down, you're insulting my intelligence. I know exactly what went on and I have hard evidence to prove it; your sexual shenanigans were recorded. The good news is there's no need for Beth or the American people to learn about your current sexual adventures; you just have to be sensible. Now sit down and listen."

Caswell collapsed into his chair, head in hands, his heart was thumping with anger, thoughts were cramming his head, fear was tying knots in his stomach.

"It's like this Jack, I don't give a damn about your relationship with Diane, believe me."

The President said nothing, gripped by fear his tongue had frozen; his mouth dry.

"You've had a good Presidency and I don't want to ruin it; we've had our fair share of scandals in the White House and the country doesn't need another one. All you have to do is play ball and give your unequivocal support for my Middle East initiative, and whatever follows on from it. Do what I say, and I promise you that poor Beth, your children and the American people, will never learn about this sordid business from me. Do you understand?"

Caswell didn't answer; he sat with his head bowed, overwhelmed by fear and shame.

"So, just to summarise; I **will** go to Iraq, and you **will** persuade Congress to come up with the investment needed. You will also play down any fears about oil and military bases. Now that's not too big a price to pay to carry on as the President of the United States of America and go out with an unblemished record. Is it Jack?"

Lincoln held a finger to his ear. "I'm not hearing you, Jack."

Caswell knew there was no way out at this moment in time; he had to play ball and live to fight another day. His mind was coming out of its paralysis; he had to find the source of Lincoln's information and destroy it. He nodded, acknowledging his submission to Lincoln's demands. "You've got me by the balls; I don't appear to have any alternative."

Lincoln smiled and sank back in his chair; he had won. "Good, then we can move forward as though nothing has happened. And you might like to give some thought to what world issue I should tackle next. You can take all the credit for the Middle East initiative by the way; I'm not interested in personal glory. You will have to brief our British friends about what's happening; they are still our staunchest allies. I'm sure your friend the Prime Minister will be delighted."

Caswell nodded his head; he was starting to recover from his shock. "You're calling the shots, for the moment at least."

"Good, I'll leave you to it. Anything else you want to discuss? No?"

Caswell shook his head.

"OK, Jack, I'll leave you in peace. Call me anytime you have something to discuss."

The President finally found the resolve to raise his head and look his one-time friend in the eye. "Who else knows about Diane and me?"

"No-one and it'll stay that way as long as you co-operate."

"And this evidence you've got?"

Lincoln smiled broadly. "It's safe, very safe; don't go getting any foolish ideas on that front." Lincoln turned back as he reached the door, lowering his voice, "Oh Jack, just one thing I meant to ask, curiosity really."

"Yes, what's that?" Caswell's voice croaked.

"Judging by Diane's squeals, you did quite a job last night; I just wondered if you were taking anything to aid your performance?"

Caswell jumped to his feet his eyes blazing. "Fuck you; get out before I throw you out."

Lincoln eyed him disparagingly. "You're not man enough. You can keep that particular secret. Love to Beth by the way; we must all get together sometime. And remember, Jack, I can bring you down anytime I feel like it."

Caswell sank back into his chair, his thoughts working overtime. He was safe for now. *How had Lincoln found out so much? Was he really the only one who knew? Could he trust him to keep his mouth shut? And not just for the present, but in the days going forward? What further demands might emerge? Christ what a mess I'm in.*

He lifted the phone and punched in Diane Phelps' number. "I need you back here right away."

"Can it wait Jack, I'm about to go out."

"No, it won't fucking wait, get in here now."

"Calm down Jack; I'm on my way." *Temper, temper Jack, who's shaken your cage?*

CHAPTER 13

Later in the Oval Office

"Go straight in Diane, the President is expecting you. He's not in good humour I'm afraid, been snappy and edgy since his meeting with the Vice-President."

Mary O'Halloran had been told to cancel all appointments; Jack Caswell had been brusque with her unlike him and had offered no explanation as to what was troubling him.

"Close the door and sit down, Diane; we have a one helluva problem on our hands."

She could tell from his furrowed brow and drawn features that he was fraught with anxiety; something major had gone awry. She put her arm round his shoulders and sought to relieve the President's anxieties.

"Don't worry Jack, whatever it is we can handle it."

The President's reaction took her aback. "Don't fucking patronise me Diane, it's too serious for fucking platitudes; Lincoln knows about us."

Her eyes widened; momentarily she was incapable of reply, grappling with the President's words. "That's not possible Jack, he can't know; we've been too careful."

"For Christ's sake Diane, listen to me; he knows. Got it?"

She nodded; hope battling against the reality of the situation, her thoughts trawling the implications of Caswell's revelation.

"He knows we got together last night, knows what we had to drink; probably knows how many shags we had."

"But how, Jack?"

The President shrugged his shoulders, "Who knows? He picked up that we were meeting, somehow guessed at what was going on and then I suppose he recorded what happened."

"Did he show you the tape or whatever?"

Caswell shook his head.

"So, we can't be certain he does have a recording."

"Damn it Diane, get real. He knew exactly what went on and says he has the evidence to prove it; I believe him. You're not suggesting he was hiding under the bed for fucks sake."

Caswell wrung his hands in despair. "Christ if this gets out, I'm finished as a political figure and I doubt if I could hang on to my marriage. Poor Beth, she would be devastated."

She reached forward and took his hand, risking rebuttal again, but this time he didn't pull away.

"Jack, let's take this a step at a time; forgive the questions but I need to know more before I can help. What exactly does he want out of this? He does want something, I assume?"

Caswell nodded. "At the moment, all he's asking for is my co-operation with this mission of his to put the world right at America's expense. This Middle East thing is already out of my control; Lincoln's driving it in the fast lane. He's got me by the balls and he's going to squeeze hard every time he wants something. This is a fucking disaster, Diane."

"Take it easy Jack, we're not beaten yet. We need some dirt to counteract what he's got; some piece of shit he wouldn't want to hit the fan. I'll get the CIA and FBI to speed up your request for his personal files. There's bound to be something he wouldn't want to make public, either for his sake or Carol's, you'll see."

"And suppose there isn't, just suppose there isn't?"

Phelps realised she was looking at a very frightened man and was surprised to see the President beginning to fray so quickly in the face of personal adversity. "There's always a way Jack, there's always a final solution; it's purely a matter of how far you're prepared to go to resolve this difficulty."

Caswell looked closely at his lover, seeing for the first time the tougher edge to her character. Her expression was steely, clinical. His heart rate soared as he realised what she might be suggesting. He was afraid to voice his thoughts, wanted to be sure what she meant.

"What exactly are you getting at, Diane?"

"You know exactly what I'm getting at Jack."

The President shook his head, this wasn't happening.

"We have to do whatever is necessary Jack; we can't let your career, or your marriage, go down the pan. But first things first, I'll expedite the reports and see what we've got. In the meantime, it might be as well to have my office, his office and the overnight room searched for surveillance devices; maybe his home too if it can be accessed without his knowledge. We need to track down those tapes. I'll try to find out if he's been officially issued with any recording devices."

Caswell was nervous. "Christ Diane, I don't know; checking out the Vice-President is risky in the first degree. And as for breaking into his house, I don't think that's possible. I can't think on what pretence I could do that. Even if Lincoln didn't know, others would. I'd have to come up with a good story and I can't think of one."

"You'll find one, Jack, you've been telling good stories all through your career. You've got time; he's not going anywhere with this as long as you play ball with the Middle East thing. He's not your usual blackmailer looking for an easy buck; it seems to me if he's left alone to pursue this ambition of his he'll be happy to overlook our relationship. He needs your support as much as you need his silence. It'll all work out, you'll see."

"I hope so, Diane, but it could become a different story if he raises the stakes too high. Christ, he's always going to be a time bomb waiting to go off. What happens when I'm no longer President?"

"The higher the stakes, Jack, the more extreme the remedy we might have to employ."

"What exactly are you getting at, Diane; spell it out? I don't think I like what I'm hearing." Caswell's gut was churning; this was all beginning to sound like a CIA nightmare.

Once again it surprised her how easily the great man had begun to crumble; she could see she was going to have to take control of the situation. She put a comforting arm round his shoulder again, pulling his head to her breast as a mother does when comforting a child. "Jack, it's been a terrible shock, I can see that, but he'll keep quiet as long as you further his Middle East initiative. If he succeeds with that, I'll have to make sure you get all the credit. Meanwhile, we try to turn up some dirt on him and try to find those tapes. If it all goes pear-shaped, we will have to come up with a more permanent solution and I can deal with that. You look after me and I'll look after you."

Caswell saw the logic in her approach and began to calm down. "You're right, we can work this out; Lincoln can't get anywhere without my backing."

"That's better Jack." She bent forward and kissed him. "I'll go now; I've got some thinking to do."

Caswell nodded; he felt more relaxed. "Come back to me when you've got a plan, and while you're at it, come up with another assignment for him; preferably one that carries a lot of risk." His eyes followed her as she turned to leave; he felt apprehensive, uneasy. *What exactly do you mean Diane, 'a more permanent solution'?*

Phelps was deep in thought as she left the President's office; she was thinking of her own career. If Caswell went down, she would go down; this all had to be cleared up before the current Presidency came to an end. *We'll have to find a permanent solution to you John Lincoln. Even as she thought, a way out of the mess was being born in her thoughts.*

Vice-President's Office, Tuesday

Lincoln picked up the most confidential of his direct line telephones, its number known to only a handful of people. He hoped it was the call he had been waiting for, the one that would set the Middle East process rolling.

"Marak speaking, Mr Lincoln; I have some news for you." The Prime Minister of Egypt spoke excellent English, one of the legacies of two successful years at Oxford University.

"Good morning, Prime Minister; thank you for getting back to me so quickly. I assume you have made some progress with the meetings?"

"Better than just progress; I think I have what you would refer to as a complete package."

"That's wonderful news, tell me more." Lincoln was tingling with excitement; a complete package implied the inclusion of Iraq.

"There will be four meetings; the first on Monday of next week here in Cairo, which I will attend along with a representative of Jordan. On Tuesday you will journey from Cairo to Riyadh, where you will meet with high-ranking representatives from Bahrain, Oman, Kuwait, United Arab Emirates, Qatar, Yemen and of course your host Saudi Arabia. From Riyadh, you will travel to Damascus late on Tuesday afternoon to meet with representatives from Syria, Lebanon and Iran.

Saddam Hussein has agreed to meet with you on Wednesday, but as yet has given no details as to where the meeting will take place, although it will be in Baghdad. I have placed an aircraft at your disposal; I thought that one of your President's planes would be somewhat conspicuous flying around the Middle East and could prove a tempting target."

Lincoln appreciated Marak's caution although his usual USAF escort would have ensured his safety. "Excellent, you seem to have covered everything. And there are no dissenters?"

"No dissenters Mr Lincoln, but some reluctant participants; I'm afraid not everyone trusts your motives, or should I say, those of your country. They are attending because everyone wants the Arab-Israeli problems resolved. I do not know who will be representing each country but, in every instance, it will be a Head of State or a Head of Government, possibly both. I am right in saying that you are coming on your own and will not be accompanied by Advisors?"

"That is correct; it's just me versus the entire Middle East on this occasion."

Gamal Marak forced a laugh, "I have to be frank, Mr Lincoln. I am wary of Iraq; there is I feel some risk to your personal safety. Saddam will not meet outside Iraq and I think that is understandable, but equally he will not host a meeting with other leaders in attendance. For your part, you will not be allowed to take your own security guards into the country. I told him that this was an unreasonable imposition, but he insists that it be a condition of your visit."

"That is worrying, but you can tell him that I accept his conditions and place my safety entirely in his hands. I'm sure he recognises the consequences that will follow if anything was to happen to the Vice-President of the United States; President Caswell's retaliation would be unbounded and brutal."

Marak sounded a warning note. "I doubt if he would cause you any physical harm but, as a hostage, who knows what he might demand for your return."

"It's a risk I'm prepared to take."

"A brave decision, Mr Lincoln; I will pray for your safety. I will send you details of the meetings by Diplomatic Courier as soon as they become available. I assume that I am now free to distribute the Draft Proposals?"

"Most certainly, and thank you for all you've done, I look forward to meeting you next week."

"And I you, Mr Lincoln. By the way I assume that President Caswell will be confirming his personal support? I have no wish to give offence, you are well respected of course, but he is after all the President."

"I assure you he will give my mission his unqualified support, Mr Marak; the President is fully behind this initiative." *As long as I have those recordings.*

"That's re-assuring Mr Lincoln, I'll bid you farewell; do come back to me for any clarifications when you receive the Diplomatic Bag and studied the papers."

"Will do. That reminds me, it would be best if communications are addressed to me personally; I wouldn't want it to get delayed in the President's mail."

Oval Office, Thursday

"I've had the feedback on Lincoln's FBI and CIA files." Diane Phelps was downbeat and could scarcely hide her disappointment. "Not good news I'm afraid Jack; there's absolutely nothing we can use. If you believe the files, the guy is as pure as the driven snow. There's not a sniff of scandal in his private, business or political life."

Caswell was incredulous, "That can't be Diane, I had cause to look at them when I chose him as my running mate for Vice-President; he was a naughty boy in his early years of married life. I can't remember the details, didn't have to; I knew where to find them."

"There's nothing Jack, believe me, at least nothing in the version I've been given."

"What do you mean, 'the version you were given'?"

"There are gaps in the files and some of the discs have been wiped clean in places In fact. it looks like his personal files have been sterilised by a professional."

Caswell looked aghast. "But who could do that? What do Oliver and Lionel have to say?"

"They're as puzzled as we are, Jack. Apparently, you were the last person to access the files. They've carried out every conceivable access check on the originals and the back-ups. Nobody has been near them since you; it's a real mystery."

Caswell was puzzled. *Could Lincoln, Dacre and Jackson be ganging up on him? Was it a conspiracy to bring him down?*

Phelps sought to downplay the issue, "Forget it for now, Jack, how it happened doesn't matter; the fact is, we don't have anything on him or on his wife for that matter. Carol seems to have spent her entire life practising for sainthood."

"Looks like we're stuck behind the eight ball?"

She nodded glumly. "I don't suppose you've come up with anything?"

"Not a thing Diane, his home and his office were as clean as the proverbial whistle. I spun the Security guys a tale that I had received a tip-off from a reliable source that the Vice-President's belongings might have been tampered with when he was overseas. I asked them to check for chemicals, listening and tracking devices. I made it clear that this was not to be made known to anyone, including the Vice-President. Fortunately, Carol was away overnight for a charity raising event in Philadelphia. Looks like Lincoln is more streetwise than I gave him credit for; I guess for the moment we have to go along with him, but I've told Olly and Lionel to keep looking. We **can** trust those two, can't we?"

She shrugged. "I think so, but you know them better than me, Jack. We could always try an old-fashioned honey trap on his next trip away. I'm sure we could find some Embassy girl who would like to accelerate her career. A lot of guys will stray if the circumstances are right; you did." She gave him a knowing look and flashed her eyes at him.

Caswell wasn't amused., "Cut it out Diane, I'm in no mood for flippancy; this is far too serious. Anyway, I can't see Lincoln falling for a femme fatale, he'll be on his guard 24/7. But you can set one up if you think you can pull it off. No hold it; on second thoughts it's too risky, forget it. He's off to the Middle East next week; let's see if we can come up with something whilst he's away."

Phelps had hoped the President would come up with a radical solution to the Lincoln problem and was disappointed at his apparent lack of enterprise. For her part, she had come up with an idea. "By the way, I've given some thought to Lincoln's next assignment."

Caswell looked at her expectantly. "I'm listening."

"I think we should dispatch him to solve the Northern Ireland problem. It has the potential to be high risk; there are lots of competing extremist factions over there. You never know, one of the loose cannons might do us a favour and provide a final solution to our problem. We can see that the wrong kind of news gets into the right hands; it's not difficult to stir up the Real IRA."

Caswell's eyes narrowed at the use of the term 'final solution.' He didn't want to be party to any 'final solution'. He was getting into dangerous waters, but he wanted out of the hole he was in. *What alternative do I have?* 'I'll go along with that suggestion, Diane. I'll make some calls and offer Lincoln's services as a mediator; play on the special relationship and all that kind of thing. Leave it with me. You spent time in Ireland, if my memory serves me right."

Phelps nodded, smiling at the memories it evoked. "I attended Trinity College in Dublin for a year, in the course of my degree; I studied the period from the 1918 uprising to the present day. I met a lot of interesting people on both sides of the divide, made some useful contacts."

Caswell looked at her anxiously; he didn't want to go any further with their conversation. "Let's leave that for now, I'll come back to you when I'm ready."

She smiled. "In the meantime, how's about some therapy, there's nothing more stress relieving than good old-fashioned sex?"

Caswell eyed the woman seated in front of him, her cleavage, those legs, her moist lips; he knew he should be putting an end to their liaison, but lust was driving him on.

"Nothing's changed for us; we go on as usual; the damage is done. As it happens, I was wondering if you were free this evening, around seven? Beth's off to some women's charity affair."

Phelps ran her tongue over her lips. *Men were so predictable.* "See you later then Jack."

The Oval Office, Friday

Lincoln had requested a meeting with the President, primarily to brief him on his forthcoming trip, but also to build some bridges; business had to go on. The two men faced each other uneasily across the President's desk.

"Sit down John, let's make this quick." Caswell's voice was formal, tense; he made no effort to conceal his antagonism.

"Jack, let's get this straight. Whatever I might think about you personally, I still respect the Office of the President. I'm here to brief you on my arrangements for the Middle East trip. As President you should be interested."

"Don't tell me my job, John," Caswell rasped. "I've got friends; I know as much about this trip as you do. Air Force One is being prepared to fly you to Cairo and, assuming that bastard Saddam lets you leave, it will be there to bring you back."

Lincoln pursed his lips. "I guess he could do you one big favour if he wanted to; what a pity you're not on speaking terms."

"You're right, maybe I should do a deal with him; I'll give that some thought. I understand Marak is placing a plane at your disposal for the internal flights; let's hope the air space is safe. I would hate to see some stray missile take you out of the sky."

"So, there's nothing I can tell you Jack?"

"Not a thing." Caswell scowled and stood, making it clear that the meeting was over.

"And I don't suppose you're going to wish me luck?" Lincoln extended his hand but Caswell put his hands in his pockets, waiting pointedly for him to leave. Lincoln shook his head and placed a hand on the President's shoulder, squeezing gently. "There's really no need for us to be enemies Jack, we can still work together."

Caswell shrugged the hand off, showing his annoyance. "Go to hell."

But Lincoln's brief contact had achieved its goal; the President's most recent experiences had flooded into his thoughts. "Just one little bit of advice before I go."

Caswell stared at his one-time friend, wondering what was to come.

"You're wasting the Agency's resources checking me out. You'll never find the recordings and anyway, there's nothing in my past which would be of use to you. My personal records, scrutinised so carefully by the FBI and the CIA, will reveal I have a clean slate. Lincoln smiled broadly, "I know that, because I wiped them clean myself."

Caswell felt his cheeks go red. *How could he know about the searches he'd arranged? The FBI had carried them out covertly.*

Lincoln grinned wickedly, openly relishing the President's embarrassment. "I've got some friends too Jack."

"But how could....?" Caswell choked back his words, knowing they could only serve to acknowledge his guilt.

"Let's just say a little bird told me, and leave it at that. See you around." Lincoln knew he was sewing seeds of doubt in the President's mind, knew the man would be driven to distraction wondering who he could trust.

When Lincoln had gone Caswell slammed his clenched fist onto his desk in frustration; he felt neutered. Somehow, by whatever means, he had to regain control. He buzzed Mary

O'Halloran. "Mary, get me the British Prime Minister on the phone please"

As he walked along the corridor to his office Lincoln puzzled over his personal files. The Executive had pulled them and found nothing; they were clean. How could that be? Even as he framed the question in his mind the answer came to him. *Thank you, Lord. I guess I can rely on you to keep that air space safe for me.*

Cairo-Riyadh-Damascus

The series of meetings began on Monday afternoon in Cairo and continued until Tuesday night in Damascus following a morning session in Riyadh. The Arabs were excellent hosts and the set pieces had gone remarkably well. Lincoln had been struck by their diversity; some wore Western suits others wore traditional Arab attire. Some focussed on the past, others looked more to the future; there were differing points of view on matters of detail but, in the end, all had agreed to support the initiative.

It was the side issues that generated most concerns; America's motives were questioned at length and he had been dismayed at the deep-seated mistrust that existed in everyone he met, including those he would have regarded as allies. Time and time again he had to re-assure them that security of oil was not the driving force behind the negotiations, and that America would not insist on maintaining military bases in the Region unless requested to do so.

They had listened patiently and debate had been mannerly, but he doubted if they were entirely convinced by what he had to say; sadly, history was on their side. However, late on Tuesday evening he finally secured their commitment, albeit he still had to meet Saddam Hussein. Moreover, through the process of thought transference during numerous handshakes, Lincoln had gained a deep insight into the hopes and fears of twelve Middle Eastern leaders.

Lincoln was learning how to control his newly acquired gift; he was now able to channel it to retrieve only those areas in which he had an interest. There was no need to intrude upon everyone's personal affairs unless it was essential to the task in hand.

The meetings with the Middle East rulers and Prime Ministers had gone extraordinarily well. To a man the supported his proposals for a Peace Accord one hundred per cent. Lincoln was overjoyed, everything he had hoped for had been achieved. His hosts had been helpful and constructive in every way and outside the meetings their hospitality had been lavish.

During his time in Syria, he had been particularly heartened by its President's concern for his safety whilst in Iraq. "Those of us with some influence, have been in touch with the Iraqi leadership to give a good account of your approach, Mr Vice-President. I personally offered to accompany you to your meeting with Saddam, but my offer was declined. I indicated that I, and my fellow leaders, would very angry if any mishap were to befall you during your visit. We do not anticipate any risk to your safety, but Saddam is Saddam, and you must be wary at all times."

"Do you personally believe he has weapons of mass destruction?" Lincoln had risked the question, and had expected a response veiled in diplomacy, but his host's reply had been direct.

The Syrian hesitated then nodded; he trusted the American. "Most of us believe that he does, but as to where they are located, I know not None of us do. Maybe we are all wrong in our belief, maybe he doesn't have them"

Prime Minister Marak who had kindly agreed to chair the meetings accompanied Lincoln to Damascus Airport and walked alongside him to the aircraft steps. 'You have done well, John, I wish you good luck with Saddam Hussein. I promise you that my fellow leaders and I will isolate him if any harm to befalls you. Incidentally, arrangement have been made for you have fighter jet escort as far as the Iraqi border; that's as close as we can go."

Lincoln proffered his hand. "Thank you for all your help, it's greatly appreciated. I will let you know how I get on with

Saddam when I get back. I would just add that I was astounded by at the level of co-operation and support everyone has offered. I am very grateful; I could not have asked for more."

Marak smiled broadly, 'I think ninety per cent of it was genuine; we all want your Peace Accord proposals to succeed and are determined that no blame shall fall on any us if it fails. Good luck, John.'

Baghdad Airport

The Egyptian executive jet touched down at Baghdad Airport at 14.05; it was scheduled to make the return flight at 18.00. Lincoln had less than four hours to complete his business. As things stood, he didn't need Saddam's support now that fourteen of the region's leaders were all pulling in the same direction, but he wanted to meet the man. Sooner or later, he had to be dealt with.

Baghdad Airport was bathed in bright sunshine, the temperature very high for the time of year. The main terminal building, shimmering in the heat, was a considerable distance away, ensuring that the plane's landing had been unlikely to attract other than casual attention. There was no red carpet, no welcoming committee and no line of limousines waiting to transport him to the venue for the meeting. Lincoln smiled wryly; he had vetoed publicity and his request had been met in the extreme.

A solitary army Colonel strode forward to meet him at the foot of the aircraft steps, stopping, clicking his heels together and saluting in traditional manner. There were no pleasantries. "Your transport is ready, Mr Lincoln." An outstretched arm and pointing finger indicated that his transport was to be a dust-covered jeep-like army vehicle. Two heavily armoured escort vehicles stood alongside.

Lincoln frowned to show his disapproval; he was irritated at this blatant show of disrespect but either he got into the vehicle or returned to the plane to sit it out. He put on his broadest smile.

"Certainly Colonel, lead on. Always wanted to travel in one of these, didn't realise they were still in service, this must be a museum piece."

The comment was ignored; the Colonel held open the rear door and wore a detached look as the Vice-President of the United States climbed on board. He then took his place alongside the driver and the vehicle pulled away immediately; the escorts took up station front and rear.

Baghdad was cleaner, brighter and better organised than he had anticipated. Ancient and modern architecture blended together harmoniously and there was no evidence of decay or poverty. He did wonder if the route had been carefully chosen to show the best of the city; but why not, most Authorities would do the same.

The interior of the vehicle was hot and stuffy and the window wouldn't open; he could feel his temperature rising steadily, his clothes begin to stick to his skin. The uncomfortable journey lasted for thirty minutes and Lincoln was relieved when they slowed to pass through a pair of huge iron gates controlling the entrance to the beautiful building beyond.

Saddam Hussein's Residential Palace, Baghdad

"Please follow me Mr Lincoln, I'll take you into the Palace."

Lincoln looked admiringly at the sheer scale of the rich architecture of the Palace; compared to it, the White House was, just as its name suggested, a rather plain white house. The impressive externals of the Palace were exceeded by its internal grandeur and décor. To his relief it was air-conditioned and the cool air caused a shiver to run down his body.

"Please take a seat Mr Lincoln; I'll advise the President of your arrival."

Lincoln took a seat near one of the panoramic windows looking out onto a courtyard of palms, exotic plants, fountains, ornamental pools and running water. The room in which he sat was the essence of pure luxury; marble flooring, fine Persian carpets, opulent furnishings and decoration with gold gilt featuring prominently. *Sanctions aren't much in evidence here. OK Saddam, I'm duly impressed, let's be having you.*

As he looked round, for the first time on his trip he felt lonely, a touch uncertain, and for a moment wished he was accompanied by his usual entourage of advisors. Five minutes went by, then ten; he was being taught some kind of a lesson. As fifteen minutes approached, he rose to his feet, anger mounting rapidly, determined to knock upon every door in turn when suddenly one opened and an army General strode purposefully towards him.

Another subterfuge had taken place. *You bastards, you had me under surveillance waiting for me to lose patience.*

"Our apologies Mr Lincoln, the President received an unexpected telephone call of relevance to our meeting. He is ready to receive you now, unless you wish to make yourself comfortable; the facilities are nearby?"

"No thank you. Let's get down to business."

"As you wish, please follow me."

Lincoln followed the General along a seemingly never-ending mirrored corridor, eventually arriving at a pair of carved wooden doors both of which the General pushed open, grandly ushering him in. Entering he saw that the room beyond was illuminated by six crystal chandeliers; there were no windows. Immediately ahead was a wooden table, some ten metres in length and lined on either side by gold gilt silk-upholstered chairs. To his left at the centre of the table sat three men, all dressed similarly in white tropical suits.

As he drew near, he could hardly believe what he was seeing; the three men were all of identical appearance. Western Intelligence had long since established that Saddam had a number of doubles, perhaps as many as six. *But why are three of you attending this meeting?*

He tried to show no surprise, stifling the question that nearly escaped his lips, and decided to treat the situation as perfectly normal.

The General interrupted his thoughts. "A demonstration to confirm what you probably already know, Mr Lincoln; the President has a number of doubles. I think you will agree that they are identical; in the event of....shall we say an accident, the West could never be sure of the outcome."

Lincoln shrugged. "I understand perfectly, General. I'm pleased to say that President Caswell has no need for such subterfuge. Can I assume that the real President is in attendance and I am to be introduced?"

"You should assume nothing Mr Lincoln. I'm going to leave now."

Lincoln took the initiative, he knew what he had to do, and reaching across the table, extended his hand to the man nearest. "Good afternoon gentlemen, I'm John Lincoln. Thank you for agreeing to see me." To his relief the three men stood and shook hands in turn, each smiling and nodding in a meaningless display of goodwill. But the ritual served its purpose, His mind search revealed that Saddam Hussein was present and sat on his right.

The man seated to his left spoke first. "Do you bring greetings from your President, Mr Lincoln?"

He was being tested right from the start. *Diplomacy or honesty? Which was the best approach?* Lincoln shook his head. "I have to confess that I do not. Whilst President Caswell supports this initiative, he feels that both sides must develop mutual trust before he would feel able to establish a more courteous relationship."

The man seated immediately opposite spoke. "If you do not have trust, is there any point to this meeting? Presumably if we do not believe what the other has to say we will not be using our time usefully?"

"I do not agree Mr President. Trust is something which should be earned, not conferred. Trust is a journey upon which we must both embark. I have asked to meet with you and you have agreed; we have each taken the first step along that journey. I hope others will follow where we lead. I assume that you harboured some hope for the outcome of this meeting or we would not be sitting here now?"

The real Saddam Hussein pursed his lips. "Perhaps our attendance has more to do with curiosity than hope or trust. Or it could be that we saw this as a unique opportunity; the Vice-

President of the United States alone in Iraq, entirely unprotected."

Lincoln smiled broadly. "That is where I have demonstrated my trust; I believe that you will observe the customary principles of diplomacy, irrespective of the barriers that currently exist between our countries."

Saddam nodded, glancing at the man on the left who took his cue.

"Let us move on to the purpose of your visit Mr Lincoln. We have studied your proposals and, quite simply, **if** the Palestinians and the Israelis can reach an agreement on the basis described, and **if** indeed there is support from the other Arab Leaders, we will raise no significant objections. We do have some reservations which require a response before we can be seen as fully committed to the Peace Accord."

Lincoln's heart nearly stalled, this apparent acquiescence was beyond his most optimistic expectations. "You will of course make your own enquiries, but if I have correctly interpreted the views expressed at the meetings in Cairo and Riyadh, I think you will find that there is unanimous support for the proposals. I believe that some of your fellow leaders have already made contact in this regard?" He looked at each man in turn but there was no sign of confirmation; his statement was not acknowledged. "Might I enquire as to the precise nature of your reservations?"

The man immediately opposite responded to his enquiry, "They are threefold; oil, military bases and the current sanctions against Iraq."

"Not Jerusalem?" Lincoln expressed his surprise.

The man on his left replied, "We are happy to let the Jordanians deal with that issue. Jerusalem is of no importance to Iraq; we will support whatever outcome emerges. Your proposals seem to be equitable, though whether they are practicable is another matter."

"Thank you, Mr President, I see that as a valuable step forward." Lincoln continued, seeking to reassure the Iraqis by explaining America's position with regard to oil and military bases, answering questions as they arose. It was a repetition of the meetings with the other Middle Eastern leaders. He ended by stating, "In summary, I acknowledge that this represents a change in policy on the part of the United States and its allies, but I can assure you it is a genuine effort to establish lasting peace in the Middle East."

The lookalike in the middle nodded. "But of course Mr Lincoln, and one which requires us to put our trust in President Caswell, who has hitherto been severely critical of my country and my policies."

"I accept that Mr President; your fellow Leaders are prepared to exercise that trust."

"Ah yes, but they have not suffered as we have. You have yet to state your position regarding the sanctions imposed on Iraq. Subject to your satisfactory response on this matter, Iraq might feel able to give its support to your proposals."

Lincoln felt like punching the air but gave no indication of his feelings; instead, he looked at each of the other two men in turn, seeking their affirmation. The man on his left nodded, but Saddam hesitated as though considering his response then replied. "Agreed, but the matter of sanctions must be addressed in parallel with the implementation of your Peace Accord should it ultimately be accepted."

His elation took a somersault into despondency; it appeared Iraq's support was about to evaporate. Sanctions were in the main the prerogative of the United Nations. "I'm sorry but I have no mandate to even discuss sanctions, nor the authority to agree to their termination; these are the sole responsibility of the United Nations. The United States will concur with the lifting of sanctions but cannot speak on behalf of the United Nations."

The man on his left thumped the table violently. "They are American sanctions supported by your British lapdogs. If you agree to their lifting no-one will object."

The man immediately opposite nodded vigorously, anger creeping into his voice. "We are making concessions and you are offering nothing in return; this is incredible. The sanctions are inhumane and unjustified; they violate the human rights of all Iraqi people especially the old, the sick and children."

Lincoln shook his head, nonplussed. "With respect, you have not made any concessions as such; you have offered your support to a Peace Accord which has the support of all the other Arab nations. It could proceed without your agreement. But if you do give your support, the United States will ask the United Nations to lift the sanctions. This is an important first step to full recognition of your country by the West."

Saddam Hussein snorted, "A meeting held in secret is hardly recognition."

Lincoln was on the back foot, the outcome of the meeting hung in the balance. "I accept your criticism, but it is the best I could achieve at this time. When I return to America, I will afford your participation full recognition. However, the only way to put an end to sanctions is to support the proposals and convince the world that Iraq has no weapons of mass destruction."

The look-alike in the middle responded angrily. "It is not the world we have to convince, or even the United Nations; it is America and America alone. President Caswell wants to see me deposed and a puppet put in my place for one reason and one reason only, oil. There are no weapons of mass destruction in Iraq. How many times do I have to say this?"

Lincoln paused before replying, considering his words carefully. "Mr President, your position is well understood, but you have to acknowledge that in the very recent past you did have such weapons, and the world is anxious to ensure that these no longer exist. Some proof has to be provided and, therefore, unfettered access must be given to the United Nations' Inspectors, only then will the understandable concern that exists be removed. All I can do is to report what you have told me; I cannot offer a solution to the current impasse.

The sole purpose of my visit is to seek your support for the Peace Accord. If you cannot give that support you will be the only Arab country to refuse, and Iraq will be isolated from its brother nations. If on the other hand you are silent on the issue, it will be judged as support, but you will not receive the credit for your co-operation. I entreat you to give your support; in the event you do, I'm certain that the United Nations attitude towards sanctions will soften."

The real Saddam Hussein spoke softly. "I would agree that those are our options." He turned to face his two doubles, raising an eyebrow, inviting their response. The man in the centre took his cue. "Iraq will not allow itself to be isolated from its neighbours by American manoeuvring, we will support the proposals. We expect you to report favourably on these negotiations and urge the United Nations to lift all sanctions."

Lincoln looked into the eyes of the fake Saddam. "Thank you sincerely, Mr President. I see this as an important step on the way to a rapprochement between our two countries. I personally am exceedingly grateful for your co-operation. And now, with your leave, I fear I must make my way back to the airport."

The double on the left nodded, "Of course and I will ensure that your transport for the return journey is more comfortable. There was clearly a misunderstanding regarding your arrival." The man smiled. "I do apologise." He rose, crossed to the double doors, wrenched them open and barked a command at the attendant guard.

"Your transport is available Mr Lincoln. Please, if you will come with me, I will take you to it."

Lincoln shook hands with the other two men, probing deeply into the mind of the real Saddam Hussein, siphoning off the information he required. When he had finished, he had one request to make. "There is just one thing occurs to me M, I wonder if there is a means by which I could contact you directly within the next twenty-four hours? I will be reporting to President Caswell during my flight and there might be good reason to inform you of his response to the outcome of this meeting."

The real Saddam stroked his chin and looked at the Vice-President questioningly.

You didn't expect to be asked that, did you? Lincoln held his breath waiting for the reply.

Saddam Hussein came to a decision and wrote down a satellite telephone number handing it to Lincoln. "This number will be operational for the next twelve hours after which it will cease to function. My curiosity is aroused; I look forward to hearing from you."

"I had hoped for twenty-four hours."

"You have twelve Mr Lincoln."

The journey back to the airport was made in a Rolls Royce and on arrival Lincoln found that a red carpet covered the short walk to the aircraft boarding steps. Iraqi soldiers lined either side and stood to attention as he passed. He took a last look round and enjoyed a feeling of wellbeing; good progress had been made and he had a feeling of accomplishment as he settled down for the three-hour flight to Cairo. Iraq's support wasn't essential to the Israeli-Palestinian Peace Accord but it had been important to meet Saddam Hussein.

Lincoln had requested that formalities on landing in Cairo were kept to a minimum and the American Ambassador to Egypt was the only official in attendance when he stepped onto the tarmac. Air Force One stood nearby ready for immediate take-off.

As they strolled across the tarmac, the Ambassador, Tom Kominski engaged in small talk; he knew not to ask searching questions, but nevertheless he was curious about the visit to Iraq.

"Was your trip worthwhile, Mr Vice-President?"

The two men had never met hence the formality. "Call me John. I think so Tom, but there are no certainties in Middle East politics, as you well know. We'll know the outcome within the next forty-eight hours; I'm sorry I can't say more at this time."

"I understand; I look forward to reading the dispatches in due course. Have a pleasant trip home."

Lincoln's first action on boarding Air Force One was to request a simple meal of burgers and fries; he'd been wined and dined well by his Arab hosts, but was ready for some American home cooking. Afterwards he fell into a deep sleep, the tensions of the last three days had drained his energies and he needed to recharge his batteries. He asked to be wakened after five hours

by which time the flight would be crossing the North Atlantic
and he could then carry out the next phase of his plan.

CHAPTER 14

Mid-Atlantic

Air Force One was half way across the big pond when the Flight Steward attempted to rouse Lincoln. "Your wake-up call as requested Mr Vice-President."

After a second request without response, the attendant shook Lincoln's shoulder. "Waken up Mr Vice-President; I've brought a cup of coffee for you. Can I get you anything to eat?"

Lincoln forced away the cobwebs and rubbed his eyes. "Gosh that was a great sleep. Coffee will do just fine, Sam; I'll catch up on food later. I've got some business I must attend to. Give me a time check on Washington please."

The Steward glanced at the twin-dialled bedside clock. "It's just after 15.00 hours back home; the white dial always shows the time back home, the yellow is set to where you're headed or, in this case, where you've left behind.

Lincoln clicked his fingers. "Of course, I forgot that; I'm not fully awake yet."

When the Orderly had gone, Lincoln adjusted his watch to Washington time, it was something that somehow always made him feel closer to home. As he showered and shaved, he pondered on what he had to do over the course of the next hour; it was make-or-break time.

He had four telephone calls to make, one personal and three others related to his trip, the latter probably the most important of his political life. The calls could have been made from the comfort of his bed but psychologically he felt the need to be formally dressed when he was engaged in serious business.

His first call was to his wife. "Hi Honey, it's me; I'm on my way back, we're about half way across the Atlantic. I've missed you, looking forward to getting home."

"I've missed you too, the house seems empty without you. Will you be coming straight home or will you be calling in on the President?"

"I'm heading right back to you, Honey, Jack Caswell can wait. We should touch down in about four hours, so all being well I'll be with you around 8pm."

"How did the trip go?" She spoke the question softly, concerned that maybe her husband's plans hadn't come to fruition.

"Everything has gone just fine. Better than I could have wished for if I'm really honest about it, but there's more to do. In fact, I've got to cut this call short. I'm sorry but I've got to fit into a time slot. I'll tell you all about it when I get back; I hope you understand it's important. I love you."

"That's OK Honey, you do what you've got to do; I can wait another few hours to hear your news. I think I'll put a bottle of champagne on ice, sounds like we have something to celebrate."

Lincoln put the phone down and buzzed through to the Communications Officer. "Dave, get me the Chief of General Staff on the line, hopefully he's at the Pentagon but no matter where he is or what he's doing I want to talk to him."

Dave Wilson pursed his lips. "I'll do my best."

The phone rang just five minutes later. "I have the Chief of General Staff on the line Mr Vice-President."

"Put him through, Dave."

"Hello Hal, sorry if I've dragged you away from something important, but this is vital and I'm tied into a time slot."

Five-star General Harold Davidson and Lincoln were old friends. They had been students together at Princeton and had played on the same football team; their lives had crossed and run in parallel for many years. Their respective roles meant that they regularly attended the same meetings and by choice they met socially with their wives.

"No problem, I was in one of those darn cost-cutting meetings John, but no matter; besides, I always feel important when I'm hauled out by the President or the Vice-President, especially when those present seem determined to plough the same old field for the umpteenth time. So how can I help?"

"Hal, I'll tell you up front. You're going to have to trust me on this one; I just haven't got time to go into the whole scenario. I'd like you to record what I'm going to say; that way you'll have some back-up if this goes pear-shaped. It'll save you making notes."

The General laughed. "I'm intrigued, hold a sec. OK, recorder running, fire away."

"You've heard about my trip?"

"Well," Davidson was hesitant. "I've heard two stories; one, you've been going round the Middle East trying to establish a Peace Accord between the Israelis and the Palestinians."

"And the other story? I'm intrigued."

"Some folks are saying that the President sent you off on a wild goose chase to get you out of his hair. Sorry about that, John."

"You're spot on with the first shot, and it's fair to say there's more than a lick of truth with the second. What I'm going to ask comes as a direct result of those talks and, if you're prepared to do what I ask, we might just establish peace in the Middle East."

Hal Davidson's ears pricked up; this was history in the making. "Now **I'm** intrigued. Fire away; I'll help if I can."

Lincoln outlined what he had in mind and sat back waiting for the Chief of General Staff's reaction, worried as the seconds passed that his friend was searching out words to refuse his request.

When Davidson finally spoke, he sounded cautious. "I'm going to meet resistance with this John, especially since I can't give out the background details; I've got day-to-day command, but this kind of request usually comes out of a meeting involving the Defence Secretary and other such notables. But what the hell - you're the Vice-President and I'm supposed to be in command at this end. I'm willing to take the risk of upsetting someone if you are."

Lincoln didn't hide his relief. "Great Hal, I'm in your debt; I owe you big time. Have you got that recorder running? I'm going to read out some data and it's going to take a few minutes."

When he had finished dictating, Lincoln felt relieved that he had been able to pass on the vital information he possessed to a senior member of the military. "That's the lot, Hal. How long will you need?"

"I'll get the process started as soon as we go off line; my guess is that it'll take about an hour or so to programme the computer."

"Thanks, I owe you big time. If this comes off, we'll celebrate in style, I promise I'll be in touch when the dust settles."

Lincoln buzzed Communications again. "Dave, I'm keeping you busy this flight; get me this number please. I'll stay on line whilst you dial up; I want to take this call direct." Lincoln read out the number.

"Hmm, a satellite phone; no problem but they're not reliable."

The Vice-President listened as the connection rang out praying it would be answered. After what seemed an eternity, the ringing ceased as the handset was picked up.

The voice spoke angrily in Arabic. Lincoln no idea what had been said but he recognised the voice and knew that its owner understood English.

"Mr President, Lincoln speaking. I realise that the hour is late and I apologise, but I must converse with you."

"It is after 11pm locally Mr Lincoln; I'm making ready to retire. When I gave you this number, I did not expect to be contacted at such an inhospitable hour."

"I apologise again Mr President, the time difference between us does present practical difficulties and I had transatlantic calls to make before I could speak with you in meaningful fashion. I also considered it prudent to be safely over the Atlantic Ocean when I spoke to you; well away from what one might refer to as hostile air space."

The Arab voiced his impatience, a young beauty was awaiting him. "Come to the point and be brief if you will, the hour is late."

"Thank you. Firstly, I believe you to be the authentic Saddam Hussein; you sat on my right at our meeting, is that not so?"

"I did indeed attend that meeting." The Arab answered obtusely.

"Mr President, it's important that you acknowledge that I am conversing with the real Saddam Hussein. I am, am I not?"

There was a long pause before the voice spoke again. "Very well, let us assume for the present that you are correct, though I cannot see how you might benefit from such knowledge."

"I'll come straight to the point Mr President; I want you to listen very carefully to the information I'm about to give you. I'm going to recite fourteen locations and, as the real Saddam Hussein, you will recognise their significance."

When he had completed his statement Lincoln could almost feel the chilled silence at the other end of the telephone; he could imagine the body blow he had dealt the Iraqi leader. The fourteen map references he had provided were the locations of the sources of weapons of mass destruction. The locations had been extracted from the very heart of Saddam's innermost memories during the meeting at the palace.

Eventually the Arab regained his composure. "Very interesting Mr Lincoln but you are misinformed; I have nothing further to say."

Lincoln let out a long audible sigh of exasperation. "Mr President, please don't insult me; the source of my information is impeccable. How many of your generals are aware of **all** fourteen locations? Before I continue to authenticate my assertion, and hopefully persuade you not to indulge in further pointless blustering, I would advise you that the Pentagon has put all fourteen sites under satellite surveillance. And, I would expect ground-based observers to be in position over the course of the next few hours.

You will appreciate that the Allies have many agents working under cover in your midst, including disaffected Iraqis.

Perhaps if I provide further detail, you will acknowledge that the locations I have described are genuine and recognise the perilous situation in which you are now placed. I will give two examples. There are three tons of Anthrax stored in a sealed vault below the Department of Biology in the University of Baghdad. It has been there since 1994. You have a total of four laboratories engaged in the production of biochemical weapons; the largest of these is a complex twenty metres below the Palace in which we held our meeting. This laboratory is operated by permanently resident staff undertaking six months tours of duty. These technicians are effectively sealed underground and alternate with a similar group when each tour of duty ends. The Director of the laboratory is Professor Tariq. Now, need I go further?"

Saddam's voice quivered with the anger he was fighting to control. "Let us assume for one moment that your information is correct; what precisely would you expect me to do? It seems to me that your President will immediately launch air and missile strikes followed by a land-based assault."

"President Caswell is not aware of the situation as I speak, and I would suggest that broadly speaking you have three options. You could start some kind of war in the Middle East and fight until you are defeated, a certain outcome. You can wait for the United Nations inspectors to identify the whereabouts of the weapons; I'll tell them where to look. America and its Allies will then have justification for declaring war on Iraq, with its inevitable outcome. And then there is a third option, the one I hope you will prefer."

He paused, waiting for Saddam's reaction. "I'm listening Mr Lincoln, continue."

"It's simple really Mr President. You tell the Inspectors where the weapons are located."

Saddam snarled into the phone. "And thereby prove to the World that I am the liar the Americans have always accused me of being. Such a solution is unthinkable."

Lincoln had anticipated how the Arab leader would respond and had a solution to his dilemma.

"It's not for me to offer a solution, but I would have thought that you could arrange for one or more high-ranking military officers of your choosing to take the blame; you might even have them summarily executed as enemies of the State. I can't imagine that your conscience would balk at such a suggestion."

Lincoln felt a pang of guilt, at how readily he was condemning to death individuals he didn't even know. But it was for the greater good, and in truth he felt little sympathy for any member of the Iraqi regime. He was sure that anyone close to the Iraqi dictator would have perpetrated many atrocities against the local people; it was rough justice. He told himself that in this case the ends justified the means; achieving peace in the Middle East was all that mattered. Words from the New Testament came to him 'love thy enemy' *I wonder if you approve of how I'm going about this God?*

Saddam considered the proposition before him; it presented the possibility of survival and who knows what the morrow might bring. "Let us continue with your hypothesis for the moment Mr Lincoln; would not President Caswell exploit the situation to achieve my downfall?"

"I give you my assurance that he will not exploit the situation, but I'm afraid that acknowledgement of these biological weapons is not the full price I'm demanding for your survival and that of your country."

"What else?" The Arab spat out his question.

"I'm requiring that you resign, on ill-health grounds if you wish, and that you put in place democratic elections, based on one man, one vote. Such elections are to take place within six months from today, with neutral observers and all the usual safeguards."

"Such a solution is impossible; I will never agree to it; never." Saddam voice quivered with anger. "My people would never agree."

It was time for Lincoln to play his final card. "It's your call; if that's all you have to say I'll notify President Caswell and the United Nations of the situation when we terminate this call. I very much regret that you are missing a golden opportunity to salvage something out of this hole you've dug for yourself. You have the chance to escape with a vestige of credit; I strongly urge you to reconsider."

Saddam was beaten and he knew it, he also knew that he would be able to organise a comfortable future for himself; he was a very rich man. "This is blackmail, nothing less than blackmail."

It was now or never; Lincoln threw down the gauntlet. "It is whatever you want to call it. I have nothing further to say; I'm going to terminate this call."

"No wait." The Iraqi leader finally cracked. "I will need some time to put these arrangements in place."

"You agree to my proposals without qualification?"

"Yes, damn you, yes; I have no alternative."

"Then I give you just three hours to contact President Caswell with your confession and negotiate the process with him. I repeat three hours. After that it will most certainly be too late."

Saddam went silent again, going cap in hand to Caswell would be a shaming process. "Me, phone President Caswell? I would prefer to deal with the United Nations Inspectors."

"Sorry, the President is part of the deal and, as you reminded me at our meeting, America is calling the shots."

"You'll guarantee that he will be reasonable?"

"You have my word; he will accept your story on this. What I can't promise is how the United Nations will react, but they are likely to follow the President's lead."

"Fuck the United Nations! America, in the form of President Caswell, controls my destiny."

Lincoln felt his heart begin to pound; he had won. "Thank you, Mr President. I'm going to telephone President Caswell immediately after this call with details of what we have agreed. Within three hours you will contact him at the White House and negotiate the best deal you can. But remember, you must confess to the weapons of mass destruction and reveal where they're hidden. You must also advise that you are resigning and that you will be putting in place democratic elections. What you can negotiate on, is how this situation is publicised, and how the process is managed here on in. Is that understood?"

"Perfectly, Mr Lincoln."

Saddam slammed down the telephone. He had some very unpleasant duties to perform, close friends and subordinates would have to be eliminated. But no matter, it was his survival that mattered now and, after all, politics was a dirty business.

Lincoln was euphoric; it seemed like he was on the verge of settling the major conflicts of the Middle East at a stroke. But even as he thrilled to his success, he remembered the power behind him; the glory wasn't his alone. *Thank you, Lord.* And the game wasn't over yet; there was one more hurdle to clear.

"Dave, another one for you; get me the President please. Tell them it's important, he's to be pulled out of a meeting if needs be."

While he waited for the return call, Lincoln rehearsed what he was going to say, it was essential that Caswell treated Saddam's capitulation with magnanimity.

"Mr Vice-President, I'm ready to put you through."

"OK Dave, go ahead."

Mary O'Halloran's cheerful voice could have been coming from next door. "How are you, John?"

"I'm fine Mary; all the better for hearing you. I hope that the President is available?"

"You're in luck; you've caught him between meetings. He's dealing with a mug of coffee at the moment; I'll put you through."

"Hello John." The President's voice was flat, disinterested; the customary pleasantries weren't on offer.

Lincoln ignored the frosty reception; Caswell was in for the shock of his life. "I've got some good news Jack, well it's good for the world and our country; hopefully you'll agree."

"Spill it, I'll judge whether it's good or otherwise."

"Firstly, all Leaders, and I do mean all of them, are signed up to the Israeli-Palestinian Peace Proposals."

"Including that bastard Saddam Hussein?"

"Yes Jack, including him. I'll come back to Iraq when I've dealt with the other issues. As far as oil is concerned, the market will determine the price with no favours or arm-twisting in either direction. With regard to military bases, we're free to negotiate country by country with no pre-conditions or pressures on either side. I've given my word as Vice-President of the United States."

"Sounds like you've sold us out just like I expected. Over time we're going to lose our position of pre-eminence in the Middle East. The Arabs will blackmail the hell out of us once the threat of war in the Middle East has gone."

"That's typical of your blinkered attitude, Jack; I think it's a reasonable price to pay for peace and I believe the America people will agree. You should be delighted that we won't be bringing our boys home in body bags or having to bomb innocent people into oblivion. And now for the big one; Saddam is going to contact you within the next three hours and you're going to give him a hearing."

"You're out of your fucking mind, Lincoln." Caswell spat out the words, his face contorted with anger.

"Shut up and listen, Jack, and remember your position here; don't have me going into your extra-curricular activities. You **will** give him a hearing or pay the price; you know what I'm referring to. Just remember I can phone Beth from here just as easily as I can phone you. You're going to listen to a confession. He's going to tell you about weapons of mass destruction; he's even going to tell you where he's hidden them."

Caswell was astounded; he couldn't believe what he was hearing. "If this is all real and not just one of your fantasies, I'll flatten his entire infra-structure once and for all. That's if he phones me, which I doubt. If he does, he'll be discredited for all time. I'll….."

"Hold it right there, Jack; you're getting ahead of yourself. Now hear me out and listen carefully, this is a one-time story. "First off, I know where all the sites are and I've instructed Hal Davidson to monitor them using our satellite systems; Saddam can't move in or out of them without our knowledge. We're also moving people in on the ground even as we speak."

Caswell couldn't comprehend what he was hearing. "How come you've found out all this? How come he told you? I can't believe it."

"Stick with the big picture Jack, leave the nuts and bolts to me. The guy is going to resign, probably on ill-health grounds and put in place democratic elections."

Caswell snorted. "You've fallen out of your fuckin' tree; either that or he's topped you up with a load of happy-baccy. He'll never give up power."

"It's all arranged Jack; all you have to do is negotiate the fine details. But there's more; I'm not finished yet."

"Don't tell me, let me guess; he's going to continue the fairy story and give half of his oil revenues to the Red Cross."

"Very funny Jack, you should be a comedian; come to think of it, it wouldn't take much to polish up your act. Saddam is going to confess but he'll scapegoat some of his henchmen and claim it was all done behind his back."

"That sounds more like the conniving bastard I know. Who's going to believe him?"

"For a start, you are Jack. And you're going to persuade others to follow your lead."

"You're out of your mind; if he confesses to what you've told me, I'll annihilate him."

"Wrong again Jack; you are going to believe him and you are going to negotiate with him or I'll have my own story to tell, to Beth, to the Media, to the Senate, to Congress; think about it."

Caswell wasn't sure which way to jump. If he went to war on Iraq maybe the Diane Phelps affair could be submerged even if Lincoln did expose him, but he knew in his heart that it was wishful thinking. Instead, he said weakly. "I'm beginning to wonder whose side you're on."

"What I'm doing is in the best interests of world peace. If you sabotage this deal, you'll end up on the scrap heap with Saddam; I'll certainly use my media empire to put you there."

There was no response from Caswell; his thoughts were in turmoil.

Lincoln pressed again. "I'm not hearing you, Jack."

"Fuck you, you've got me by the balls and you know it."

"Of course I do, and don't you forget it; I can put on an almighty squeeze if I have to."

The President sighed; he was beaten. "OK, I'll play ball but if he tries to pull a fast one, I'll attack Iraq tomorrow."

Lincoln relaxed; he had won the day. It was time for him to be magnanimous, time to play on the President's vanity. "There is some good news in all this for you personally, Jack. As long as you play ball and move the process in the right direction you can take all the credit for the deal. If you play your cards right you might even win the Nobel Peace Prize."

Caswell weighed Lincoln's words carefully and began to see some blue sky emerging out of the gloom. *A Nobel Peace Prize.* "And what about you? Surely you want some of the kudos?"

"Not a cent's worth, I've just been your runner, Jack; you've been the mastermind. I'm sure Diane can advise you on how to secure maximum glory."

Caswell fell silent; he saw the opportunity that was opening up. If he played his cards right, he could establish himself as a major statesman in the history of world politics. He would be up there with Roosevelt and Churchill.

Lincoln smiled. "I can almost hear your brain cells working, Jack. You're starting to see the big picture, well at least the bit that has you centre stage. Am I right?"

"I'll do what you say this time, Lincoln, but it won't always be that way, I promise you. Now maybe we should clear this line in case your friend is trying to get through."

"Saddam's not my friend, Jack; he's just a player in the game. I'll be in touch when I get back."

Caswell put the phone down and reflected on the scenario that was opening up. He would have to act quickly, grab the glory, before the news leaked out from other sources.

"Mary."

"Yes Mr President?"

"Get a hold of Diane Phelps, Rebecca Wright, Al Weinberger and Hal Davidson; put them all on standby for a meeting with me in a few hours time. Tell them to cancel everything else, no excuses. And keep my line clear for a call from Saddam Hussein."

"I'm sorry Mr President I didn't catch the last name."

"You heard right, Mary, Saddam Hussein is going to honour us with a call. Make sure every word of the conversation is recorded."

"Dave, I'm working you hard this flight, I've got another task for you."

"Go ahead, Sir, communications are my business."

Lincoln sent a simple transmission to the twelve Arab leaders he had met in Riyadh, Cairo and Damascus, along with copies to Caswell, Palestine's Abdul Musrat and Israel's Ezer Dayan.

Everyone is now on board with the Peace Accord. President Caswell will personally lead negotiations henceforth. He will also be making an important announcement regarding the situation in Iraq following contact with Saddam Hussein.

Please involve me if any of my undertakings require further support, confirmation or clarification.

Thank you for your help, you are making history
Good Luck
John Lincoln, Vice-President of the United States.

Lincoln felt like jumping for joy; he had pulled Caswell very firmly onto a hook from which there was no escape. He knew he was jumping the gun. Conceivably Saddam might not keep his word but, in that event, Caswell could pursue the destruction of the biological weapons in any way he chose.

"Mr President," Mary O'Halloran voice quavered with excitement, she sensed a moment of history in the making "it's him; Saddam Hussein is on the line for you."

"Put him through Mary."

"President Caswell." He was calm, matter-of-fact; he had steeled himself for this moment. Whatever his personal feelings he knew he had no option but to do a deal and that email of

Lincoln's to the Arab leaders had tightened the noose round his neck.

"Saddam Hussein, President of Iraq." The Arab spoke confidently, trying to maintain his dignity.

"I know who you are and what you do." Caswell growled. "I have to confess that I don't like you much and I trust you even less, but I'm going to try to do business with you. I suggest that you come straight to the point."

The Iraqi's voice did not betray the humiliation he felt at going cap in hand to Caswell.

"Very well; I'll speak in your language; I know you have no Arabic. I'm calling at the request of Vice-President Lincoln to inform you of very recent and very unfortunate discoveries in my country. I hasten to explain that I had no personal knowledge of these matters. The perpetrators have already been punished; in fact, they have been executed, such is the enormity of their crime. What they have revealed explains many of the misunderstandings between our two countries."

You lying conniving bastard. Caswell wanted to respond but he put a brake on his tongue. It was happening; he could see his elevation to political legend taking shape. He could imagine the Nobel Peace Prize ceremony; he'd been there for Jimmy Carter's.

Saddam continued, his voice revealing no trace of defeat or contrition. "I wish to inform you that I have discovered a number of sources of what you would consider to be weapons of mass destruction."

Caswell interrupted; he wasn't going to make it too easy. "You're saying that these are concealed within Iraq?"

"That is correct."

"How many of these sources are there?"

After a momentary hesitation Saddam responded in a hushed voice. "Fourteen."

Caswell echoed the information. "Fourteen. And you knew nothing about them? How could this happen without your knowledge?"

Saddam moistened his lips; stress had left his mouth dry. "The deception was carried out by individuals at the highest level. People I trusted; traitors who had aspirations to the Presidency. But let us put the past behind us; I'm prepared to have the sites inspected and any weapons destroyed."

"I applaud the fact that you've made this revelation, though I'm puzzled as to how it all came to light." Caswell was enjoying having the upper hand and was determine to humiliate the dictator.

Saddam gritted his teeth and replied lamely. "I have no explanation as to how those responsible were able to conceal their misdeeds; my Chief of Internal Security was complicit in the deception. Fortunately, one of those involved became an informer, though he too has been court marshalled and executed."

Caswell reflected on his conversation with Lincoln, so far there had been no mention of resignation. "You must be highly embarrassed at these revelations; they must be politically damaging."

The President of Iraq recognised that the moment of his demise had arrived and faced it bravely. "Of that there is no doubt and I will do the honourable thing. I will advise the people of Iraq that I have decided to resign due to the revelations as a matter of honour but also in part due to my failing health. I will announce shortly that democratic elections are to be held and I might endorse my son's candidature for Presidency."

Caswell smiled gleefully. "I welcome your decision but the United Nations will of course want to have neutral observers at these elections and be certain that the system of Government is indeed democratic. I personally wouldn't like the idea of your son carrying on where you left off; let's have some real change."

Saddam protested. "In a democracy my son would be free to campaign for the Presidency, would he not?" We will of course invite impartial observers to the election process but our system of government is entirely an internal matter."

"I can live with your son's candidacy, but approval of your system of government by an external Body is essential, although it need not be visible." Caswell was determined to secure maximum co-operation from the Arab.

Hussein took his cue. "If such approval could be given in secret, then it could perhaps be accommodated."

Caswell had one more element of the negotiation to put in place - the time scale for implementation. "We seem to have reached an accord and I believe a time scale of six months has been discussed?"

The Iraqi protested. "That doesn't give me much time; there are many arrangements to put in place."

"I have every confidence in you Mr President. You are still in charge in Iraq until you resign; I'm sure you'll meet no opposition to your proposals." Caswell tried to keep sarcasm out of his voice and sound statesmanlike. It was time to begin a new chapter and he was determined to derive maximum personal benefit from the situation that now existed. The Nobel Prize for Peace would be a fitting tribute to his political career.

Saddam replied tersely. "Very well, I will proceed on the basis we have discussed."

Caswell sank back in his chair; he had screwed everything he wanted out of Saddam. "We seem to have agreed a way forward. For my part, immediately following your announcement, I will welcome your statement and put in hand the immediate inspection of the weapons sites. I think that we have gone far enough for today; we will no doubt talk again in the near future. This is the birth of a rewarding era for the Iraqi people and for the Middle East in general."

The two men ended their conversation; one elated, the other despondent, each contemplating the days that lay ahead.

CHAPTER 15

The Oval Office

Thirty minutes later, Mary O'Halloran ushered Weinberger, Wright, Davidson and Phelps into the Oval Office. They sat open-mouthed as the President poured out his news taking as much credit from the situation as he dared. He sought to separate Lincoln's meetings with the Israelis and the Palestinians from Saddam Hussein's capitulation, claiming that the latter was a victory for his policy of military build-up.

Weinberger and Wright had reservations as to Saddam's sincerity but having made their views known, in the end bowed to Caswell's pressure and Davidson's logic.

Phelps echoed her master's voice pointing out that it was a win-win outcome all the way round. "Saddam forced out of power, democracy in Iraq, no military casualties, no massive expenditure on war, real prospects of peace in the Middle East and a complete vindication of the President's policies. The President can afford to be magnanimous in his acceptance of Saddam Hussein's confession and leave it to the world press to go for the dictator's jugular; we'll give them every encouragement of course."

Caswell nodded approvingly, adding that the military build-up would continue until the United Nations inspectors had completed their work; America would remain in the driving seat.

Weinberger sighed. He had to go along with the proposal, but it all seemed too good to be true. "I hope we're not being suckered Jack; he's a crafty son of a bitch."

The President looked questioningly at his Secretary of State. "Meaning what Al?"

"Well, he can see a war coming he can't win, so he gives up some of his weapons and keeps the rest on ice. Next, he resigns, puts in a puppet Government, waits for things to quieten down, and bides his time to fight another day. A leopard doesn't change its spots, Jack."

Caswell's guts tightened; maybe Saddam **was** playing a strategic game. *Christ, you had better be right Lincoln.* "It's possible Al, we'll remain on the alert but in the meantime, we run with my scenario."

The President could see the obvious; the demise of Saddam would fill the headlines. The Palestine negotiations would be sidelined. They had reached other agreements in the past, all had subsequently unravelled; the public had seen it all before. But Iraq was different; this was his chance for glory and he wasn't going to let it go. "OK guys, that's all for now. I'll keep you informed. Diane, you hang on, I need some advice on how to handle this with the media."

Weinberger turned as he reached the door. "Just remember what I said Jack, I don't trust the bastard."

Left alone, Phelps hugged her lover and kissed him. "You handled that beautifully Jack, I'm proud of you." She pulled him close and pressed her lips to his. Caswell felt his emotions gather but there were more important matters to hand and he pulled back. "Later darling, later."

She pouted but moved away to an armchair; she could wait if he could. "I can't believe that Lincoln has pulled this off Jack, it's uncanny. Who's feeding him all this inside information? How come he's got every leader in the Middle East eating out of his hand? He's good but he's not that good."

"I don't know and right now I don't care. I just want to make sure that I get as much credit for the whole show as I can. I want you to glue yourself to Iraqi television alongside an interpreter, and report back with every detail, every nuance of Saddam's speech. Then brief me on an immediate response. Pull out all the stops; I want an announcement from the Oval Office on all TV channels all round the world. I want to address a special meeting of the United Nations. I'll report to the Senate and Congress giving Lincoln a fair mention in those forums but play down his role everywhere else. Got me? And whilst you're at it, give some thought to any groundwork I should be doing to secure the Nobel Peace Prize."

She had to smile at her lover's blatant glory seeking but it suited her; his future was her future. "Will do Jack, but first things first. Let's get you centre stage before we start lobbying for awards. And don't forget Lincoln, he's still a potential problem for us."

Caswell shrugged. "He'll have to be dealt with sometime but, if he delivers goodies like this, maybe we should learn to work with him."

"Don't be naïve, this honeymoon won't last; sooner or later he'll ask for something you're not prepared to give, and if you say no, he'll pull the trigger. The aftermath could overshadow anything you've achieved, especially if he explained how these Middle East Agreements were really brought about. Your chances of a Nobel Prize would evaporate in an instant."

Caswell came back down to earth. "I haven't forgotten. I've cleared the way for him get involved in the Irish question; that should keep him out of our hair for a while. If you can come up with anything that will bring a more permanent answer to our situation, just go ahead."

Phelps seized her opportunity. "OK Jack, I'll take that as an executive order. Now, this adrenaline-charged atmosphere has stirred me up, when do we get some quality time?" She rubbed her thumb along her lips suggestively.

Caswell smiled. "I won't leave it too long I promise."

Washington Airport

Air Force One touched down at 19.03 and a weary but happy Vice-President went straight home. He longed to share his experiences with Carol; she was the only one with whom he could relive in full the enormity of what was happening. He knew he could never tell his story to the whole world, but maybe someday he could write about it all in the guise of fiction.

She listened attentively, sitting quietly in the corner of the bathroom whilst her husband relaxed in an aromatic foam-filled bath. The single candle somehow brought an air of quiet solemnity to the occasion as he tried to explain his inner feelings.

"So much has been achieved in so little time Honey, it's awesome. I still don't understand why it's happened to me."

"There really is no need to understand everything, John. Sometimes faith should be enough."

"I wish I had your simple beliefs."

"Someday you will Honey, you'll see."

When the telling and questioning was over, she looked at him with an expression near to reverence. "Truly you've been chosen to do God's work. You make sure he gets some of the credit. Have you thanked him?"

Lincoln felt awkward. "Not in the way I should, and I'm afraid the good Lord will only get such credit as Caswell doesn't take to himself."

"No matter about him as long as you bear in mind the power behind you, and remember always that what the Lord gives, the Lord can take away."

"I'll never forget, I'm just so afraid I'll get it wrong sooner or later. How much of this is down to me? Am I just a puppet or am I setting the agenda?"

His wife shook her head a little sadly. "You have got to learn that we are all in his hands John; we only do what he lets us do."

Lincoln sighed. "Sometimes I wonder how he would handle things if he had returned as himself."

Next Day: Oval Office

The President was feeling pleased with himself; it was all happening; the public relations machinery was in full flow. Saddam Hussein had delivered his message to his people; there was no turning back. "I've got to hand it to you John; I never thought I'd see the day when every nation in the Middle East was singing from the same hymn sheet. If this comes to fruition our Presidency will go down as one of the greatest in American history."

Lincoln offered a note of caution. "It's going well, but keep your hand on the tiller. It's not over yet. Who knows what chicanery might be afoot behind the scenes in Iraq."

Caswell shook his head. "I feel confident there's going to be a lasting settlement. I even managed to be civil to that bastard Saddam; I reckon the deal is done and dusted. He's made his broadcast by the way; the media is full of it."

Lincoln couldn't resist a gibe. "And full of you too Jack. Maybe it's time you stopped calling him a bastard and changed that mindset of yours; it'll help with future relationships. It's going to be your show here on in; I'm dropping right out of the picture."

Caswell could hardly believe his luck. "What do you mean, dropping out completely?"

"Exactly that Jack; I'm out. It's your baby now, but if you renege on any of my undertakings, the Middle East leaders will come to me to sort them out, and I guess you can work out my reaction. I'm happy for you to be in the limelight and I won't steal any of your glory; just make sure you deliver. I'm sure your mistress will give you all the assistance you need both in bed and out of it."

"OK, OK, I've got the picture. Leave her out of it, please"

"Glad to see we understand each other Jack, make sure you keep it that way."

Caswell changed the subject. "I've got another assignment for you, a big one but if you can bring peace in the Middle East, this will be child's play. I want you go to Ireland and use your skills to solve the Ulster problem; the Loyalists and Republicans are further apart than ever. The UK Prime Minister is expecting a call from you when you're ready. I've never understood why Reagan and Clinton involved themselves so much in the Irish question, but it's expected of us."

Lincoln laughed out loud. "You know damn well why they want us on board. For one thing Great Britain is our oldest and most loyal ally and the American-Irish vote was essential to that pair. Congratulations, you've handed me another poison chalice, thank you very much. Who came up with that one, you or Diane? But don't worry I'll take it on; an end to the problems in that corner of the Western world is long overdue."

Caswell shrugged, "Whatever you say, although I'm not convinced that the various factions really want peace; too many of them are making a nice living out of the situation, including some politicians. Is there anything you want me to do?"

Lincoln dwelt on the question; he wasn't keen on Caswell's involvement but there were protocols to be observed and he was the President. "Two things; advise the Prime Minister and the Taoiseach that I want to go over there just as soon as they'll have me. Use your charm, or muscle, to make sure it happens within the next two or three weeks. No fuss, no publicity. I want a low-key visit with everything minimal; it can be kept below the radar and seen as a holiday trip. The other bit of help I need is access to telephone contacts for the Republican and Loyalist factions. I'm guessing that either you or Oliver Dacre at the CIA can come up with that."

Caswell raised an eyebrow. "To what purpose?"

"I want to talk to all parties in the same room at the same time."

Caswell shook his head. "I can't see that happening. They hate each other's guts or at least they like to give that impression."

"Of course they do, they've got to maintain their public image. But they co-operate on some levels; they agree boundaries for drug peddling, they don't rob the same banks and they avoid out-and-out warfare like the plague. I think they stopped fighting for ideals a long time ago."

"I don't disagree but, I doubt if the Command Councils, or whatever they call themselves, will want to meet with you unless you've got something to offer."

"I'm not going there bearing gifts. I'm going with an open mind to listen then see what I can do to bridge the gap. They've got nothing to lose, and they get to meet the Vice-President of the United States; something to tell their grandchildren about."

"Have it your way, both Prime Ministers will be cautious, maybe even suspicious; they won't give you a blank cheque."

"I've just told you I don't want anything from anybody; bear in mind their peace talks have stalled and it needs something to break the log jam. I feel it's time to get back to basics and ask the various factions what they really want."

Caswell shook his head. "It's all been done, it's all on record; disarming the IRA is the key and they won't fall into line as long as British troops remain in Ulster. It's a real chicken and egg situation; one that's proved irreconcilable up to now."

Lincoln responded dismissively. "Yeah, yeah, you said that about Palestine and you said it about Iraq. Twist arms if you have to, call in some favours. You know the score, just make sure the Prime Minister and the Taoiseach back me up when I need them to. In the meantime, just leave me to it."

"OK, I'll do what I can." Caswell was unconvinced, but he had nothing to lose and everything to gain."

Back in his office Lincoln reflected on his encounter with Caswell; his newly acquired power was developing and he had accessed Caswell's thoughts without direct physical contact. *Perhaps it works on those with whom I've already established contact, like the channel remains open.* But there had been something he hadn't got to the heart of; he had sensed some kind of threat as though Caswell meant him harm. Perhaps that wasn't altogether surprising. There had been many times in the past when he'd wished some obnoxious politician would disappear. He tried to dismiss the thought from his mind, but was he being given a warning?

CHAPTER 16

The White House

Lincoln put his coffee down and picked up the phone. It was Caswell.

"It's me, I've got some news for you on the Irish trip."

"Good news I hope, Jack?"

"The Prime Minister and Taoiseach have agreed to your visit; it won't be publicised and security will be minimal, just as you requested. They asked me to remind you that it's a difficult time for them; the Northern Ireland Assembly is under suspension and all sides are very sensitive. They liked your idea of describing the trip as a holiday."

"Suits me, I can pretend I'm tracing my ancestry if anyone gets nosy."

Caswell went down the wrong path. "You being black I can't see that working too well; you'll have to do better than that."

Lincoln sighed. "Only joking, Jack; try not to lose your sense of humour along with everything else."

"Ah, I see; very droll I must say. They are genuinely anxious about you rocking the boat; they've staked their reputations on the current Peace Process and they don't want to take a step backwards, so be careful about what you promise."

Lincoln was slightly irritated by the unnecessary caution and he let sarcasm surface. "Thanks Jack, tell them how pleased I am to have their confidence. I'll do whatever I have to do to achieve a successful outcome. Did you have any luck with the contact numbers?"

"Only partial success and everybody pulled out all the stops, I assure you. Nobody is co-operating over there; the Loyalists and Republican paramilitaries have cut themselves off from direct political contact. The best that could be arranged is for you to set yourself up somewhere and then contact an intermediary with your number. I'll give you his number before you go. After that you await their pleasure and hope they'll want to speak to you. And there's no good grousing about it, that's how it is."

Lincoln was disappointed. "So essentially, I get to make one phone call, then sit in my hotel room and wait."

"It's the only game in town; take it or leave it. You can still choose not to go."

"One thing is certain, I'm going. I'll brief you when I work out exactly what I'm going to do."

"Have it your way, let me know when you need a plane laid on."

Back in his office Lincoln stood at his window and looked out onto the White House lawn, reflecting on his undertaking. The Vice-President of America would be heading for Ireland without a team of advisors, no personal minders and very little security provision by his hosts. *I must be mad; upset the wrong people and they won't hesitate to assassinate me.* It was just as dangerous as the Middle East, perhaps more so. He was putting himself in a vulnerable position but he would go and, as Carol often reminded him, '*Put yourself in God's hands, you won't go far wrong.*'

If Carol were to be believed, God had chosen him and he was doing God's work so everything would be OK. *I sure do hope my wife has got it right, Lord.*

The following day Caswell phoned again. "Hi John, do you want Mary to book you into a hotel?"

Lincoln smiled. *You just want to know my whereabouts, Jack.* "No thanks, that's kind of her, but I'll look round for a place when I get there. You can get Air Force One on standby for take-off tomorrow night. I intend to fly out around seven tomorrow evening."

"Christ you're not giving your hosts much notice. By the way where are you headed? Belfast or Dublin?

"I haven't made my mind up, I'll brief the flight people tomorrow, but it will be one of those airports."

"Why the secrecy? I'm beginning to think you don't trust me?"

"I guess that's it exactly Jack. I don't trust you."

"Have it your way; I'll let your hosts know that you'll be arriving tomorrow morning.

Ireland Car Rental

"Leary's Car Rentals, Rosemary speaking, how may I help you?"

"I'd like to reserve a car for the day after tomorrow; I'll pick it up around 9.00am."

"Certainly sir. Can I have your name, address and driving licence details? I'll also need a credit card number."

Lincoln advised that he was an American citizen and provided the requested details. When he finished his call, he sat back satisfied; the woman hadn't made any comment when he'd given his name, not even when he had given his Washington home address. *I guess the Vice-President isn't too well known over there.*

He pondered on booking a hotel, but decided not to; it was out of season and he could pick somewhere to his liking on the day.

Washington Airport, Air Force One, 19.30

"Welcome on board, Mr Vice-President. Nice to see this baby put in some real flying time; I hope you continue your globe-trotting." The pilot spoke from the heart; flying the President was prestigious, but there weren't too many trips away and sitting around on standby was a real bore.

Lincoln nodded, "If things go to plan Captain, you'll be spending a lot more time in the air."

"Suits me; I wonder, could I be advised of our actual destination in Ireland; I have to file a flight plan?"

"Of course, Captain, we're bound for Shannon Airport."

Shannon Airport is located in the Republic of Ireland, in County Clare, just fifteen miles to the Northwest of Limerick.

In choosing Shannon, Lincoln believed he was less likely to be recognised there than if he landed in the Republic's main airport, Dublin, or at Belfast International in Ulster.

Lincoln retired immediately to the Presidential suite for the night and settled down to read the detailed briefing notes prepared by the American Ambassador to Ireland and the two political leaders. He was relieved to find that both leaders shared a common approach. He asked to be wakened at 06.00 local time; the United Kingdom was five hours ahead which meant Air Force One should by then be an hour or so from the Irish coast.

Later

In the event he woke at 5.30am and had showered and dressed when the Flight Attendant knocked on his cabin door. He took a few minutes to drink his coffee, then made his way along to the flight deck.

Captain Edwards was surprised when the cabin door opened and the Vice-President greeted him with a cheery "Good morning."

"Good morning, Mr Vice-President. Nothing wrong I hope?"

Lincoln shook his head.

"That's a relief, I hope you slept well? We had some turbulence during the night."

"Didn't notice it Captain, I slept the sleep of the dead. Am I right that local time is five hours ahead, making it 06.04am?"

"That's correct; we'll be putting down in about an hour."

"Good. There's a reason for my presence, a small change of plan."

"Change of plan?" The Captain echoed the Vice-President's words. "Meaning exactly what, Sir?"

"I want to divert to Knock International Airport."

Edwards hesitated; he didn't want to challenge the Vice-President. "That might not be possible; we do have an authorised flight plan."

"Make it possible, Captain." Lincoln adopted an uncompromising expression. "Pretend it's a security issue if you have to, or imagine that Shannon is fog-bound. I guess that in such circumstances a diversion would be routine."

"I'll do my best." Edwards took no immediate action, clearly waiting for Lincoln to leave.

"Don't mind me, just go right ahead and contact Air Traffic Control to make the arrangements. I'm sure they'll be delighted to accommodate Air Force One, but I'll hang around just in case there is a problem."

"There's also ground security to be considered; you are the Vice-President."

"Security is all taken care of, just carry out my instructions please."

Edwards accepted the tone of finality in the Vice-President's voice and contacted the Air Traffic Control. As Lincoln had anticipated, there were no difficulties obtaining permission to divert, and he remained on the flight deck whilst Edwards turned the aircraft North and set course for his new destination.

With only fifteen minutes flying time remaining Lincoln returned to his quarters. He had acted on instinct, not knowing whether or not, the Captain was under orders to report back to the White House. Edwards was the President's personal pilot and his allegiance would understandably be to Caswell. Lincoln knew that satellite tracking would reveal the plane's flight path to anyone watching, but some last-minute changes might help to ensure he wouldn't be followed from the airport.

Knock International Airport

The airport opened in 1985 and lies a few miles from Kilkenny in County Mayo, in the Republic of Ireland. From there Lincoln would head North on the N17 to Sligo, then East to his final destination, the small town of Warrenpoint at the head of Carlingford Lough. A tourist centre, popular with yachtsmen, Warrenpoint is in the Province of Ulster not far from the border with the Republic. It was ideally located for the business he hoped to conduct over the course of the next few days.

Air Force One landed shortly after eight-o'clock local time; Lincoln wasted no time in getting off having thanked the crew for a pleasant trip. He wanted to clear the airport promptly, just in case there were any unwanted observers.

He didn't escape attention completely; the Airport Manager was there to greet him, astonished at the unplanned arrival of Air Force One. As soon as he saw Lincoln, he knew it wasn't the President. *Who are you? You must be important whoever you are.* The official was surprised to see that the new arrival was unaccompanied. *Where are your advisers? Why, no security staff? Perhaps you're not a VIP after all, but you look important and it was, after all, Air Force One.* Questions flooded his mind, his visitor's bearing and confident manner suggested importance and surely not just anybody got to travel in the President's plane. *No, you're definitely top brass.*

Paddy Flynn's voice betrayed his nervousness as he introduced himself. "Paddy Flynn, Airport Manager, Sir. Welcome to Ireland."

"John Lincoln, Vice-President of the United States."

Christ the Vice-President, he was right out of the top drawer. Flynn gazed at the man facing him in awe as he shook hands. "I'm sorry there isn't a red carpet, Mr Lincoln."

"No problem, Mr Flynn, this is a very low-key visit and not one I want to publicise. I'm afraid I can't offer an explanation, at least not one that would be truthful."

Flynn shuffled his feet. *What was he supposed to do now?*

Lincoln detected his discomfort and took the lead. "I wonder if you could take me across to the Car Rental area, Leary's to be specific; we can talk as we go."

Flynn nodded. *Sure now, that's easy enough but the Vice-President hiring a car and driving? Was this real? Should he ask for an explanation? No, best not.* "Yes Mr Lincoln, follow me please."

Lincoln put an arm round his host's shoulder and lowered his voice to a whisper. "Mr Flynn, I wonder if this visit could remain confidential for the next week or so, after which the reason for secrecy will become clear. I appreciate Air Traffic Control and others will have seen Air Force One land but I want my presence here kept out of the media. It's all a bit sensitive at the present time. I hope you understand?"

Flynn was a willing conspirator and eager to please. *Christ, the Vice-President of the United States was taking him into his confidence; just wait till he told the lads down the pub.*

"Of course I do Mr Lincoln."

As the years went by, in true Irish fashion, he would embroider the story of his brief encounter out of all recognition to the actual event. It wasn't everybody got to meet the Vice-President of the United States and be asked to be his confidant. Yes, he'd have a thing or two to tell his children and his grandchildren.

Lincoln was passed through Car Rental with maximum efficiency and without apparent recognition. The woman on duty eyed the Airport Manager hovering in the background, wondering why he was accompanying the black American but made no comment. She would ask Paddy what was going on when the American had gone.

"Thank you for your help, Mr Flynn, I know I can rely on you." Lincoln winked knowingly.

Flynn tapped the side of his nose with his forefinger. "You can, Sir, believe me. Not one word will pass these lips, never fear; not even the priest himself will know till the time is right."

It was eight-thirty when Lincoln set out on his 130mile drive to Warrenpoint. The flight had gone well and he enjoyed being unencumbered by protocol or bureaucracy. The car was small by his standards, but comfortable, and he quickly settled back to enjoy the journey through some beautiful Irish scenery. It took him a few miles to get used to driving on the left and he was pleased he had specified an automatic, not having used a gear-stick for many years.

The tranquillity offered by the green rolling countryside seemed so much at odds with the problems that had pervaded the country for so many years. He drove at a comfortable speed, totally oblivious of other road-users; he didn't think there was any chance of being followed. He was wrong; he had overlooked the fact that his calls from the White House might be monitored, a procedure instituted on Caswell's instructions. They had known all along that he would be picking up a hire car from Knock International Airport. The man following him had even managed to ascertain what vehicle he would be allocated, and had pulled in behind him at a discreet distance when he exited the Airport.

Warrenpoint

The journey was uneventful and he covered the distance to Warrenpoint in less than five hours, including a stop for a sandwich and the mandatory pint of Guinness in a traditional Irish whitewashed pub on the outskirts of Ballygawley.

The drive through Warrenpoint itself, a smallish town, didn't take long and he made a mental note of the few hotels on offer as he went along, eventually settling on The Castle which transpired to have twenty rooms and a five-star rating. It didn't in any way resemble a castle, but it was set on the top of a hill overlooking the sea so maybe in the distant past it had been the site of a fortress of some kind.

Lincoln parked his car behind the hotel and ignoring the rear access, made his way back round to the front entrance taking deep breaths of the salt-laden sea air as he went. The young woman behind the Reception Desk looked up as he entered, smiling a welcome. "Good afternoon, Sir, how can I help you?"

"I'd like the best room available please, preferably one overlooking the sea."

"Certainly, do you have a reservation?"

"No, I don't, I'm travelling around your beautiful country, just booking in wherever takes my fancy." Lincoln hoped he sounded like a typical American tourist.

"And how long do you think you'll be with us?"

"I guess a week in the first instance, longer if I feel like it."

The Receptionist, Maureen O'Farrell, studied her computer screen. "There's a choice of two rooms. A small but comfortable single facing the sea or a luxury double with views to the countryside at the rear of the hotel; you can see the Mourne Mountains in the distance."

He ditched his preference for a sea view; a room described as small in the UK would be tiny by his standards. "I'll have the double please."

"It is more expensive, of course" She smiled and put on an apologetic expression.

Lincoln shrugged. "That's not a problem, I'm happier with a bit of space around me."

The usual registration formalities were completed smoothly, she barely glanced at his passport; they dealt with many American tourists in Warrenpoint. A few minutes later he was ushered into his room by a leprechaun of a porter who pocketed his tip with a cheery grin and wished him a 'rewarding visit.'

Lincoln stretched out in a hot bath, unaware that one floor below him, Reception had another visitor, a tall well-dressed man wearing a tweed overcoat and a trilby hat. He flashed his fake police warrant card at Maureen O'Farrell and extracted the information he required.

"It's routine, nothing to be concerned about. In fact, based on what you've told me I'm pretty sure it's not the person we're interested in. I'm sorry to have bothered you. Best not say anything to Mr Lincoln; we wouldn't want him to get the wrong impression of the Old Country. We wouldn't want to appear to be nosy or inhospitable, would we?"

The young woman was flustered and shook her head anxiously; she hadn't been in the job long and didn't really know how she was expected to deal with a situation of this kind. "No, no, of course not."

When the man had gone, she wondered if she should have called the manager but it was too late now; she didn't want to be told off, best to forget all about it.

CHAPTER 17

A Farmhouse near Newry

Donal McGuire was pissed off; he'd been summoned at short notice, told to drop everything and report to his local Commander. *Why the Hell couldn't they plan ahead? They had fuck all else to do but plan and dream, or so it seemed to him.* If he had the guts, he'd get out of the IRA, but he was afraid to voice his feelings; he was trapped. He had promised to take his wife to the pictures that very evening and now he would have to disappoint her. *Bastards!*

"I wish you could get out, Donal." Kate McGuire was a slightly built, pretty woman in her thirtieth year, a year younger than her husband.

"So do I, but until they decide to let me go, I'm stuck. And you really shouldn't know I'm with them; you must never admit you know to anyone, never."

"I know, I know." She looked at him anxiously. "Donal, you never do anything really bad, do you?"

He smiled at her reassuringly. "Of course not, Sweetheart, I just help out with little jobs now and again. Don't be worrying that pretty head of yours. If I can get back early, we'll still go out, and if it's too late we'll go tomorrow; provided your mother can still look after the girls."

As his car bumped along the narrow-rutted farm track McGuire wondered if he could ever break away from the paramilitaries. *Perhaps he should broach the subject with the man he was about to meet. He had been young when he'd joined, idealistic, full of airy-fairy dreams; it had been different then. Life had moved on, he was married now and blessed with two adorable daughters, both at school. He had responsibilities now and he was happy. He'd served the IRA well; surely, they would understand? Yes, he'd ask the man if the opportunity arose, but he knew in his heart he wouldn't. They would consider him to be a traitor, a deserter. No, they would never let him go; he knew too much and was too good at what he did.*

A blue Volvo stood in front of the stone-built farmhouse; the man was there. He pulled up alongside, got out, walked along the front and knocked on the door.

"Come on in Donal." His local Commander, Jimmy McGimpsey had been keeping watch whilst he sat warming his hands at the peat fire. No one lived in the farmhouse; it was remote and had been acquired for clandestine meetings such as this.

"It's a cold one today, Jimmy."

"That it is. You're a shade early."

"Better that than late. What's this about? I'm keen to get done and get back home; I was planning on taking Kate out tonight."

"Aye well, this is **really** important Donal."

McGuire bridled. "Taking my wife out is important to me, Jimmy."

The other man stared at him. "This is IRA business; nothing is more important than IRA business. You should know that. Relax, pour yourself a measure of whiskey; I've got another guest coming."

"But..." Donal made to protest, his line of work was a solitary business and the fewer involved in it the better.

McGimpsey held a finger to his lips in reproof. "This time it's different."

A series of loud raps on the door stilled further conversation.

"Right on time. Come in." Jimmy shouted.

The door opened and Donal was taken aback as he watched the new arrival enter. This was man's work, how come a woman was involved? She couldn't possibly do what he did.

"What the fuck is she doing here?"

Mary Larkin was stunningly attractive, the sun shone through the open doorway causing her shoulder length hair to shine like burnished gold. Her face was almost angelic and had little need for make-up. And she had a woman's body, a real woman's body, not the stick insect frame of those that routinely adorned the fashion magazines.

She smiled at Donal's outburst. "Close your gob Donal, it detracts from those handsome features of yours."

"What's going on Jimmy? Why is she here?"

"I could ask why you're here Donal, except that I've got enough common sense to figure it out for myself." Mary Larkin raised her eyebrows, posing an unasked question.

McGimpsey, sat back enjoying the exchange. but it was time to quieten things down. "She's in the same line of business as you Donal, and every bit as good; some say better, though not myself I hasten to add."

Mary Larkin and Donal McGuire appraised each other. They had met from time to time at various rallies; but neither had known the nature of each other's involvement until now.

"No one ever walked away from one of my assignments." Donal was a bit of a chauvinist and getting angry; it was starting to dawn on him that he would be working with a woman. *How could a woman possibly have his kind of expertise?*

Larkin laughed out loud. "Sure now, I'm in no doubt as to who's best; Jimmy." She enjoyed baiting the male ego at the best of times and she sensed McGuire was an easy victim.

McGimpsey intervened. "Enough the pair of you, time will be the judge of who's best. Personally, neither of you would get my vote, but a man's got to work with what he's got. Sit down both of you and listen carefully; I only want to go through this once, then we're out of here."

"First off, the job is to be done tomorrow morning."

Donal and Mary glanced at each other. "Short notice Jimmy." she ventured. "We usually like to get to know the site and set up the rifles."

"You'll manage." He held up a photograph. "The target is this man. As you can see, he won't be difficult to recognise in these parts."

Mary giggled. "I hope you're not a racist Jimmy. Has he bothered you? Or is this your answer to the immigrant problem?"

"Ha, ha. Very funny, I don't say. Just take a good look at the photograph; **you** probably think all black people look the same."

"I'd know soon enough if it was Denzil Washington or Mike Tyson had his hand on my arse; this guy is more of a Morgan Freeman type."

Donal flinched; he hated to hear a woman swear.

McGimpsey nodded. "He's staying at the Castle Hotel in Warrenpoint. His car is parked at the rear of the hotel; note that it's a silver Ford Mondeo. You'll take him out tomorrow morning at the public telephone box on Killylee Lane. You'll be working at around three to four hundred metres depending on where you choose to set yourselves up. I could do the job myself at that distance."

Donal was puzzled, "So why two of us Jimmy? This is child's play; even Mary couldn't miss at that range."

"There are two of you because I say so; I'm taking no chances on this one."

Donal shook his head. "Who is he? He must be very important or he's done us a nasty disservice along the way."

"His name is John Lincoln."

Donal shrugged, "Never heard of him. What does he do for a living?"

"He's the Vice-President of the United States."

"Yeah, yeah, and I'm Peter Fucking O'Toole."

McGuire said nothing, waiting for the full impact of his revelation to sink home.

"Fuck me. You aren't kidding, are you Jimmy?" Mary was excited; she got a high from killing and the more important the target the bigger the thrill.

"But why Jimmy?" Donal was uneasy; there would be a massive outcry in the aftermath of the killing. "We don't usually do anything to antagonise the United States, and he'll be surrounded by security. We'll be lucky to get a clear shot, and even luckier to get away free. They'll have helicopters, perimeter guards; it won't work. And come to think of it, what's he doing at a public telephone box anyway?"

McGuire raised a warning finger. "You're asking too many questions. There won't be any security, this is an informal visit; that's why you haven't seen any mention of it in the news. The whys and wherefores of this operation are none of your concern. You will do the job and get out, and make no mention of it to anyone, either inside or outside the organisation. Is that clear now? Any slip-ups and you'll find yourself in an unmarked grave and maybe your family alongside you. This operation is top secret, and known only to a handful of us, and it must stay that way. We'll be making sure that the Loyalists take the blame. We'll gain maximum political advantage."

Donal nodded. He knew better than to continue his challenge but his stomach knotted at the prospect of what lay ahead; the Authorities north and south of the border and the CIA wouldn't let up on this one. Christ they were still arguing about who killed Kennedy.

McGimpsey turned to the woman. "And you, Mary, have you got any problems with what you're being asked to do?"

"Fuck me, no Jimmy."

Donal flinched again and gave voice to his feelings. "That's the second time you've said 'fuck me' I'm beginning to think it's an invitation."

"You can dream, Donal, you wouldn't have the balls for it. Best go home to your wife, poor thing doesn't know any better."

"Cut it out you two." McGimpsey spread a map on the floor. "You'll meet at Mawhinney's Cottage at eight tomorrow morning; it's not occupied at the moment but it's kitted out and liveable. You'll leave one car there and make your way to here and park your vehicle off road." He pointed to both locations on the map, an area they were both familiar with.

"From there you'll climb to the top of the hill to this point and pick your spot. You'll find you have a clear view of the telephone box. Lincoln will drive along the lane from Warrenpoint, in a silver Mondeo as I said earlier. If all goes to plan, he should get there at 9.30."

A thought struck Mary. "Hold on Jimmy, just how can you guarantee that he'll be there?"

"That's my personal task Mary. He'll be there, believe me. Now, any further questions?"

Donal shook his head keen to get back to his wife; if he got away soon, he might just get back in time for the pictures. "No, I'm clear; if that's all I'll be going."

Mary snorted. "Fuck me Donal you're losing it; don't you think we'll need weapons?"

"I knew what Jimmy meant carrot-top. No gun, no job, it goes without saying. You rile me once more and you'll find yourself well and truly fucked, and I won't be fussy what end I choose."

She laughed at him. "With what you've got between your legs I'd doubt if I'd notice."

McGimpsey lost patience. "Shut it you two, I'm beginning to wish I hadn't picked you pair for this job. I've got two rifles, both to be abandoned when the job's done. Sling them into the middle of the mill pond on the way back to the car; doesn't matter if they're found."

"What have you got for us?" Larkin's eyes shone with excitement.

"Donal's got a SakoTRG21, it's accurate at twice the range you'll be working at."

"I've used one before; it's a good piece of equipment, I'm more than happy." Donal nodded his approval.

"And for you Mary, we've got the British Army's standard sniping rifle."

She smiled, giving a thumbs up. "Great, the Accuracy International L96A1; I assume it's the long-range version."

McGimpsey nodded appreciatively. "I'm impressed Mary, you know your weapons." He handed her a carrier bag. "Get going and don't do anything to get stopped carrying that. Just one last thing. We've put two marksmen on this job to be absolutely certain of a kill; if you fail, you'll pay with your lives. I mean that. And remember what I told you, never speak of this operation to anyone, inside or outside the organisation."

The ever-present smile left Mary's face; she knew it wasn't an empty threat.

McGimpsey nodded at her. "You can go now Mary; I want a word with Donal."

When she had gone the IRA Commander studied Donal McGuire, pouring two whiskeys as he gave thought to his words. "You should curb that tongue of yours; Mary is a good operative and hasn't let us down this far. If I'm any judge, you don't seem too happy about this job? You're usually detached and professional, as a good marksman has to be."

"Killing the Vice-President of the United States will have serious ramifications, of course I don't like it, Jimmy."

"The whole purpose of our work is to make those in power uncomfortable; it's the only way to achieve change. We aren't killing people for target practice. When the news hits the headlines, no politician in these islands will feel safe; they'll be glad to come to an agreement with us."

"Maybe if it was a British politician I'd understand, but American?"

McGimpsey shook his head. "Makes no difference where he's from as long as he's a big name. It's time we made a big hit; there's a danger of us going soft. Cheer up and don't get stopped on your way back to that lovely wife of yours.",

"Have it your way, Jimmy."

Donal lifted the sports bag containing the Sako and made his way to the door; he was about to step outside when McGimpsey called after him. "Donal, bear in mind what I told Mary. I wasn't joking; if Lincoln isn't dead this time tomorrow, you'll both be executed. And as I said, keep your mouth shut"

Castle Hotel, Warrenpoint

Lincoln picked up the telephone in his room and dialled the contact number he had been given.

"Hello, who's speaking please?"

"John Lincoln."

"I'm afraid I don't know the name. Are you sure you have the right number?"

"It was given to me by a friend."

"Is that right now?"

"It is indeed. I'm phoning from the Castle Hotel in Warrenpoint."

"I'm sorry Mr Lincoln there seems to have been a mistake. I can only suggest that you check the number."

The dialling tone took over as the man at the other end put down his phone. Lincoln wasn't concerned; he'd known what to expect. It was up to them now; all he could do now, was sit and wait. His immediate business completed he went for a pre-dinner stroll around Warrenpoint, and stood for a while watching the yachts bobbing up and down on the incoming tide. How peaceful it all seemed. How could Ireland continue to tear itself apart after so many years? What a destructive cocktail, power, politics and religion had produced.

Half an hour later he returned to the hotel and made his way to the dining room. There were ten other guests present as he took his place, four couples and two men dining alone. One or two caught his eye as he settled down, but nobody appeared to have any real interest in his presence.

He took his time over his fulsome meal, sipping contentedly on a reasonable red wine and was last to leave the dining room. It was too early to retire and he made his way to the bar to kill some time, and sample the best whiskey they had on offer. Two of the couples had found secluded corners and obviously wouldn't welcome company, so he stationed himself at the bar and enjoined the barman in conversation.

Seamus Moloney, judging by his non-stop prattle, had kissed the legendary Blarney Stone several times over and the next hour flew past, by which time the effects of alcohol and a long day finally dictated that he should find the comfort of his bed.

Lincoln heard the sound as he pushed open the door to his room; there was something on the floor scraping across the carpet. Switching on the light he immediately saw the envelope. The note inside contained typed instructions.

Tomorrow morning, turn right when you leave the hotel, then take the third turning on the left into Killylee Lane. Drive for one mile until you see a telephone box on the right-hand side. Arrive at 09.30. You will find a mobile telephone inside. Wait there until it rings and answer it.

175

CHAPTER 18

Mawhinney's Cottage. Next day

At eight the following morning Donal McGuire pulled up outside the remote cottage; its original owner, Paddy Mawhinney, had long since departed this world. It was small but comfortable and was always available as a safe house for those in need of it. As far as the authorities were concerned it was a holiday home in the ownership of a local farmer.

Mary Larkin came out immediately; dressed in jeans and a grey wool sweater. Donal eyed her curves and felt his pulse quicken. *God but you're a looker Mary Larkin. I'll give you that.*

"Good morning, Mary."

"Good morning, Donal."

They were both tense, yesterday's sexist banter was consigned to the backburner, this was business.

The morning sun shone through her auburn hair causing it to shimmer and sparkle; Donal breathed an inner sigh and pursed his lips. *Given the opportunity Mary Larkin, I'd have you on your back. He loved his wife dearly, but Mary was an exceptional woman and very bed-worthy*

"Who'll be driving Donal?"

"I'm happy to, if that's alright with you?"

"You're being very polite this morning; you must have had a good night?" She raised an eyebrow, asking a question she knew wouldn't be answered, smiling when she saw him redden just a touch.

"I slept very well Mary, if that's what you're asking? I'm saving my energy for the job in hand."

"Fuck me Donal, how much energy does it take to pull a trigger?"

'Fuck me.' the words swam round in his head. *If only you were asking Mary.* He shook his head. "I wish you wouldn't swear Mary, it doesn't suit you."

Something made her bite back one of usual retorts. "For you Donal, I'll think about it."

He smiled at her. "I'd really appreciate it if you would."

Larkin turned on her heel and walked to her car, leaving him staring after her. He watched as she transferred the bag containing the L96 rifle into the boot of his car. They had time in hand but they set off anyway, keen to be doing something. Their destination was only twenty minutes away, ample time to let their tensions subside.

Donal knew exactly where he was headed. Larkin for once was silent, she asked no questions, offered no directions for the route; he would have been the same, the job was in progress and they would both act as professionals should.

McGimpsey had chosen their parking place carefully; they could pull off the road and conceal the car behind a thick hedgerow.

Mary jumped out of the car and pushed open the gate to the field. Donal reversed in leaving the car ready for an immediate getaway. She closed the gate, pleased that it swung easily and quietly on its hinges. It had in fact been oiled two days ago by McGimpsey himself.

One hundred metres away, at the far end of the field, a hill rose steeply to provide the vantage view that they needed for the task in hand. They set out, passing a pond on the way.

"I guess that's where Jimmy wants us to dump the rifles."

Larkin nodded. "I guess so. Seems a shame, they're first-class guns."

They climbed the hill quickly and were both breathing heavily when they reached the top.

"Well, that's the hard bit done I reckon."

"You know Mary, your voice is very sexy when you breathe heavily."

"Don't you be getting any ideas; keep your mind on the job." She chided him but in truth, she harboured the notion of a fling, not that she'd tell him that.

"Never fear Mary, my mind has been on the job since I first saw you this morning." He grinned at her.

She smiled back at him, "Now why do I get a feeling we're not talking about the same job?"

"Can't imagine."

The other side of the hill from the field sloped down gently to a post and wire fence running alongside Killylee Lane and, just as Jimmy had told them, there was a clear view of the telephone box. By 08.45 they had both set up their rifles, each firing a few imaginary practice shots. There wasn't a cloud in the sky, there was no wind to speak of and, with the sun behind them, conditions were ideal.

"I'd guess about three hundred and forty or fifty metres Donal; what's your reckoning?"

"I'll go along with that; well inside the accuracy of these two beasts. It's not much harder than a fairground shot if our target stands still. But I wish to God it was a different target though."

Mary grimaced. "You've got no sense of history. Not everybody gets a chance to shoot the Vice-President of the United States. And if I did happen to get arrested, at least I'll go down making headlines all round the world; remember the Kennedy headlines."

"I suppose so. Nothing to do now but to wait for our man to turn up. Thank God it's a bright morning and mild with it; I hate hanging around."

Larkin rolled over onto her back and gazed up at the sky. A blade of grass between her teeth, she watched small wispy clouds drifting across the blue sky, somewhere a lark was singing. "It's lovely here. We never take time to enjoy places like this."

Donal found himself looking at her, his thoughts lustful as he watched the gentle rise and fall of her breasts.

"We were always out playing in the fields when we were young." She continued to reminisce, unaware of his attention.

"Take the bull by the horns Donal; faint heart never won fair lady." he muttered to himself.

She must have half heard him and turned her head. "What was that you said Donal? I didn't quite hear you."

"I was just thinking that our man won't be here for at least half an hour; plenty of time for a good shag if you're interested?"

Her eyes widened; she could scarcely believe what she'd heard. "What? In your fucking dreams Donal; you disappoint me. Is that really the best you can come out with? I feel sorry for your poor wife. Get your mind back on the job. Come to think of it, what would Kate have to say if she knew this was how you behaved?"

He smiled broadly at her. "Sure now, I wouldn't be telling my wife; it would be our little secret."

"Dream on, you've been reading too many chicklits if you think that's the way to win a woman over."

"I'll carry on dreaming then, but if ever you change your mind ……"

She interrupted him. "Bury it Donal, we've got work to do."

"Car coming." Donal caught a flash of a car in the distance as it turned into the lane.

She glanced at her watch. "It's only ten minutes after nine; he's early if it's him."

They listened to the progress of the car, both mentally preparing themselves for the kill but as it came into view at the end of the hedgerow, they saw that it was white, not silver.

"False alarm, damn it." Mary frowned, disappointed; waiting was the worst aspect of any assignment.

The white Vauxhall Viva pulled up alongside the telephone box and a small fat man dressed in workman's overalls got out and went inside. Seconds later he pushed his way out of the box, got back in his car and drove away.

"He was quick whatever he was doing; he couldn't have made a call. I wonder what he was up to?"

Donal adjusted the focus on the Sako's telescopic sight and looked into the interior of the telephone box, not sure what he was looking for. There wasn't anything immediately obvious, but then he spotted it, a mobile phone partially concealed behind the handset. He smiled. *Very clever Jimmy.*

"The bait is in place Mary; that guy has just dropped off a mobile and I'll bet our man is coming here to pick it up and receive a call. And of course the call is timed for…..?" He looked at her waiting for an answer.

"Nine thirty; as you say, he's a clever guy our Jimmy."

At nine twenty-six, Lincoln's silver Mondeo turned into Kilklee Lane; the moment had come.

Donal took up prone position and sighted his target. "All set Mary?" There was no need to ask, he knew she was as ready as he.

Her eyes glinted. "Can't wait, this really gives me a buzz."

"You still on for the head shot?"

She nodded and her eyes fixed on the approaching target; her lips drawn tight.

"Good luck. I'll hit him in the heart or the spine, depending on which way he's facing."

The Mondeo pulled up, its silver bodywork glinting in the sunshine, silence once more as the engine died. Lincoln got out and gazed round, his eyes searching for observers. He gave no regard to the top of the hill; he didn't really expect to be under surveillance. Looking into the sun, he wouldn't have spotted his would-be assassins in any case.

Satisfied that he wasn't being watched, he moved closer to the box and looked through the glazing for the mobile, immediately catching sight of it behind the handset. He pulled the door open wedging it with his foot, reaching forward to retrieve the mobile, then looked around again, wondering if some unseen watcher was about to dial.

The moment for the assassination had arrived; Lincoln stood perfectly framed in the doorway of the telephone box, just as they had anticipated he would.

"One, two, three, fire." Mary Larkin spoke softly without emotion.

The two shots rang out in unison, sounding as one; two bullets sped towards their victim, reaching Lincoln even as he heard the loud crack that filled the area for a split second.

McGuire and Larkin had barely a glimpse of their victim falling as they rose quickly to their feet with their rifles; there was no need to hang about, their priority now was to get clear of the area. They didn't leave any evidence, no cigarette ends, no sweet or gum wrappers; only the flattened grass signalled their presence. They ran down the hill towards their car; it had been easy.

"The guns, Mary." He stopped at the pond shouting to her as she was about to run on.

"Shit, I nearly forgot; I still think it's a shame to dump them."

"Orders, Mary"

He threw the Sako into the middle of the pond, watching as it sank and disappeared without a trace; the Accuracy International followed.

"I might come back for that when I'm an old lady; it'll be worth something someday."

Jimmy McGimpsey knew the pond well; it was deep and fed by an underground spring and hadn't dried out in his lifetime. The guns would soon be covered with mud and weed, and if they were found, no matter; they couldn't be traced back to their users.

"I'll get the gate." Mary pulled it open, closing it again when the car was through, then climbed into the front seat. Donal breathed a sigh of relief; they would be well clear of the area before the body was found.

"Well done, Mary, a good job."

He had watched her as she climbed into the car, her eyes shone with excitement, adrenaline coursing through her body She was on a high. Without a word he leaned over and kissed her, lingering, tasting her lips, pulling away before she could make protest. "I hope we get the chance to work together again; I get lonely doing our kind of work."

She looked at him, unsure of his motive, a change from his antagonism the previous evening. "You surprise me, I thought you objected to me being a marksman."

He shrugged. "Maybe I was wrong about that. I can see it might be an advantage in some circumstances." With a laugh, he engaged gear and the car pulled away. They drove in silence for a while neither sure what to say.

Mary was first to break the silence. "Why did you do that back there?"

"Do what exactly?" He smiled but didn't take his eyes of the road.

"Kiss me in that way; it wasn't the usual congratulatory peck on the cheek."

He took a sideways glance at her. "It wasn't meant to be. Truth is you're a very attractive woman; I fancy you and like as not, I'll not be getting the chance to kiss you again."

She said nothing, wanted to come up with a spiteful retort, but none came and the moment passed. Donal was a handsome man, a very handsome man; his kiss had aroused her, maybe just maybe…

A House in Armagh.

McGimpsey glanced at the kitchen clock whilst his wife cleared up after breakfast; it was just leaving nine-forty. He smiled and whispered to himself. *'Bye, bye Mr Lincoln.'* One hundred thousand dollars had been banked for him in a Boston account. Diane Phelps, allegedly on the authority of the President, had paid the money into an Irish Heritage Fund, ostensibly set up to promote Irish-American relations. Questions were rarely asked about how such money was ultimately used. There were many similar donations, most finding their way to the IRA through nominated cultural advisers.

The IRA Council would never know about this particular transaction, unless McGuire or Larkin spoke out of turn, and he had put the fear of death into them. He would have to make a phone call later in the day claiming responsibility on behalf of the Ulster Freedom Fighters, a militant loyalist group. Diane Phelps had promised him that she would leak a statement to media contacts in the USA, indicating that informed sources had attributed the assassination to a loyalist splinter group.

McGimsey had been introduced to Phelps when she attended Dublin University studying twentieth century Irish politics; he had been her conduit for the IRA's perspective. They'd got on well together and their relationship had led to a short torrid affair, ending when she went back to the States. They hadn't maintained contact and he'd only become aware of her again when she got the White House job. Her telephone call had come out of the blue and he'd been wary when she had asked if he still had IRA connections. He had been stunned when she asked outright if he could arrange Lincoln's assassination during a visit to the Republic. She had refused to discuss why anyone wanted the Vice-President dead other than, *just politics.'*

Phelps hadn't asked any questions when he had offered to make the necessary arrangements personally, making it clear that it be carried out without the knowledge of the IRA Council. The price he had put on the job hadn't been challenged and half of his fee had already been credited to the Boston bank account. The balance would be paid when Lincoln's death was announced.

"You look like the cat that got the cream, Jimmy; what's making you so pleased with yourself?" Peggy McGimpsey broke into her husband's thoughts.

"Well, if you must know, I was thinking it would be nice to go to America for a holiday this year."

"You're dreaming, Jimmy, we couldn't afford it."

He winked at her. "Don't you be too sure, Peggy. I hear that Boston is well worth a visit." He had to make the trip to collect his money and what better cover than a holiday.

Killylee Lane

Lincoln lay still for a few moments, pretending he was dead, his reflexes and army training taking over. He let a few minutes pass, then pushed himself to his feet nervously, praying that his assailant had left the scene. 'Bastards.' He'd been set up; an attempt had been made on his life. *But why? And who was behind it? Republicans or Loyalists? The contact number he had been given supposedly belonged to an intermediary serving both sides of the divide. Which was responsible and why?'*

He had heard two shots, more or less simultaneous; one had shattered the door glazing. *Two misses, strange. And why was there no follow up to check if he was dead?* The thought made him shrink down again and adopt a defensive position.

Lincoln guessed that the shots had come from the hilltop, less than four hundred metres distance; a simple shot for a proficient marksman. *Whoever you are, you were confident of a hit. You didn't hang around to check out I was dead. I guess you saw me fall and concluded that you had been successful.* He voiced a thought aloud. "It doesn't make sense; a maximum of range of four hundred metres, no wind, a stationary target, clear visibility; all in all, an easy target." *Perhaps they intended to miss and it had been a warning. But to what purpose? And why two shots, one would have been warning enough.* Lincoln shook his head, "A real mystery."

The planted mobile rang interrupting his thoughts; he took the call automatically. "Hello, John Lincoln speaking.'

"Good morning, Mr Lincoln."

The voice was matter-of-fact; there was no note of surprise at finding him alive. "Sorry I'm a few minutes late; thank you for being punctual, a rare quality nowadays especially in a person as important as yourself. The meeting you have requested has been arranged for the day after tomorrow, Thursday."

Lincoln forced his thoughts back to the job in hand. "Both parties will be there?"

The man laughed, "There are more than just two parties involved; all the paramilitary groups, loyalist and republican, have promised to be there. You're quite a draw Mr Lincoln. But bear in mind I'm just passing on the message, I'm not offering guarantees. You'll appreciate my position, I'm sure."

"Where will the meeting take place?"

The man at the other end of the line chuckled. "Ach now, you wouldn't really expect me to be telling you that; sure, we hardly know each other. You'll be picked up from where you're standing this very minute and taken to the rendezvous. Be there at ten on Thursday morning."

Lincoln's thoughts were racing. *The telephone box isn't my favourite meeting place given recent events. Should I mention the shooting? If I do it might cause concern at the other end and put the meeting in jeopardy.* He decided to go along with the arrangements for the moment.

"I'll be here. What about my car, do I follow? What happens exactly?"

"I've got no part in that Mr Lincoln. Just turn up and leave the rest to them."

"How can I get in touch with you if I need to?"

"You can't; even the previous contact number isn't in use now. Be there on Thursday and let matters take their course. I'm going now, just one thing more. Destroy the phone you're holding, take your heel to it. Goodbye."

Lincoln carried out his instructions; perhaps even now he was being watched. He was starting to feel he couldn't trust anyone.

Back in his car Lincoln reflected on what had taken place. The telephone caller had shown no surprise and had gone on to set up the meeting; he had expected him to be alive and remain alive at least until Thursday. But how many people had known he'd be there that morning? He had no way of knowing how the various factions operated. Was there a loose cannon on the scene hoping that his assassination would bury the Peace Process once and for all? It was possible, but on the other hand both Republicans and Loyalists dealt harshly with renegade members. And nothing could explain how two shots had missed him unless the marksmen were just unskilled amateurs.

Lincoln started the car up and was moving away when the explanation came to him; it wasn't luck, he was being protected. He looked skywards and spoke reverently. "I guess I'll never be sure of what happened, but thank you Lord; it seems like I'm going to need a helping hand more often than I thought."

He didn't mention the incident when he got back to the hotel or report it to the Police. He couldn't afford to put himself into the media limelight; once involved, the news hounds wouldn't let go.

CHAPTER 19

The Oval Office

"Well Diane, what have you got for me?"

Caswell and his Head of Communications were having one of their routine business meetings.

"Nothing of any consequence Jack, there are still a number of interviews scheduled to deal with progress in the Middle East. They're a chore, but you have to do them to keep your name in the frame for that Nobel Peace Prize you hanker after."

"No problem, keep them coming."

"You're doing exceedingly well in the popularity polls; as far as the American people are concerned you could probably walk on water."

Caswell felt smug; things were going his way again. "Keep them thinking that way Diane, that's what I pay you for."

"That's my job, Jack though I'm open to all sorts of new assignments." She winked at his boss. "I'm at your disposal, anytime, day or night." She locked her gaze on the President waiting for a response; it was over a week since they had last spent time together.

Caswell nodded. "I'll try to get along to your office this evening; I've been real busy all day."

"Sure Jack, I understand. I'll see you when the coast clears. We'll have things to talk about, I'm sure." She let a smile play round her lips. "Any news from Lincoln?"

"Nope, not a word, although I know he's settled in a small touristy town by the name of Warrenpoint; he's been pretty cagey about this trip. No matter, he won't get anywhere over there with that lot; the Irish are genetically programmed to self-destruct. The name rang a bell with me and I looked it up: it's where Queen Elizabeth's uncle, Lord Mountbatten, was assassinated by the IRA"

Phelps shook her head, "I wasn't aware of that, what a co-incidence."

Carswell looked at her sharply. "What do you mean, **a co-incidence**?"

"Nothing, just Lincoln being there, that's all." Inwardly she swore at herself; Carswell would remember her slip-up when news got out of Lincoln's assassination. "Don't be too sure that Lincoln won't make progress over there, he pulled it off in the Middle East against all the odds. We mustn't underestimate him."

"True, and if he hits the big time in Ulster, I'll be the first to congratulate him, and of course steal the credit."

"I'll go now, I'm around if anything breaks. See you this evening and I want you on your worst behaviour."

Mawhinney's Cottage

Donal pulled up alongside Mary's car and waited for her to get out. She turned to face him, studying his expression, trying to make her mind up. Her body was tingling, speaking to her. *Was it the excitement of the kill, or was it lustful thoughts?*

"I've got a bottle of Champagne in the boot of my car if you're interested Donal? How's about we go inside and celebrate?"

"Champagne?" His expression showed his surprise.

"It's a little ritual of mine; I always crack a bottle after a mission. Usually I'm on my own; it'll be nice to share it for a change."

Donal's eyes gleamed with anticipation, but he tried to keep the eagerness out of his voice. "Anything to please a lady."

"So, I'm a lady now, am I? Does this mark a new beginning to our relationship I ask myself?"

"Let's go in and find out."

"Put a light to the fire Donal; you'll find matches on the mantelpiece. I'll see if I can find some glasses."

She was away some time and the fire had developed a healthy roar by the time she returned. He could see that she had tidied up her hair and re-done her lipstick. She saw him smile and was pleased that her efforts hadn't gone unnoticed.

"You look ravishing Mary; that auburn hair of yours must be the finest in all Ireland."

She looked away from him, for some reason embarrassed at the compliment, and unsure what to say. Instead, she found escape in the dancing flames of the fire.

"You're a dab hand with a fire, Donal. Sorry about these glasses, they're the best I could find." She held up two plain tumblers.

"Champagne is my favourite tipple whatever the glass."

"You surprise me; I thought you would be a beer and whiskey man. It's my favourite too, and it isn't every day that we get to toast the assassination of the Vice-President of the United States."

She popped the cork and filled the glasses watching as it bubbled to the rim. "To the Cause." She chinked his glass.

"Aye, and to better times."

"And what would better times be for you, Donal?"

He took another sip then lowered his glass slowly, letting his eyes find hers, conveying his desire before he spoke. "At this moment it would be making love with you, Mary Larkin."

"Well now, making love sounds a more attractive proposition than shagging any day of the week." She touched his glass with hers and took a sip, holding his gaze for a moment, then turning away without saying anything. She crossed the room to a door and went inside leaving him confused. *Did she expect him to follow? What was expected of him?*

He reasoned it was the bedroom; it was going to happen. He had started to cross to the room but stopped when the door opened and she returned carrying a duvet. "Here in front of the fire Donal, where it's warm." She smiled at him and waited for his reaction, shrugging when she got no response. "And it'll be more romantic." She spread the duvet on the floor and stepped onto it inviting him to join her.

He hesitated. A warning bell had rung somewhere. He didn't want romance; he didn't want anything permanent. She saw his hesitancy and gave out a soft, throaty laugh. "Don't panic, it's a good romantic shag I'm after, not a confession of undying love. You're not my first fling and you'll not be my last."

He smiled at her frankness. "But maybe Mary Larkin, just maybe, I could be your best."

"That as they say is all to play for and there's only one way to find out."

She started to take off her sweater but he stopped her. "No, let me, please."

He knelt at her feet and took off her shoes and socks, rising then to pull her sweater over her head and was reaching round to undo her bra when she stopped him. "I'll have to start on you or I'll be standing here ballock naked and you'll still have your kit on peering at me. Let's get those shoes and socks off for a start; I hate men who keep their socks on."

She moved close and pulled his shirt off over his head, then stood back waiting for him to remove her bra. He kissed her breasts hungrily; the urgency overwhelmed them both; suddenly they were pulling and dragging at each other's clothing. Finally, they could delay no longer and sank naked onto the duvet where he reached for her, pulling her onto him till her body stretched and ground against him. His lips found hers, tongues flicking and pushing, exploring.

He cupped her breast in his hand and dropped his mouth downwards taking her nipples in turn between his lips, whilst he searched between her thighs. She responded urgently, grabbing at him, pulling him into her. "Come on to me, Donal, come on to me." Her voice strained with emotion, her quick breaths catching her words, her nails digging into his back. "I want you now."

"Not yet Mary, not yet, this might never happen again; I don't want to rush it, I want it to be special."

She shook her head violently, pulling his head forward; her tongue filling his mouth, whilst her hands tugged urging him to satisfy her. "Please, please, we've got all day to be special."

"Don't rush me, I'm going to teach you the alphabet."

Her eyes rolled and she shook her head violently, continuing to pull at him. He wasn't making sense. "Alphabet? What fucking alphabet?"

He straddled her, pinning her arms to the floor. "This is my alphabet, Mary. I take each letter in turn like this." With his tongue he traced an A on her forehead, then a B on her lips saying each letter in turn as he moved around her body. His tongue reached her breasts, circling her nipples. "It always needs more than one O."

"Hurry Donal, I'm nearly there." Sensational tremors were running through her body; it seemed every erotic zone was on red alert. He travelled down the soft roundness of her body every letter sending shock waves through her body.

"Yes, yes, yes." She didn't want him inside her now she just needed to finish the journey he was taking her on. Finally, it was over and he felt her tensions ebb away in tiny waves as her ecstasy subsided."

"My guess is you enjoyed that?"

"Jesus, I hope you never run out of letters."

"You'll maybe find that out another time, Mary Larkin."

His hands were working at her again, lifting her to meet him. She relaxed as he began his movements then joined his rhythm, her back arching seeking more penetration. Those feelings were gathering again, she was losing control. *Christ where did they come from, where do they go?* 'His strokes were deeper, faster, becoming desperate; he too had lost control. Tiny moans and groans escaped their lips as they travelled through waves of pleasure, both seeking ultimate ecstasy, finally finding it together then collapsing spent of passion.

Afterwards, Donal threw some more logs onto the fire and they sat quietly watching the growing flames, their arms around each other, both remembering the passion they had just shared. Eventually she stood up and smiled at him. "I'm going to get us another glass of champagne. I've got something else to celebrate."

He smiled and looked at her enquiringly.

"It's never been like that for me, and I doubt if it ever will be again." She saw the doubt in his eyes. "I mean it."

His eyes travelled over her as she filled their glasses, admiring the sensual symmetry of her body. They had just made love, but already he wanted her again. She sat down opposite him lotus fashion and handed him his champagne.

"Here's to better times, if better times there can be." Her eyes held her meaning.

"Aye, it's been quite a day one way and another." He sipped at his glass. "You're a beautiful woman Mary, and I can say that with total honesty now I've seen the best of you. To better times indeed." He raised his glass and smiled. "And judging by the look of this fella," he looked down, grinning unashamedly as her eyes followed his. "I think maybe they're here; but this time round I'm banking on you doing most of the work."

She knew what he wanted and sat across him, taking him inside her, pulling him close, her arms round him, her lips on his; lifting and lowering herself, slowly at first savouring each moment, quickening as passion fuelled excitement, seeking the contact she wanted. They let out little groans and growls of mounting satisfaction, their senses swimming as they strove towards their climax, deeper this time after their first bout of frenzied passion.

Neither of them heard the door open, or saw the lone figure step inside. The man stood watching as they writhed together, smiling when Mary let out one final cry of rapture before sinking into her partner's embrace. They remained locked together savouring their closeness then sat back, gazing at each other in contentment, wanting the bond they had found to last a while longer.

Clap! Clap! Clap! The couple swivelled round to track the sound. "I wish you two could do everything as well as you shag; I'd be a happy man indeed."

Two surprised faces found themselves looking at the man who moments ago had dispassionately witnessed their copulation.

"I see you came out on top Mary; that's no surprise I suppose."

"What the fuck are you doing here, McGimpsey?"

Mary pushed herself away and reached for Donal's shirt, rising to her feet and covering her nakedness.

McGimpsey laughed. "A bit late to be covering up Mary; I've seen it all, and heard it all, for that matter."

Donal pushed himself to his feet, anger mounting, preparing for an assault. The intruder recognised his intentions and pulled a revolver from a shoulder holster. "Don't be foolish, there's a good lad."

"What do you want, Jimmy?" Mary's anxiety was growing as she looked at the gun pointed at them and recognised the menace in the man's voice.

"I'm a man of my word; you must understand that."

Donal butted in. "Meaning what McGimpsey? Get to the fucking point, or are you just a sad perverted Peeping Tom?"

"Lincoln... isn't... dead" McGimpsey spoke softly, deliberately, watching as their expressions changed, saw the surprise register. "Our two best marksmen and you both missed. Now how can that be I asked myself? And do you know what? I couldn't come up with a satisfactory answer. I reached the conclusion that for some reason or other you wanted to miss."

Donal and Mary stared vacantly, mouths open and shocked by the revelation.

"Nothing to say, cat got your tongues? Well, he lives, you die."

"No that can't be, he's dead, we saw him fall; honest. We took him out, he's a gonner." Donal knew that death was staring him in the face.

"Is he now? Well, the good Lord has handed out another resurrection; the man is back in his hotel probably having a stiff drink to celebrate his return from the dead."

Mary shook her head. "I can't understand it, Jimmy. We couldn't miss at that range, not both of us. Give us another shot at it, I promise you he won't survive a second attempt. We'll get him this very night."

"Too late."

He fingered the trigger, smiling as a red ragged hole opened up in Donal's forehead, spinning him round; knocking him to the floor.

Mary Larkin let the shirt fall slowly from her hands and stared aghast at the man standing in front of her. "You bastard, you've killed him, you've killed him. We both couldn't have missed; we saw him fall. We couldn't miss from that distance, I tell you. You must have supplied some crap ammunition; that must be it."

McGimpsey snorted. "You're clutching at straws Mary, but I've got to give it to you, you're a beauty when you're angry; I expect you know that. I don't suppose you fancy one last ride on the hobbyhorse? No? Well perhaps not, it would be disrespectful with Donal lying there with half his head blown away. I'm sorry Mary; sure, tis a terrible waste."

The gun kicked again, the bullet tearing into her heart; Mary Larkin was dying as she slumped to the floor. She looked up as her killer leaned over her. "Sorry, it won't take long. I hope you're not in pain? I couldn't bear the thought of putting a bullet in that pretty head of yours." McGimpsey wiped his gun clean of fingerprints and manoeuvred it into Donal's grip. *A little job for the forensics team when they find the bodies.*

As he drove away McGimpsey smiled grimly. *The Police will have fun with that one; a crime of passion, that's what it'll look like. No more than the pair of you deserve; you've cost me a small fortune. Like as not I won't get the chance of such easy money again. Bastards! Thank God I got paid half up front. A shame really, I've lost two useful compatriots. What a fucking mess, Jimmy boy.* He spoke to himself as he drove, wondering how the Council would react? *Must remember to give Kate McGuire my condolences when the time comes. I wonder if Mary has anybody close?*

Lincoln spent the next day as a tourist, walking in the Mourne Mountains, admiring the beauty of the area. He knew that he was exposing himself to further danger but, somehow, he felt safe; he was in the very best of hands.

He dined in the Hotel again, retiring to his room fairly early to give thought to the next day's meeting. The last thing he did was watch CNN on television; by chance it featured Jack Caswell telling his audience how he had achieved peace in the Middle East. "Good old Jack, that's my boy, always the opportunist."

The rendezvous

After breakfast next morning Lincoln set out again to Killylee Lane, wondering what the fates had in store for him this time round. He felt totally calm; he was a player in some grand plan and everything would work out no matter what. He slowed as the telephone box came into view; they were waiting for him. He coasted to a halt behind a black BMW, remaining behind the wheel until two of its three occupants got out. If they were armed their guns weren't on display and he felt relieved that there was no immediate threat to his person.

The taller of the two men, slim with a mop of black curly hair, greeted him cheerfully enough. "Top of the morning to you, Mr Lincoln. We won't hang about if you don't mind. Please get in the BMW, you'll find a blindfold on the back seat; I'd be obliged if you would put it on."

Lincoln hesitated and glanced at his car. "Don't worry about your car, Daniel here will follow along behind if you'll give him the keys."

Daniel was a fresh-faced young man, around seventeen. He smiled broadly as he stepped forward quickly, extending a hand for the keys. The events of the day before were still fresh in Lincoln's thoughts. "How do I know I can trust you?" He bit his lip at the futility of the question even as he asked it.

The tall man shrugged. "You don't Mr Lincoln, simple as that. It's up to you what you do; you asked for the meeting. If you want to meet us, get in the car. If you don't, go back to the hotel or take another walk in the Mournes. You seemed to have enjoyed the great outdoors yesterday by all accounts."

So, he had been watched. Lincoln nodded. "Sorry, you're right of course; here's the keys." He tossed them to the younger man and moved forward to the BMW.

The man smiled broadly. "No problem, sure there's no harm in being cautious." He pulled open the car door. "After you. Daniel, check out Mr Lincoln's car."

Daniel nodded eagerly. He was newly recruited to the Cause and this was important work. He pulled an electronic scanner from a pocket and passed it back and forth over the Mondeo, then underneath, searching for a tracker or mike. He then did the same with the interior.

"Now who's not being trusting?" Lincoln couldn't resist comment.

The tall man smiled. "Point taken; thing is we might trust your good self, but you mix with some very nosy people. I'm sure you understand. CIA, MI5, folks like that."

The young man completed his task and gave a thumbs-up. "All clear Colm, we can go."

"Put your blindfold on Mr Lincoln, and we'll be on our way. It's about a thirty minutes drive from here. Daniel will be right behind us."

"Where are we going?"

"Not somewhere you would know even if I told you, but we'll be staying north of the border if that's of any help to you."

CHAPTER 20

Drumena Lodge

The lodge stood in the centre of a fifty-acre pine forest, itself part of an estate of two hundred acres. A gravel drive, nearly two miles long, led to it from the main road. Used for small conferences and management training. It was in the ownership of Loyalist sympathisers and made available from time to time for meetings such as today's. Its isolated location served its purposes well.

The Republicans had a similar establishment in the south and another in the north. Each side knew about the other's premises but, as for so many matters, they were included in the quid pro quo arrangements that existed between the two sides. They had long since learned that tit-for-tat actions didn't bring any tangible or lasting benefit either side. Any gain was short-lived and led to the inevitable reprisals which, in turn, inexorably escalated out of all proportion to the original trespass. Political gain was much more likely to be achieved by striking at Government forces and commercial targets, rather than warring between themselves.

Drumena Lodge was comprised of three timber buildings, constructed in harmony with their forest setting. It had a wild west look about it. The centre block housed the conference room and its supporting administrative and ancillary facilities. The smaller blocks to the left and right provided overnight accommodation.

Two men stood in the entrance to the centre block, eyeing each other with a mixture of respect and curiosity; it had been a long time since their paths had crossed. They belonged to different sides of the political and religious divide; this was the first occasion they had met in peaceful circumstances for many years.

Seamus Rafferty, Republican, Chief of Staff of the IRA and, by the good graces of others, served as chairman and convenor when circumstances required republican factions to gather together. A role that had become increasingly difficult as the Provos gained strength and other extremist splinter groups came into being. But, at the end of the day, the IRA was still the major force behind the republican Cause.

He was a very ordinary looking man who would pass as any child's grandfather. Average in every respect of his physical build, his once black hair now turning to grey. His eyes were his strongest feature, sea green and searching, set deep in a face worn by experience and a fair share of heartache. He had been a killer in his younger days and could still serve a death sentence on those whom he considered had damaged the IRA, irrespective of their allegiances; numerous republican supporters had been removed from the equation when they had stepped too far out of line. In spite of his history, he attended Chapel every Sunday and many thought he was a good Catholic.

The man opposite was Ronnie Collins, a Loyalist, and Commander-in-Chief of the Ulster Defence Army, commonly known as the UDA. Currently it was his responsibility to convene the Protestant factions when the need arose. Nowadays they all seemed to have their own agenda, although they all claimed loyalty to the Crown and continued union with the United Kingdom remained their Cause.

He was the younger of the two Taller and heavily made; his face bore the scars of many encounters and sat below a head of closely cropped ginger hair. He looked, and was, hard and uncompromising, ruthless in pursuit of his enemies; he would give or ask no quarter.

"It's been a while, Ronnie."

"Eighteen months, Seamus, my shoulder still aches from the wound you inflicted."

Rafferty laughed. "Fair's fair Ronnie, my leg still gives me gyp where you put a bullet in it; I thought my end had come yon night."

It was Collins's turn to smile. "Aye, I suppose we're even after a fashion. I'm glad those days have gone; I've slept a little easier since we reached an accommodation between ourselves. To tell the truth I'm more worried about some of my own side nowadays."

"I know the feeling, I wish the fanatics amongst us would learn from the past but no sign of it; sad thing is, they're gaining ground."

They both turned at the sound of approaching vehicles; a small convoy came into sight as it rounded a bend in the forest road.

"I don't know if those are yours or mine Seamus, but I suppose we'd better go our separate ways; there are those who wouldn't approve of us passing the time of day."

"Right enough." The Republican sighed. "I'll see you across the table; it should be an interesting day."

Ten minutes later, all those invited had assembled in the conference room, gathering in little groups around a long table, lined by chairs upholstered in blue.

"Not your colour Seamus." Collins called across.

"No matter Ronnie, I'll be putting my arse on it, and I'll be sure to release a fart or two."

Both men laughed though not everyone appreciated friendly banter between sworn enemies.

Every active faction was represented, old and new, large and small, moderate and extreme; the word had gone round that all the players in the game were welcome.

The mediator, Andy O'Donnell, a political newspaper columnist, trusted by both sides, had achieved the impossible; he'd got them all to attend and had taken care to ensure that the thirty representatives present were equally divided between Loyalists and Republicans. They were all men; there was no place for a woman at the top table of Ireland's extremist groups. They had given an undertaking not to carry weapons, but there was little trust amongst them, and many had ignored the instruction. Conversations halted midstream, dying away completely when the door opened and those present saw that the latest arrival wasn't one of theirs.

Lincoln looked round the room waiting for whispered comments to die away. For most this was the first time they had seen the Vice-President of the United States; somehow photographs and newsreels had passed them by. He could almost feel the intensity of their appraisal. "Good morning gentlemen." He swung his gaze around the room. "Thank you for being here; I appreciate your presence especially in view of the short notice."

Some responded, some grunted; others just looked on impassively studying the black man who represented the most powerful country in the world. His brief, less than enthusiastic welcome was over and, some made to be seated but he forestalled their intent.

"I wonder if you could remain where you are for a little longer. I'd like to move round the room and meet each of you in turn, at least shake hands before we begin our discussions. We might not want to by the time the meeting is over."

He smiled at them softening his words. He wasn't motivated by courtesy alone; he was about to invoke his telepathic powers again. Lincoln took his time as he shook hands with each man, ascertaining their loyalties, exchanging brief comments and absorbing their inner thoughts. By the time he had completed the process, three key themes had emerged.

The main players had fairly clear views on the terms of a permanent solution to Ulster's future. The larger groups were confident that they could force the smaller, generally more extreme groups, to comply with the terms of any agreement reached. He learned the location of many, perhaps all, weapons and explosives stores. Lincoln continued to be amazed at the information his brain could receive and be available for recall whenever required.

There was one revelation that startled him. When Jimmy McGimpsey, member of the IRA Council, introduced himself, Lincoln learned that the failed attempt on his life had been commissioned by Diane Phelps. None of the others present knew of the incident, including Sean Rafferty also a member of the Council. Surely Caswell wouldn't have sanctioned such an act? Lincoln felt chilled by the very thought, but it was something he would deal with when he got back to Washington; he had to keep his mind on the business immediately in front of him.

"Thanks for that, guys; I guess we can all take our seats now. I'll sit at the head of the table sandwiched between those representing Republican interests on my left, with Loyalist sympathisers to my right. Can I ask that if there are any physical hostilities planned, you give me prior notice so that I can get the hell out of here?" Lincoln's humour drew a few smiles and he sensed the tensions around the table relax as the men took their seats. He looked round the sea of faces, making sure he had their attention then formally opened the proceedings.

"Now I know that it's a sensitive issue, since many of you are independent, but I'd like to identify a chairman or lead representative for each side."

Rafferty raised his hand. "I'll fulfil that function for Republican interests, purely on the basis that I'm the oldest."

Collins gave a wave. "And I'll do likewise for Loyalist interests, on the basis that I'm the ugliest."

The room resounded with "Hear! Hear!"

Lincoln used the moment. "Well now, that's one thing you all seem to be agreed upon. I would just confirm that the entire proceeds of this meeting are confidential. There will be no Press statements released, unless you decide otherwise, and I'm talking about a unanimous vote, not by majority" He glanced at his watch; it was a few minutes short of eleven.

"If everyone is ready, we'll make a start. I'll begin by explaining why I'm here and I would just confirm what you probably already know; I have no security presence either here or at my hotel. I've come entirely alone. I represent the President but I have no pre-determined agenda other than the big one, to try to promote peace. As you might guess, I have no Irish ancestry; my roots lie in American slavery. I act independently of the Prime Minister and the Taoiseach; I'm entirely a free agent. I want to listen to what you have to say, then try to use my good offices to steer us to common ground; I guess you've heard that kind of thing before?"

Heads nodded all round the table.

"Right off I'd like to establish two principles. One, when someone is speaking, he's allowed to speak uninterrupted. Two, if we reach a point where we agree on something, large or small, we honour our undertakings. Anyone who dissents from those principles should make themselves known now, and maybe it would be best if they left the meeting."

Lincoln paused and looked around the table. Most gave some indication of assent; nobody stood to leave. "Good. It seems to me, as an uninformed outsider, that the gaps between you fall into two categories, those of administration and those of principle. I'll say it right up front; I don't think this is the forum for solving nitty-gritty administrative issues; it should confine itself to the resolution of principles."

Rafferty spoke up immediately. "That's a problem right off. We don't know what you're calling administration and what you're referring to as principles."

Lincoln smiled. "A good point. I'm not absolutely clear either, Mr Rafferty, but I would say that in general, matters of administration **should be** the remit of a local democratically elected Body. Such a Body wouldn't exist until the matters of principle were resolved. If all the principles had been hammered out to conclusion in the past, instead of being fudged, perhaps the present Northern Ireland forum wouldn't be suspended now."

Collins interjected. "Comfort words Mr Lincoln, a mite strong on rhetoric and lacking in real substance; we still don't know what your principles are. In my mind principles should be few in number, administrative issues are infinite."

Lincoln seized the opportunity that had opened up; he could move the meeting forward more quickly than he had expected.

"Fair enough Mr Collins, I accept the criticism. To start the ball rolling I'll outline what I believe are the principles and you can all shoot me down. Here goes.

"One, democracy is founded on one man, one vote which would lead to an elected forum to govern Northern Ireland. I see nothing wrong with the current electoral arrangements, so I would say that you already have one principle in place.

"Two, occupation of the Province by British Army personnel should cease.

"Three, all illegal weapons and explosives should be handed over to an agreed authority or be verifiably put beyond use; I have in mind filming the destruction or having it observed by mutually agreed monitors. In a democratic society, there is no need for either of the foregoing, and as long as they exist there is no democracy in Ulster in the true sense of the word.

Lincoln paused and looked round the table; faces stared back; expressions attentive but not giving much away. Clearly, they were listening and there were no challenges to his assertions. "So far, so good, we seem to have a measure of agreement."

He paused and looked around inviting dissent but none came. "Let's pull away another layer and try to get to the root of the differences. Let's hope I understand the history. You already have an elected Assembly; I'm going to suggest that you stick with it for the next ten years, and that it remains accountable to, and funded by, the British Parliament."

There were murmurs of dissent amongst Republican interests, who continued to believe that the British Parliament strongly favoured the Loyalists.

Lincoln nodded. "I see that I've struck a nerve. But the current assembly and its responsibilities, were the subject of the Good Friday Agreement; it is the basis on which the electorate turned out to vote. I don't see that those gathered around this table have a mandate to set that aside, whether you like it or not." Again, he paused to look round at those assembled, locking his gaze for a few seconds on the two Chairmen, inviting their challenge.

When none came, he continued. "But let me go on to what should happen at the end of that ten years of British involvement. I believe there should be a referendum to determine whether the existing system of Government should continue, or whether Ulster should become an independent

State. In the latter event it could have membership of the European Union and/or the Commonwealth, should it so desire. Such a referendum would be held every ten years."

On his left some Republicans were shaking their heads, others sensed there was more to come and gave no indication of their views. Loyalists appeared to be receptive to the principle, or at least there was no outward rejection of the proposal.

"I can see that Republican representatives aren't enthusiastic, presumably because this doesn't allow for a United Ireland. I would argue, why should it? I personally accept that there is an argument for a United Ireland, and I would give the people of Ulster a chance to have their say in the event that the aforesaid referendum resulted in a majority vote for an independent State. This new independent State, Ulster, would hold a referendum, on its fifth anniversary of its existence and would offer three alternatives.

To remain an Independent State
To re-unite with Great Britain
To unite with the Republic to form a United Ireland

"Such a referendum would be in two stages; the option with the lowest votes cast would be eliminated after the first ballot with the second ballot reverting to a simple two-horse race. I would just add, that I think that, where re-unification with either country is the chosen option, the people of the country involved, the Republic of Ireland and British electorates should have a vote on whether they want to unite with you. There's nothing to say the either of them would want you on board again, given the headaches you've caused both over the years.

"In the event of support for a United Ireland, opportunity could be taken to look at how Ulster might function. Is there for instance, scope to operate on a federal basis, using the ancient Provinces of Ulster, Munster, Connaught and Leinster as a model? But that of course is an administrative matter, not a principle at this stage." In essence gentlemen what I'm proposing is simple. **Government of the people, by the people, for the people** as was once said by somebody much cleverer than me. In other words, democracy rules not weapons or guns.

He had fired their imagination; an uneasy silence filled the room. The proposals went beyond anything previously put on the table. It was difficult to argue with real democratic principles.

"Loyalists are currently holding out for continuing union with the United Kingdom, but that was as much to do with not joining with the Republic as anything else, and there might be some benefits in being independent. The Republic has flourished under huge injections of European money, and perhaps Ulster could do just as well.

"Republicans want a United Ireland, but it would only work if the vast majority of the people in Ulster were in support; independence might provide a viable alternative and maybe in the long run, free of British interference, prove to be a stepping stone to unification."

Rafferty was first to speak. "That last proposal is too big for any of us to respond to off the cuff, but from a Republican viewpoint, I'll grant that it warrants careful consideration. I can see it has a glimmer of merit, but fifteen years would be too long to wait for a vote on a United Ireland. What's your thoughts on this Ronnie?"

Ronnie wasn't the most eloquent of individuals, nor a visionary, but Rafferty had sounded both reasonable and genuine, and the proposal had a ring of fair play about it.

"I'd personally be happy to wait for a hundred years for on a vote for a United Ireland, but maybe it's time to move forward. Fifteen years is not that long, bearing in mind we've been at this for the best part of a century. Sure, it takes most politicians a week to make their mind up on whether to fart or not. And come to think of it, independence might bring unexpected rewards, given the generosity of the European Union. But maybe we're getting in front of ourselves; there are still the other principles to be considered. For instance, when are the Republicans going to give up their weapons?" He stared across at Rafferty.

Rafferty snorted. "I could ask you Loyalists the same question, and when is the British Army getting off our streets?"

Lincoln interceded. "Hold it guys, we'll come back to weapons and the army; let's keep to the principles of government for now. We'll deal with those other issues, I promise." He was pleased at the progress being made, both sides were talking; debate was on a reasonable level. Over the course of the next hour he promoted discussion, making sure the smaller factions participated, and, when everyone had had their say, it seemed to him there was a general acceptance of the principles he had set out, including the referendum proposals. It was time to focus on the hitherto intractable problems of disarmament and the departure of British soldiers from Irish soil.

"OK, there's a measure of agreement about the nature of the future governance of the province; let's draw a line under that for the time being and take a look at the other two principles which I would articulate as follows.

There's the Republican view which goes something like this, "Trust us, remove the Army and then we'll put our weapons beyond use."

The British Government, supported by the Loyalists, will say something along the lines "We've got every right to be here, this is a British province. When the weapons have gone there will be no need for us to be here and the Army can leave these soils."

"Now, as an outsider, at this stage I trust both sides, and I can't see that it matters which side acts first, as long as both sides keep their promises. To be honest I don't really understand why both sides of the equation can't be scaled down in parallel. Maybe you could enlighten me on that one?" Lincoln had his own ideas on the subject but it was theirs he wanted to hear.

Collins spoke first. "The problem is, John, nobody knows just what weapons the IRA and their like possess. You can see soldiers, when they leave its indisputable; that's not the case with weapons."

Rafferty responded immediately, but his tone of voice carried a touch of reason.

"Republicans aren't the only ones with weapons, Ronnie, as you well know. How would we know if Loyalists had got rid of theirs? We're not going to put ourselves at risk, and you wouldn't expect us to."

Lincoln intervened. "We would have to ensure there was an intermediary in place that you both trusted and respected, to oversee the process."

Eddie McGuiness, a Loyalist extremist sneered. "For fuck's sake, don't be so naïve, Lincoln. Any intermediary would only know what he's told; he'll never be able to certify that all the weapons have been destroyed."

Lincoln shook his head. "I appreciate the point you're making, but we have to get to a solution. We need trust on both sides, or you will all still be in the same old rut a hundred years from now, and that cannot be in the interests of the people you claim to represent."

The debate ranged round the table; sometimes reasoned, sometimes heated, always passionate, but it seemed to Lincoln to be going round in circles with neither side giving ground. When it was clear everyone had had their say, he called them to order. "Gentlemen, we're getting nowhere. It's nearly one-o'clock and I don't know about you but I'm getting hungry, and when my belly's empty I'm unreasonable. I suggest that we break for lunch and assemble again at two?"

He looked round the table at a mass of nodding heads. "Good, that's another thing we've agreed. Apparently, there are two separate rooms with a supply of sandwiches. No alcohol at my request; I don't want a war on my hands. With your indulgence I'm going to suggest that Seamus and Ronnie lead discussion on the Referendum proposals over lunch. I've summarised the options in this handout; there's a copy for everybody. Come back at 2pm with views and suggestions; we'll toss a coin for who presents first."

'Might I suggest an alternative, Mr Lincoln?"

"Go ahead, Mr.Rafferty."

"You come to each of us in turn, in our respective rooms, and hear what we have to say. Then we all meet up at two-thirty or so. You can come to us first; I'll trust you not to reveal our ideas to the Loyalists. That way when we join up you can lead discussions."

Jimmy McSweeney, a bitter Provo snarled. "You might trust him Seamus, but how do you know I do?"

Rafferty half rose from his seat, his eyes steely. "You don't trust anybody Jimmy; if you've got a better idea spit it out."

McSweeney backed off. "I didn't say I didn't trust Mr Lincoln; I was just pointing out that you should consult the rest of us before you make commitments on our behalf."

Rafferty pursed his lips and thought for a second. "You're right Jimmy, I accept your admonishment. Do I have your permission?"

The Provo nodded grudgingly.

Collins raised his hand, looking round as he spoke. "I think it's alright with us. How will you be spending your time, John?"

Lincoln chuckled, "I'm going to pray for some enlightenment, then I'm going to apply it to the weapons versus the Army conundrum which seems to be the main issue preventing progress. I declare this session closed."

He watched as the leaders of Ireland's terrorist factions filed quietly out of the room; their expressions gave no impression of their thinking. His thoughts racing; if the arms and army issues couldn't be resolved, the meeting would prove to be a waste of time and effort.

CHAPTER 21

Drumena Lodge, lunch break

Lincoln sat alone, eating a sandwich, reflecting on the discussions of the last few hours. He had witnessed at first hand the deep-seated intransigence that existed between the paramilitaries resulting in the current stalemate, and no doubt countless others in the past. It wasn't all gloom; there seemed to be some common ground with regard to the constitutional proposals. Although these would have to be approved by the British and Irish Governments. He saw no problem there; they would likely agree to any solution that brought an end to the divisions that were so damaging to Ulster and its people. But and it was a massive but, the old blockages remained - putting weapons beyond use and the withdrawal of the British army. He couldn't accept, wouldn't accept that there wasn't scope for resolution. He wasn't prepared to let his initiative end in failure.

He readily understood why the British Government couldn't withdraw its troops before disarmament took place; giving into terrorists was something no country could be seen to do. And the paramilitaries were essentially terrorists, no matter what their ideals.

On the other hand, he could understand why the IRA didn't want to give up their weapons before the Brits left Ulster; that would be construed as their defeat. The Irish had long memories, and history showed that they had suffered badly under British rule in the distant past.

What he couldn't understand was their reluctance to take the final steps to peace; the past was past. So much had changed in recent years and yet the old hatreds still festered below the surface. Perhaps the IRA wasn't able to deliver? Perhaps its organisation was so fractured by factional disagreements, it was no longer functional? *Dear Lord, please help me to a solution, show me how to overcome this intractable problem.*

One thing he had to do was talk to the British Prime Minister. He checked the Downing Street number in his diary and dialled on his mobile.

"Downing Street; who's calling please?"

"John Lincoln, Vice-President of the United States. Could I speak to the Prime Minister please? It's a matter of some urgency."

The number he had been given was known to very few and it guaranteed access although the two men had never met. "You're in luck Mr Vice-President the PM is between meetings. If you hold on, I'll put you through."

Lincoln breathed a sigh of relief; the PM could have been anywhere. A few seconds passed then the voice spoke again. "Go ahead; you're through to the Prime Minister."

"Prime Minister, it's John Lincoln, we really must meet up sometime. I'm very sorry but I don't have much time; I'll get right to the point if you don't mind."

"Suits me, I'm due into another meeting shortly."

"I know you've been briefed on my initiative and I'm phoning in that regard for some informal advice. I'm right in a middle of a meeting with both sides and need your take on the age-old problem of IRA weapons."

"I can guess what you might want to ask me, but go ahead."

"I was wondering why the option of withdrawing troops, in parallel with weapons reduction ending up at a zero base, hasn't been adopted?"

"It's a solution I could live with, but the IRA insists that theirs has to be the final act; in effect all troops must leave the province before they completely disarm. This wasn't acceptable to me, or to the Loyalists, so it hasn't been pursued."

It was as Lincoln had expected - he knew that the IRA had given an undertaking to disarm under the terms of the Good Friday Agreement but there had been no mention of exactly when - as ever the devil was in the detail.

"And what about the current process to put weapons beyond use?"

The PM sighed, "Minimum destruction, countless obstacles, all sorts of delaying tactics; I don't know how the Mediator manages to stick with it. At the present rate of progress, it'll be twenty years before we've got rid of what we know they've got. And our Intelligence Services have picked up that they are keeping lines of arms supply open, which doesn't imbue me with much confidence for the future."

"I fully understand your position, but let me pluck at a non-existent straw. If they did agree to a rapid disarmament, would you pull your troops out immediately?"

"Mr Vice-President, I've got better things for British troops to do; I'd issue orders for them to withdraw tomorrow given half a chance."

"Thank you for that Prime Minister. Strictly informally, the political future of Ulster, what's your stance on that?"

"I've stated on numerous occasions that it's up to the people of Ulster to determine their future. Her Majesty's Government will not sell them out; the ballot box, their ballot box, will be the final arbiter."

"Thank you. I guess that's all I need to know for now."

"Mr Vice-President, I realise that you'll be hoping for a positive outcome from your talks, but a word of caution. Please don't raise any unrealistic expectations. And I'd appreciate being kept informed of any proposals before they get set in tablets of stone."

"Of course; I'll be in touch when this meeting ends. Thank you for speaking to me."

Lincoln slumped forward over the desk in front of him, his head in his hands. *I'm between a rock and a hard place. I need some kind of a miracle and I haven't got one in my repertoire. I need a helping hand on this one.* He turned in his chair and looked skywards through the window, "If you're listening Lord. I could do with some help, preferably within the next half an hour."

For the next half an hour he ran through scenarios, lines of persuasion, American investment strategies and other inducements, but none seemed plausible given the nature of those he was dealing with. He had nothing new to offer; he was back to wishing and hoping for something to emerge round the table.

He stood to stretch and as he gazed aimlessly out of the window, saw a car approaching at speed and screech to a halt in front of the entrance. Its occupant got out immediately and rushed into the building, his expression one of anger. *Oh, oh, looks like trouble.* Lincoln's stomach knotted; he felt his teeth grind together.

The man Lincoln had observed was the IRA's Quartermaster General, Paddy Lynch, and he was seeking Seamus Rafferty.

Something had gone seriously wrong and it was still happening; two more cars were approaching the Lodge at speed, sloppy parking, doors left open, men racing into the building.

Lincoln swallowed and felt his mouth go dry. *Oh, oh, this looks like a crisis.* Mentally, he braced himself for a stormy session ahead, but he didn't go to investigate. *Best if I leave them to it; let the dust settle.'*

Paddy Lynch hammered on the door to the room where the Republicans were meeting, then made his way in without waiting for a reply. "Sorry," he offered a general apology for his interruption, "this can't wait I'm afraid." He scanned the sea of faces for Seamus Rafferty, and moved to his side.

"What brings you here Paddy? Jesus, you look like you've seen a banshee."

Lynch garbled out his story in a whispered voice and watched the blood drain from his compatriot's face. "That can't be, there's some mistake." Rafferty shook his head in disbelief. "It just isn't possible."

"It's true, Seamus, there's no doubt about it. They.ve all been destroyed, every last one of them.'

As they were speaking, the other two very agitated men who had just arrived, burst into the room seeking directions; one asked for Ronnie Collins, the other for Jimmy McSweeney.

Rafferty guessed at what was happening and felt fury rise within. "They're across the corridor in the room opposite."

The men turned, almost bumping into each other in their haste, and made their way out of the room.

Meanwhile, outside in the car park, two more men arrived and raced into the building. Lincoln watched the activity; something big was going down. Sooner or later, they would come to him; he could feel his heartbeat gather pace. He sat down to wait the inevitable confrontation.

Seamus Rafferty led all of the Republicans across to the Loyalist gathering and hammered on the door. "Ronnie Collins, come out here you bastard. I want to talk to you, come out."

The Loyalist had received the same news as Rafferty and he too had jumped to the obvious conclusion, that the other side was to blame. Collins pulled a gun from his jacket pocket and hauled open the door, the others gathering behind him.

Rafferty didn't flinch at the sight of the gun. "You and your lot are finished Ronnie; this is all out war. All agreements are off."

The Loyalist waved his gun in the Republican's face. "You fucking bet its war, you're lucky I don't blow your head off right this minute. This is just like the IRA, sneaky bastards that you are. First you set up a truce, pretend to destroy your weapons, then you declare war. But you won't beat us; every Protestant in Ulster will rise against you now."

Realisation began to dawn on Rafferty; Collins's reaction didn't make sense. He raised his hands in peacekeeping mode. "Hold on Ronnie, calm down for a minute and listen. Let's think about it, I reckon we're both in the same boat."

The Loyalist snarled back. "Me? Me? In the same boat as a Fenian, you're out of your fucking mind. What the hell do you mean?"

Rafferty maintained his calm. "If I'm right, all your weapons have gone up in smoke and you think we arranged it, right?"

Collins nodded, waiting for his protagonist to go on. "I'm listening."

"That's exactly what's happened to our gear; every cache has been hit on both sides of the border and we're blaming your lot. Some bastard is trying to set us at each others' throats."

Collins lowered his gun reluctantly as it dawned on him what had taken place. "We've been stitched up nicely and there's only one candidate I can think of - our friendly visitor from the United States. There was always something fishy about this meeting right from the start. He turned up out of the blue, Mr Nice Guy, everybody's friend. Fuck the bastard. It's all too much of a co-incidence, let's go get him."

Rafferty wasn't sure but someone was to blame. "No rough stuff, let's hear what he has to say."

Collins pushed past without comment, now wasn't the time to let a Republican call the shots.

Lincoln steeled himself when the door was flung open and Collins made his entry followed closely by Rafferty; he could see the others gathering in the corridor behind them. They were like a mob, seething with anger; a number of handguns were in evidence; they weren't supposed to be carrying guns, but now wasn't the time to remind them. One gun though did worry him, the one clenched in Ronnie Collins's fist and pointed straight at him. *I hope you're still around, God.*

"What have you been up to you crooked bastard, you and your British friends?" Ronnie Collins was shouting, frothing at the mouth. "This is all one big set-up and you're pulling the strings."

Lincoln pushed himself up from his chair, taking his time, striving to retain an appearance of calm puzzlement that belied his racing heartbeat. He looked his accuser in the eye, unflinching. "I haven't the faintest idea what you are talking about." He fought to keep fear from his voice though he knew his life was hanging by a thread. They wouldn't hesitate to kill him; death was their favoured punishment.

"Liar!" Collins was livid. "Let's execute the Yankee bastard." He looked around at the others inviting their support.

Lincoln remained outwardly calm. "Execute me if you must, but at least tell me what I'm accused of."

'Don't play the fucking innocent." Collins retorted.

Something in the American's demeanour rang true with Rafferty, "It's not an unreasonable request Ronnie."

Lincoln seized the lifeline. "Bear in mind I came here alone, no security, no guards and there's no back-up racing to my rescue. If I've done something to offend you this much, I've taken one hell of a risk; I'm well aware of your reputation for summary justice."

Even Collins began to see the logic and allowed his anger to subside, pocketing his gun and exchanging puzzled glances with Rafferty. *Fuck it, the Yank was right. It didn't make sense for him to be this foolhardy.*

He raised his hands in supplication, nodding his head. "I suppose he's got a point Seamus; he's not an idiot."

Rafferty nodded in agreement. "That he has, but it sure is one hell of a co-incidence given what we've been talking about."

Lincoln spoke softly trying to nurture the temporary calm. "Look, I came here in good faith, I think you know that. I now find myself effectively your prisoner for something of which I'm totally unaware. Let's approach this step by step and begin with you guys telling me exactly what has happened to get you so steamed up."

Rafferty shrugged. "He's not going anywhere Ronnie; there's nothing to be lost by talking this through."

The Loyalist's anger was ebbing away the more he thought about the situation; his initial certainty had deserted him. The others behind him had quietened down. Even the redoubtable Jimmy McSweeney spoke up, surprising everyone.

"I reckon we should give him a chance Ronnie."

Collins nodded. "Alright Mr Lincoln, we'll play it your way for the moment.

Lincoln listened intently as the various factions revealed that somehow, and simultaneously it seemed, their weapon deposits had been destroyed. When everyone had had his say, Rafferty summed up. "So, there it is Mr Lincoln. There have been a series of simultaneous explosions on both sides of the border resulting in the destruction of all our weapon stocks, large and small. In the circumstances, you'll understand why it's hard for us to accept that they're not connected with the timing of this meeting."

Lincoln was completely dumfounded; his prayers had been answered in an almighty fashion. "It's a mighty strange coincidence I can't deny it. Nor can I explain it. Keep in mind that I didn't know either the precise timing, or the venue for this meeting until yesterday. I swear that these occurrences had nothing to do with me, nor the United States Administration, nor any of its Agencies. I confess though that I prayed for a solution to the weapons issue as I sat in this room; prayed in fact that they didn't exist. Maybe the good Lord has answered my prayer"

Collins sneered. "I wouldn't expect you to own up to it, but blaming the Almighty is hardly credible. Unless you want me to believe that the Saviour swept down out of the sky to do Uncle Sam's bidding? You'll need to come up with a better excuse than that."

Lincoln shook his head. "You've got me wrong, Mr Collins, I'm not making any excuses; in fact, I'm delighted that the weapons have been put beyond use, but I can't claim the credit. If I was in your position, I'd want to know precisely how, whosoever is responsible, managed to find out the whereabouts of every weapons' cache on *both* sides of the divide? And, having got hold of that information, how did they manage to plant explosives without anyone's knowledge? And somehow, manage to get them all to be activated during the course of this meeting? And finally, if they were able to obtain that kind of information, how come they didn't put a bomb under this very building and take us all out of the game?"

Lincoln's questions struck home and demanded answers that nobody present could give. The men were still angry, but deflated and uncertain what to do; they stood silently awaiting a lead.

Rafferty stroked his chin, perplexed by this totally inconceivable turn of events, his thoughts grappling with what the IRA Council would expect of him in this situation. "Those questions require answers right enough and we're going to begin the inquest right here and now." He turned to Ronnie Collins, "I suggest," he then made a point of addressing McSweeney, "if that's alright with you Jimmy, that we all go back to the Conference Room and bring our minds to bear on this state of affairs? It seems that on this occasion we are all on the same side, or at least we might have a common enemy."

McSweeney reacted instantly. "And while we're talking, what about out friend here?"

Rafferty scratched his head. "I believe him. As far as I'm concerned, he can go."

"What? You're fucking crazy. He's the biggest fucking hostage we'll ever get our hands on."

"Hostage for what exactly, Jimmy?" Collins snarled, the idea appealed, but to what purpose.

"For whatever we want Ronnie, that's what." McSweeney stood his ground.

Rafferty, who had watched the exchange with some pleasure, intervened. "And what exactly do *we* want Jimmy? Loyalist, Republican, IRA, Provo, UVF, UDA; we'd all want something different."

McSweeney hesitated, not even sure of what he wanted. Collins came to a decision. "I go along with Seamus. We'd never agree and all hell will break loose if we kidnap the Vice-President."

McSweeney sneered at the two men. "Are you two bastards going soft? This is a golden opportunity."

Collins pushed his revolver into McSweeney's face. "Don't bad-mouth me, Jimmy. If you want the guy, you have him but we're not part of it on this side."

"Nor us," added Rafferty, looking around the Republicans, pleased to see heads being shaken all round. "Is there anyone wants to help Jimmy kidnap the Vice-President?"

There were no volunteers.

Collins lowered his gun and grinned. "Looks like you've won yourself a prize Jimmy. He's all yours; we'll leave you to it."

McSweeney swallowed and faced up to his isolation. "I think you're all fucking chicken, but I won't break ranks. We need a united front at times like this."

Rafferty turned Lincoln. "Looks like you are free to leave, but if we do find out that you had any involvement in this business, your days are numbered. Understand? Now, have you got your car keys?"

Lincoln breathed a sigh of relief; he was safe for the moment. "yes, thank you. I can understand how you must be feeling, but I'm not going to run away now; there's unfinished business to attend to."

Rafferty shook his head. "I don't think it's appropriate to continue with these talks after what's happened."

Lincoln drew a deep breath; in a flash it had come to him what he had to do. He understood full well why this opportunity had been created for him. He held up his hands, inviting silence, waited until the conversations that had broken out died away.

"I know that this is a highly sensitive time and you're all very angry, but what's done is done. I think you could make huge political capital out of this situation. There's a chance for you all to solve Northern Ireland's problems once and for all. You can do what successive politicians have failed to do if you move quickly."

"And how would we be doing that Mr Lincoln?" Rafferty asked the obvious question.

Lincoln grasped the opportunity that had been created and put forward his grand plan. "It's simple really, the weapons are gone and nothing can change that. News will leak out sooner or later; in fact, in all probability both Governments will already know. Don't let them gain the upper hand; you lot can take the credit for what has happened. Make an announcement to the effect that you have destroyed your weapons and demand that British troops get out of Ulster immediately. And, if you can all agree on a formula, put forward your Constitutional proposals at the same time. It'll be one in the eye for the Politicians; it'll raise the standing of the paramilitaries to new levels."

He watched briefly as they digested what he was suggesting before going on. "I'll give you my backing, and I'm certain the President himself will weigh in. I'll get on to the Prime Minister and the Taoiseach as soon as you allow me."

Collins and Rafferty exchanged glances, and the latter spoke. "You're sure that the British and Irish Governments will go along with this, Mr Lincoln? We have nothing left to bargain with; they might crack down hard if they know we're at our weakest."

"They won't, I promise you. The President has a great deal of influence; if nothing else he can make huge sums of money available for investment."

"Are you certain of this? We'd have to be certain that the President was on board."

"Yes Mr Collins, I'm certain. I guarantee it."

Collins and Rafferty looked at the men gathered round them; they said nothing, their expressions impassive. The Loyalist nodded his head a fraction. "I think we have to discuss the Vice-President's proposal in private Seamus; it's a big step to take. Mr Lincoln, you're free to go, we'll get word to you about our decision."

"I'd prefer to remain here if you don't object?"

Collins shrugged. "Suit yourself. OK Seamus, back to the Conference Room it is."

As the men turned and filed along the corridor to the Conference Room, Lincoln observed Collins draw Rafferty aside, saw the two men exchange comments, then go into a vacant room closing the door behind them. *Now what are you two cooking up, I wonder? No matter I'll find out soon enough.*

Inside the room the two men faced each other, Republican and Loyalist, sworn enemies but with a common self-interest. Collins was first to speak.

"I'll come right to the point Seamus. I don't like this at all. Our two sides have learned to live with each other and we've carved the province up to our mutual advantage. We exercise considerable influence in our respective communities Some respect us, others fear us, either way we're pretty important. Agreed?"

Rafferty nodded; his thoughts had run along the same lines.

Collins continued. "I'm not sure I want to give all that up, peace or no peace. There's good money being made out of the drug trade; our status shields us from the full force of the law. It could all be lost if we go down the road Lincoln's suggesting."

Rafferty grinned. "Well now I'm not sure that we could call it *good* money, but like you I'm happy with my way of life just as it is. I'm all for the Cause as long as it doesn't affect the penny in my pocket. There's no need for us to fight, and no need to reach a settlement. Aren't we all brothers within the European Community anyway?"

Collins grinned broadly. "God but you talk a load of shit sometimes Seamus, but it seems we are agreed. Let's get back to the others and steer them to the right conclusion."

The two men shook hands and winked at each other.

Lincoln saw the two men re-appear smiling, walking side by side, chatting. *That looks hopeful. I wonder what kind of a deal you two have cooked up.*

Half an hour went by, then an hour. Lincoln grew more impatient by the minute but there was nothing he could do but sit it out. Then at last the wait was over, a soft knock on the door and Rafferty entered closely followed by Collins. The Republican looked anxious.

"I'll come right to the point; I'm sorry, Mr Lincoln, they wouldn't go along with it. Almost to a man they're looking for some kind of revenge. They can't see how we can trust anybody given what's happened today. It's best if you get away from here while you can."

Rafferty appeared glum and genuine in his regret.

Collins joined in. "We did our best Mr Lincoln and we'll keep trying but it doesn't look good, for the moment anyway. It's too big for most of them if you ask me. Most of the lads respect you, and they're not blaming you as I speak, but I'd go if I was you. Their mood could change; a rumour, a wrong word here and there and who knows."

Lincoln was dismayed. "What are you two going to do?"

"The only thing we can really." Rafferty retained his crestfallen expression. "We're going to condemn this breach of trust whilst Peace talks were in progress. We're going to blame the Brits and we're going to claim that only some of the weapons were destroyed."

Lincoln waved his finger angrily. "No. I can't go along with that. I'll have to put a different viewpoint."

Rafferty nodded. "Of course you will Mr Lincoln, but for sure that won't change anything; we'll still be here and you'll be on the other side of the Atlantic. As for the weapons, they're easy enough to come by nowadays if we need them. I promise you that Ronnie and I will work hard promoting those ideas of yours, maybe next time we'll reach a better conclusion." Rafferty extended his hand. "As Ronnie said, best if you go now. I'm not sure about some of the hotheads."

Collins put his hand on Lincoln's shoulder. "Sorry, it was a good try. No hard feelings."

Lincoln shook hands with both men in turn, nodding sadly, looking into their eyes. "It's a pity it has to end this way, but its not all over yet I assure you; I won't let the progress we've made be in vain. No matter what anybody says or does, peace will come to Ulster, believe me. Those who are against peace will be vanquished." He looked deeply into the eyes of each man in turn, then without further comment he pushed his way past them and made his way out of the building.

Collins shrugged. "There goes a very unhappy man Seamus. Still, I can't see what he can do now. Vanquished? What did he mean by that? Sounded a bit religious to me; probably reading too much Bible, or maybe I should say babble." He laughed.

Rafferty nodded. "He's like all the others, Ronnie; they can only do what we let them do. Now let's get back to the lads and tell them what nasty things he had to say; stir them up a bit more."

Collins put his arm round his one-time enemy's shoulder. "You're a wicked bugger, Seamus."

"You bastards! You lying, cheating, conniving, evil bastards! I hope you all rot in hell."

Lincoln sat in his car volubly cursing the two men who had just betrayed him. He'd extracted the whole sorry truth from them as he shook their hands. He was totally devastated by the lack of integrity shown by both sides of the current paramilitary leadership. He looked over to the Conference Centre and ranted at a non-existent audience.

"Damn you; your predecessors of years gone bye would be ashamed of you. Will there ever be a settlement in Ulster whilst people like you remain in command? You've replaced the ideals of the Cause and the Union with self-serving power and greed? Damn you. Damn you all. I wish you had all been blown up with your weapons."

In the instant he spoke the words, there was a series of massive explosions and Drumena Lodge was turned into a raging fireball. Shattered glass and building debris were thrown thirty metres into the air; Lincoln flinched as some struck the car. Flames engulfed the three buildings, their wooden construction feeding the inferno. Natural human reaction took over; he had to render assistance. He opened his car door and started to get out, but froze when he heard the horrific cries of pain and death as searing flames ravaged human flesh. There was nothing he or anyone could do.

Lincoln sat transfixed by the scene unfolding in front of him. Nobody could escape from the building; all those men would perish. He lowered his head into his hands, covering his eyes to shut out the scene in front of him. "What have I done? What have I done? Dear Lord, I didn't want this to happen, I didn't." *I think you did, John. It was your prayer that was answered*

He pulled out his mobile; he had to summon the Emergency Services. He started to punch in 999 then realised he didn't know where he was, he'd been driven there blindfolded; there could be a number of Drumena Lodges in Ulster

It would have made little difference if he had been able to summon the Emergency Services, cries for help were already dying away; all those men would be burned to cinders and the building reduced to a heap of charred timbers by the time they arrived.

Lincoln decided to drive down to the main road and look for a landmark so that he could give proper directions. He needed to escape the dreadful scene of devastation in front of him, get away from the stench of burning flesh that was already pervading the air. As he drove down the long access road through the forest, his conscience plagued him; all those men burned alive. It was true they were all extremists, but they were also fathers, husbands, sons. He felt certain that his plea, his prayer, had resulted in their deaths; he couldn't let them die in vain.

CHAPTER 22

Washington, the previous day.

Diane Phelps answered an early evening call on her mobile, her most private one. Only a few people had the number. "It's Diane, who's calling please?"

"It's Jimmy, is it all right to talk?" McGimpsey knew to be cautious.

"Go ahead."

"I'm afraid my operatives didn't complete the task."

Phelps groaned her disappointment. "Christ, why not?"

"I don't know and they can't explain. I'm afraid they've left our employment and won't be coming back."

"What now?" She was starting to think about her investment.

McGimpsey wanted nothing more to do with the affair and sought to bring a close to the episode. "I doubt if another opportunity will arise, it's too risky; the Council are looking into what happened. It would be more than my life's worth if they suspected my involvement. I can tell you that your man is going to a hush-hush meeting tomorrow with all the protagonists."

"Couldn't you arrange for something to happen whilst he's there? This is important to me, very important."

"Forget it Diane, you're going to have to deal me out of this one."

"What about the cash?"

McGimpsey chuckled. "As they say, me darling, you've lost your deposit You backed the wrong horse this time round. Obviously, in the circumstances, the outstanding balance needn't be paid."

Her anger mounting, she shouted at him. "You'll have to return what you've been paid." She heard him laugh as he rung off. "Fuck it, fuck it, fuck it."

County Antrim near Drumena Lodge

Lincoln reached the main road – turn left, or turn right? He had no idea where he was; his thoughts travelled back to his journey from Warrenpoint. He'd been blindfolded but he was fairly sure the car had turned left off the main road onto the forest drive; he could recall the crunch of the wheels on the gravel. He turned right, looking back at the sign as he did so, 'Drumena Lodge'.

A mile further on, he arrived on the edge of the tiny village of Ballybellew. He now had a fix on where he was and could put the plan he had conceived into action. It was time to make another telephone call. He wondered for a moment if it really was his plan, or was he just a tool. *Who's pulling the strings, you or me Lord?* His mobile displayed a strong signal and he punched in the number.

"Downing Street, how can I help you?"

"Hello, this is John Lincoln again, Vice-President of America, I phoned earlier and spoke to the Prime Minister. I need to speak to him again on the same matter. It's extremely urgent."

"The Prime Minister is in Cabinet, I'll put you through to his Private Secretary."

"I don't want his Private Secretary," Lincoln snapped, "I have to speak to the Prime Minister. I'm sorry if I sound rude but it really is urgent."

The telephonist gritted her teeth. *'Vice-President or not, I have my instructions.'* "I'll put you through Mr Vice-President."

"The Prime Minister's Private Secretary speaking, William Parker. How can I help you Mr Vice-President?"

Lincoln breathed in deeply, stifling his impatience. "I'm sorry Mr Parker but you can't help me. I must speak to the Prime Minister in person. I assure you it's an emergency and I know he would want to take this call. The matter involved is highly sensitive."

"Could you give me some idea of the nature of your call, Mr Lincoln and I'll see what I can do? He has a standing order to the effect that he's not to be disturbed whilst in Cabinet. Could he return your call as soon as he's free?"

Lincoln snapped. "Damn it, I told you that this is an emergency. Mr Parker, please tell him I'm on the line. I suggest that you pretend that a missile has hit Big Ben or put it down to that 'special relationship' we're always referring to. Just get me through."

There was a momentary silence at the other end of the line. "Very well Mr Vice-President, I'll do my best."

"Mr Lincoln, Ralph here. I'm sorry I wasn't available. It sounds as though you have a problem, how can I help?"

"Sorry about this, Ralph, but we **all** have a problem; there have been dramatic events here in Armagh within the last hour. I honestly can't explain how they came about. But I believe there's just a slim chance we could use them to bring about peace in Northern Ireland, and I do mean a permanent peace. It's essential we act quickly; it will require immediate and careful handling."

The PM drew a sharp breath; it all sounded ominous. "You have my full attention; please explain and I'll do everything in my power to help."

Lincoln described the events he had witnessed and outlined how he believed they could be used to advantage. When he finished, he held his breath, readied himself for further explanation and persuasion; in his experience the Brits were over-cautious when big decisions had to be made.

To his surprise the Prime Minister barely hesitated. "To call this a shock, John, is the understatement of the century, but I agree we must seize the opportunity. It'll need your direct involvement; this will put your diplomatic skills to the test. And of course we'll have to get the Taoiseach on board as well."

Lincoln smiled broadly. "I'll be only too pleased to see this through to a successful outcome. What do you have in mind?"

"There isn't time to go into it in depth, but we must hit the broadcasting media tonight. I'll need you to join me in London; the three of us will have to appear on television together if this is going to stand any chance of success. We have one major problem, in that there will be no paramilitary representatives available to join us; we'll have to come up with a plausible reason for their absence. We'll need to cover that angle somehow. John, I wonder, could you make your way to Belfast International Airport and I'll arrange an RAF flight to London for you. Also, it would be ideal if you could phone the Taoiseach and tell him what you've told me? Tell him I'll be in touch shortly. I've got things to do; I've just had an idea on how to handle all this."

Lincoln demurred. "Wouldn't it be better if I drove to Dublin and you joined us there? It would probably look better if the announcement was made in the Republic in any case."

The PM didn't hesitate. "Of course, you're absolutely right; now why didn't I think of that? I'm going to arrange for Drumena Lodge to be sealed off and get a cover story put in place, so don't worry about that dimension."

Heaven

The Old Man had witnessed the events and had considered intervening, but hesitated and the moment had gone. The Council would learn soon enough what had taken place and it would not approve, could not approve. There would be argument, then censure. Many would see the occurrences as an abuse of power and a breach of commandment; it would not suffice that the intent was good. They all believed that life was sacrosanct. You may have taken a step too far my son.

Drumena Lodge, later.

Less than an hour after Lincoln's telephone call to the Prime Minister an armoured personnel carrier turned into the forest road to Drumena Lodge and stopped just inside the gates. Two men, dressed in Police uniforms, got out of the vehicle and positioned themselves at the entrance to the site The vehicle then continued along the forest drive until it rounded a bend and could no longer be seen from the entrance, at which point it halted. Its occupants were under strict instructions not to go anywhere near the Lodge, having regard to the very sensitive nature of the negotiations that were taking place inside. The driver turned the vehicle around to face back the way it had come then pulled of the track. Six men in military uniform got out of the carrier and deployed themselves; they were there to deal with any intruders who bypassed their colleagues guarding the entrance.

Dublin, later.

The Prime Minister and the Taoiseach flanked the Vice-President as they sat facing a line of television cameras. They were ready for a broadcast that would be made simultaneously on all channels in both countries. A link to CNN in the United States had been put in place. Beyond the cameras were two rows of responsible political analysts and journalists, many of whom had travelled with the Prime Minister on his flight from Heathrow to Ireland. They had been summoned at short notice but not been briefed on the purpose of the broadcast; it was obvious to everyone that something big was breaking, and they wanted to be part of it.

Lincoln took a sip of water, watching for the ten seconds warning that he was about to go on air, taking his cue when it arrived. "Ladies and gentlemen, thank you for watching this broadcast, and thanks also to the journalists and others who have joined us in the studio. The Taoiseach and Prime Minister have invited me to make this announcement, and I'm proud to be involved in what I believe to be a momentous occasion. I am here to tell you that Loyalist and Republican paramilitaries have today, of their own volition, destroyed their entire stock of weapons and explosives. The British Army has commenced an immediate withdrawal from Northern Ireland. Details of the withdrawal are being finalised as I speak to you. Hostilities in Northern Ireland are at an end with immediate effect and a new era of peace has begun.

"The Prime Minister has issued instructions that the withdrawal process is to be completed within six weeks. All, I stress, **all**, Army command posts will be dismantled by the end of the year. The Northern Ireland Assembly will be reconvened by order of Parliament and effectively it can resume responsibilities immediately."

Many in the assembled media stood up, vying for attention, before Lincoln could complete his statement. Hands were raised seeking attention; journalists shouted question after question.

Lincoln raised his hands to silence them. "Yes, yes, I'm sure that you have many questions, but I have more news to impart, news which is of equal importance to the foregoing. Dealing with the weapons was a courageous step, a vital step, but in my view, it dealt with past differences; the future also has to be addressed. In that regard, I have an important announcement, a historic announcement."

Journalists fell silent and waited expectantly; history was being made and they were part of it. Lincoln reported on the nature of the negotiations that had taken place at Drumena Lodge and how a basis for the future government of Northern Ireland had been reached. He congratulated the paramilitary leaders on their co-operation and shared vision for the future.

"There are still details to be hammered out and a number of administrative issues to be resolved but I'm confident that before morning all outstanding matters will be resolved. In fact, as I speak, those involved are still working together; had an agreement not been so close they would have been represented here tonight. The final package of proposals will be presented to the Governments of Great Britain, the Republic of Ireland and the Northern Ireland Assembly for discussion and hopefully adoption. Both the Taoiseach and the Prime Minister have studied a draft of the current proposals and are confident of their acceptance. That's all from me at this time; I'm now going to hand you over to them."

Both politicians made short statements, affording congratulations to the Vice-President and all the Parties involved. They confirmed their support for the proposals; details would be issued as soon as the paramilitaries concluded their discussions. They both ended their statements with fulsome praise of the Vice-President's powers of negotiation and mediation.

The three men then faced a barrage of questions with Lincoln taking the lion's share. The broadcast ran well beyond its allotted time, but all went well; the die was now cast. Many top Loyalist and Republican politicians and paramilitaries would have seen the broadcast and their reaction would be crucial. They would no doubt be trying to reach their contacts at Drumena Lodge. How would they react when they couldn't make contact? The next twenty-four hours would be crucial

The White House, late evening

"Diane, have you caught the news? Lincoln has pulled it off in Ireland. And would you believe it, the bastard hasn't had the courtesy to phone me. It's absolutely incredible; he's got more luck than the Devil himself. See how you can use the situation to my advantage. This scenario will be well received by Irish-Americans; it'll be worth thousands of votes." Caswell was genuinely excited; it would all help when the Nobel Committee was deciding who should get the Peace Prize.

Phelps' eyes narrowed; Lincoln had triumphed again; the barrier between her and the Presidency was greater than eve. *Fuck you McGimpsey*

"He sure is lucky Jack, lucky beyond belief. I'll get to work on the publicity but lots of folks are beginning to pick up on his involvement in world affairs; it's becoming increasingly difficult for you to steal all the credit. You know what Abe Lincoln had to say about, fooling all of the people all of the time; people out there will start to wonder who's calling the shots in the White House."

"Forget the health warning. Get on with the job, that's what I pay you for Go to it. And whilst you're at it, get me a transcript of anything coming out of Ireland; I need to be well briefed."

"I'll get right on it, Jack, you can rely on me. Are we getting together later?"

She was disappointed when he shrugged. "We'll have to see how the Irish situation develops,"

"I'll leave it with you Jack." *Christ don't tell me you're going off the boil already.*

230

Drumena Lodge, nearing midnight.

The Army team securing access to Drumena Lodge had been withdrawn before midnight. No explanation had been given not that anybody cared; it would be more comfortable back in the barracks. The Police Service of Northern Ireland had been asked to secure access to the estate and a manned vehicle had taken up station at every entrance.

At the main entrance, one of the two Policemen on duty, Mike Nolan, leaned back in his seat and shivered. "Keep the engine running Tommy, it's going to be a long, cold night. It's ironic when you think of it, us guarding that lot. I bet they've got more guns at that meeting than we have in our bloody Station."

Tommy Burns nodded, "That's for sure, but we'll keep well away from them. We can take turns to sleep the night through."

At 0200 a three-man SAS team, carrying loads of gear, led by Sergeant Eddie Ross approached Drumena Lodge. They had made their way cross-country and the police were not aware of their presence. This was a covert operation and only two very senior officers knew of the SAS involvement. Their orders were simple; kill anyone found alive at the Lodge and make sure that all the buildings were burnt to the ground. They hadn't been told what to expect, but as they got nearer to the lodge, they encountered the unmistakeable smell of burnt flesh and caught glimpses of smouldering embers.

"Looks like someone has had a bonfire, Sarge."

"Yeah." Eddie Ross was puzzled. The smell was pungent, one he had experienced on other occasions. "Smells like a few bodies have encountered a barbecue; somebody got here before us."

Minutes later they arrived at the edge of the clearing around the complex that had once been Drumena Lodge.

"Fuck me Sarge, what do we do now?"

"What we always do, follow orders; check out the site and deal with any survivors."

Smoke still rose here and there from the collapsed ruins, now and then there was a small flicker of flame fanned by the occasional breath of wind. Sparks rose as they trampled quickly through the remains, scanning the collapsed structure for unlikely signs of life. The smell of burned flesh seemed to grow ever-stronger. It soon became clear that there were no survivors. All that remained of what been the cream of Ireland's paramilitary leadership was charred flesh and grey ash.

"Christ, what's gone on here Sarge?"

Ross shook his head. "Looks to me like some bugger has been very careless with his matches. There's more to this than meets the eye, but we're going to do what we were told to do and say nothing. And I mean say nothing." He was remembering his Commanding Officer's last words. *I'm not sure what you'll find when you reach the target, just carry out your instructions and when you come back simply report 'mission accomplished', that's all I'll need to know. If you don't accomplish your mission don't come back. Understood Sergeant?'*

"Not much for us to do Sarge, it's all been done."

"We have our orders Corporal; set the incendiary charges in what's left of all three buildings. Go to it. And disperse those empty alcohol bottles around the site."

"What's the point Sarge?"

"One, because we've been told to, and two, because I don't want to carry all this fucking stuff four miles across country again. Now get fucking moving."

Twenty minutes later the Sergeant and his men gathered together, the incendiary charges were in place and ready for ignition. The old-style ignitable running fuse would leave no traces in the ensuing conflagration.

Ross flicked his lighter and applied it to the fuse, watching intently as it started its slow journey towards the first of the incendiary charges, igniting the other fuses on its way.

The men immediately ran back to the edge of the clearing and watched the initial ignition; others followed almost immediately sending huge flames into the air. The fire wouldn't last long; there was very little material left to burn.

"OK men, let's get moving."

Five minutes later they heard the explosion. "That's it guys, job complete Quicken the pace, let's get clear of this area."

The explosive charge did exactly what it was intended to do. "Waken up Mike; there's been some kind of an explosion at the Lodge."

Police Sergeant Mike Nolan shook his head to clear the lingering effects of his sleep. "Are you certain Tommy? I didn't hear anything."

"Definitely. It came from the direction of the Lodge."

"OK. Radio Headquarters; tell them we're going to investigate."

SAS Base

Back at their Base, SAS Sergeant Eddie Ross was reporting to his Commanding Officer.

"Mission accomplished Sergeant?"

"Yes Sir, but there's something I think you should know"

"I know all I need to know Sergeant. You've done the job, now its best that you forget all about it. I'd just remind you of your obligations under the Official Secrets Act."

"Yes Sir, understood Sir."

"That's a good chap. Now you and the men get your heads down, have a good night's sleep."

When the Sergeant had gone, Colonel Charles Greening telephoned the number he had been given; he hadn't been told who would answer and had been told not to ask.

"Yes?"

"Colonel Greening here. Mission accomplished."

"Thank you, Colonel."

Drumena Lodge, 2.45am

Mike Nolan and Tommy Burns could see the flames through the trees as they sped along the forest drive.

"Looks like there's a major fire Tommy; we must alert the Emergency Services."

Nolan pulled the car to a halt safely away from the flames and got out.

"Christ the Lodge has all but gone, those timber building must have gone up like wildfire. Where is everybody?" Nolan was puzzled, something didn't seem right

The two policemen gazed around the area, then circled the building, shouting as they went. "Doesn't look like anybody got out alive; I don't understand how this could have happened in such a short space of time. Poor bastards, that's burning flesh we can smell; we have a disaster on our hands."

Burns rubbed his belly, "I feel like throwing up."

Nolan nodded. "Join the club. Do you know what puzzles me?"

Burns shrugged. "Tell me."

"It's all ground floor construction, presumably with adequate means of escape, but not a single person managed to get out. How do you explain that?"

Nolan thought for a second. "We don't really know that nobody escaped, Tommy. I'll bet all those bastards were stoned out of their minds; look at all those shattered bottles.2

"Hmm, maybe, though somehow, I don't buy it."

The first fire appliance screeched to a halt alongside the police car, men spilling from its interior, going immediately into their routine, preparing to set up lighting and connect hoses.

The Senior Fire Officer shook his head. "Forget it lads, we're too late, there's nothing we can do here; there isn't even anything to make safe. I can't understand why it's gone so quickly."

The fire engine's powerful searchlight played over what was left of the lodge, pausing here and there as it picked out what appeared to be the charred remains of a body.

The SFO joined up with Nolan. "We're going back to the Station, Sergeant. This is a complete write off as far as we're concerned. It'll burn itself out in no time at all. We'll be more useful back at the Station, this won't be the call we get before our shift is over. You'll have seen the charred remains; this is a potential crime scene. I assume you'll secure the site; it'll keep Forensics engaged for six months or more. We'll be back first thing in the morning to help ascertain what set this lot off."

Northern Ireland Office, earlier

Meantime, through the Police network, news had reached the Northern Ireland Office and instructions had been given to seal off the entire area. The Secretary of State for Northern Ireland had not been briefed on the cover up that was in progress and immediately contacted Downing Street. The Prime Minister was woken from his sleep by his Aide and played his part well, his portrayal of surprise and horror was convincing; he ordered an immediate investigation. The media was not to be informed; he would deal with all announcements personally. He instructed his Aide to inform the Taoiseach. The Aide was puzzled but asked no questions; he would learn more when the Prime Minister issued his statement.

London and Dublin: 0800 hours

In simultaneous broadcasts the Prime Minister and the Taoiseach addressed their respective countries for the second time in twelve hours.

Tragedy had struck; a devastating fire had burned Drumena Lodge to the ground. As far as was known, everyone taking part in the Peace talks appeared to have lost their lives. The fire had taken place during the hours of darkness; investigation of cause had been deferred until first light. Early indications suggested that there had been a massive explosion, probably due to accidental ignition of a major gas leak. No further information was available at this time.

Efforts were being made to determine exactly who had attended the meeting, which had of course been held in secret with the Vice-President of the United States initially in attendance. At the request of the Vice-President and the Paramilitaries, neither Government had been represented at the meeting. A telephone number would be given at the end of the broadcast for anyone who might have information about anyone attending.

Sympathy was extended to all the relatives and friends of those lost in this terrible accident. It was devastating to think that those who had lost their lives taking Ireland into a new era had not lived to gain the recognition they deserved. Both Governments would work together to provide a fitting memorial to the victims and the British Army would begin its withdrawal from Ulster in the near future.

The Prime Minister and the Taoiseach expressed their determination to ensure that those who had sacrificed their lives in pursuit of peace had not died in vain. They called upon all communities on both sides of the border to work together to build on the progress that had been made; a permanent peace must be secured in honour of those lost in the fire.

Vice-President Lincoln was returning to America but remained available to offer any assistance required of him. He was too shocked to address the media; the memories of the men with whom he had negotiated were too fresh in his mind.

Throughout Ireland

What was left of the leadership of paramilitary forces was confused; they couldn't understand how the weapons had come to be destroyed so quickly and without consultation. Who had carried out the destruction? Who had given the orders? Nobody was coming forward with any information; Government sources appeared to be equally mystified.

The political settlement had come out of the blue; it hadn't been discussed within the ranks. An emergency IRA Council had been formed and would issue a formal statement in due course. The big question was what to do now? British troop withdrawals were already underway. The Northern Ireland Assembly had gone into session. The protestant paramilitaries were saying little but appeared the accept the peace initiatives. There was overwhelming support for the peace proposals in the Press and within the Public, both in the north and in the south.

Could it really be a coincidence that the cream of the paramilitary leadership has been extinguished in the blink of an eye, on the very day they had lost all their weapons? The whole business smelled of a carefully orchestrated operation by the one of the Government Agencies but there was little they could do for the present. The dissidents didn't want to be isolated and there was no real reason not to go along with the new order of things. After all, if they didn't like how things worked out, they could start all over again. Their predecessors had started with nothing and so could they.

CHAPTER 23

Washington

Carol Lincoln threw her arms around her husband. "Welcome home Honey. You look like you've lived a lifetime in this past week. I've followed progress on television and everyone is praising **you,** though crafty Jack Caswell is making sure he gets his share of the limelight."

She studied her husband; he looked tired and strained, and sadness showed in his eyes.

"I never want to go through anything like that again Carol. I pray to God it's been worth it."

"You're tired Honey, you'll feel better when you've been home for a while. Give yourself some space. The tragedy isn't of your making; you need time to reflect and weigh things in the balance. There are many souls all over Ireland who will sleep more soundly in the days to come; a whole country can look forward to a happier future because of what you've achieved."

"You don't understand." He spoke sombrely, his eyes glistening with tears. "Because of what I've done, at least thirty men have died, maybe as many as thirty-six; they weren't sure of the numbers when I left. There are a lot of children without fathers, wives without husbands, mothers and fathers without sons all because of me. What a horrific way to die."

"Because of you John?" She looked at him puzzled. "I don't understand, Honey."

"Yes, because of me. I gathered them there, I….." He faltered, afraid to say the words that would reveal his guilt. "I don't know if I can handle this."

She knew he was deeply troubled, but wasn't sure how to help. "When you're ready you must tell me the whole story Just bear in mind, the Lord was watching over you, He knew what was happening. Whatever is troubling you is known to Him."

"Oh, how I wish I had your faith, Carol. Somehow, I just feel that I'm to blame. I caused this whole tragedy; I made it happen."

"Tell me about it when you're ready, maybe I can help."

Lincoln looked at his wife wondering what to do. *What would she think? How would it affect her simple beliefs if she knew what had really happened?* He shook his head and knew he could never bring himself to tell her. "Not now Honey, maybe someday I'll tell you all about it."

Oval Office: Next day

Another triumph John, you're building quite a reputation as a peacemaker. Our friends across the pond think the sun shines out of that black arse of yours." Caswell was upbeat.

Lincoln had made the Prime Minister and the Taoiseach promise that the truth about the events at Drumena Lodge would never be revealed, an undertaking they were more than happy to give.

"I thought you might like to offer to fund the rebuilding of Drumena Lodge and erect a memorial to those men, Jack? Who knows they might rename the whole forest after you? The Jack Caswell National Park how does that sound?"

Such was his vanity that Jack Caswell's enthusiasm was roused immediately. "I like that idea; I'll follow it up this afternoon. What's on your agenda now? What part of the world are you going to save from doom and disaster next?"

Lincoln pursed his lips. "I'm not sure Jack. I'm going to give myself some time to work that one out."

"Well, the whole world is your oyster, John. Africa, the Indian sub-continent, or perhaps you could start on the borders of the European Community and travel east. Then there's those North Korean bastards, they need sorted out."

Lincoln shook his head; he was still feeling the pain of Drumena Lodge and deeply worried about the power he could unleash. A power he was no longer sure he could control.

"I'll let you know in due course; I'm not rushing into anything. Though it's nice to see that you are beginning to appreciate my efforts. There's just one thing puzzling me about my Irish experience, Jack; someone took a couple of shots at me early on. I made enquiries, but nobody on the paramilitary side seemed to be responsible."

Caswell gaped; his eyes widened; his surprise seemed genuine. "Christ John, thank God you didn't take a hit. It must have been one of the extreme factions; there are so many splinter groups over there, and they don't all want peace. Can't say I'm surprised; I did say you should have some security."

"I'm not sure who it was, Jack, but I promise I'll be following it up one way and another."

"Sure thing, I certainly would. Let me know if you need any help."

Lincoln searched Caswell's thoughts and was relieved to find that he had no knowledge of Diane Phelps' duplicity.

Heaven

The Old Man sat with the Council; he had been put under great pressure. 'Divine power had been abused. Long-standing principles had been put aside, the sanctity of life ignored. The sixth Commandment had been ignored - Thou shalt not kill.'

He had argued that all through time, wars had ensued and many had given their lives that Good might triumph over Evil. The situation had been a kind of war; the resultant peace would ensure that many would live who might otherwise have perished. Communities would flourish; normality would be restored. People might have more concern for their fellow man.

Members of the Council had argued that this hadn't really been a war amongst men, divine power had been used.

The Old Man had countered that a mortal being had been the driving force; it was his solutions that had been allowed to succeed. It hadn't been a question of Divine Will.

The Council had not been wholly persuaded to his way of thinking but, in the end, he had worn them down, and they had accepted that the work should continue for the time being. But the divide was growing and his authority was being seriously challenged for the first time in history. "Be careful my son, the end does not always justify the means."

Washington

In the months following his experience in Ireland, Lincoln sought tirelessly to develop his role throughout the world as an arbitrator and peacemaker; always willing to take on the smaller tasks as well as those that earned banner headlines. There was a never-ending demand for his services. Although still Vice-President of the United States he was increasingly referred to as 'ambassador extraordinaire'; the world had adopted him as its own.

For his part he remained full of doubts as to the role he had inherited and was never quite sure where the boundaries of his powers lay. *Who was in control? Himself or some divine spirit? Was he directing whatever course of action he found himself engaged in, or was he the one being directed by a greater force? Could he access whatever forces he believed he required, willy-nilly, or would they only be given to him if his actions were sanctioned by a divine power?* There were no voices whispering to him, no guidance being given. There were times when he felt very much alone.

As ever it was Carol who came to his rescue and relieved his anxieties. *'He's always in command, John, He charts the course for you to follow. Have faith and things will always turn out for the best.'*

If only he had her faith. For Carol everything was black or white, right or wrong, good or evil; there were no shades of grey, no compromises, no murky dealings. But however hard Lincoln tried, he could not believe that, somehow, he could do no wrong. He was human, he was fallible, the disaster which had occurred in Northern Ireland continued to haunt him.

However, progress was being made and, although relationships between Israel and the Palestinians continued to be volatile, both sides continued step by step along a diplomatic path which was inexorably leading to peaceful co-existence. Although he had had to intervene twice when policy in the

Knesset was on the verge of taking a wrong turn in respect of the Israeli settlements in Palestine.

Two hard-liners had reverted to their old ways and were rallying support for their cause. He had covertly used the media to bring about their downfall. One was removed from power when details of his corrupt dealings during his tenure as Defence Minister were revealed; the other resigned when the western press exposed his sexual proclivities involving underage children of both sexes.

Lincoln had contacted Dayan and Musrat to advise them that he was the source of the revelations and that he wouldn't hesitate to bring other failings to the attention of the media if it proved necessary. It wasn't diplomatic pressure - it was blackmail, pure and simple and it brought the result he wanted. But was it right? Would the ends always justify the means? Where did that invisible dividing line lie?

Meanwhile, in Ireland the newly established Peace Accord had proceeded apace with both sides of the divide co-operating fully to fashion a new Ulster. Perhaps they had finally tired of the long struggle and a century of strife was at last coming to an end? Or was it perhaps, as some commentators had suggested, the old paramilitary leadership were living in fear of their lives.

The tragic events at Drumena Lodge had shocked everyone connected with terrorism and paramilitaries had dwindled in number. The lengthy investigations that followed the tragedy had failed to identify what had caused the fire; whether it was arson or accident hadn't been established. As ever it suited the media to conjure up all sorts of conspiracy theories; most were certain that the fire and the weapons disposal incidents were co-ordinated. But by whom remained a mystery.

The paramilitary leadership on both sides of the divide had concluded that the Intelligence Services of both Governments, perhaps with CIA involvement, had carried out the operation and that assassinations would continue if terrorist acts persisted. It seemed to them irrefutable that their networks and command structure had been penetrated by the Intelligence Services, though no moles were ever found. In the end, all sides had agreed to pursue political solutions to their grievances. So far, this latest peace accord was working.

The situation in Iraq had been carefully managed and the country was on the verge of electing a new Government. Lincoln had used the knowledge extracted from Saddam to inform Caswell where the Iraqi leader had secreted the weapons of mass destruction, and the huge financial resources stolen over the years. The President had pragmatically struck a deal with the deposed family; they would be allowed to retain a substantial sum provided they left Iraq. The sum involved would be sufficient for them to continue to live the lavish lifestyle to which they were accustomed.

Caswell had been ruthless in one regard; one condition of the settlement required Saddam to dispose of such members of the previous leadership as the Americans required. The dictator and his sons accepted the deal; it probably suited them since they were able to eliminate a number of potential enemies.

Following the leadership cull, arrangements were made for Saddam and his families to resettle in Saudi Arabia; Caswell warned, that if they stepped out of line, he wouldn't hesitate to have them eliminated by covert action. In truth it was a solution he might pursue in any event with the co-operation of the Saudis; politics was a dirty business.

Lincoln had then turned his attention to the Indian sub-continent and had been instrumental in restoring full diplomatic relations between India, Pakistan and Bangladesh when he came up with a border solutions acceptable to all regimes. As part of the deal, he had persuaded the Senate and Congress to fund a joint satellite programme to improve communications and border surveillance in both countries. He had followed his usual practice of meeting the lead politicians and persuading them, willingly or otherwise, to do his will and reach agreement.

Notwithstanding the pressures he had exerted, it had seemed to him that both parties had been looking for a way out of the hole they had dug for themselves; all he had to do was act as the honest broker. It still helped though that the United States was still oiling the wheels through the medium of overseas aid. Not that Uncle Sam was losing out, bilateral trade agreements ensured otherwise.

The Lincoln Residence

Another important initiative began unexpectedly when Carol joined him in the garden early one evening. "Those poor people in North Korea, as if they didn't have enough problems."

He looked at her expectantly; he'd been looking for a way to get involved in a rapprochement between the two Koreas.

The Communist North's nuclear development programme continued to be seen as an ongoing threat to the Region; Caswell's threats had made no impact on the determination of the regime to advance its knowledge of atomic power. As they saw it, they had the right to generate sufficient electricity for their country's needs and, in the absence of adequate supplies of oil or gas largely due to American diplomatic pressure, it was difficult to see what alternatives remained open to them.

"Why, what's happened, Honey?"

"News has just leaked out that a virulent virus is sweeping through their country. They estimate that over one hundred thousand people have died already and if they can't stop it millions will die. I would have thought you would have known, Honey? The CIA has its fingers in every pie as far as I can see."

"Sounds nasty, but Caswell hasn't mentioned it. Not that he would see the need to tell me. I'll see what I can find out tomorrow when I meet up with him." *Was this the opportunity he had been looking for? Where had this hitherto unknown virus come from? Surely it was a sign, an invitation for him to get involved? It had to be.*

The White House

The President sat alone in the Oval Office waiting for his Vice-President, letting his thoughts drift over his relationship with Diane Phelps. He still enjoyed their sessions but they were beginning to lose their novelty status; excitement and passion were on the wane.

And, more to the point, there were times when she was in danger of forgetting who was boss; she'd had to be taken down a peg or two. On the other hand, she did deal the media superbly, and had built up all the right contacts over the years. He valued her communication skills but had a fear of what she might do if he was to call a halt to their affair.

Caswell kept hoping that she would drift off into some new partnership and they could end their liaison by mutual agreement, but there was no indication that this was on the cards. Moreover, he had his eye on a gorgeous young blond Research Assistant who had recently joined the White House staff.

A knock on the door interrupted his thoughts and Lincoln stuck his head round the door.

"Good morning, Jack, I wonder if I could have a few minutes of your time? I'll come straight to the point if you don't mind."

The two men had all but dispensed with social niceties both recognising, given their relationship, that it was waste of time. "I caught the News last night. Were you aware of this virus spreading through North Korea?"

Caswell nodded. "Sure, reports have been coming in for some time. All good news as far as I'm concerned. The more of those little bastards that get wasted the better."

Lincoln stepped into the office and closed the door behind him. Caswell's outlook on world affairs in general continued to anger and frustrate him; he just didn't seem to move forward in his thinking. "Have you learned nothing Jack? Isn't there a single vestige of humanity inside that head of yours?"

"You know John, you sound more like the Pope each time I see you. That job looks like it's coming up soon, you should put your name down for it. Anyway, there's nothing I can do even if I had the slightest inclination. Our people reckon this virus is ten times worse than Ebola. It's airborne, it can be transmitted by touch; you name it and it can do it."

"How come we know so much about it?"

"The South Koreans managed to get hold of a few blood samples and we're working with them to produce a vaccine but not getting too far."

Lincoln nodded. "That's good as far as it goes; I assume if we do come up with a vaccine, we'll share it with the North Koreans?"

Caswell smiled wanly. "Of course we will, of course we will. Tell you what, you can put on your Dr Kildare outfit and go round giving them all a jab. Seriously, we'll do all we can to help out, believe me."

Lincoln knew that Caswell was telling him what he wanted to hear. Knew too that he had no intention of helping the North Koreans unless there was something in it for America. He wasn't sure what he could do but something was telling him that he had to involve himself.

"I'm going to take a trip over there, Jack; I'll be away for a few days, maybe a week."

Caswell shrugged; the further away his Vice-President was the better. "Suit yourself, I hadn't realised that clinical research was one of your talents. Just make sure you don't come back with an infection; I might have to put you in quarantine for a month." He laughed out loud at his idea. "If it did nothing else it would keep you out of my hair."

Lincoln returned to his office and picked up a phone. "Carol, it's your ever-loving husband calling. I'm on the move again; could you pack a bag for me, Honey? I've got to go away for a few days."

She guessed where he was going. "You're going to North Korea to see if you can help with that plague over there, aren't you? I knew you would."

"Sometimes I think you know more about me than I do. I'm actually heading for South Korea; I've got the germ of an idea floating round in my head. Bye for now, I'll be home shortly."

Seoul, South Korea
Twenty-four hours later, courtesy of Air Force One, Lincoln landed in Seoul and was welcomed by a small honour guard and

driven to the National Assembly building. As was now his practice, he had requested minimum ceremony, publicity or security. Thirty minutes later he sat opposite the Prime Minister of South Korea, Kim Jeng Pol.

"This is an unexpected honour Mr Vice-President, one which is welcome."

"The honour is mine, Prime Minister. Thank you for agreeing to see me at such short notice."

The two men exchanged pleasantries for fifteen minutes before it dawned on Lincoln that his host was too polite to enquire as to the reason for his visit. "Prime Minister, I'm sure you are wondering why I'm here and I confess that there is a particular reason for the timing of this visit."

"I thought there might be; go on Mr Lincoln, I'm intrigued."

"We are both aware of the problems in North Korea at this time." He paused, looking for confirmation, wondering how his host would receive his enquiry; the two nations still mistrusted each other.

"You are alluding to Virus NKX1?"

"I wasn't aware of its classification, but yes."

"And what exactly is the nature of your interest Mr Lincoln?"

"Purely humanitarian. I'd like to visit the laboratory where the virus is being investigated."

The Prime Minister frowned, "Might I enquire as to why you should want to do this?"

"I want to ensure that your researchers are receiving maximum co-operation from the American scientists who are working on the formulation of a vaccine. I understand that this virus is virulent and early discovery of a vaccine is essential if we are to avoid a world-wide pandemic."

Kim Jeng Pol's expression betrayed his scepticism. "I would have thought that a simple telephone call could have fulfilled that purpose, Mr Vice-President. I venture that you are not telling me the whole reason behind your interest but I will nevertheless arrange access for you. The laboratory is not far; you could go now if you wish? Alas I have other business to attend to and will not be able to accompany you. Apologies."

Lincoln was embarrassed; his host had immediately seen through his shallow deception and had shamed him further by offering his assistance nonetheless. "Prime Minister, might I put a direct question to you?"

Kim Jeng Pol smiled wanly. "I am powerless to prevent your question Mr Lincoln but I need not answer it unless I wish."

Lincoln smiled at his host's philosophical response. "Understood Prime Minister, my question is this. In the event that a vaccine for virus NKX1 is found, what action would you take?"

Kim Jeng Pol's brow furrowed, but he replied without hesitation. "A strange question since the answer is self-evident, Mr Lincoln. We would immediately commence mass production of the vaccine. Surely that goes without saying? The virus will spread to my country sooner or later and we must be ready to combat it. Sadly, our capacity to produce large quantities is limited. But the question is of course hypothetical since we have barely begun the research necessary to identify and create a vaccine."

"Prime Minister, if it will help, I give you my assurance that when a vaccine is found I will do everything in my power to ensure that American pharmaceutical companies make available their production resources. Might I assume for the moment, that your scientists are successful in discovering a vaccine; would you share your knowledge with North Korea?"

"Mr Vice-President, my lifelong aim has been to re-unite our two countries, South or North, we are all Koreans. The current regime in the North is, shall we say, misguided, and I hope the future will bring change. I deplore the needless sacrifice of life in any circumstance."

"You have given me a Statesman's answer, Prime Minister. You must excuse the tactlessness of my enquiry. There are those in position of great power who do not share your outlook."

The Korean smiled sagely. "Ah, I begin to understand. From what you imply, I assume that President Caswell may not be fully appraised as to the reason for your visit."

"That is indeed the case."

Kim Jeng Pol nodded. "I will arrange for your visit to the laboratory but will say as little as possible about the nature of your visit, though I will be issuing a formal statement about the good relationship between our two countries."

Within the hour Lincoln was being shown round South Korea's National Laboratory of Biology. He listened carefully to the scientist's understanding of the virus and was pleased to learn of the respect and co-operation between the Americans and the South Koreans. Much of his visit was spent looking through glazed screens into key laboratories and speaking to research staff. He had listened carefully to all that had been said and asked many questions to further his understanding of the problems faced by researchers when seeking to develop a vaccine.

Before he left, he spoke privately with Professor Tae Kyu Sam, a Virologist of world standing, giving him his private telephone number and promising assistance if he required further investment or Western equipment.

"I fear that my need on this occasion is not for resources Mr Vice-President, it is for enlightenment."

The moment had come. *I need your help, Lord, please assist Professor Tae Kyu Sam to discover a vaccine.* Lincoln extended his hand and engaged in a longer than normal handshake, relieved when he felt a strange pulse of energy flow through his arm. He smiled broadly.

"Something tells me that you're going to make a breakthrough very soon Professor."

The scientist shook his head in puzzlement as the American made his way out of the laboratory. *What a strange remark? If only it were to be the case.*

As Lincoln journeyed back to Prime Minister Kim Jeng Pol's residence, he prayed hard that the idea he'd nurtured before he left Washington would come to pass.

Oval Office, two weeks later

Lincoln was meeting up with Caswell for a routine exchange of ideas.

"I suppose you've heard the news from South Korea, John?"

"No, I haven't checked my mail or calls this morning. Tell me."

"Apparently some Professor out there has discovered a vaccine for that virus that's been doing the rounds in North Korea. I can't believe that they could come up with a solution so quickly; it usually takes years."

"That's wonderful news, Jack; potentially hundreds of thousands of lives will be saved."

The President was less enthusiastic. "Yeah, apparently so, and guess what? Kim Jeng Pol has given the know-how to the North Koreans without even consulting me, or making any demands on them. Not a single concession demanded in return. It sounds like the kind of thing you would do. I don't suppose you put him up to it?"

"I didn't need to, Jack. Thank God, unlike some folks, he has some regard for his fellow man. I applaud his actions unreservedly and so should you. Anyway, the vaccine wasn't even discovered when I was there. I'm sure your spies will have told you that."

Caswell nodded thoughtfully. "Yeah, I guess this is one miracle you can't claim the credit for. Looks like the Professor just got lucky."

Lincoln smiled. "It sure, looks that way."

The Lincoln Residence

Over dinner that evening Lincoln told his wife about the vaccine.

"The good Lord works in mysterious ways, Honey. Let us hope that this is a watershed for those two countries and they will work together in the future. You must be pleased; I suspect you lent a helping hand somewhere along the way."

"You know better than that, I can't claim any credit, other than by being a conduit; I'm still terribly mixed up about this whole situation I find myself in."

"I know you are Honey but you've achieved so much and there's more to be done. Just accept that you've been chosen to do the Lord's work and get on with it. Now, finish up that dinner, I feel like an early night." Her broad grin told him that tiredness wasn't the reason behind her early retirement.

Not everything Lincoln touched turned to gold; there was one country where he hadn't enjoyed any success, China. No matter how hard he'd tried, his overtures had been rebuffed. He was desperate to establish a closer relationship with China; he believed that its destiny was to replace America as the most powerful nation on Earth. But so far, they had not been receptive to his approaches.

As ever, he shared his problems with Carol and, during one of their conversations she had suggested he learned Mandarin. "The Chinese are an ancient and proud civilisation; they would appreciate you talking to them in their own language. It's one of the few nations that doesn't need Uncle Sam's blessing, why should they have to speak English all the time. We should meet them half way."

He shook his head. "No, Darling, we get by perfectly well using interpreters; there's no need for me to learn Mandarin. In any case, I'm like most Americans, hopeless at foreign languages"

His wife had chided him. "That's one of our problems; **we** don't make the effort but we're happy enough for them to learn English. It's no wonder they make things difficult for us. I think you should at least give it a try. It would show that you **are** different and demonstrate how serious you are."

In the weeks that followed, Lincoln had given the matter some thought, and decided to take his wife's advice. He engaged a personal tutor and devoted two hours each day in an attempt to gain a working vocabulary; his powers didn't seem to help on this occasion. It soon became clear that he wasn't going to master Mandarin through divine intervention. Progress had been slow initially but at the end of two months he felt brave enough to try out his new skill. He contacted the Chinese Ambassador to Washington to meet to exchange views and his efforts at speaking Mandarin had been well received. *As ever you were right, Carol.*

News got round, and his diplomatic efforts started to be rewarded when previously closed doors began to open. He still needed the services of an interpreter during serious negotiations, but so did his hosts on those occasions. He began to attend more informal events put on by Chinese entrepreneurs and it was during these that his Mandarin brought dividends.

Nevertheless, although relationships blossomed, his achievements were limited. He had emphasised the need for environmental prudence, openly citing his own country as the worst offender on the planet, and suggested that America and China should both comply with the Kyoto Treaty. Chinese representatives had listened patiently but had given no indication of their intentions.

Elsewhere throughout the world he used his powers endlessly in pursuit of equity and peace, never ceasing to be astonished and repulsed by what he discovered in the inner sanctums of world leaders and those close to them. Corruption was commonplace, and he didn't hesitate to point investigative journalists in a direction that would ensure the downfall of those in question. Corruption was distasteful but understandable; greed was mankind's universal weakness. When he found it, Lincoln resolutely sought its punishment especially where it resulted in the exploitation of people. He was totally unforgiving where the abuse of children was involved or the trafficking of drugs.

In some of the African countries, where politicians and the like seemed to be impervious to exposure, he had convinced himself that he had to take direct action. He took the view that the ends justified the means. Lives ended inexplicably - by suicide, sudden fatal illness or dramatic accident. *Lord, I pray I'm following your will, that I'm on the right path.*

He never discussed such actions with Carol; some inner part of him knew that his actions were wrong. *Tell me Lord, how can it be right for evil to flourish at the expense of the innocent? Sometimes, taking life seems to be the only way to protect those who can't defend themselves. Please help me, Lord; I'm so confused at times.*

Heaven

The Old Man looked on, wondering yet again if he should intervene, wondering too how he should intervene. But in the end, he had avoided making a decision and turned his attention to other matters. He either had to trust his son, or bring him back. He was managing to avoid the Council, but the time would inevitably come when he would have to face it; fortunately, the Universe is large and his many responsibilities enabled him to defer the confrontation that undoubtedly lay ahead.

California

There was another attempt on Lincoln's life; a missile struck the executive jet in which he was travelling as it began its approach to a small airport in California. Inexplicably the missile failed to explode. The plane had lost altitude rapidly but, thankfully, the pilot had miraculously regained control and made an emergency landing at a nearby landing strip.

"That's as close as we'll ever be to death, Mr Vice-President." The pilot had told him. "We were lucky to get down safely."

Lincoln's heart was pounding. "I guess God was looking over your shoulder." *Thank you pilot and thank you too God.* The Newspapers blamed Al Queda but the culprit was never apprehended.

The White House

Diane Phelps wasn't surprised at the attempt on Lincoln's life; she had hoped one would be made. She had deliberately let slip the Vice-President's itinerary during an interview with a well-known Arab sympathiser.

However, Caswell had been shocked by the attempt and had revealed no knowledge of the incident when Lincoln had accessed the President's inner thoughts.

The assassination attempt would have remained a mystery had Lincoln not scanned Phelps during an ambassadorial social gathering at the White House. He had reasoned it had to be someone who had detailed knowledge of his travel arrangements - someone who would benefit from his demise - someone with many contacts and someone with political ambitions. The White House, Head of Communications, ticked all the boxes

It was now clear to him that Phelps had somehow convinced herself that she was acting with the President's approval, but, since Caswell wasn't aware of what was going on, she had to be acting on her own volition. Lincoln wasn't sure what to do about her but she would have to be watched; she was clearly ruthless and ambitious and would do anything to further her political career. The Irish assassination attempt and the missile incident had both resulted in failure, but Lincoln was sure there would more attempts on his life. *What will you try next Diane? Little do you know that you're wasting your time; my protector is all-powerful. But what do I do about you? Eliminate? Expose? Or do I do nothing?*

CHAPTER 24

Oval Office: Summer 2003

The President had unexpectedly asked Lincoln to call in for a chat. "Thanks for dropping in John, with your globetrotting we don't get to see each other as much as we used to."

Caswell's smile was at its brightest. "How's Carol these days? It seems an age since we all got together socially."

Lincoln returned his smile, wondering what he wanted. "Nine months more or less, Jack. Perhaps we should fix up dinner some place in town? Diane wouldn't be jealous, would she?" He couldn't resist the gibe.

Caswell refused to take the bait and even forced a laugh. "No, she won't mind; she's pretty broad-minded and we're not quite as close as we were. I'll get Beth to ring Carol and fix a date. I asked you to call in because I thought you should be the first to know; I'm going forward for a second term."

Lincoln nodded. "I expected you to and to be honest, you've been a good President in most respects; better than most. You deserve another term in the Oval Office, and judging by current polls, it'll be a landslide. The country is very proud of its Nobel Peace Prize winner; if we can keep your relationship with Diane out of the public eye it should be plain sailing."

Caswell flinched at his Vice-President's scarcely veiled threat. "Thanks for the testimony, John, I appreciate it. I've been wondering about my running mate."

Lincoln raised an eyebrow, *So, that's what this meeting is about.* "No need to wonder Jack; I'll be there at your side same as last time. You aren't thinking about breaking up a winning team or are you?"

Caswell forced disappointment out of his voice; he'd hoped that Lincoln might want to pursue his venture to create a New World order unshackled by his White House obligations.

"Not at all John; I just wanted to be sure that are happy to continue as Vice-President. Though the way I see it, you've outgrown the job. You've been so successful in pursuit of your own agenda, I thought maybe you might like to be free of the White House, and me for that matter."

Lincoln didn't hide his cynicism. "I see. I step down and leave the way clear for who Jack? You wouldn't be thinking of making your bed mate your running mate?"

"You've got me all wrong John, honest. I've made no decision pending this meeting. In any case, I don't think she's up to the job."

"My, my, had a lover's tiff?"

"Not exactly, but nothing lasts forever. You know how it is."

Lincoln smiled. "That's just fine, but I suspect she's got a firm hold of your balls and I'm not thinking pleasure-wise. She'll exact a hefty price for her services and that includes keeping her mouth shut. But that's your problem. As for me I'm going to carry on doing what I'm doing now; I'm not sure whether you see that as good news or bad news. On the other hand, you'll be relieved to know I won't be running against you, so I won't need to release any unsavoury allegations to the Washington Post about your pedigree."

Caswell couldn't hide his relief. His face broke into a smile; a second term was in the bag. "Thanks for that, I appreciate it; we've managed to work pretty well together despite our differences."

Lincoln nodded. "I'm happy with how things are at the moment. All we have to do is keep them that way."

Privately Lincoln had given serious thought to running for the Presidency, but his personal mission demanded most of his time; time that wouldn't be available if he sat in the Oval Office. America needed a strong President at home, as well as abroad and despite his shortcomings Caswell exercised his power astutely both in the Senate and in Congress. More importantly, from his point of view, Caswell was there to be used when he needed him.

The President smiled. "That's fine by me, John; you would be the people's choice for my running mate according to the polls. It'll be great to have you on board. It's a dream ticket, together we'll be unstoppable. When the other candidates get to know you're on board they'll withdraw; it'll be the first walkover since George Washington was elected unopposed back in 1792."

"Nice of you to say that Jack, thank you. I look forward to working with you. Not sure how Diane will receive the news though. By the way, whilst you and she are working on your policies for the campaign, there are three issues I'd like you to cover. You should aim to include them in your State of the Union speech next January."

Caswell gulped, felt his mouth go dry. "What have you got in mind? Nothing too radical I hope, we don't want to disillusion all that support out there."

Lincoln nodded. "Oh, it's radical alright. It's at the cutting edge of policy but I know we can pull it off; just like you did for your oil friends when you negotiated that pipeline through Afghanistan."

"What are you getting at?"

"Don't play the innocent Jack; you covered your tracks well, but my sources knew how to follow them. You're collecting a pay-off through the award of the pipeline construction contract to Overland Oil Corporation, amounting to one half of one per cent of the oil flow revenue for the first five years. It's all concealed in a Swiss Trust in Beth's name."

Caswell slumped back in his chair bewildered. *Where was the bastard getting his information from?*

Lincoln grinned at the President's discomfort. "Don't worry, distasteful as it is, as long as you play ball with me, I'll keep my mouth firmly shut. I've kept quiet about Diane, haven't I? You should have been more careful about the terms of that Trust, Jack; if Beth got to hear about Diane she could walk away with the loot."

Caswell grimaced. "OK, OK, John; don't pile it on. Just what do you want?"

"That's better Jack, I knew I could count on you. We'll have to work on the detail but I'm looking at three major areas."

The President felt sweat surface on his brow, he could feel a headache coming on. "Go on," he sighed "spit it out; don't keep me in suspense."

"I take it you don't want to guess then?"

Lincoln was extracting maximum pleasure out of the President's discomfiture. "Three big issues Jack:

Third World Debt
Planet Earth and its finite resources
Reform of the United Nations."

"Christ John, get real; I want to win another term. I can guess what you have in mind and all I can see is dollars draining away from Uncle Sam. You know the mind of voters as well as I do. Hhit them in their pocket and they'll bite back at the ballot box."

Lincoln didn't budge. "It's not negotiable, but think about it. If you don't do what I want you're finished anyway; give it a try and you might just go down as the greatest reformer of all time. I'm a realist. You can put on whatever spin you want when you're making speeches, just make sure those matters are on the agenda. And when the campaign's over, and you're safely back in the White House, I'll make sure you deliver."

Caswell was livid. "Fuck you John, fuck you good and proper. You're in the driving seat for now, but just bear in mind that everything in this world isn't under the control of the United States. There are other countries out there with vested interests."

Lincoln snorted. "Good to hear you acknowledge the fact that the entire world isn't made out of American Pie; there's hope for you yet. I promise that others will follow your lead, so go to it. History will see you as a hero. In any case just think of the logic....." He paused making sure he had the President's full attention.

"The Third World is crippled servicing its debt, but its nickels and dimes to America and the others in the G7. In some cases, the entire Gross National Product of the poorer nations is taken up just paying interest charges. If they can't afford to develop, they can't afford to purchase all the things we'd like to sell them; and then what happens? They get envious of our wealth, then what? They become terrorists. Then we spend billions bombing them; then more billions rebuilding their economy. It's a cycle we've got to break."

Caswell looked at him glumly. "Go on, tell me more."

Lincoln continued. "Planet Earth speaks for itself. Its resources are finite and we've got to conserve those resources for future generations, your children and mine. And we have to help the developing nations to do the same. You are going to revisit the Kyoto Treaty and make it work. As for the United Nations, leave that to me; I'll come up with some proposals to make it more effective. That place makes me so angry; the number of resolutions that aren't implemented is ridiculous."

Caswell shook his head. "Damn it, I don't understand you. Most of those people you're so soft on are corrupt to the core, half the aid is siphoned off before it ever gets to those it was meant for."

Lincoln clapped his hands. "Sounds like the pot calling the kettle black; you know all about corruption that's for sure. But we're still going to do our best to change things. I'm sure you can come up with some safeguards; think about it and run them past me"

Caswell was inwardly fuming but he was cornered. "Have it your fucking way; it'll be the end of both our careers. We'll see how much support you get when Joe Public starts to work out how much your insane dreams are going to cost them in taxes." The President had raised his voice; his hands were shaking with anger.

Lincoln was unmoved. "Calm down Jack, you'll give yourself a coronary. Get used to the ideas, make them work You can do it if anybody can, believe me."

Heaven

The Old Man looked on. 'You mean well but you want too much too soon my son. Mankind needs time, it does not learn easily or quickly; you are asking more than they are capable of giving. Still, the Council will welcome your intentions and, hopefully, give you more time. Many still have concerns about your work.'

The Oval Office, next day.

Diane Phelps sat opposite Caswell, the presidential desk forming a barrier he was going to need. She wanted to know the outcome of his latest meeting with Lincoln.

Caswell was uneasy, there was a question he dreaded. "Well, he's forced me to commit to three more of those new world ideas of his."

'Don't keep me in suspense, what are these new ideas?"

"Writing off Third World Debt, Planet Earth, essentially the Kyoto Agreement and more, and one I can't argue with - the reform of the United Nations."

Phelps laughed, shaking her head. 'He's crackers, the voters won't go for it. Our people won't put their hands in their pockets to bale out the Third World."

"We wouldn't be alone in the venture. The G7 and others would pitch in; it's not the first time it's been muted in private sessions."

Phelps shook her head, "Can't see it happening, and as for greening the planet, there are too many oil interests around the world, not least in the USA. It might happen someday but not in our lifetime. And as for the United Nations, good luck! Nobody will give a dime; it needs a good kick up the proverbial. But, interesting as all that may be, it's not the news I'm interested in."

The moment Caswell had dreaded had arrived, there was no place to hide. "I'm sorry, Diane, truly sorry, but he wants to be my running mate for another term. He's refused outright to stand down."

Phelps was dismayed. 'So why didn't you give him a push, you're the fucking President."

"I tried, but he's adamant. He knows too much, knows all about us and threatened to go public. I'd lose the Party's nomination, Beth would walk out, and you would be consigned to the scrap heap."

Phelp's eyes glinted, "I know about us too, Jack, and don't you forget it. I might resign and write my memoirs, do some chat shows – millions would want to know what the President was like in bed."

Caswell was between a rock and a very hard place. "I can't see what else I can do. I'm gutted. Believe me I wanted you as my running mate. I'd be more than happy to get Lincoln out of my hair.'

Phelps patted the desk with her finger for emphasis. 'I want to be Vice-President, Jack, and I won't take no for an answer."

"Let me think about it and I'll get back to you when I come up with something."

Phelps eyed Caswell, unyielding. "You'll meet me tonight in the overnight suite and we do what we always do. Afterwards we'll talk this through to a solution. The alternative is I tender my resignation now and start work on my memoirs."

Caswell was beaten and he knew it. "Have it your way, Diane; see you at seven."

Diane Phelps' Office, Later

Phelps was very disappointed, her dreams of becoming Vice-President were evaporating. She could see Carswell's dilemma and for her there was only one solution – Lincoln had to be dealt with; permanently dealt with. She had made arrangements twice and Lincoln had somehow survived, but his luck couldn't last forever. If Caswell didn't come up with a solution this evening, she would have a third try at Lincoln's assassination. But how? She didn't have an answer as yet but she would come up with one – she had to.

The Oval Office, later

Caswell sat deep in thought, as he had done since Phelps left his office an hour earlier. In truth, he admired her abilities with the media and wanted her to carry on in her current role, but he no longer wanted her as a mistress. He couldn't get rid of her; she knew too much and it would be difficult to explain. She was too good at her job; even if she kept her mouth shut the public would be suspicious. As for Lincoln, the proverbial thorn in his flesh, he couldn't sack him; he knew too much and had brought results – a Nobel Prize not to say the least. What was that old saying – *Oh what a tangled web we weave, when first we practise to deceive.* Whoever came up with that one certainly knew what they were talking about. He thought on for another hour and was on the point of taking a break when a thought came to him – it wasn't the perfect answer but it would do for now.

The Overnight Suite, 7pm.

Caswell was sitting on the sofa when Phelps entered the overnight suite, locking the door behind her. Caswell had removed his jacket, taken of his tie and had a bottle of champagne on ice. He rose immediately and kissed her. "Good to see you. Sorry we parted in bad terms earlier. Can I pour you a drink?" he motioned at the champagne, her favourite drink.

"Sure can, have we got something to celebrate?"

"You can decide that later on, Darling. First things first"

Phelps was confused but, dammit, she wanted to make love. His close proximity stirred her emotions whether she wanted or not. She watched as Caswell filled their glasses, passing her one.

"To us." He clinked her glass and quaffed it down. He pulled her close, lips and hands at work. "We'll talk later. I have a proposal to put before you."

Their sex was passionate, urgent, Caswell was more forceful than usual. Phelps wasn't complaining; it was a good sign. Afterwards they dressed and sat with a mug of coffee in hand. Phelps was first to raise the subject Caswell had been avoiding.

"OK, Jack, we've both satisfied our lust, that side of our partnership is nigh on perfect. Let's hear your proposal, good or bad."

Caswell drew a deep breath. "The way I see it I'm piggy in the middle – Lincoln can bring us both down and probably win the nomination and the Presidency – agreed?"

Phelps nodded, warily, "Agreed." She left it that; didn't add anything, didn't ask anything – he was centre stage.

"So, if I chose you as my running mate, our political careers would be over."

Phelps felt impatience stirring; they had been down this path. "Tell me something I don't know, Jack."

"Be patient, Sweetheart, I'm getting there."

Phelps all but flinched. He'd never used the term sweetheart, their relationship was about sex and power not love. "I'm listening."

"I'll come to the point. I want to ensure you get to be my Vice-President."

Phelps smiled broadly; this was good news but the way Caswell had phrased it didn't sound right. "Good news, Jack but I sense there is more to come."

There was no going back now. "There is more to come, Diane, hear me out before you react."

Phelps sighed she had been right to be wary, Caswell was about to deliver his punchline.

"If we are to survive, we both have to gain Lincoln's trust – there is no alternative. Tomorrow, I'm going to make an announcement confirming John as my running mate for the next election." He saw her eyes flash, her fists clench. "Hold on, Diane, hear me out. We win the election, we send him off on his three missions, and six to nine months into my Presidency one or two things happen."

Phelps was looking at him expectantly.

Caswell took a deep breath. "If his missions are going well you can arrange for his demise. If they aren't going well, he takes his own life, with your assistance of course. Failure would be a bitter pill to swallow for a man of his standing. In the meantime, from now on we seek to co-operate with Lincoln, build good relations and win his trust 100%. What do you think? Are you on board or not?

Phelps nodded. "Sounds good to me with one condition."

"And that is?"

"I get to decide when he gets taken out?"

Caswell smiled broadly. "We have a deal. Shall I crack another bottle?"

"Much as I'd like to, Jack, I think I want to get home and have a bath. See you in the morning. I'll leave you to tidy up and change the sheets etc." She kissed him lightly. "See you around; I'll get working on your campaign."

As she walked back to her office Phelps was deep in thought. *Could she trust Caswell? Probably, he has most to lose if things went wrong. But if you do cross me Jack, I'll make sure you suffer big time.*

CHAPTER 26

Washington

The lead up to the election had gone well, Caswell had made his pitch to the effect there was no need to 'make America great again, it was already great' and he was going to make it greater still. He won by a landslide. The headline trio, Caswell, Lincoln and Phelps had proved themselves invincible; Caswell had won a second term with the largest majority in history.

Superficially, Lincoln and Phelps had built a good working relationship, though Lincoln, whilst acknowledging her skills as a campaign manager and publicist, still hadn't developed an iota of trust in her. Phelps for her part was following Caswell's orders and waiting for the right opportunity to come along. Lincoln had suspended his ability to access their innermost thoughts; campaigning was a dirty business and he didn't want to find himself at daily loggerheads with his colleagues. His public standing was high, but he had his own agenda and needed Caswell in power to achieve his goals

Oval Office: November 2003

The two men sat facing each other just three days after the election results, Caswell was had been snowed under with congratulatory telephone calls, cards and emails.

Lincoln had been surprised at the result. "I still can't believe the size of that majority; the people really are on our side. Just think, another four years in office and then you can start writing your memoirs."

Caswell's face wore a smile of deep satisfaction. "You're right and what a story I'll have to tell. I'm really looking forward to this term, the economy is in good shape, unemployment is low, exports are booming and I've got healthy majorities in both Houses. Getting legislation through shouldn't be a problem."

"Let's hope so. I trust you haven't made too many promises to those cronies of yours; what we promised during the campaign has to be delivered or I'll have my own story to tell."

Caswell glanced anxiously at his Vice-President. "You're still serious about those ambitions of yours?"

Lincoln nodded vigorously. "You bet I am and we're going to start today. You're going to gather the G7 and the G20 together and you're going to persuade them to give an undertaking to wipe out Third World debt over the course of the next three years."

"Three years?" Caswell was shocked; this was well beyond what he'd expected. "Be reasonable John, that's impossible. Even if we could afford it, we'd never get it through both Houses."

"We can afford it and we'll get it through. I'm sure you've got lots of favours you can call in; just let me know where the blockages are and I'll see what I can do. I own a very influential media machine and I'll use it if I have to."

Caswell knew it would serve no purpose to argue and conceded. "OK, have it your way; I'll give it a go, but no promises."

"Correction, Jack; it is a promise, be sure of that. G7 is due to meet later in the year and that's when the announcement will be made. So best get started on the domestic front and I'll do a round of shuttle diplomacy with the other G7 members. We'll review where we are up to with this in six month's time."

The Oval Office: May 2004

Lincoln enjoyed a great feeling of wellbeing Six months of negotiations with G7 members had come to fruition; they had promised to participate in the elimination, or at least substantial reduction, of Third-World debt. He had taken soundings with members of the G20, and, with a little informed arm-twisting, most were on board. He was now looking to Caswell to deliver his side of the bargain.

"I've done my bit Jack; the other members of G7 are going to follow your lead and most of the G20 members are supportive. In fact, I was told that the idea had been discussed in the past, but Uncle Sam's representatives, including yourself, had always poured cold water on any suggestion of dealing with Third World debt."

The President shuffled some papers. "I confess and I still think it's a waste of time. They'll squander away any benefits, and I suspect a lot of the aid would find its way into the hands of corrupt officials. We've loaned them money in the past and they don't pay up when the time comes."

"I know all that and how interest on loans accumulate; they go sky high, become unaffordable and the cycle of defaulting on loans continues. It's not that they don't want to repay their loans, it's because they can't. We are going to break that cycle; renege on your promise at your peril.'

Caswell shook his head. 'Believe or not, I want to honour my promise but there are powerful voices in both Houses who won't let this happen. Honest, I've done my best."

Lincoln had accessed Caswell's thoughts and knew that the man opposite was telling the truth. "I believe you Jack, so this is how we're going to deal with the situation. You're going to hold a barbecue or a buffet lunch at Camp David and invite the opposition along with their partners. We'll see if we can't persuade them to change their minds. I guess you'll need to invite some supporters as well so it's not too obvious what we're up to."

The President shook his head. "It won't work. I've pushed and prodded as hard as I dare, even offered some incentives, but the resistance won't go away."

Lincoln leaned menacingly over the presidential desk. 'And I won't go away either. Do what I say, get those invitations sent out. I've saved you some trouble; I've made a list of those who you expect to speak against the proposal."

Lincoln had carried out his own research during recent visits to the Senate and Congress to ascertain the extent of support and opposition. He handed over a list. "I reckon there are twelve Senators and twenty Congressmen we need to persuade. If we can turn most of them, others will follow and we'll win the vote comfortably."

Caswell studied the list, and swallowed, they were all there. "But how did….. ?"

"How did I what? Get to know who was against the proposal? Let's just say I have my media contacts. And there's this list as well Jack."

He handed the President another list. "You'll recognise the names listed here, I'm sure."

Caswell looked at the list his hand trembling as he read. He looked up guiltily, not sure what to say.

"You got it, Jack. Those are the individuals you encouraged to speak against the proposal, even though they were happy with it. You're going to tell them you've reconsidered and want them to support the motion when it comes along. And I'm warning you for the last time; don't fuck with me. Don't pull this kind of stunt again, I'll always find out what's going on and I'll bring you down if I have to. And guess what happens if you're impeached? That's right, the Vice-President takes over. Last chance Jack, I mean it."

Caswell gulped, his face was a picture of despair, his tone forlorn. "OK, I've got it, I'll get to work on it right away."

Camp David: June 2004

The cream of America's elected representatives, makers and shakers, had gathered at the President's invitation, safely tucked away from the eyes of the media. Blue skies and a warm sun favoured the occasion; the men had dressed casually at the President's suggestion; the ladies were as always, dressed expensively.

"Nice idea Mr President; it's been a while since we've had an informal gathering of this nature." Senator Malvern's slow Southern drawl had lured many an opponent into underestimating his abilities.

Caswell smiled. "It's always nice to entertain friends, Senator."

Lincoln joined the two men, squeezing the Senator's shoulder in greeting. "Been a while Senator. How's that boy of yours getting on? Charles, isn't it? I met him during a visit to his College. I admired his vision for the World. Wants to work in Africa for a spell if I remember rightly?"

Malvern smiled disarmingly. "He's young, idealistic. He'll learn sooner or later that some people just can't be helped."

"Aw, that's a shame, I had hoped that you would share his views on lending the under-privileged a helping hand."

"As the Good Book says, Mr Vice-President, every man should carry his own burden. Charity begins at home as far as I am concerned."

Lincoln nodded agreeably. "The Good Book, as you refer to the Bible, says a lot more than that, as you well know. The Saviour was always very kind to those in need. Are you still making pictures by the way?"

Senator Malvern half-choked on his cocktail. "Pictures? What pictures are you referring to?"

Lincoln leaned forward and whispered into the Senator's ear. "Don't worry Senator, you can carry on making your sordid little skin-flicks, but make sure you support the President on Third World debt or your little secret will become front page news. Understand me?"

The Senator had gone a shade paler; suddenly his years showed. "I reckon I've got the message Lincoln. Come to think of it, the Good Book says we should help our brothers all we can."

Caswell hadn't heard Lincoln's threat but the Senator's expression told him that he had gained another supporter.

"Must circulate." Lincoln turned to leave. "Give my regards to that boy of yours Senator. Now, why don't you run along and discuss Third World Debt with the President."

Lincoln selected his next target. "Congressman Ratcliffe, Edward as I recall, I hope you're enjoying yourself."

"Sure am; what about yourself?"

"Likewise. You must be a happy man; your stockholdings must be sky-rocketing in value?"

Ratcliffe was tall and rangy with a mop of ginger hair. "I make a little bit here and there, but how come you're so interested in my financial affairs, Mr Vice-President?"

"I'm always interested in folk's good fortune Congressman, and yours is a fairy story really. Nominee buys thousands of shares in a mediocre building company then out of the blue it's awarded a multi-million-dollar State contract. Share values soar, nominee does very well. As I say, it would be a fairy story but for the fact that you Chaired the committee that awarded the contract. I believe that you used your casting vote? Then held back on the announcement until you bought the shares."

"I don't know what you're suggesting Lincoln. I believed I was awarding the contract to the company best equipped to undertake the project."

Lincoln winked. "Of course you did, Congressman but I'm not sure the media would see it that way if the details ever came out."

"What are you after? Spell it out?" Ratcliffe's face had reddened, his fists were clenched as though readying to throw a punch at his accuser.

"Calm down Ed, striking the Vice-President could have serious repercussions; I'd kick the shit out of you. You can relax this time round. I'm not really interested in your shady dealings; you can keep your gains if you do me one favour."

The Congressman stared at the Vice-President, smiling as he sensed a painless solution was on its way. "So, what do you want, a slice of the action?"

"Money is of no interest to me; I could buy and sell you a hundred times over. I just want you to wander over there and tell the President that you've decided to support the Third World Debt proposal."

"And that's all you want?" Ratcliffe was incredulous.

"That's all."

Congressman Ratcliffe shrugged his shoulders. "I'll go and tell him now. I don't give a fuck one way or the other."

Lincoln spotted his next victim. "Why Emily, how nice to see you; it's been too long."

Senator Emily Jackson was nearing sixty but most would have placed her around forty There wasn't a line to be seen around her wide hazel eyes. "We need more good-looking women in politics."

"Why bless you John, I'll take that as a compliment; you always were a charmer. I'm pleased to see that you're spending some of your valuable time in the good old USA for a change. Is Carol here today?"

Lincoln smiled, "No she had some charity work to do, and truth to tell she doesn't much care for political gatherings. As for me, I tend to go where I can do most good Emily, which is why I'm here at Camp David today. How's that husband of yours, still printing millions?"

"He's very, very rich John, eat your heart out. He makes more than I can spend that's the only pity."

She wasn't exaggerating; Abner Jackson was a Texas oil magnate who had used his wealth and influence to indulge his wife's ambition to achieve success in politics. To be fair to her, she had worked hard and had developed into a formidable politician.

Lincoln reached forward and took her hand, taking her by surprise; she tried to pull away but he held firm. "You've been a very busy lady, Emily. Some of those young men can barely cope with your attentions." He released her hand and she stood back, her eyes wide, her mouth gaping wide as she tried to digest the Vice-President's accusation.

"I don't know what you're getting at. What young men?"

"Too many to put names to Emily. I suspect you couldn't name half of them. Your latest companion is one Carlos Mendoza, before him there was Tony Prince. I wonder, does Abner know that you regularly go cruising on the look out for young studs? That blonde wig you wear for the occasion isn't much of a disguise."

Fear showed in her eyes and she looked round to ensure they weren't being overhead.

"Don't worry Emily. Nobody can hear us and I promise I won't breathe a word to Abner if you can help me out."

"What do you want, a bit on the side? I don't usually go in for coloureds but there's always the exception." Her face set in defiance, she almost hissed at him, "You men are all the same, all out for an easy mark."

"You certainly fall into that category Emily, but I'll pass if you don't mind."

He glanced over her shoulder. "Oh look, I do believe Abner is headed this way. I must ask him what he thinks of your recreational activities?"

She looked round and saw that her husband was indeed making his way towards her and turned back to Lincoln her eyes pleading. "Please, it would kill him if he knew."

"My silence is easily bought, Emily. All you have to do is to tell Jack Caswell that he can count on your vote on the Third World Debt issue. If you can do that, I can overlook your little transgressions."

"That's nothing less than blackmail!"

"What else would you expect from a coloured guy, Emily? Hi Abner, how are you doing?"

"I'm in good shape Mr Vice-President. Now what are you two cooking up?"

Emily Jackson grabbed her husband's arm in a show of affection, "Nothing much Honey; I was just telling John that I've decided to support Jack Caswell on that Third World Debt business."

Abner nodded, "Good idea, see if you can get him to write off your credit card debt whilst he's at it." He laughed gleefully at his own humour.

Lincoln took his leave. "Sorry but I have to circulate. I want to catch up with Congressman Bonnetti. "Good hunting Emily."

Lincoln had spotted Andy Bonnetti heading indoors and followed, weaving his way across the lawn, exchanging hellos with those who caught his eye. He guessed that the Congressman was headed for the Men's Room and made his way there. There was nobody else around and he made a pretence of washing his hands whilst Bonnetti busied himself at the urinal.

"Andy, it is you, isn't it?" He called over his shoulder

The Congressman half turned, "Yeah, it's me John; nice occasion. Not often I get to socialise with so many colleagues. We ought to do this more often."

Bonnetti was in his mid-thirties and had made his name as a journalist before turning to politics.

"I would have thought that you get to see plenty of them at your coke parties Andy?"

Bonnetti swung half way round, his eyes narrowing, a scowl spoiling his handsome features.

Lincoln turned to face him and pointed downwards. "Careful Andy or you'll piss on those designer trousers of yours."

"What is it with you Lincoln? Spell it out?"

"Don't be so uppity Andy; I just heard that you had quite a little set-up going at those parties of yours. I hear that there's free coke and lots of young lovelies; I know for a fact that some of them are underage."

Bonnetti eyed Lincoln cautiously. "What about it?"

Lincoln winked. "I hear tell that Congressmen Sanders, Wilson and McKay are regular players."

"Who have you been talking to Lincoln? What's your interest? You can have an invite if that's what you're looking for?"

"No thanks Andy, I don't fancy you or your wife. I hear she puts herself about at those orgies just as much as you do. I'm not into wife-swapping. I was just wondering where my civic duties lie; the people ought to know about their elected representatives' interests, don't you agree? As an ex-journalist you should know what a good story it would make. Come to think of it, I'm looking for some good political dirt to liven up my networks."

Bonnetti took a threatening step forward and wagged a warning finger. "You wouldn't dare, you can't prove anything."

Lincoln smiled. "I assure you I have all the evidence I need. Tune into my channels next week if you don't believe me."

The Congressman began to back-pedal. "Can't we discuss this, John; it's just some harmless fun after all?"

"Pull your zip up Andy; I can't really see why women are attracted to you. There isn't going to be any discussion, I'll tell you exactly what I want."

"Enlighten me."

"I want you and your cokehead cronies to support the President when the Third World Debt Bill comes before Congress."

The Congressman stifled a laugh. "Is that what this is about? Arm-twisting to drum up support for the President?"

He pulled his zip up. "Sure, he can have my vote, and I'll talk to the others. Now will you excuse me, I want to wash my hands."

"Just make sure you and your friends deliver, or I promise you'll make the headlines. One more thing Bonnetti, put an end to underage invitations."

Lincoln continued to engage the politicians on the list for the rest of the afternoon and the all too familiar story of human frailty or corruption emerged in all but eight of the thirty-two politicians targeted. *How did some of these people get into politics?*

Later

When all the guests had gone, Lincoln met up with the President to check on progress.

Caswell shook his head. "I wish I knew how you do it John; folks have been coming up to me all afternoon claiming that they're having second thoughts about the Third World Motion. You must have a big hold over these people."

"It's a one-off exercise Jack; just put it down to friendly persuasion. I reckon that there are twenty-four converts to your cause, ten Senators and fourteen Congressmen. That represents a big swing in the voting numbers and, by my reckoning, it's enough to get the Motion through."

Caswell nodded glumly. "You're sure you can rely on them?"

"Just as sure as I can rely on you Jack; cheer up, it's a victory."

The President poured himself a Jack Daniels and looked out over the lawn; waiters were clearing tables, chatting cheerfully as they went about their work. "I'm still not sure about this; the Finance world won't like it. The economy is strong but this kind of thing gives the money men the jitters."

Lincoln shook his head, "Its peanuts and you know it is. It's a tiny ripple in the great scheme of things, little more than a fleabite where the combined wealth of the G7 and G20 is concerned. We can afford it; sell it to both Houses, I know you can. Lift everybody's horizons. Good old Uncle Sam, we're the good guys. Go heavy on the rhetoric, instil some vision; show the World what a statesman you are." Lincoln paused, looking for a new tack, he could see Caswell wasn't convinced. "Think about it. If we can unshackle these countries, they'll be our friends for a long time to come. It'll create future markets for our products. And if their living conditions improve, there's less chance of terrorism being nurtured. Added to that the world will see you as a real visionary, a stateman extraordinaire. Who knows - maybe another Nobel Prize will follow."

Caswell's face broke into a smile, "You're right as always, John, I'll give it my best shot. Whilst we're talking about this, just out of interest; we have the G7 and the G20 but what does the G stand for; I've never heard it mentioned?"

'Simple, Jack, it stands for Group.''

Barcelona : November 2004

G7, supported by the G20, announced that it would eliminate Third World debt over the course of the next four years.

Caswell was excusing the extended period to his Vice-President. "I know you wanted it achieved in three years, John but it was the best I could negotiate with the others. Financial climates have changed since we started out on this."

Lincoln patted the President's shoulder. "Never mind, you can surprise them by writing off America's chunk in three, just as you promised me, and just as Senate and Congress agreed. I'll revisit our G7 partners and see what I can come up with. Now, don't you feel good? The biggest benefactor the World has ever known? You will surely be a contender for another Nobel Prize."

Caswell allowed himself a wry smile. "Fuck it, do you never let up?

The Vice-President shook his head slowly, raising an eyebrow. "Just do it Jack."

"OK, OK, you win as usual. God help me. At home I'm seen as going soft, overseas I'm becoming a hero."

"I guess that's the way of it. Now that we've got Third World Debt out of the way we must talk about the next steps in our campaign."

Caswell rolled his eyes in despair. "Please, not now; don't spoil my day completely."

CHAPTER 27

Heaven

The Old Man was looking forward to the next meeting with the Council; many had acknowledged that the situation on Earth had improved greatly, and for the moment there was a grudging acceptance that perhaps the Return had been justified after all. He would have to tread carefully though, there were still those who continued to be unhappy about the methods that had been employed.

He would point out that the Old Testament had once taught 'an eye for an eye, a tooth for a tooth'; surely using fire to fight fire was not unreasonable in pursuit of a greater good? Millions were already benefiting from what had been achieved this far. Inevitably He would been asked 'where is the line to be drawn?' and would answer 'we will know where when the time comes.' Sadly, deep down, he believed that the line had already been crossed.

The Overnight Suite: November 2004

Caswell and Phelps were still lovers. Much to his surprise, the young blonde staffer he had had his eye on, had rebuffed his advances, so he had rekindled his desire for Phelps.

"That was great, Jack, your performance has gone up a level. Are you on some kind of booster? One of those Chinese herbs.'

"No need, Babe, the only incentive I need is right here in bed with me."

Phelps smiled broadly and snuggled in close Now seemed a good time to approach a difficult matter. "Jack, I know you won't want to hear this, but…."

He interrupted her. "You're not going to tell me you're pregnant!?"

"Don't be silly, I don't want kids with you or any other man. I want to remind you of the promise you made in the lead up to your election – about me becoming the Vice-President."

Caswell gulped. "I do want you as my Vice-President but I just haven't come up with a way to make it happen."

"We both know how to make it happen – Lincoln has got to have a fatal accident, that's all. Just give me the go ahead and I'll make it happen."

To her astonishment Caswell didn't rebuff her suggestion outright. "OK, you have my permission to do whatever you have in mind; you can decide where and how. But I want to decide when, and right now I need him, America needs him and, arguably, the World needs him."

"Needs him for what, Jack?"

"Greening this planet of ours. I've just read the latest scientific reports on the state of the environment and with the latest rise in the average world temperature, we've gone into the red zone. Time is running out, Diane."

Phelps sighed, she had read the same reports. What Caswell had said was true. "So, what are you suggesting?"

"The main thing is to get China to sign up to the Kyoto Agreement and the only chance of that coming about is for Lincoln to use that charm on the Chinese. If he can get the China on board, I'm sure I could persuade our people to redouble our efforts to reduce greenhouse gas emissions. We're as bad as China when it comes to ruining the environment.

"And think about it. If he were to achieve that, he could drop out of the picture completely. You could arrange that when the time was right. You would be my choice for Vice-President, and you would inherit a great world-wide scenario. The Presidency would be yours for the taking when my term of Office came to an end."

Phelps' thought processes were working overtime. What Caswell had described did sound very plausible; there was just one thing missing - timescale."

Sounds great, Jack; I just have one problem with what you've just put forward – timescale. When is Lincoln going to embark on this mission; when is he heading for China?"

"I intend to meet with him when he gets back from his current trip to Africa, probably early January. How does that suit?"

"Sounds good to me. Just make sure it happens or I'll take control of the timescale; I have plans for our Mr. Lincoln. Now all this talk of power politics has made me randy, let's get our mind back on the job."

January 2005: Oval Office

"Happy New Year and welcome back, John. I hope your trip to Africa brought results."

"Happy new Year to you Jack, especially so on the second anniversary of your Presidency."

Caswell had given up trying to resist his Vice-President's demands; Lincoln always seemed to be a step ahead. Besides, he had done well out of Lincoln's efforts and Diane had seen to it that he had been given undue credit for his Vice-President's many successes. He had stolen the limelight whenever he could, and promoted the belief that his hand was always on the tiller. Lincoln didn't seem to mind and relationships had been on the up for over a year.

Caswell had to acknowledge that the political climate around the globe was changing for the better, and at a much quicker rate than he could ever have imagined. America was winning friends and countries were coming to expect a fair deal from Uncle Sam. Better still, contrary to what he had feared, the effect on the economy overall had been negligible. There was an added bonus; it seemed that when the outside world praised the President, the electorate felt good about itself and, as a result, worked harder and spent more. *Maybe the voters felt it demonstrated how clever it was of them to elect him as President.*

Lincoln smiled and sat down opposite the Caswell. 'My visit to Africa went well. I wasn't there asking for anything from them, and that makes it easy. Our debt relief programme is serving them well and there's much less corruption around. I made it clear to them, if I discovered any corruption, our financial support would end instantly and high tariffs would be applied to their exports. A harsh warning but all the nations I visited acknowledged that it was a justifiable policy.”

“Sounds good, John, you sure know how to win them over. Now I have some good news for you. I’m preparing my State of the Union Address and I want to advance a major appeal for America to save the Planet. But I need China on board, or at least listening to the argument for reducing carbon dioxide emissions and all those other noxious gases. If you can get our Chinese friends to go down the same route, I’m sure folks at home will fall into line.”

Lincoln smiled broadly, he was completely taken aback, this was total unexpected. “It’s a wish come true to hear you say what you’ve just said, Jack, thank you. You’ve made my job so much easier. I promise you I’ll give it my best shot, but the Chinese won’t roll over, they’ll take a lot of persuading.

“I’ve been thinking about our approach and I think you should make recycling and greenhouse gas emissions the responsibility of individual States. I’ll help you persuade State Governors to go along with the idea. Maybe we could offer a big incentive for the best performer? Americans like a competition, especially if it brings a prize at the end of the process. Really poor performers could be subject to a small Federal tax levy, maybe one that would be re-invested locally to reduce energy consumption. I’ll leave those thoughts with you.”

“Thanks for those ideas, John, but I’m thinking on an even bigger prize. I am going to sign up to the Kyoto Agreement, of course, but I want China to sign up as well. I want you to go over there and use persuasion or threat; big tariffs on their exports would be a frightener. I should never have pulled out of it; I know that now. My reasoning was misguided and I was desperate to win a second Term. I recognise it’s a major U-turn but it’s one that’s essential; the latest environment reports have convinced me. Our people know what signing up to Kyoto means; I spelt it out for them when we withdrew. They won’t like it when it starts to hit their pockets but we might just win them over if we can persuade China and others to join in.”

Lincoln patted the desk in front of him and gave Carswell the thumbs up. "I'd better get going, I have a lot of work to do. Thanks again, Jack I'm going to give it everything I've got.

Lincoln stood and was half way across to the door when Caswell called out. "John, come back please, there's one other matter I want to raise."

Lincoln turned and was surprised at the look of apprehension, fear almost, he saw on Caswell's face. "What's wrong? I've never seen you look so troubled. How can I help.'

"It's Diane, she's desperate to be my Vice-President mate and I've fobbed her off but you know the hold she has over me. She's insisting that she gets to be Vice-President before my time is out. I've strung her along best I can and she's agreed to wait until after your visit to China. After that I think she's so desperate she'll try to arrange your assassination. God forgive me, I should never have let it get this far. I'm so sorry, John.'

"It comes as no surprise, Jack. It won't be the first time she's tried; there have been two attempts that I know off. Say nothing of our conversation, I'll deal with. Diane."

"Be careful, John, she's dangerous. Watch your back, please.'

January 2005: State of the Union Address

Caswell was coming to the end of his State of the Union Address; he had pulled out all the stops and delivered a rousing upbeat speech. Lincoln had to give the man credit; he was a great speechmaker and knew how to engage with his audience.

"….. and that is why I have decided to sign up to the Kyoto Agreement. I do it not for today's Americans, I do it for our children, and for their children. I invite China and other nations to join with America in a quest for a better Earth. I will be asking Vice-President Lincoln to make this initiative his top priority, such is the importance I afford this issue."

The applause from the assembled politicians was polite. The rapturous adulation of previous years was missing but he'd done it and he now had to deliver. *Don't let me down John; we need another one of your miracles.*

281

Oval Office: Next day

"How has my Address gone down, Diane?" Caswell was worried; he had known that the politicians would be lukewarm about his Kyoto undertaking but he could handle them. It was Public's reaction that concerned him.

Diane Phelps pursed her lips. "You've just about got away with it, Jack. Laying it on the children always tugs at the public's conscience, but it's finely balanced. I reckon the Polls will swing your way when you announce those big investments in energy research, especially if you choose your States carefully; dollars always buy votes. The National Energy Competition will be a winner if the reward is big enough. The World stage is going to be important too, we need some or all of the other non-signatories to the Treaty to follow your lead. Do that and you'll be home and dry. China is key, get China on board and you'll win the day."

Caswell smiled wryly. "I guess we have to pin our hopes on Lincoln's trip to China for that. Which reminds me, did we ever get an inkling of where he gets his inside information? It can't all be attributed to his media contacts; some of the stuff is way above that level. If I didn't know better, I'd think there was a leak right here in the White House."

Phelps squirmed. "I haven't come up with anything you would regard as tangible."

Caswell sensed she was holding something back. "Out with it, Diane. If you haven't got anything tangible, just what have you got?"

"Well," she said hesitantly, "I got a contact at the Pentagon to run some scenarios through Oracle, all hypothetical of course. Basically, we asked it what were the most likely sources of access to your most classified knowledge, both personal and State."

Caswell recalled that Oracle had cost nearly a billion dollars. It was an advanced computer the Pentagon used to evaluate hypotheses; it was unhampered by human bias or the diplomatic consequences of its analyses. It examined situations as described and dealt with them on the basis of pure rationale.

Caswell nodded. "Good idea, so what did it come up with?"

Phelps pulled a face. "Well, it didn't really come up with any concrete answers. You know computers as well as I do, *'insufficient data to reach a conclusion'* was the message on the bottom line."

Caswell's face showed his disappointment, "Damn."

Phelps paused for a moment, unsure whether to go on or not. "But it did come up with three possibilities."

Caswell sighed and showed his irritation. "Move on for Christ's sake; don't spin it out."

"Patience, I'm getting to it. It came up with three possibilities, two of them fairly predictable." She licked her lips nervously; she knew the President wasn't going to be pleased.

"First off it suggested that it might be a well-placed ally, like say the British Prime Minister. I guess you tell him most things?"

Caswell snorted. "Absolute rubbish; I don't tell him everything and I can't see he'd have a motive. Next?"

"It also suggested that the source could be a close confidant, here in the White House or within your family."

Caswell paused, exploring the possibilities in his mind. "Well, it's not Beth, of that, I'm sure; she barely knows a Republican from a Democrat. But a straightforward leak is a possibility. The leak would have to be at the highest level, someone with access to all my mail and papers. When I think about it, Mary O'Halloran fits the bill or,....." He hesitated, looking at Phelps closely, searching her expression for a reaction to his barely concealed accusation, "or you. I know it's not Mary, she's as loyal and trustworthy as the day is long."

Phelps reacted angrily, "Well I can assure you it's not me Jack. Don't forget the information Lincoln has got could damage me as much as you. I need you Jack, my future is in your hands; you can trust me completely, in bed and out of it."

Caswell snorted. "I don't trust anybody, completely."

Phelps smiled and pouted. "Not even little old me?"

Caswell raised an eyebrow. "You're too ambitious and unprincipled to be trusted completely Diane, but I don't think for one moment you would betray me. At least not whilst you harbour notions of advancing your political career. You mentioned three possibilities, what's the third one?"

"You're not going to like it."

Caswell made no reply and waited for her to go on.

"Oracle came up with the term, *involuntary telepathy.*"

"What in the hell is that exactly?"

"Well basically it means that without wanting to, you somehow convey your thoughts to a third party, Lincoln in this case. In other words, Lincoln can read your mind."

Caswell banged his fist on the desk, anger in his voice. "Jesus Christ, that machine cost us nearly a billion dollars and it comes up with an answer out of science fiction. That's fucking great, John Lincoln is a mind-reader, now I've heard everything. Oracle is like all computers, rubbish in, rubbish out."

Phelps moved round behind him nuzzling his ear, both hands caressing his chest. "I guess we just have to hope that somewhere along the way Lincoln meets with an accident, a terminal accident."

Caswell pulled away and swivelled round.

"Don't panic, nothing will happen till he gets back from China. For the moment, it's just a line on my wish list. You must admit it would be simpler if he wasn't around."

"Right now, I need him to deliver on his promises."

"Whatever you say Jack, but you know what we agreed. Sometime down the line, it's going to happen."

"We already have an understanding, don't speak to me about this subject again. Understood?

Phelps understood, the buck was entirely in her court, Caswell agreed, he just didn't want to talk about it. "You need to relax Jack, have some fun. What say I call in to see you later on?"

"Sorry, really sorry, I promised Beth I'd get back early tonight."

"Then it'll just have to be tomorrow. Don't let me down or I'll be thinking you've gone off me, and that wouldn't be at all good."

Caswell's eyes narrowed at the scarcely concealed threat but he said nothing.

CHAPTER 28

Beijing: February 2005

Lincoln visited the capital of China ostensibly to enquire if a Presidential visit by Jack Caswell would be welcome. To his relief, Head of State Chiang Zongji, advised that such a visit would be welcome, provided a reciprocal visit to the United States took place within the following twelve months.

"President Caswell would be honoured, Sir; he expressed such a hope before I left." Lincoln was lying but he knew it would please his host. His Chinese vocabulary and pronunciation had improved over the months and he now rarely referred to the interpreter provided by his host. He had invoked his telepathic powers and to his surprise found that Chiang Zongii had an impeccable background. *A clean politician, good for you. Not that it helps me much.*

"Perhaps these two historic visits could be used to signal to the world a strengthening of our relationships, perhaps even herald some partnership initiatives."

"Partnership Mr Lincoln? What kind of partnership do you envisage?"

"I had in mind Commerce and Research, perhaps Anti-Terrorist Activity."

Chiang Zongii smiled enigmatically and leaned back in his chair; *the American was fishing for something, but what?*

"Trade between our two countries is already growing rapidly and we try to build closer trade links whenever the opportunity presents. Our arrangements to counter terrorist attacks are, I would assert, well developed although we do not always publicise our successes. I cannot help but observe that you make no mention of Human Rights; most visiting leaders inevitably raise this subject, yet you do not. This surprises me Mr Lincoln. I had thought that the unfortunate events of Tiananmen Square were still uppermost in the minds of Western politicians?"

Lincoln abhorred what happened in Tiananmen Square but now wasn't the time to dwell on the past. "Tiananmen Square was a tragedy Sir, but it was a tragedy which occurred sixteen years ago, and I think that the Republic has moved on since then. I am sure that all countries can improve their democratic processes to allow their people a greater voice, and that of course includes China."

The Chinese leader smiled and inclined his head. "A diplomatic reply Mr Lincoln and I believe you are sincere. Kim Jeng Pol has spoken well of you and considers that you are to be trusted."

It was Lincoln's turn to incline his head. "That was generous of him. He found your assistance in facilitating discussions with North Korea to be invaluable."

"We will continue to do what we can; the two countries have developed a much greater understanding following the NKX1 outbreak. You mentioned Research as an area for partnership and presumably this might involve investment?"

Lincoln smiled. So often money oiled the wheels of politics, and even a country as great as China was not immune. "Provided we could identify suitable projects I'm sure that appropriate investment would follow. I see opportunities in Space Science, Medicine and Renewable Energy. Any or all of these would involve long term partnerships, don't you agree? The entire world could benefit from the joint resources of our two great countries."

China's Head of State allowed a trace of a smile to cross his lips; he liked this American. "Then we must see what we can do, Mr Lincoln. You continue to surprise me; you have made no mention of the troublesome Kyoto Agreement."

Lincoln nodded and spread his hands. "As you are aware Sir, America has only just re-signed the Agreement; it is not for me to preach the wisdom of ecology. I readily acknowledge that America is a major source of atmospheric pollution, and we must all do what we can to reduce our carbon footprint. Obviously, we hope that all countries will sign the Agreement in due course, including China."

Chiang Zongji shook his head. "I am afraid that China is not ready to sign the Agreement. We have far to go in our development before we can afford the expensive goal of becoming energy efficient. The population of China is huge; it increases by fifteen million each year and this adds to our need for resources. And we mustn't forget that China has become the world's workshop; everyone benefits from our inexpensive products and inevitably this fuels demand for energy."

Lincoln nodded his understanding. "I understand the difficulties but perhaps you could give a tangible signal of your intentions to reduce China's carbon footprint? For instance, you might enter into a partnership with America to research forms of renewable energy. There would be benefits for China as well as for this small planet of ours. I also believe that China should receive greater reward for its exports, and I would work towards that goal if I could claim that higher costs were reflected in more investment in sustainability."

Chiang Zongji threw back his head and laughed; this was what the American wanted - this was why he had come to China. "Do you perhaps play chess, Mr Lincoln? I think you would be a worthy opponent. I make no promises, but I will give further thought to this partnership you speak off, perhaps in time for President Caswell's visit."

"Thank you, Sir, I can ask no more."

As he shook hands Lincoln knew that the Chinese leader would be true to his word.

Beijing: August 2005

President Caswell's State visit to China was an overwhelming success and concluded in the signing of a Joint Statement which promised collaborative research into a wide range of matters, including renewable forms of energy and an important undertaking by China to review the terms of the Kyoto Agreement. It was a small concession but the spin-doctors ensured that it was seen as a triumph for the President's diplomatic skills.

Caswell had around eighteen months left of his Presidency and was giving thought to his future when he retired from political life. He was America's golden boy, there were good times ahead. Or were there? There was a fly in the ointment, two flies in fact; Diane Phelps and John Lincoln; they both new too much about the darker side of his life. Either or both could at any time spill the beans about the misdeeds of his Presidency. A couple of days before he had boarded Air Force One for Beijing, Phelps had told him that she had decided it was time to deal with Lincoln, on a permanent basis. He hadn't dissented but hadn't enquired what she had in mind; if she was successful, one of the threats to his future would be eliminated. That would leave Phelps and he'd had an idea in mind how to deal with her.

Oval Office; January 2006

Caswell and Lincoln sat together in the Oval Office drinking coffee and reflecting on World affairs. The Vice-President was looking ahead to the President's retirement.

"Just twelve months to go Jack, then you can put your feet up on that ranch of yours or travel the World in style earning exorbitant fees for speaking at public engagements. Or are you going to take time out to write your memoirs?"

Tensions between the two men had eased since the China trip and, as the end of his Presidency drew nearer, Caswell had grown more relaxed about Lincoln's excursions; they all seemed to end up to his benefit. He was indeed going to publish his memoirs and make sure he did so before the man opposite decided to do the same.

Caswell smiled. "Never thought I'd say it but I'm looking forward to getting out of politics; I've seen it all and done it all. And what about you John? No doubt you'll be looking to step into my shoes?"

To his surprise Lincoln shrugged. "Who knows Jack, I haven't made my mind up on that one. It has its attractions, but I enjoy what I'm doing now and I reckon I've made a difference over the last three or four years."

"I'll grant you that, but I doubt you would have fared so well without the backing of the President of the United States, willing or otherwise? Granted you set the direction of travel but I had to pull the levers. You were right though, and America's standing in the world has never been higher, albeit our wallet is a touch lighter than it used to be. You've been a real maverick and I've picked up a bundle of grey hairs along the way."

Lincoln didn't quite see it that way. Caswell had often been a barrier to progress as far as he was concerned and he wasn't going to give him a pat on the back. He had the ultimate silent partner and was sure he could have made it all happen, with or without the President's cooperation.

"It's been worth it, Jack; our economy is strong and our efforts will pay big dividends in the long term. And we mustn't forget, you did get a Nobel Prize out of it."

Caswell wasn't looking for an argument, but he believed he was right and stood his ground. "Having me in your corner, willing or otherwise, suited you too John; that's how politics work. Seriously, if the White House doesn't back you when I'm no longer in office, it won't be easy for you to stride the world making change. Do give some thought to running for the Presidency." In truth Caswell didn't care whether or not Lincoln would run for the Presidency, he just wanted to be sure of Lincoln's plans.

Lincoln nodded. "I will, Jack. Now to the point of my visit; we've got one more mission, you and I, before you leave Office."

Caswell sighed resignedly. "I'll try not to dissent. Go ahead, strike fear into my heart yet again. What are you after now?"

"As I told you previously, I want to restructure the United Nations, make it more democratic and effective."

Caswell shook his head. "Making it more democratic won't make it more effective, you know that; it'll grind to a halt if everybody has a say in everything. You've seen it in action; it talks itself to a standstill time and time again. It produces Resolution after Resolution that it never enforces, unless Uncle Sam takes control that is. It's nothing more than a debating society."

Lincoln responded firmly. "It's the only world forum we have, and we need it for all its faults. We owe it to our children and their children, to make it an effective body. If we don't succeed, America will end up being the world's policeman in perpetuity, or at least until someone takes that role away from us. And who knows who that might be or where it might lead? I agree, it doesn't have a shining history, but the fundamental concept of the United Nations can't be faulted and it's up to its members to make it work."

Caswell rubbed his face in his hands in despair. "OK have it your way. What have you got in mind? Just how do you think you are going to make it more effective? I know from experience it's a waste of time arguing with you once you get the bit between your teeth."

Lincoln had given a lot of thought to a solution; it couldn't be too radical and it had to be relevant to the smaller nations. The influence of the larger nations had to be reduced and there was a need for greater geographic autonomy over local issues.

"The way I see it, the United Nations should be broken down into six blocks; the Americas, Asia, Europe and Russia, Africa, the Indian Sub-continent and Australia-Oceania.

There would be six Security Councils, one for each Block, dealing with matters in their own sphere of operation. Above them there would be the United Nations Executive Council, UNEC, composed of one representative from each of the geographic blocks. There would be a permanent Secretary-General managing the Executive Council; Chairmanship of the other Councils would be on a rotation basis."

Caswell shrugged. "I could live with that, doesn't seem too radical. We know that those blocks, as you describe them already hold informal meetings behind the scenes; they've scuppered many resolutions."

Lincoln was surprised at getting the President's agreement so readily and continued enthusiastically. "There would be a lot of autonomy and devolved power. Regions would have to sort out their own problems, America wouldn't have its finger in every pie, and there would be no permanent members on the Executive Council."

Caswell shook his head violently. "No way! We need to sit at the top table; we need to be at that level, we need to have the power to veto. We won't be the only ones who feel that way; Britain and France won't go along with it. In fact, I doubt if any of the current permanent members will; they'll all cling to the status it brings."

Lincoln frowned. "I'm disappointed in you Jack. I had hoped that by now you would have stopped worrying about America calling the shots in every arena. The USA is the most powerful nation on this planet and will be for a long time to come; we have the technology and the wealth to ensure our position of pre-eminence. In the final analysis we can do what we want, when we want to, and being on or off the Security Council doesn't affect that."

Caswell cupped his chin in his hands and leaned forward on his desk. "I give up John. So just how do you think this restructuring is going to be achieved? Are you about to produce that magic wand of yours again, or just rely on a miracle this time?"

Lincoln, aped Caswell and leaned forward, resting his chin on his cupped hands.

"It's going to be brought about by example and persuasion, same as always. Anyway, I reckon there aren't too many countries that will object to power being shared out on a more equitable basis. More countries are going to get the opportunity to sit at the top table and that must be good for democracy. I suspect the main opposition will come from our own politicians and we can deal with that."

Lincoln winked at the President. "We can, can't we? You understand me, don't you? And, as I see it, the European Union will deal with Britain and France, which leaves Russia and China as possible objectors. But if everyone else comes into line I doubt if they would stand alone against the proposal. It's like a row of dominoes; one falls they all fall."

Caswell looked at his Vice-President admiringly. "Is this the end of your crusade John or do you have some other ideals hidden away in that head of yours?"

Lincoln grinned broadly. "Nothing that can't wait Jack, but world-wide disarmament, at least at nuclear and missile level, must be the ultimate goal. A long-term plan to scale down weapons to tactical level would be wonderful, just the thing for a reformed United Nations to cut its teeth on."

Caswell looked at his Vice-President in astonishment. "You're not serious, are you? No country will give up its means of defence. The small fry might, but very few countries will ultimately agree to leave their borders without defence. If I were you, I wouldn't even give that idea an airing."

Lincoln was adamant. "It's a tough one, I grant you, but a strong United Nations would be their best defence and mankind can't go on fighting wars forever."

Caswell laughed. "Come off it, John, get your feet back on the ground. Mankind has fought wars since the beginning of time, it's in the genes. Some things will never change. Forget it, listen to me for once."

"I'll leave it for now, but sooner or later, I'll try to make it happen. Best get used to the idea."

"And will you run for the President?"

Lincoln shrugged. "I don't know; I'll think it over tonight and come back to you with a decision tomorrow."

"And that's a promise, John?"

"'It's a promise."

"Just one thing; I'd like Diane to be present. She'll have to handle the announcement and might have some questions to ask?"

Lincoln shrugged. "No problem. She has many faults but she's a good publicist."

CHAPTER 29

Oval Office: Next morning

Caswell and Phelps were waiting for Lincoln when Mary O'Halloran ushered him into the Oval Office. They both wished him good morning as he took his seat opposite the President. Phelps sat on his left and he moved his seat a little so he could see both their expressions when he responded to their questions.

Caswell was first to speak, "I hope you got a good night's sleep, John. It's quite a decision you have to make; it would have kept me awake all night."

"I had no problem getting off to sleep, Jack, I made my mind up before I went to bed."

Phelps nodded, "Smart move, I always try to clear my thoughts before I settle down for the night."

Caswell leaned forward expectantly. OK, we've covered the pleasantries, what decision have you come to?"

"I'm going to leave US politics and devote my time to the United Nations. I won't be running for the Presidency this time round."

He had barely finished his reply when Phelps asked for more detail in a not too polite manner. "We're all going to leave politics sooner or later. When exactly are you going to make your exodus?'

"If you hadn't dived in so quickly, Diane, I'd have gone on to tell you. Don't let your ambitions get the better of you."

Phelps bit on her tongue. "Apologies but it's not myself I was thinking about. I was thinking about Jack and what he'd have to do if you handed in your resignation today. Sorry if I've offended you.'

Caswell interceded his voice soft. "So, what have you decided, John?"

Lincoln smiled, "I'm sure you'll be delighted to know that I'm going to stay on as Vice-President for the remainder of your Presidency."

Caswell smiled broadly, "Thank you, John; I thank you, America thanks you. It's the answer I hoped for."

Lincoln had watched for Phelps' reaction out of the corner of his eye and to his surprise she hadn't displayed any sign of disappointment. Inwardly, Phelps was fuming, *bastard,* but she knew she had to turn on the charm. "That's great news, you two are the best Presidential team in White House history. It will be my privilege to present this wonderful news to our people. Everyone is a winner today."

Lincoln nodded respectfully. 'Thank you for those generous words, Diane. I've got nothing to add so I'll go now and get on with planning my United Nations campaign."

Phelps raised her hand. 'Please keep me briefed on that, John, I'll help in any way I can with publicity. A random thought has just occurred to me, an event that maybe you can help me with."

'Try me out, I'll help if I can"

'You were in the Air Force, if I recall correctly?"

Lincoln nodded. *What are you up to?* Caswell looked on, a puzzled expression on his face. "I served five years in the Air Force, why do you ask?"

"Ever done a parachute jump?"

"Where is this leading, Diane?"

Caswell butted in, "Yeah, what are you on about? Let us in on it.'

"I'm doing a parachute jump on 4th July and wondered if John would like to join me. I'm raising money for UNICEF, and just thought with John's interests in the welfare of children throughout the world, he might like to join in. I want to raise as much as I can, and I'm sure his participation would push charitable giving through the roof. If he doesn't feel like taking part, he can at least be my first sponsor."

Caswell thumped his desk. "No way is the Vice-President taking part in a risky venture like that. What the hell are you thinking about?"

"Hold on, Jack, it's my decision and I'd very much like to take part. And as for sponsorship, I'll donate fifty thousand dollars and give the event maximum publicity via my media outlets. Now how much are you putting on the table, Mr President?'

"You're mad, John, fucking mad." He shook his head sensing Lincoln was determined. "I'll match your fifty grand."

"Fantastic, you guys are so generous. I've just had another thought. Let's keep quiet about John doing the jump, just headline that it's a masked celebrity and create a bit of a mystery."

Lincoln nodded. "I like that idea: I'll leave the publicity side to you. Can you let me have details of the jump - when, where and what height are we jumping from?'

Phelps was over the moon; everything was going as she hoped. Lincoln's days were numbered. "The jump is on Independence Day, 4th July: we jump from a helicopter into Central Park in New York. Provided weather conditions are good we'll jump from about eight thousand feet."

Lincoln glanced at his watch. "Sounds great. I have a meeting soon, must go. We'll talk through the details nearer the time, Diane, bye for now." *I wonder what you have in store for me, Diane? I hope my Guardian Angel has the date in his diary.*

Lincoln's United Nations Campaign
January to June 2006

In the six months that followed, Lincoln shuttled tirelessly from continent to continent, often with Carol at his side, manoeuvring and manipulating, pressuring and persuading, blackmailing and bribing those in power, towards a new United Nations. It proved more difficult than he had anticipated; everyone accepted the concept but the administrative detail and bureaucracy hindered the process.

Election methods, rotation frequencies, veto versus majority voting, levels of autonomy, big countries with their huge populations versus small countries, rich versus poor, the regularity of meetings, information sharing. The chain of obstacles had been relentless. One obstacle after another seemed to emerge, often forcing him to retrace his steps. There were times when he thought the whole process would grind to a halt. It was a veritable nightmare. *Please God help me, don't let me fail now.*

Eventually, frustrated and disillusioned, he had resorted to the liberal use of his powers, convincing himself that he had been given them to use as he saw fit. Recalcitrant politicians were eliminated; others were deposed or discredited as he relentlessly pursued his objective.

Time and time again he felt himself grappling with his conscience, as he struggled to make decisions, but increasingly he told himself that the ends justified the means. In the end he stopped questioning what was right and what was wrong; his will would be done no matter what. *What I'm doing must be right. I am the junior partner after all, the Lord's will be done.*

He didn't tell Carol of his dark side and wondered if she had guessed at the truth. She told him increasingly often, *'that might wasn't right'* and of the need to remember the Bible's teachings. Eventually she had given up and become detached. Wherever they were, she insisted on going to a local church to pray and he knew she was struggling to deal with the moral and ethical dilemma she had been drawn into by some of her husband's actions. He feared he was losing her. Worse still, had lost her.

Heaven

The Old Man faced the Council again; many had approached him individually voicing their concern and demanding a formal assembly of all members. He knew the time had come; the Council's collective patience was finally exhausted.

"He must be brought back or at the very least His powers curtailed. Good must triumph over evil, but not at any price. There are lines that must not be crossed, whatever the circumstances. We must abide by our own moral and ethical codes and comply with our own teachings. We think He should be brought back."

The Old Man knew they were right, yet still sought to excuse what was happening. "Earth has improved; it is a better place for his interventions."

"That cannot be denied, but lives are being taken simply because they do not share his vision at this time. The right to free choice has been transcended by his will. People are being sacrificed for no other reason than they believe that their world should be governed in a different way. If you wanted humankind to act mindlessly without choice, you should have made it so. They have to evolve in their own way and at their own speed. There has been too much interference by your son."

The Old Man looked round seeking support but saw none. "I have to disagree. In the grand design of life on Earth, these are small departures from our ideals: many will benefit greatly if his plans are fulfilled. Mankind will take a giant step forward."

Murmurs of protest challenged his statement; heads shook in disagreement, dissent showed in every face. He scanned their faces for support, but disapproval was unanimous.

"I do not want to stop his work. We can learn much for the future, a vast universe lies beyond Earth."

The Council was not persuaded. "You must bring him back. He is becoming a God on Earth, rendering everyone subservient to his will; something we have all sought to avoid through the ages. We want mankind to follow the path of righteousness through faith in the Almighty not under the duress of brutality."

The Old Man tried again. "But above all he is a force for good."

*One of the most senior and respected members of the Council rose to his feet, signalling others to be silent. "I believe I speak for us all. He is a force for whatever **He believes**. His values have become distorted since the transfer took place; divinity has been tainted by human failings. He sets aside our laws whenever **He chooses**. This situation cannot be allowed to continue. You must curtail his powers."*

The Old Man shook his head. "I cannot."

"You must, we are all agreed".

The Old Man looked round the Council of Elders, representatives of all time, leaders and visionaries of the great Religions and Beliefs. Not one offered support, all sat grim-faced, waiting for the only decision they would accept. He had finally lost; he knew the moment had come.

"Very well, I will do what you ask, but first he must complete his latest venture."

"But...." the Elder spokesman began to protest.

The Old Man stared at the speaker. "Enough, I have made my decision. Let us now give our thoughts to other places in the universe."

CHAPTER 30

The White House: 4th July 2006

A US Air Force helicopter had landed on the South Lawn and stood idling, its rotor blades spinning slowly as Lincoln and Phelps walked towards it. Phelps was dressed in a star-spangled jump suit as was Lincoln. Lincoln however was gloved and masked so that no-one could see his skin colour and perhaps deduce it was the Vice-President. The donations had reached nearly sixty-million dollars, money had flowed in from all round the world.

Phelps had come up with a brilliant idea; an on-line twenty dollars a shot to guess who the celebrity was and it had produced nearly fifteen million dollars with guesses ranging from Taylor Swift and Billie Eilish to Justin Bieber and Bruno Mars.

We got ourselves a beautiful day for it, John. Sunny but not too hot, and thank God, no wind."

"We sure did, Diane, just a reminder that I'm not supposed to talk in case someone recognises my voice."

"You're right, I'll shut up. Good luck with the jump."

"Thanks, you too."

It was 10.15am and they were due to make their jump over Central Park at Noon. The pilot had a fifteen minutes margin, not that the timing had to be perfect. Phelps had arranged for the parachutes to be provided and handed one to Lincoln when they met up. He had of course scanned her and knew that his had been tampered with. The main chute wouldn't deploy and the pull cord for the back-up chute was jammed. Whoever used it would hit the ground hard. He now had to find a way of switching the chutes when they got to the plane. He had thought about calling off his jump on some pretence, but in the end decided she was going to die at her own hand. *You're out to get me, Diane, so quid pro quo.*

When they reached the helicopter Lincoln slung his chute over his left shoulder and invited Phelps to climb on board first, taking her chute in his right hand to make it easy for her. As she heaved herself upwards, he quickly swapped the chutes; the die was cast.

The pilot welcomed them on board, and when they had settled, got permission for immediate take-off. Caswell had arranged for a security escort to accompany them on the hour and half flight to Central Park. The flight passed quickly, neither speaking to the other. Each wondering what the other was thinking. No matter what spin you put on it they were both erstwhile cold-blooded murderers.

New York Central Park.

The park was full of spectators. Bands were playing in several areas, cheerleading girls were strutting their stuff, it was the carnival of the year. Crowds let out a huge cheer when the three helicopters appeared in the sky a thousand feet above the twenty feet diameter target set up for the parachutists. The two escort helicopters peeled away to remain on station some distance away and the lead aircraft began its climb to eight thousand feet.

"We are have reached eight thousand feet, please take your places and confirm when you are ready." The pilot had to shout his instructions.

Lincoln moved to the left exit, Phelps to the right, both shouting 'Ready' when they were in place.

The pilot shouted again, "Jump on my count of three." There was a short pause, "Three, two, one, go"

Phelps and Lincoln launched themselves, taking up traditional arms and legs outstretched sky diving positions. Lincoln was impressed, Phelps had obviously had training and knew how to manoeuvre herself into position opposite him.

The crowds below were cheering loudly, media telescopic lenses were capturing the action for television, viewers were glued to their screens.

Phelps and Lincoln made no effort to speak, the rush of air and his face mask would make it impossible to hear each other. Moments passed, both keeping an eye on their altimeters, seven thousand, six thousand, five thousand it was time to deploy their chutes.

Lincoln saluted Phelps and pulled away to put a goodly distance between them. At four thousand feet he gave her a thumbs up and pulled his rip cord; the chute deployed immediately and he was wrenched upwards into a vertical position.

Phelps followed suit, shocked when her chute didn't open. She was descending rapidly and reached for her back-up ripcord. She knew in an instant what had happened - Lincoln had switched the chutes. Her face filled with dread as she tugged in vain, she knew she had less than two minutes to live.

Lincoln covered his eyes briefly, not through any feeling of remorse or horror at what he was witnessing; he knew he was on camera and it would be what was expected. Phelps hit the ground outside the target, her life was over. Military medical staff were rushing towards the body, the crowd was silent. This was an Independence Day they would want to forget but would remember for the rest of their lives.

Army personnel surrounded the target watching Lincoln's descent, ready to help when he landed. He touched ground just inside the circle and a Sergeant ran over to assist him out of the parachute harness.

"Well done. Are you OK?"

Shielded by the Sergeant, Lincoln pulled down his mask. "Do you know who I am, Sergeant?"

Sergeant Fairweather gaped at him for a second. "Oh my God! Yes, Sir." He saluted, "Yes, Mr Vice-President, Sir."

"At ease, Sergeant, I don't want to attract attention. Get me outta here, soon as."

Fairweather looked around as Lincoln pulled his mask back up. "There's an ambulance over there, let's get you in it, Sir.

Here, let me pretend to help you, put your arm round my shoulder and limp, make out you're a casualty."

"That's quick thinking, Sergeant. I'll see you get a Commendation when this is all over."

Instructions were given to the Ambulance driver, and Lincoln was taken to the nearest military landing strip where he was picked up by a helicopter and flown back to the South Lawn.

The White House.

Jack and Beth Caswell sat aghast in front of their television listening to the reports of the incident. Phelps fall and landing had been blacked out. Beth was in tears she had screamed and buried her face in his chest. The Caswell's house phone rang and the President eased his wife out of his arms to take the call. "Caswell speaking - Yes, I was watching. - I see. - Give instructions that the other parachutist is to be brought to my private quarters in the White House."

Jack Caswell returned to the sofa and cradled his still sobbing wife in his arms. "There, there, Pet. A tragedy, but sadly these things happen in life. It was Diane's parachute that didn't open. We can be thankful that John got down safely. I will ensure there is a formal investigation to determine why her parachute didn't open. She will be a great loss to the White House, her campaign strategies won me two campaigns; I'll be forever grateful to her."

Inwardly Caswell felt a sense of relief, Diane knew too much and she was gone. *You won't be writing those tell-tale memoirs now, Diane.* One of the thorns in his flesh had been removed.

Later

A White House staffer dutifully escorted Lincoln to Caswell's private residence albeit he had no need of a guide. Caswell was waiting for him in his lounge when he was shown in. A tearful Beth Caswell had excused herself.

"Thank you, Charlotte, you can go home now. Come in, John. You must be shaken to the core; grab a seat. Can I get you a drink?

"I could do with one, Jack. A good measure of your best Scotch wouldn't go amiss. It's been a draining experience."

"Coming up, right away; I'll join you."

The two men sat alongside each other on a comfortable settee; Lincoln took a long sip of whisky. "I needed that; I feel like slumping right here and sleeping for the next twenty-four hours."

"You're welcome to stay the night; I'll send a car for Carol, I'm sure she would want to be with you."

"I won't thank you, Jack, I want to get home; I'm here at your request."

"Of course, understood. What's your view of what happened?"

"Somebody screwed up when they packed the chute, simple as that. Diane brought two packs and gave me first choice." *How easy it was to lie.* "It could have been me lying in the morgue, God was with me." *At least that's the truth, John.* "The jump went normal until we dropped to five thousand feet, we gave ourselves some distance apart and pulled our ripcords. The rest is history, mine opened, hers didn't. She died a horrible death and I sit here talking about it."

Lincoln yawned and finished off his whisky. "Sorry, Jack, I'm beat, this has taken a lot out of me. I'm gonna go, get out of this suit and have a bath."

"Don't blame you, John, it's been a rough day. There's a car waiting for you outside; I'll see you out."

"Thanks, but no need. I'll see myself out and leave you to prepare your tribute to Diane."

Lincoln Residence later

Caswell had phoned ahead and Carol was there waiting on the porch for Lincoln when he arrived back. "Come here." She put her arms around him and pulled him close. "You poor darling, what a horrible day it's been for you. That poor woman.

I forbid you to ever do that kind of thing again. Bless the Lord for looking after you. Now get out of that silly costume; I've run a bath for you and there's a whisky waiting for you. Go ahead, I'll join you soon."

Oval Office: August 2006

Jack Caswell's eyes had been glued to the television screen for most of the day. The United Nations was in session in New York and he was watching the televised all-channel debate being broadcast live from a special meeting. Maybe the most important in its history. Every nation on earth was represented and there was only one subject on the agenda; re-structuring of the United Nations itself. They were debating the merits of John Lincoln's proposals and he had just finished addressing the chamber earlier. He had then excused himself to allow representatives unfettered debate, free from his forbidding presence. He had worked tirelessly for weeks lobbying for support and there was nothing more he could do. His final plea had been made in private to his spiritual partner; a simple *Please let it happen, Lord.*

Later

Caswell stood up and bowed ceremoniously when Lincoln entered the Oval Office.

"I can't believe you've pulled it off John, a reconstituted United Nations; I didn't think it possible. It's a miracle, that's the only way to describe it. Whether it'll be any better than its predecessor remains to be seen. I thought you were going to lose out to the Security Council veto at one stage, but somehow you pulled it off. The Brits were easily persuaded when Uncle Sam supported the motion - the Russkis want to strengthen relationships with Europe - the Chinese saw an opportunity to dominate Asia. I thought France would use their veto to defeat the Motion.

"As I understood it, the Frech contingent was split but I think Lafarge was minded to exercise his veto. Fate smiled on you when he had a heart attack. I'm sure the French were wavering. Still, it's all done and dusted now and I just hope it's as effective as you imagine it will be. It still looks like one big talk shop to me. But congratulations, John It's your baby; everybody knows you're the architect behind this new political edifice. Has a date been set for the inaugural ceremony?"

Lincoln shook his head. "The current Secretary-General is working on it; looks like it could be in the summer of next year. Construction and conversion works are already in hand to get the new Regional Centres completed as soon as possible."

Caswell raised his eyebrows. "That quick? Exciting times John. You know, sometimes I wish I could be around to play in these great new arenas of yours, but my days are numbered. I'll be watching with interest from the sidelines though. Which brings me to the big question, domestic politics. You know what's coming. Are you going to change your decision and enter the race for the Presidency? The polls reckon folks aren't committing their support one way or another until they're sure you're not running. You're our biggest hitter and they don't like to see you running out on Uncle Sam, much as they admire you."

Lincoln shook his head emphatically. "No Jack, count me out. I've got other ideas for the future."

Caswell was dumbfounded. "I still can't believe you're jumping ship; the Presidency is the most powerful office on earth and it's yours for the asking. I'm astonished that you don't want to experience it for at least one term. Our people want you to lead them, and you would be making history as the first black President. Whatever our differences I believe you are by far the best candidate; think about it, please."

"Sorry Jack, I've got other plans; the World has moved on in these last few years and I want to move with it."

Caswell sat back in his chair, smiling. "You really believe in this new order of things, don't you John? I've never quite believed you. Always wondered what your agenda was deep down, but I guess I've got to accept that you're sincere. And to be fair, your approach has worked for the betterment of the world this far. But sooner or later mankind reverts to type, and it'll all start to fall apart, you'll see. The way I see it, equality is wonderful, democracy is wonderful, but in their perfect form they are unattainable ideals."

Caswell drew breath and continued. "And what happens when these ideals fail because countries just can't agree, or some renegade dictator won't comply? What happens then? You won't agree, but I'll tell you anyway. You need a big fucking stick to bring them into line. And guess who's got the biggest stick? Good Old Uncle Sam, and as far as I'm concerned, long may it be that way. When push comes to shove, the United Nations will sit on its hands and debate - no action, just debate."

Lincoln sighed. "We have to move on from the big stick, there are too many would-be big sticks in this world of ours nowadays. We waste billions developing ever-bigger sticks, sticks that we never use. We have to develop appropriate sanctions, Jack."

Caswell shook his head. "Sanctions never work, they always hurt the wrong people; dictators go on living in luxury and the poor grovel in the gutter."

Lincon nodded, "I appreciate what you're saying, but I want the world to follow our lead and adopt our values because we're right, not because we've got the biggest muscle."

The President's concern was genuine. "So, you really are going to carry on crusading? What happens when you're not Vice-President? Do you think you'll be successful without a power-base? People all over the world listened to you, because of who you were; they could see Uncle Sam looking over your shoulder. When I leave office, you'll be just another retired politician; the new President will have their own views and you could end up being at odds with your own country. Let's face it you had to blackmail me into co-operating with you; the next incumbent might not have a skeleton in his cupboard."

Lincoln nodded his agreement. "I understand all that and I've given it a lot of thought; I know what I want. The United Nations is going to need a new Executive Secretary-General and I'm looking in that direction."

Caswell grimaced in disapproval. "Well first off, if history is anything to judge by, the job's got no teeth. They usually want that post to be occupied by a squeaky-clean unknown from some backwater country. Somebody who has never said boo to a goose and isn't likely to start now."

Lincoln shook his head and smiled broadly. "But that's it, there won't be a tradition for the new United Nations to follow; it's a whole new ball game. And I'm black, and pretty well squeaky-clean as you know, Jack. You and the late Diane Phelps tried hard enough to come up with something damaging and failed. Even our old friends at the FBI and CIA couldn't rake up any muck on me, or my family."

The President nodded, acknowledging his guilt. "Sorry about all that, I was running scared and protecting my interests. I always respected you; it wasn't personal."

"Another thing Jack, I hope you learned a lesson from your relationship with Diane and haven't got involved with one of those lovely young staffers you've got working for you?"

Caswell gulped. "I have to confess, I thought about it, but I learned my lesson. Diane wanted me to get rid of you and appoint her as my new Vice-President, then go on to support her selection as the Party's next Presidential candidate. Said she would go public about our affair if I didn't. If I'm honest, it was a stroke of good fortune for me when her parachute didn't open. I've had her office and home searched from top to bottom, every scrap of paper has been recovered by the CIA and brought to me. I've got about ten boxes to go through to make sure there is nothing incriminating."

Lincoln spun a bit of devilment, "We never did find out what happened to her parachute, but you certainly had the motive."

Caswell protested, "Hold on, don't go pinning that on me. How could I have known what chute pack she was going to pick; you told me that she supplied the chutes for the jump. It could just as easily have been you lying in the morgue. As it happens, it suits me; Diane threatened to blackmail me on more than one occasion. You're the only one whose memoirs could embarrass me now."

"You've got nothing to fear from me, I promise. That reminds me, I've got a present for you."

The President watched as Lincoln walked over to the bookcase and reached down behind two ancient volumes to remove two small brown envelopes.

"For you with my compliments, Jack and no hard feelings I hope?"

Caswell tore open each envelope in turn, and lifted the two objects that fell onto his desk. He looked up and raised his eyebrows questioningly, light beginning to dawn. "Are these little babies what I think they are?"

"Yip, they're the recordings you wish had never been made. I shouldn't play them with anyone around, best destroy them."

Caswell burst out laughing. "You crafty bastard, so that's where you hid them. I had the White House searched high and low for these and they were right under my nose all the time"

Lincoln wagged a friendly finger. "And you searched my home, my Lawyer's office and my Bank deposit safe; you violated my civil liberties in a big way."

Caswell shrugged. "No apologies on that score; you were blackmailing me big time. It was self-preservation pure and simple. That reminds me; whilst we're having this heart to heart, there's just one thing I'd like to know. How have you managed to get the inside track on so many dealings?"

"You'll never know. You don't know a fraction of what's gone on in the last five years or so. I'm going now. We're starting a new future; the slate is wiped clean all round. I have one last confession to make. I know that you encouraged Diane to take me out of the game. She arranged for my parachute pack to be tampered with. I found out and switched them."

Caswell opened his mouth but words wouldn't form. Lincoln raised a finger to his lips, "Don't say anything, Jack, it's all worked out for the best."

Caswell watched as Lincoln left the office and relaxed back in his chair, a happy man. He couldn't believe that he was holding the evidence that he had feared for so long. His marriage and his reputation were safe; he could enjoy his retirement in knowledge that nobody would ever learn about his sexual indiscretions.

CHAPTER 31

The Oval Office: November 2006

Jack Caswell sat alongside Beth in the Oval Office watching through the night as Presidential Election results were announced.

"Do you think your Party will win, Jack?"

"It doesn't look good; polls in the swing States have been consistently against us. I'm glad I'm out of this one."

"Me too, darling, I've got some big holiday plans in mind for us next year."

"I look forward to hearing about them, a long break is something we both need. I can assure you we'll be regular travellers judging by the invites I've been receiving. And most of them are all expenses paid."

September 2007

The six buildings serving the Regional Executives of the United Nations opened simultaneously; the different time zones presented some difficulties but symbolically it promoted Lincoln's 'one world' concept. It had had just over a month to set up the Regional Councils and choose their Regional Secretary; it wasn't difficult, negotiations and bargaining had been in progress for months.

October 2007: United Nations

The Headquarters of the United Nations Executive Council was sited in the old UN building in New York and opened by Lee Ming, the current Secretary-General.

Heaven

The Old Man had been requested to attend an emergency meeting of the Council to explain why its wishes had not been carried out and had acknowledged his tardiness. "I will fulfil your wishes soon. His work on Earth is nearly complete."

There had been objections "Powers continue to be abused. Would you favour others as you have favoured your Son? When will you bring him back?"

"It will be soon."

The Council was displeased. Its wishes were being blatantly disregarded but what could it do?

January 2008

Peter Ridgemont, one time movie star from Delaware had won the presidential election with a narrow majority. His Vice-President was Gregory Liskard a Californian billionaire. Both men were white, married and upright citizens in the true tradition of American politics.

Following their inauguration, Jack Caswell retired to his ranch to write his memoirs and participate in the lucrative speech making circuit. He and Beth would go on to enjoy the many free holidays he'd been offered at the end of his Presidency

United Nations : April, 2008

"Fellow delegates to the General Assembly, Honoured Guests, I give you the new Executive Secretary-General of the United Nations, John Lincoln."

Lincoln stepped forward to the podium amidst the glare of flashing cameras; the moment he had waited for had finally arrived. He had been the unanimous choice of the six new Regional Assemblies. Everyone rose to their feet. The applause was deafening such was their respect for the man who had done so much to establish a new World order.

"Thank you, thank you, thank you so much."

Lincoln was elated; his personal ambition had been achieved. "This is a great day, not just for me, it is a great day for the United Nations and for the world. Today represents a new beginning, it provides a new opportunity for us all to build a planet our children and their children can be proud of. We must put the mistakes of history behind us, learn from them and move forward. Together we can build a world where freedom is universal; a world free of slavery.

"I want to see freedom of choice for everyone, freedom from hunger, freedom from oppression, freedom from aggression. I want to see equality of opportunity to be the right of every man, woman and child on this planet. Ideals I hear you say. Yes, they are ideals, but these are ideals we must strive for. Never again must we settle for what is expedient at the expense of what is right.

"Who amongst you can reject the concept of a world in which there is food for everyone, a world where everyone has access to proper healthcare, a world where everyone receives education?

"I want a world in which everyone has the opportunity to earn a livelihood to support their family. I want a world of sustainable resources. I want a world of democracy and interdependence. In my world, peoples and nations will not be exploited by rich multi-national organisations. The sovereignty of countries will be respected and those who are wealthy will help those who are poor.

"Many share these ideals and working together we can turn them into realities. In the months and years that lie ahead I'll be calling on nations to invest in these ideals and to reduce expenditure on defence and weapons of destruction. I want our new United Nations to be synonymous with action and achievement. I do not want endless debate followed by inactivity, something we've all been guilty off. I ask you all to join with me in building a better tomorrow for our children, our children's children and the generations which follow them."

The Assembly dutifully rose to its feet to give the standing ovation, which everyone expected. Lincoln returned to his seat and sat smiling; he at least believed it was a new beginning.

The representative of the European Regional Council, Sir Ian Ogilvy, whispered to his opposite number from the Council for the Americas, Thomas Landers. "I hope he doesn't really believe in all that stuff; a bit of rhetoric is all right in its place, but most of his speech was pie in the sky in my view."

Landers shook his head. "I'm afraid he's very serious about it all Sir Ian. He doesn't seem to have taken on board that there's a new Administration in the White House and he doesn't have Jack Caswell at his elbow. I can't see the new President bankrolling his more outlandish ideas at the expense of the US taxpayer; Pete Ridgemont will focus on domestic politics, at least for his first term."

Sir Ian nodded. "Can't say I blame him. Charity begins at home, except of course for the special relationship." He added with a twinkle in his eye."

The American laughed, and put on an English accent. "But of course old chap."

Heaven

The Old Man had watched events unfolding from afar and had gone back to the Council, proud of the progress his son had made. Grudgingly, the Council had agreed that the venture had in the end been worthwhile, but remained concerned that there might be further abuse of power.

The Old Man warned his son, "You must be careful how you use your powers in the future, my Son; the Council remains very unhappy about your presence on Earth.

United Nations: June 2008

Lincoln pressed on with his ambitions for a better world and within a month he had produced a Charter for the destruction of nuclear weapons and other weapons of mass destruction. He declared that he wanted the Charter to be adopted one year hence on the first anniversary of the establishment of the new United Nations.

The Charter called upon all nations to reduce their expenditure on weapons of mass destruction and defence by twenty percent each year over the next five years. All existing missiles and warheads, together with nuclear, chemical and biological weapons, were to be destroyed. Research into such weapons was to be discontinued and permanently banned.

The Charter required full compliance by all nations. There was provision for monitoring and enforcement; Lincoln was determined that there should be no weapons which could fall into the wrong hands.

In the months that followed Lincoln canvassed relentlessly for acceptance of the Charter. Despite the warning he had been given, he continued to use his powers mercilessly; those who objected were blackmailed into agreement or eliminated. But even he was finding it impossible to secure lasting commitment. There were times when he had procured agreement of leaders, who were subsequently deposed by others unfavourable to his cause and he had to start again.

He managed to establish that the issue was so fundamental that every country should be allowed to vote at the anniversary session, rather than through the Regional Councils. He also secured agreement that the Charter should be adopted if eighty percent of all delegates voted in favour. As the Anniversary session drew near, he intensified his efforts, shuttling back and forth from one country to another, sometimes despairing that he would never succeed in gathering the necessary support.

Carol was always at his side, offering words of comfort and encouragement, always telling him to rely on the Lord. "Have faith, the Lord's will be done. You will succeed if he wants you to succeed."

"I must succeed Carol; the future of the world depends on it. Can't you see?"

"These great changes take time. You have pointed them in the right direction but they must be free to choose their own destiny. The Bible tells us that. Look how long it took the West to put an end to slavery."

"No, no Carol, the time is now, that's why I was chosen. They must do what I want."

She shook her head slowly. "It's not what you want John, it's what the Lord wants."

"But I speak for Him. They must do what I want or accept the consequences."

Carol Lincoln was troubled and looked into her husband's eyes, they seemed to stare through her as though he was obsessed. She sought to calm him, lowering her voice to a whisper, fearful of how he might react. "Consequences? What consequences, John? You sound like a dictator."

"You'll see, you'll see."

Meeting after meeting followed as he sought out those opposed to the Charter, and as the Anniversary Session drew near, he felt confident that he had done enough to win the day.

United Nations: Anniversary Session, April, 2009

On the day of the vote Lincoln watched from the podium as speaker after speaker spoke in favour of the Charter. A few spoke passionately against it. Others stressed the need for caution.

He knew that in spite of his efforts, the vote would be finely balanced and he made a forceful closing speech in favour of the resolution, ending with a threat.

"I will speak plainly, if you fail to support this Charter you are condemning millions of children, some of them yours, to an early death. Vote against it, say no and you will be betraying your children's future and the very future of Earth itself."

The votes would be counted electronically, a system he had insisted be installed in all United Nation chambers in the hope that the smaller nations could vote secretly against their neighbours and the more influential, larger, richer nations without fear of reprisal.

The time came to vote, and at his signal, each delegate pressed one of the two shielded buttons.

Within minutes the electronic display screen showed the result, 39% For, 61% Against.

The Resolution was lost; he had failed and had failed badly. Many had failed to honour the undertakings they had given him; many had lied by speaking for the Resolution but had secretly voted against.

In that moment he realised, for the first time, that his divine power could not guarantee success; the organisation he had set up to control the new world order had failed him.

A furious Lincoln rose to his feet to formally acknowledge the outcome. He was livid and made no attempt to hide his wrath as he spoke.

"Fellow delegates, Honoured Guests, it is a black, black day for the world. Your lack of resolve on this issue is unforgivable. The Resolution has been defeated and I have no recourse but to accept your decision. To the 39% who voted for Peace and a better world, I give my grateful thanks; the 61% who voted against must live with their shame.

"Many of you have hidden behind the anonymity of the electronic voting system, but I know who you are. Many of you have failed to honour your promises to me but, worse than that, you have betrayed our planet. Mark my words, your children will pay the price of your deceit and cowardice. You have failed to kindle hope for the future, and by your decision you have condemned many children to a life of poverty or early death and the risk of a nuclear war. A fate that all of you here present today believe will not befall your children, all of whom are protected by the positions and privileges that you enjoy."

Lincoln threw discretion to the wind; anger and a wish for retribution consumed him. "But I warn the guilty among you that the forces of good will not be denied; you will live to rue this day, your deceit will not go unpunished. Mark my words, the sins of the fathers will be visited upon the children."

The stunned delegates initially sat in silence, shocked by his intemperance and threatening language, then rose to protest angrily. Fists were shaken angrily, boos rang out, some delegates left the auditorium. The media were feverishly making telephone calls; television viewers were stunned. Government Officials all round the world were preparing their response to Lincoln's outrageous behaviour.

The British delegate whispered to his American colleague. "What in Heaven's name possessed him? How can he know who voted against the Resolution? Thank God he's one of yours; I think he's off his rocker."

The American nodded. "No doubt about it; it's time we started canvassing for a replacement Secretary-General"

Carol Lincoln sat in the public gallery, her head in her hands, sobbing. "My poor John, what has happened to you?" She watched as her husband stormed off the platform brushing away his aides.

Back in his office, Lincoln slumped down behind his desk to reflect on what had happened, wondering what to do next, reproaching himself for his failure. *But it hadn't been his fault, he had done all that he could; he had trusted others and been betrayed.*

As he reflected on what had taken place, vengeful thoughts fuelled his anger; his eyes glinted and dark thoughts filled his mind. "The sins of the Fathers will fall upon the Children. Let it be so" he cried, then gathered and harnessed his power; he wanted vengeance.

Around the world, his misguided ordnance began to take effect; children of delegates and of leaders of countries opposed to the Charter began to die suddenly as he focussed one by one on those who had betrayed him.

Heaven

The Old Man thoughts were interrupted by Peter, the most senior member of the Council. "Father, look at what is happening on Earth. You must intervene immediately and bring your son back now."

The Old Man acted instantly when he saw what was happening, but it was too late. Many daughters and sons, toddlers to teenagers, had already met untimely deaths. He and Peter gazed in horror at the scenes on Earth, deeply ashamed of what had occurred.

"My Son, how could you have made this happen? Your fate is sealed; you can never return to Heaven. You are lost to me forever."

"What have you done with him, Father?"

"I have sent him to a place far away, it will come to be known as Celestia. He will have to repent for his sins and begin a new life.

United Nations, later.

An hour after Lincoln's speech, a nervous Aide knocked on the door of his office and getting no reply, entered to find the Secretary-General lying on the floor behind his desk. A doctor was summoned immediately, but the only call on his skills was to pronounce that John Lincoln was dead.

A post-mortem carried out later that day revealed that he had died instantly as the result of a massive stroke.

Carol Lincoln was broken-hearted. More so, when she learned of the deaths of so many young lives. It could not be a co-incidence that their lives had been taken so soon after her husband's threats. "May God forgive you John. You meant well but you lost your way."